This is a work of fiction. All of  organizations, and events portrayed in this novel are either products of the author's imagination or are used fictitiously. **THA HOOD THA BAD & UGLY.** **Copyright ©2017 by J. Hitz.** All rights reserved. Printed in the United States of America. No part of this book may be used or reproduced in any form or by any means without written consent except in the case of brief quotations embodied in critical articles or reviews.

Kenerly Presents Publications
P.O. Box 562674
Charlotte, NC 28213

Website: www.kenerlypresents.com
Email: shauntakenerlypresents@gmail.com

ISBN-13: 978-1973967293
ISBN-10: 1973967294

Printed in The United States of America

Tha Hood Tha Bad & Ugly

J. Hitz

ACKNOWLEDGMENTS

First, I would like to give all my honors to God

Now that I got that out the way, I'd like to dedicate this book to my mother (Syverina L. Moses) R.I.P my angel. Thank you for your love, patience, and guidance. I will forever continue to be all that you invested your life in.

I'd also like to dedicate this novel to my boys Jayvon Moses and Jhmar Primm. You guys are my reason for pushing so hard everyday. May your lives be as fulfilling.

Next, I want to thank *all* my family. I love y'all to death for all the support, the likes, and the shares. Let's keep opening these doors. Gotta let'em know we want in! I just love it when we on one. Don't y'all? Lmao!

I want to send special love to my dad Jeff Clair, aunt Patricia Clair, cousin Twanna Williams, cousin Terrance Lavinge(T to tha B), cousin Kevin Fulford, and Helena West. You guys help make my coming home transition smooth, and it gave me the time to invest in this project here. Thanks I love y'all!

Ed Williams, Jo Jo Anthony, Derrik Robinson, Travis Summerville, Paulie Bosanko, Aaron Watson, Charlie Wilson, Rump, Willie Welch, Marcus "BIG MEECH"Grisby, Chris Dukes, Cebo Mc Duffy, Antonio Allen, and Terrance Elane. You guys followed me day in and day out as I wrote this book, and in one way or another your responses gave me guidance. It's all love. Ay! I got bell peppers and ice cream for *all* y'all! Lmao!

I can never end this without giving thanks to the coach, Shaunta Kenerly. You gave a brother like myself wind to flap my wings. That will always be appreciated and remembered. (Real N@#* shit) Thumbs up to Kenerly Presents and Flawless (Nikki Rountree) for believing in my talent. Terrie... I know you didn't think I forgot about you. Thanks for the dope ass tips! (Terrie L. Branch)

Last but never in the least I would like to give a very special thanks to my partner in crime April Freeman (Free). Man oh man, words can't express my gratitude. You believed in me, so all I can say is Thank you, for *everything*.

I truly apologize if there is someone(s) I left out. Not to worry, many more to come!

CHAPTER 1

It was the top of the summer, when I stepped out of that hell hole. I waited five long years for this day to come and for whatever reason, I couldn't fight the nervousness that I felt... Whoever said that the dead couldn't rise, was a fuckin' lie... My heart was pumping and beads of sweat started to form on my forehead as I began to walk down 'Free Man's Road'. Free Man's Road is what we called the two hundred foot concrete slab that separated the prison from the gate to freedom, and I swear it was feeling like it was taking forever.

As I took my last few steps, I stopped; I gazed out into the world like a hungry lion and momentarily froze. When I turned my head to the left, I looked the prison guard square in the eyes. Then he asked, "Ready playboy?" Right then, I closed my eyes, took in a deep breath, then exhaled... When I opened my eyes, I cocked a smile at the guard, and said, "Hell yea! You betta fuckin' say it!"

The guard smiled back, shook his head then yelled out. "Gate!"

I instantly heard a loud buzz then the clank of a lock. It wasn't long before I saw those huge prison gates slowly split like the Red Sea allowing me to embrace my freedom.

I savored the moment by taking slow calm strides until I saw a yellow cab that sat there as if it was waiting for me.

I opened the door and slung my lanky 6'2" frame into the backseat and got comfortable... That's when I heard a raspy Dizzy Gillespie type voice say.

"Where to youngsta?"
"Bus station."
"Bus station gone be ten, but for an even fifty, I'll get'cha to ya front door."

Chapter 2

Once I got in Nassir's crib, I took a seat admiring how well my man was doing for himself. He stood there smiling with his chest all poked out admiring his own shit with me. What can I say? That was classic Nassir for you. Always feeling himself.

Once he snapped out of his dream world he said, "Oh shit! Before I forget, I got sumt'n fo you. Go ahead have a seat, relax. I'll be right back."

He took off to a room in the back of the house and returned with a bulky manila folder and tossed it on the table.

"Dats all you fam."

I opened the envelope and emptied everything on the table.

"Dats ten racks my nigga. Dat should give you a decent head start." There laying on the table was two neatly bundled stacks of hundred dollar bills, a set of keys, and a necklace. The money was a huge blessing but what caught my attention was the necklace.

I picked the necklace up and held it so I could get a good look at the heart shaped locket that hung from the chain. It belonged to my mother. It was the only thing I had to remember her by, and when Nassir saw the look on my face he said."I went and kicked it wit'cho ole G a couple days before she passed. You know she was like a mother to me too, right? All she did was talk about her baby Adonis. She loved you more than anything fam. She wanted you to know that you was still a king"

I started to choke up a bit when Nassir told me those last words. When I was a kid, everybody used to crack jokes about me being ugly. She would hug and wipe my tears away then say, "Baby, let me tell you something about beauty. As time goes on beauty fades, but royalty? ...Royalty will last forever. So, when them kids crack their jokes, you just remember that you're my king."

I was still lost in thought when Nassir touched my shoulder saying,

"Ug you a'ight bro?"
"Yeah ummm, I'm cool, I'm cool."
"Hey fam. I didn't mean to throw you off like dat. I just—"
"It's all good bro. Don't even trip, real talk."
"Ok. Well look, you got the back room on tha right. I already left clean sheets and shit back there fo you. Towels and face rags is in tha closet in tha hallway."
"So wut all deez keys to?"
"Ah! Dig tha move. You gone love tha move Ug. Come with me."

He took me out to the backyard where I saw this big ass H2 Hummer. It had a metallic orange paint job with a pair of 24" rims on it. Nassir noticed how I looked at the truck and said,

"Aw hell naw! Dats me playa…Dats you over there."

He pointed toward an old Nissan Maxima. It wasn't fucked up or anything. But after looking at the Hummer, I felt like someone had just snatched my trick or treat basket. I tried to shake my disappointment while saying,

"Yo Nas, I thought' chu said I was gone dig the move. Wus up?"
"Hey, we can swap it out whenever you want. I like to use the Maxima when I'm droppin' shit off anyway."
"It's all good. Beggars can't be choosey."
"Dats a lie."
"Wut' chu mean."
"Well, you said beggars can't be choosey."

And that's when he walked over to the four car garage that sat in the backyard. He unlocked the door, pushed it open, pointed inside and said,

"Choose!"

I walked inside the garage and my mouth hit the floor. I was looking at two 1973 Chevy Impala's. It was me and Nassir's dream car. We had always talked about having twins. One was all white on white with custom leather sports seats, chrome grille, sunroof and 26" rims. The other was peanut butter and jelly. Candy apple red paint with tan leather interior, chrome grille, and 26" rims. I could still smell the fresh paint on both of them. I was so fixated on the cars, I didn't even notice the two Banshee four wheelers in the corner. One was white and the other was candy apple red to match the Impala's paint. Now, I was definitely diggin' the move, so after contemplating for a few minutes, I said,

"White! I want the white one."
Nassir extended his arm out and took a bow in a joking manner saying,

"Your wish is my command. Now let's go get sumtn' to eat, I'm hungry den a mufuka."

Minutes later, Nassir and I pulled up at the corner of 135th & Pulaski where one of the four local liquor stores was located, Trogan's. The store was owned by an Arab family, who also owned a chicken joint connected next door called Sharks. The"t" block next to Trogan's was 135th and Keystone. This area of Robbins was known as South Park. South Park had a crew of mixed dynasties; some were Gansta disciples, and a few were Vice Lords, and a couple were Blackstones. They were young and wild and all about their money. They loved to represent their hood, but they'd die for their block, and Trogan's was definitely a part of their block.

We pulled into the parking lot of Trogan's and sat for a few seconds while Nassir scoped out the scene making sure everything was all good. Once he was comfortable with his surroundings, he shut the truck off and said.

"Yo, you still fuck wit dat Patron?"
"Yessir."
He peeled off a hundred dollar bill and handed it to me.
"Cool, grab a fifth of Patron and some lime juice."
"Dats all?"
"Uhhhh naw. Grab some Black n' Milds and some Garcia y Vega's too. I'll get tha food. Wut' chu want?"
"Shiiiiit, grab me 6 wings fried hard, wit lemon pepper and some mild sauce." I then dipped off into the store to grab the drink.

When I came out of the store, Nassir was leaning against the truck talking to one of the South Park dudes named Racks. He was always respectful and humble, two qualities I admired in a man. Which is why he was one of the few guys I hung out with before I was locked up.

Racks was so into the conversation with Nassir he didn't even see me walk up. But as soon as he saw me he got pumped.

"Oh shit! Ugly dude, welcome home baby boy! How ya feelin'?"
"I'm good bro. I'm maintainin'."
"Dats wussup. Man, bro it's good to see you though fam.... Ay Nassir, you gone take care of me when you get back to tha town, right?"
"I got'chu my nigga, don't even trip." Racks turned back to me.
"Ay Ug, come through tha block and fuck wit'cho boy, bottle on me." He gave me and Nassir a fist bump and was out. I

made a note to get around to kickin' it with him, because to me, Racks was still one cool ass dude.

Chapter 3

It was around seven o'clock when Nassir and I got back to the house. The sun was setting and the evening summer breeze felt good. Now that the night was falling, more of the older crowd that I knew began to come out and show their faces. It was good to see some familiar faces. It's what made home, home.

Being gone for five years made a lot of names and faces sort of blurry. But there was one face that instantly got my attention, and I knew it extremely well. It was Candice, my road dog. Everybody used to think Candice and I messed around, but we were just the best of friends and loved each other's company. Candice was one of those real good friends who I could pour my heart out to. She was the first female I ever cried in front of. No matter how fucked up my day was, she always made me smile.

Candice was already walking toward the truck when I hopped out. When she saw my face, she stopped dead in her tracks, eyes wide, and mouth open. She actually looked like she just saw a ghost. It was hilarious watching her reaction and when she finally got past the shock, she screamed.

"Ahhh!... Ug, oh my God!" She ran up to me and hugged me super tight. "Heyyy baby, I see you den got a little muscle on you."
"Yeah, I was in there workin' on my sexy."
"And it's workin' nigga, look at' chu!"
That's when Nassir interrupted our little reunion and said,

"Damn Candice, Ug tha only mufuka you see out here?"
"Whateva Nassir, Wussup wit' cho ole' triflin' ass."
"Awww shit. It ain't even eight o'clock yet and you gettin' started already, huh? Fuck you, wit'cho ole bee bop scoobidy oooh

yeah face ass!" The shit was so funny we all just busted up laughing, and I do mean crying laughing.

Once we all got past the giggles, Candice gave Nassir a playful punch in the shoulder and said,

"Anyways, Ug this is my girl Toni."
Candice turned and kissed her. In the mouth! I mean like she wanted to see what was up for the night! My mouth dropped and my eyes got big as hell. Nassir watched my expression for a second then cracked up laughing saying.

"Look… at…that…nigga…face!" Then laughed some more until Toni jumped in saying,

"Don't start no shit Nassir."
"Com'on man, I ain't even on nat. It's just that Ug ain't know, I forgot to tell' em, but when y'all two did tha toung-o-war, tha look on nat nigga's face was priceless!"
I closed my mouth long enough to say with a grin.
"My bad y'all, I just got caught off guard. Damn, I guess we got a lot of catching up to do huh? Well let me take a shower and tighten up, then Im'ma come back out."
Candice said 'ok', gave me another hug and told me welcome home, then I took off to handle my scandal.

I rushed back in the house, tossed my bags, and jumped in the shower. When I got out, I threw on some tan cargo shorts, a white tank top, and some all-white Air Max.

I stepped in the living room where Nassir was rolling up some weed. I sat on the couch, reached for the Patron bottle to pour myself a shot and then took it to the head. After that, I refilled my cup with half Patron and half lime juice. I took a heavy sip and said,

"So Nas, where all this money comin' from?" Nassir cocked a smile and said,

"Man Ug, I watched deez nigga's get money for years fam. Now it's my turn."

"So wut'chu fuckin' wit?"

"Shiiiit, I'm fuckin' wit dat white."

"Wut' chu grabbin'?"

"I usually fuck wit a half a bird, sometimes tha whole thang."

"How you movin' it, bags or weight?"

"A little of both. Wut? You trying to get down?"

"I don't know. Wut da prices like?" Nassir whistled.

"Fifteen five fo tha half, thirty fo tha whole thang!" I snapped my neck back in surprise *and* disgust.

"Man get tha fuck outta here!"

"I ain't bullshittin', and tha work ain't even all dat, but I make it do wut it do tho."

I took another sip of my drink and rubbed my chin as I drifted off in thought. There wasn't a snowball's chance in hell you could get me to dish out that kind of cash for a kilo of coke. It just wasn't reality to me, so I said,

"Wus da deal on nat shit' chu smokin'?"

"Shiiiit dis dat thang right here! Nigga be hiittin' me up fo five hun-ned a zip."

"Fuck! So mufuka's got tha dope *and* weed on lock, huh?"

"I'm sayin', dis dat OG Kush, but nigga's got some reggie floatin' around fo probably about a "G" a pound."

"Who got it?"

"Tha Mo's, folk'nem in tha Old Projects, folk'nem in the Trailers, oh and tha nigga Gacy got some kill shit too!"

"Gacy?!"

"Yup."

"He still be over on tha Bay?"

"Hell Yeah, ain't nuttin' changed wit dat nigga, he still grindin'."

"Bet, I wanna try and catch up wit' em tomorrow or sumt'n and see wus poppin'."

Then Nassir lit his blunt, took a deep pull, held the smoke and said,

"Say no more. You ready to go see wut tha fuck Candice and Toni on?" I told him yes then he grabbed the other blunts he rolled while I grabbed the the drink, and we took our little party outside.

Chapter 4

It was about nine thirty when we stepped back out on the block. All you heard was the sound of crickets chirping, sounds bumping, and dogs barking from afar. The block was dark as hell, with the exception of the porch lights and the one street lamp that was posted at the alley in the middle of the block. The rest of the block consisted of burned and abandoned houses surrounded by bushes, which made this a good spot to get money.

As we maneuvered our way toward Candice's house, we noticed her and her girl Toni had already gotten their night started with a fifth of Remy. So, I just copped me a spot on the porch as Nassir passed Toni the weed and said,

"I got next." Meaning, he would serve the next customer that came to the block to buy. He then dipped off and hid his pack in the bushes.

While I sat there sipping my drink, I took in my scenery. I was lovin' it! Watching my man get money made me feel proud. He was at his high and he was happy. But what impressed me even more was watching Toni get money just like him.

I paid close attention to the both of them as they tag teamed for about an hour while Candice and I got caught up. Everything was running smoothly until the block started rockin' like crazy. I mean customers were coming at one to two minute intervals for about another hour and a half. Once the traffic calmed down I said,

"Damn, so y'all like a regular Batman & Robin, huh?"
Nassir stood up straight, put his hands on his hips, and tilted his chin, then said,
"Yes, I am Batman."

Toni said, "Batman?! You shittin' me! You just look like a bat... *man.*" And that's when Nassir kicked it off!
"Awww shit! You den got me started, wit'cho ole Cambell's soup mmm mmm good face ass."
Toni stood her ground by saying,
"Fuck you Nassir, wit' cho ole rock'em sock'em robot face ass!"
"Wut?! Fuck yo ole 'so you wanna hit people wit garbage cans,' face ass!"

They went back and forth for *a while,* until Nassir's phone started to ring. He answered, then walked off to talk in private. Toni then excused herself and took off to the bathroom. Candice and I sat in silence for a moment until I spoke saying,

"Yo girl Toni cool peeps, Candice."
"Yeah, I'm feelin' her. She makes me happy."
"Well then dats all dat matters."
"So wut about'chu Ug? Wut' chu gone do wit'cho self?"
"I don't know, probably take my ass back to school or sumt'n. Wussup you workin'?"
"Yup, I got my RN license last fall. Now I work full-time at the nursing home in Crestwood."
"Ok... ok, dats wusup. Well, I'm proud of you."
She smiled, then Nassir came back to the porch smiling saying,
"Guess wut'chall?" Simultaneously, we both said.
"Wut?!" Nassir's silly ass started crip walking and singing.
"I'm finna get some puuussaay!" Candice and I just shook our heads, then Candice got up.
"Well fella's, that's my cue."
Then Nassir's drunk ass said,
"Wut Candice, you finna get some pussy too?"
"*Bye* Nassir!!...See ya tomorrow Ug." I gave Candice a hug and a kiss on the cheek, then Nassir and I rolled out.

CHAPTER 5

It was close to 2am when we got in the house and Nassir started rolling up so more weed. He let me know that the night wasn't over and that his expecting company was bringing a friend. He also told me he had her stop at the store to buy more liquor. Man, I got excited! Five years without pussy can drive a player mad, and boy was I ready!

Twenty minutes later the doorbell rang. Nassir yelled from the back room to go ahead and open the door. It was the girls!

When I opened the door, there was this thick ass redbone with a long wavy ponytail, and a pretty smile. The other chic walked up with a bag in her hand. She was dark-skinned, petite, and sexy in all the right places. After checking them both out, I told them to come in and make themselves comfortable.

Once they came in, they sat on the couch and started making themselves a drink. I figured I'd set the mood. So, I turned the CD player on and some old school Keith Sweat came pumping out of the speakers. As if on cue, Nassir came walking in the living room in some boxers, house shoes, a robe, and a pair of Ray Ban's on his face… singing Keith Sweat's song.

'You may be young but you're ready…….. Ready to learn.'
And the girls started to giggle.
"Hey Ug, pour me a drink famo."
He stepped to the dark-skinned one and started rolling on her. I was like, what the fuck! This fool think he's a stripper! But at the same time, it let me know that the redbone was for me. Before things started to get too loose, Nassir pulled me into the kitchen to put me up on game.

"Ug the dark one is Aliyah and the redbone is Domonique. Don't get it twisted with the pretty faces bro, they col' freaks, they get down! So just roll wit me, aight?"

"A'ight cool, Aliyah and Domonique, gotcha!"

We went back in the living room and Nassir began dancing on the dark one again, only this time, a little freakier. She then started grabbing on his junk. I could see that shorty redbone was enjoying the show. So, I walked over to her and snatched off my tank top. I stood right in front of her all ripped up. Shorty reached out and ran her hands down my abs, then shivered and said,

"Damn boy, yo body sexy as hell! I reached over and grabbed my cup and downed all the liquor. I just spent five years in the joint. I didn't have time for all that dancing shit, so I just pulled my dick out ... Nassir put his head down and smacked his forehead with the palm of his hand. The girls stood there with their mouths wide open. That was when Nassir said,

"Fuck it! Strip poker den ... I lose." Nassir got asshole naked, but kept the sunglasses on. The girls followed suit and started peeling off their clothes too. Nassir followed up by reaching in the pocket of his robe and pulling out a hand full of rubbers. He tossed them in the air like parade candy, and that's when the festivities began.

For the next two hours, we did some hardcore fuckin'... tag team style. Before I knew it, I passed out. I can't remember what time the girls left, but I *do* know that Nassir welcomed me home with style.

Chapter 6

The next afternoon, I woke up lazily around one o'clock. The house was empty and so was my stomach.

I stepped into the kitchen to see what was in the fridge and I found some bacon. I decided to make myself a sandwich. While frying the bacon, I turned the television on to watch the CNN News channel. You know a playa gotta keep up with his current events.

After I finished my sandwich, I went into the bathroom to take a shower. I turned the water on and let the steam build, then I stepped in. The hot water relaxed my body and gave my mind a moment of solitude. It was something that I desperately needed, and now I was ready for my day to begin.

When I stepped out on the block, it was hot as hell. Nassir, Toni, and some young kid was sitting under a big maple tree by the bushes. I could tell that the area was groomed for hustling by the way that the grass separated itself from the dirt. I'm just glad it was under some shade.

When Nassir saw me come out of the house he waved me over to join them. And once I made it, I stood there as I listened to all three of them talk about how they needed to get more organized in their hustle. After I said what's up to everybody, I copped me a spot on an old milk crate, and just observed. Once Nassir was done playing Nino Brown he said,

"Ay Ug, dis my lil nigga Yella Boy." I gave shorty a head nod, then spoke to Nassir.
"Yo Nas, let me holla at'chu fo a minute."

I pulled him to the side and reminded him that I wanted to see what was up with Gacy and the weed. He acknowledged my request and then spoke to Toni and Yella Boy saying,

"Ay, y'all hol' it down. Me and Ug bout to bust dis move right quick." Then we hopped in the truck and took off to the bay to hook up with Gacy.

The Bay area was on a secluded dead end block off 136th Place & Kildaire. When we turned onto the block, all the guys seen Nassir's truck and threw up their three fingers representing the BD nation. The three fingers symbol was known as "The Trays" or "The Bars", and Nassir threw them back up proudly.

I looked to my right where I saw a dude in the gang way with an AK-47 assault rifle. He held it like he was ready to let go at any moment. So, I gave him a head nod letting him know that it was all good.

All of Gacy's guys watched us as we pulled to the dead end of the block where a gate separated the block from the 294 overhead expressway, which also separated the Bay from South Park.

Once we got to the end of the block Gacy walked up to the truck, shook up with Nassir, and said.

"Wut up BD?" He looked over in the passenger seat and saw me smiling back at him. "Ug, oh shit, they finally let' cho ass out, huh?!"

He walked excitedly around the truck and snatched the door open. "Show me some love nigga!"

I hopped out of the truck and we embraced like playa's. When Gacy finally stepped back and looked me over he said, "When you get out?"

"Yesterday."

"And you just comin' to see a nigga?! You bogus as hell fam."

"My bad bro, Nas kept me busy all day helpin' me get situated."

"It's all good, you still my nigga. Wut up wit it doe?"

"Shiiiiit, I'm trying to see wussup on tha greens?"

"Ahhhh, hitting tha streets runnin' huh?"

"I'm just trying to get in where I fit in."

"Ok, ok. Well, dis wut it's lookin' like… I'm dumpin' dis shit on deez weak ass nigga's fo thirteen hunnid a pound, but since I fucks wit' chu and you fresh out, I'll plug you fo a G." I looked at the weed, then rubbed my chin and said,

"Wut'chu a do fo five of' em?"

"Five? Hmmmm…… fuck it, I'll do it fo tha forty-five. Wussup?"

"How long?"

"Uhhhhh, gim'me a couple hours, I gotta hit my spot."

"Aight bet. Just hit Nas line when you ready."

Back in the truck Nassir was rolling up a blunt. I told him about the arrangement, and that Gacy would be hitting his line soon, I then leaned back in the seat and took a deep breath. Now, I needed to check my competition out.

"So Nas, tell me one mo time who else got tha weed."

"Tha Mo's, tha Folks in tha old projects and the Folks in the trailers." I didn't want to expose my hand to Gacy, cause I needed the connect, plus he was my man. I told Nassir I wanted to see what the other spots were working with. So I said,

"Hit tha Mo's up first, then we'll hit the Folks." So we rolled over to 139th to another local liquor called Frank's. Franks's sat right at the corner across the street from a local bar called the Cozy Corner. Directly behind Frank's was a ratchet glass debris scattered alley. This was where you could find the Black P Stones, also known as the Mo's.

The Mo's ran under the five point star and stayed to themselves. They were known to get into it with the G.D's from the old projects that frequently came to the store or to the bar across the street.

When we pulled into the parking lot of Frank's, I saw about ten dudes lingering in the alley behind the store. Nassir's stuck his head out of the window and yelled out.

"Ay, where Big Mo at?" One of the guys spoke up saying.
"He gone, wut' chu need?" I told Nassir to just grab a sack.
"Ay, just gim'me a sack famo." Dude came with the sack of weed and we left.

As we drove away, I checked the sack. The weed looked ok, but the sack was short as hell. I stored that info in my mind as a mental note, then we headed over to the projects.

A few minutes later, we pulled up in the old projects. This here was an all GD spot. The GD's in Robbins had a lot of members, which made them the strongest by numbers, but the weakest in unity. It was so many of them. It was more likely that they got into it with each other, nevertheless, they banged hard!

As we rode through the Old Projects, I saw people standing around *everywhere.* It started to remind me of being back in the joint on the yard, so I told Nassir to just grab the weed and keep it moving and he did. He grabbed the sack and we turned out of the old projects and shot up Clair BLVD. and turned into the trailer court.

The trailers were also an all GD spot as well as the new projects across the street. The trailers were a definite death trap, one way in and one way out.

When we pulled in, the females stood around smiling and admiring Nassir and the Hummer. The guys in the area didn't like that very much and started to mug the shit out of us.
Despite of all the ugly stares, we pulled over and once we did they got thirsty as hell. About six guys ran up to the truck and reached through the window with hands full of weed. Nas took one

sack and placed a ten dollar bill in the hand he took the weed from, the rest scattered like roaches. We could tell that they loved our money, but grew tired of our presence. So we turned the truck around, and got the fuck out of dodge!

It was like that in Robbins, shit could pop off at any given moment. Dudes in the town were name builders, and if it makes them look gangsta, then they were all for it. They were standing on making their spots notorious for money and murder!

Hours had passed and Gacy finally hit Nassir's line back. Nassir looked at his phone saw it was him and answered.

"Yo!"
"Where y'all at?"
"We on our block."
"I'm comin' yo way. I'm turning on yo block right now."
"I see you."
"Bet."

The conversation went fast and Gacy hung up quickly. He pulled in front of our house and I ran up to his Harley Davidson pickup and Gacy said,

"Wutup playboy? It's right there on the floor."
I reached in, grabbed the bag, dropped the money, and shot off toward the door of the house. Gacy wasted no time he was already turning the corner by the time I stepped in. That's how I like to do business, smooth and clean, in and out.

When I got in the house with the package, I wasted no time. I checked the weed I bought and knew exactly how I wanted to sell it. I broke each pound down in sixteen ounces a piece, then bagged up nine big ass bags off each ounce. These were my dimes. I would sell each bag for ten bucks, with a total profit of twenty-seven hundred dollars. Not bad for a start, huh?

By the time I finished bagging up, the sun was beginning to set. I smashed a bowl of Cap'n Crunch, and sat back for a second to gather my thoughts. I pondered on the fact that I may piss off a few guys with my big ass bags of weed, but fuck'em, this was business. If they weren't game for a little competition then their veins pumped bitch and they might as well wrap it up. Cause this isn't any hand holding contest. This? This is the motherfucking hood!

Chapter 7

Carlos stood in his cell looking into a stainless steel plate he called a mirror. He was brushing his hair when a tall, black, well-built guard with a beard and ponytail stopped at his cell.

"Mr. Carlos, you have a visit. I'll be back to get' cha in five minutes." Carlos smiled politely and said.
"Thank you Andre. I'll be waiting."

Exactly five minutes later Andre, the guard, returned to take Carlos to the visiting room. As he escorted Carlos down the corridor, they briefly spoke.

"You know Andre, one of these days you're going to look back and laugh at this job."
"I sure hope so Mr. Carlos, I sure hope so. Have a nice visit. I'll be waiting in the officer's station when you're finished."

Carlos entered the private room where he was greeted by his personal assistant and his attorney, Leonard Shultz, then they all sat down. Carlos looked at his assistant and immediately spoke.

"Do you have any word from my brother?"
"Your brother, ummmm, is still not happy with this whole prison situation, but he respects your judgement." Carlos chuckled.
"Yes yes, I'm not surprised. Is there anything else?"
"He says that our people in Chicago have become unmanageable." Carlos instantly stopped smiling.
"Unmanageable? What the hell does that mean?"
"He says he'll speak more in depth once you've arrived."
"Fine! So, Leonard, where are we with the development project?"

"We are still having problems with one city, but you are aware of that. Besides that, all the other city mayors have signed off, and all the contracts have been signed and sealed. The construction companies are in place and our franchisers are ready to take off."

"Beautiful! My business in this prison is done Leonard, start gathering the paper work. Meet with the warden and get me out of here." Then he looked back to his assistant. "And you! Tell my brother the seed has been planted, and we're on schedule. Leonard will let you know when to expect me. Are we clear?"

"Yes sir, crystal."

"Ok then, Leonard I want to see you by Monday morning with some news about my release."

"Yes sir." Said Leonard, then Carlos stood up and yelled for the guard.

On the way back to his cell, Carlos' mind was spinning. He was extremely pissed about the news on his Chicago venture. He knew that this was the first line of business he'd have to take care of once he was released. To Carlos an agreement was an agreement, and his people in Chicago were not living up to their word.

Once the guard secured Carlos in his cell and began to walk away, Carlos called out his name.

"Andre." The guard turned around and came back to the cell.

"What'cha need Mr. Carlos?" Carlos looked the guard in the eyes, trying to get a final feel for him before speaking, then he said,

"How would you like to become a rich man?" The guard moved closer to the steel bars and said.

"Are we talking hypothetically Mr. Carlos?"

"No Andre, we're talking Five million dollars."

The outrageous amount caught the guard's attention, and he was all ears. Money talks and bullshit doesn't have a tongue, so even though Carlos' request was extremely risky, the guard had no problem accepting Carlos' proposition. All he had to do now was let Carlos set everything in motion and wait for the word.

Later that evening, Carlos was laying on his bunk staring at the ceiling. He sat up and pulled back his mattress and grabbed a photo that he would frequently look at. He took his index finger and gently rubbed it across the faces of the couple in the picture and gazed into their eyes. He felt that looking into their eyes set forth a boundary of communication, an understanding that went deeper than anyone could ever imagine. After staring at the picture a little longer, he took a deep breath then said,

"Don't worry, everything will be as you both wanted. It will be ... perfect!"

Carlos then kissed the photo and placed it back under his mattress. He curled under a single blanket and closed his eyes, thinking of how he would handle the situation involving his associates in Chicago. He knew that it would take careful planning, but the result would be epic, and his message would be heard loud and clear.

Chapter 8

It was an early Friday evening in the hood. I'd have to say a little after six. The night was beginning, and chics were migrating around the town in cliques. Even though it was the early evening, it was still hot as hell. The females let it be known by the lack of clothing they wore. The more dark spot of the ass you saw, the more available they were for the night. Me myself, I was feeling damn good! My big ass bag of weed hustle had taken off, and I had already done a re-up with Gacy earlier today, and just finished bagging it up. So far, today had been a good day.

Toni, Yella Boy, Nassir and I sat on the block sippin' on some Coronas. I asked everybody what their plans were for the night and Toni responded by saying her and Candice would be going to the movies. Nassir tried to talk me into going to the lakefront with him and Yella Boy, but I declined. All I wanted to do was stack my money. I appreciated everything Nassir had done for me, but I couldn't see myself living off of another man. I just wasn't that type. I had to be me, ugly ass Adonis Stuffy.

An hour later the Corona's were gone and so was Toni and Candice. Yella Boy and Nassir were getting ready to take off, when Nassir extended his invitation.

"Ug, you sho you don't wanna ride out famo?"
"Naw, I'm good. I'm just tryin' to stack dis bread. You know my b-day comin' up in a few weeks. Playa gotta get right."
"Ok Ug, I see you. I don't know when you became a playa, but I feel you my nigga." Nassir began to chuckle a little saying. "Yella Boy, you strapped?" Yella Boy smiled and put on his best impression of O-Dog from *Menace II Society* and said,

"And you know it!"

"Cool, give Ug yo strap, we gone ride wit tha tek."

Yella Boy reached in his waist band and pulled out a chunky ass glock. I took it from him and looked at the imprint along the barrel of the gun. It was a .40 caliber HK. Just coming home from a five year pistol charge made me uncomfortable handling the gun, but I was better off with it than without it. Nassir watched me as I looked at the gun and said,

"Ug, let me find out' chu forgot how to used one of dem."
"Stop playin', I got dis."
Nassir said,
"Ok then Ugly Montana, we up!" And they jumped in the Hummer, pumped the sounds, and rolled out.

Hours had passed and all the weed heads in the town were satisfied for the time being. I got bored as hell and decided to hit a few blocks and see what was going on around the hood.

While I was cruising, I remembered Racks telling me to come fuck with him. So, I bent a block and headed toward the South Park area of the town to check him out.

When I pulled up on the corner of 135th Place & Keystone, which was the South Park area, it was poppin'! Crackheads were constantly coming, and the females were spread all over the block while the hustlers just thugged out. Everybody was smoking weed, drinking some kind of liquor, and having a good time.

I saw Racks leaning against his car with one of the girls standing between his legs, so I pulled over and parked in front of his car and got out. Racks was already tipsy and so into the female, he didn't even recognize me pulling up. As I walked toward him, he finally recognized me and pushed the girl away yelling.

"Ugly dude! Wus hap'nen bay-beee!" And we greeted.
"Shit famo, I'm just out cruisin' tha land."
"You want sumtn' to drank nigga? Ay ay…. Ay shawty! Get my man Ugly dude sumt'n to drink. Ug what'chu wanna drink famo?"
"You got some tequila?"
"Ay, bring'em some of dat Cabo Wabo. Ay Ug, dis shit gone knock yo noodles back bro! Straight up!"

I grabbed the cup of tequila and sipped lightly as I took in the scene. A clique of five females walked up and spoke to Racks and a few other guys standing around. Racks' little brother grabbed one of the females by the arm and said.

"Tasha, wussup wit dat butt?!" Letting her know he was interested in sex. She snatched her arm away from him and said,
"Don't be grabbin' on me like dat nigga, get tha fuck out my face!" A few people standing around started to laugh and he felt embarrassed so he said,
"Ay, fuck you bitch!"
"Bitch?! I got'cho bitch nigga! Racks you betta get'cho lil' brotha!"
"Or wut bitch! Fuck you gone do?!"
The girl pulled out her cell phone and started punching numbers. Racks' little brother Chris got furious and walked up to her and said,

"Ay, while you on tha phone tellin', tell a mufuka dis bitch!" And he slapped the shit out of the girl! A few dudes stepped up and grabbed Chris and walked him away. Racks grabbed the girl trying to see if she was ok.

"Shawty you aight?"
"I'm straight, I'm straight! It's all good, I ain't trippin'." Then she yelled out. "It's all good Chris, it's all good!" Then her and the other four females walked off.

For the life of me I couldn't tell you where the hell these dudes came from, but in less than five minutes, two cars came flying up the block and came to a quick stop right in front of the Maxima I was driving. Instantly, five guys hopped out at the same time. Out of the first car, the front passenger and the guy from the back seat stepped up. As they came closer, the front passenger held his pants by the waist as if he had no belt on. The one holding his pants scanned the crowd saying,

"Where tha fuck dat nigga at dat put his hands on my sista?!" Everybody just looked at each other like, who the fuck does this dude think he is. Then he spoke again. "Where dat bitch ass nigga Chris at?!" Then without hesitation, Chris stepped up.

"I'm right here nigga! Fuck you tryin' to do?!" Before the guy could say another word, Chris reached back and punched the guy in the face. He stumbled back holding his jaw. It all happened so fast, I couldn't believe what I was seeing. As the guy's back hit the ground, he quickly tried to regain his balance. Chris came storming at him. Then quickly without hesitation, the guy pulled a gun from his waist firing three shots, hitting Chris twice in the face and once in the chest. Then as quickly as it all happened, everything just stopped. Chris' soul had departed, and his body fell to the ground in slow motion.

Once I snapped out of the shock of reality, my mind told me to hit the ground. At that exact same time I made my move, gun blast erupted as I inched my way under Racks' car. Even though I had a pistol on me, I wasn't trying to be anyone's hero. There were enough of Racks' guys out there with guns, so I stayed where I was. The only thing that raced through my mind was, please God don't let me die tonight.

The gunfire had finally came to an end. Now, all I could hear was the pounding of the pavement by running feet, car doors slamming, cars starting, and wheels screeching. As I came from under the car, I heard this Godawful sound. I stood up, dusted myself off, and took in the scene. The same two guys that first stepped up, laid there in a huge puddle of blood, riddled with bullets. I then directed my eyes toward that awful sound. It was Racks, on his knees, rocking back and forth holding his brother's lifeless body, crying.

It didn't take long before I heard sirens, so I walked over to Racks, put my hand on his shoulder and said,

"Racks, he gone bro... Tha police comin', we oughtta' get outta here." Racks pushed me away with one arm and yelled.
"Leave me tha fuck alone!" And he kept rocking and crying. There was nothing more I could do. So, I jumped in the Maxima, took one more look at Racks holding his brother, then I got the fuck out of there before the police came.

****

It was about ten thirty when I got back to my block, and Toni was there tending to a few customers. I parked the car in front of the house and walked over to the maple tree where we usually post up. I set my eyes on a plastic chair, sat down, and stared at nothing. All I could see was Chris getting shot over and over in my mind. I was so gone, I didn't even notice that Toni came and sat down next to me, let alone hear her talking to me until she yelled my name.

"Ug!" I looked at her and she said, "Did you hear all dem gunshots? It sounded like mufukin' Iraq out here."
Then she lit a blunt as I said, "Hear it?! I saw it!" Once I said that, Candice came flying out of the house yelling.

"Ay! Ay y'all! Did y'all hear about Lil Chris?" Toni's eyes lit up then her head snapped toward me with her mouth wide open. She looked at me, then looked at her blunt. She looked at me again, then extended her arm out to me with the weed in hand.

"Ug, hit dis shit." I don't even smoke weed, but tonight I took it anyway.

While I hit the weed, Toni pulled out a fifth of *Hennesy* and a row of cups from a brown paper bag that sat on the ground next to her chair. She poured a cup and passed it to me, then Candice said,

"Ug, what' chu doin' smokin' weed? You don't smoke!"
Then Toni said, "Candice, he was over there when Chris got killed." Candice gasped, then quickly sat next to me speaking excitedly.

"Swear to God Ug, are you ok?" She leaned in and gave me a hug. When she let me go I hit the blunt again and passed it to Toni. I took a sip from my cup and told them the story in its entirety.

I've stood on the outside of the yellow tape and seen dead bodies lay on the ground from afar, but this would be the first time I had ever actually seen a life taken so up close and personal, and at the rate things were going, I didn't think it would be my last.

The three of us sat outside for a while just talking. The town was in a frenzy and everybody came looking for weed. Toni wasn't half stepping herself. Since the South Park block was shut down, all their clientele shifted to our block. That's when Nassir and Yella Boy showed up. Nassir parked the Hummer in the grass about ten feet away from the maple tree where Candice and I were sitting. Toni was moving from car to car serving customers when Nassir and Yella Boy hopped out. They ran to the bushes, grabbed their packs, and started serving customers too. Once the block cleared up, Nassir spoke,

"Damn! Wut tha fuck goin' on out here? Somebody get raided?"

I simply said,
"Hell naw, Chris got killed." Nassir cocked his head in a thinking manner, then responded.

"Chris, Chris." His eyes popped, and his mouth dropped. "You talkin' bout Lil Chris?! Racks lil brotha?!…. Daaaaamn!"
"Yeah and I was down there when it all happened." Nassir shot me a look.
"Wut?! Aw hell naw! Ay Yella Boy, grab dem blunts out da truck." And for the next twenty minutes I explained how Chris had gotten shot and how the South Park dudes turned a few of the guys from the Old Projects into swiss cheese. It was at that moment that I realized that this was going to be a *long* summer.

Around one thirty in the morning Nassir, Toni, and Yella Boy had sold out. Right then we wrapped it up and everybody went home.

When I walked through the door I headed straight for my room. I stripped down to my boxers and flopped onto my bed. I laid there thinking about my life. It was so much I wanted to do, I just couldn't put my finger on what it was. I just know I wanted to do it before someone left me stretched across the pavement like Lil Chris.

Chapter 9

I woke up the next morning still exhausted from last night. I looked at the clock to see it was five minutes past eleven. I got out of the bed and got down on my knees. I thanked God for another day of living and said a prayer for the guys who lost their lives last night. After that I did fifty push-ups, fifty sit-ups, and fifty jumping jacks. I repeated that routine for an hour then took a shower.

Once I finished, I stepped out, wrapped the towel around my waist and stared in the mirror. I looked myself in the eyes and said,

"I'm the master of my own destiny." I then cocked a little smile and hit the block to get that money.

I went through my gear and threw on some gray fleece joggers, a gray Nike t-shirt, and some all-white air force ones. I sprayed on some Roberto Cavalli cologne and tossed on my gray White Sox fitted cap then hit the block.

When I stepped outside, I jumped in the Maxima and backed it up on the shaded grass under the maple tree and sat there as I waited for some action. Fifteen minutes later Yella Boy showed up. I realized I didn't know much about him, so I took this time to get better acquainted. I found out that he was nineteen years old, which kind of threw me off. Even though he looked sort of young, he had a confident swag and a real story to tell demeanor that made him seem at least twenty-seven. He was about 5'10" with a long curly ponytail, thin goat tee, and skin so light I knew he had to be mixed, so I asked,

"Shorty wut'chu cut wit?"
He smiled and said,
"My mother was white and my father is Puerto Rican and black."

"You speak Spanish?"
"Fuck naw, but I talk dis hood shit just fine."

He went on to tell me his mother was a crackhead prostitute who died from a heroin overdose. He never knew his father and he'd been living with a foster family since he was ten years old. He admitted that they were ok people, but he was ready for his own space, and I felt him. Shit, no wonder the little homie seemed older. When I asked him what else he was trying to do with his life besides get his own spot. He said,

"On some real shit Ug, I don't even give a fuck as long as I got a pocket full of money. Shit I'm just out here livin'."
"So wut *do* you care about?"
"Just tha people I fucks wit. Nas, Toni, and Candice like the only real family I got."
"Well, you got me too shorty, and if Nas got'chu around, I know you one hunnid."

From that moment forth he wasn't just the little homie anymore, he was my new little brother. I could tell that our bond would grow stronger in time. Everything happens for a reason, and I was going to make sure I kept Yella Boy close to me at all times.

Around two in the afternoon Nassir and Toni came out on the block and Toni handed Nassir two stacks of money held together by rubber bands.

"Here, dats thirty-seven fifty a piece."
Nassir replied,
"Bet, dat nigga should be pullin' up any minute."

Seconds later, I saw Gacy's Harley Davidson pick-up come cruising up the block. He blew his horn and rolled pass as someone from the passenger seat tossed a Mc Donald's bag onto the grass in front of our house. As he drove pass a female pulled up in a white Monte Carlo and asked for Nassir. He got in the car and the car pulled over to the curb. When Toni saw that, she casually walked over, grabbed the bag off the ground, and tossed it in the garbage can. She then pulled the can into the backyard behind the privacy gate and grabbed the bag out of the can then entered the back door. Ten minutes later, Nassir hopped out of the Monte Carlo and the female drove off. Nassir looked toward Yella Boy and I then said,

"Ay Yella Boy, com'on so we can handle dis business." Yella Boy glanced at me and said,
"Com'on Ug, let me show how I do dat thang." Then the three of us went into the house, locked it down, and got ready for Yella Boy to work his magic.

We stepped in the kitchen were Toni was at the table mashing down big chunks of cocaine into powder. Yella Boy grabbed a large pot from under the countertop, then grabbed a big eight ounce Pyrex jar with the handle from the cabinet. Nassir then left the room and came back with a small digital scale. Yella Boy filled the pot half way with water and sat it on the stove then turned the flame up high. He came back to the table and started helping Toni mash the coke. That's when I asked,

"How much is dat?" Toni then replied.
"Half a brick."
Then Yella Boy said,
"I ain't gone cook it all at once. I'm just gone do a quarter thang at a time."

First, Yella Boy turned the scale on and sat an open plastic baggie on top of the scale plate. Next, he dumped large amounts of coke into the baggie until the scale read 251.2 grams. He then poured the coke into the jar adding fifty-four grams of baking soda, then started stirring it together for a good mix. After that, he sat the

Pyrex jar into the pot of boiling hot water then turned to me and said,

"Now I'm just gone let dat shit heat up." As the coke got hot, Yella Boy gave it a little stir here and there letting the cocaine's natural oils mix with the baking soda, then he said. "Ug dis how you slow cook dat thang to get a good stretch, you can't lose."

He then took a teaspoon and put eight scoops of the boiling hot water into the jar. He stirred and chopped at the coke then added eight more teaspoons of water then stirred and chopped some more. The once powder mix began to turn into a thick peanut butter like substance. After another ten minutes, the peanut butter like substance turned into a thick tan snot, then the thick snot loosened up to a thin snot. That's when Yella Boy said,

"Ug, check it out my nigga."

I looked into the jar as he kept stirring the snot. Ten minutes later, he grabbed an oven mitten from off of the counter as he kept stirring. He then took the jar out of the water and sat it on the counter as he kept stirring. He stirred and stirred until the butter knife he was using just stood still. He took a glass of ice cold water and slowly poured it over the solid crack mold. Just enough to cover the surface, then filled jar up with ice cubes and let it sit while he prepared the next batch.

Fifteen minutes had passed and most of the ice in the jar had melted. Yella Boy drained the water and ice out of the jar then wiggled the knife. It was as stiff as a dick in a pussy house.

Yella Boy turned the jar upside down and gave it a few smacks. When he turned it back over, he gave the knife a firm grip and yanked it, pulling the huge mold of crack from the jar. It came out looking like one big ass cookie. He snatched the knife from the mold, pointed at it and said,

"Crack my nigga! Dat's how you do dat shit." He turned around with a confident stride then got ready to cook the other nine ounces.

I was impressed by Yella Boy's skills. He had a lot of potential as a hustler, I just wondered if he was able to take that potential beyond the game. As I watched him, I began to get a closer picture of Nassir, Toni, and Yella Boy's relationship. What wasn't clear was the end game. When would enough be enough? Shit, who am I kidding? I needed to be asking myself that same question, but right now I knew I didn't have that answer. I just feel like if I stay humble and loyal, it would all come together in due time.

After all the business was handled, we spent the rest of our Saturday simply enjoying each other's company while we got that money. *Man* I missed this shit. Just the feeling and the rush of hustling is more euphoric than sex itself. I know many wouldn't agree with that, but I'm telling you, it takes a *real* hustler to understand what I'm saying. Cause only a real hustler will hop out that pussy to go get that paper.

Chapter 10

It was around five in the evening when Toni came back outside from taking a shower. Nassir had made a store run and we had already started sippin' on some Corona's. Toni went straight to the cooler to grab her one when she noticed four fifths of Coconut Ciroc, four big cans of Dole pineapple juice and six cans of Dole pineapple rings. She closed the top of the cooler and said,

"So, we on nat Coco-loso huh?"
Nassir replied by saying,
"Hell yeah, and hopefully I'll be doing the cha-cha all up in some pussy by tha end of the night. Know wut I'm talkin' bout?"

I sat there taking in my surroundings when I noticed Toni in some black stretch work out pants and a tight white V-neck t-shirt. I happened to take a quick look at her ass when Nassir whispered,

"Ug, wut tha fuck was dat fam?"
"Wut?"
"Bro, did you just look at Toni's ass fam?" Sort of embarrassed I quickly said,
"Huh?! Wut? Uhhh naw!" Then Nassir started getting loud.
"Awwww shit! Ug checkin' out Toni's cheeks! Hey Ug, you know dem booty pops she got on right?"
Toni slapped her ass saying,
"Fuck you nigga, dis all collard greens and cornbread. Betta act like it!... Don't listen to dat fool Ug, he just mad cause he knows he ain't gone *never* hit dis!"
And Nassir replied,
"Wuteva, don't nobody wanna hit dat weak ass pussy. I'm just saying, yesterday you was like Olive Oyl, now today you all out here like Buffy da Body. Wussup?!"
"Olive Oyl?!"

"Yeah Olive Oyl, wit'cho ole heard you was lookin' for candy man face ass."

"Mmm hmm, fuck yo ole pump up tha jam face ass."

"It's all good Toni, wait til I get dis liquor in my system, im'ma heat'cho ass up. Ay Ug, me and Yella Boy got some *real* ski-woo's comin' through in a little bit, so you ain't gotta keep lookin' at Toni's ole squarepants ass booty." And we all cracked up laughing.

After our brief comedy segment, the next few hours went by kind of quick. Although I still had thoughts of Chris being murdered still fresh in my head, I was able to enjoy the nice warm summer breeze. It relaxed my mind and calmed my nerves. It made me feel blessed to be free and alive.

A little after nine, a black Kia Sportage pulled up on the block. It was dark and we didn't recognize the vehicle, so we kept our hands on our pistols. Nassir's phone rang. Seconds later the Kia parked in front of our house and three sexy ass females walked our way. I stepped to Nassir and said,

"Wus tha move bro, how we gone play'em?"

"I just met shorty. So, I don't know wut kind of shit they on. Let's just play it by ear…oh and Ug?" I looked at Nassir and said what's up, then he said, "Wuteva you do bro, don't pull yo dick out til' I give you tha word fam?" I chuckled and said,

"I got'chu bro."

Once the ladies got over to the maple tree Nassir introduced us to the girl he knew. Her name was Nikki. She then introduced her friends Shawntay and Brittany, then Nassir introduced us.

"Y'all already know Yella boy, but dat's Toni and dats Ugly, but we call him Ug."

The ladies sort of looked at me in disbelief. I guess they couldn't imagine a man actually naming himself Ugly. It tickled me a little but I simply said,

"It's all good. Wuts already understood don't need to be explained." The line I had just dropped on them kind of broke up the uneasiness of my name. Besides, I'm sure they've seen uglier than me, and that's when our night began.

Everybody started to get comfortable with each other's company. Shawntay gravitated her way toward Yella Boy, and Brittany sort of joined in with Toni and I.

Brittany was sexy as hell. She stood about 5'9" with shoulder length hair and a caramel complexion. She almost reminded me of Sanaa Lathan. She wasn't shy by far and seemed to be enjoying herself. She kind of fit in like she'd kicked it with us before. Now, I know I'm not the cutest, but my body was bangin'. So, I pulled my go to move, and no, I didn't pull my dick out. I just peeled off my t-shirt and straightened out my tank top, and I think it got her attention. She stared at me for a second then said,

"Now, why you let people call you ugly?"
"Baby girl, ain't nuttin' cute about me."
"Maybe you just need a little encouragement." Ummm ok, was that a flirt? If it wasn't, it sure sounded like one, so I decided to give it a shot.
"Is you dat little encouragement?"
"Maybe, maybe not. Wut's your real name?"
"Aw com'on baby now, if I tell you Im'ma have to kill you."
"Well, if you do tell me you might just get the chance to kill *sumt'n*...... one day."
I smiled and replied,
"In dat case, my real name is Adonis."

"See, that wasn't hard Adonis. And now you look ten times better to me." Then I asked,
"Is dat tha liquor talkin'?"
"Nope, that's a *real* bitch talkin'"
Toni tapped me on the shoulder and said,
"Shorty got game Ug."
And I replied,
"Yeah I know, and I feel like I just got pimped."

For the rest of the night Brittany and I connected. I really wasn't looking for a girlfriend at the time, but she made me want to get to know her a little better. We were both at that level. We both understood that there was chemistry between us, but not the physical type. It was that type that allowed us to be in the moment when she could say I'm feelin' him, and I could say... damn... I'm feelin' her.

It wasn't long before twelve o'clock rolled around and Nikki had to work the next day, so the ladies were preparing to leave. Brittany gave me her number and I told her I would call. We leaned in to each other for a long hug and she said.

"Damn you smell good mmm... Ok, I gotta go just make sure you call me tomorrow, don't make me wait." We let each other go and she walked away. Then in a girly, childish like tone she said, "Bye Adonis." I didn't say anything back, I just smiled. Like I said before, what's understood doesn't need to be explained.

Once the ladies left, Nassir asked how much liquor was left. I checked the cooler and let him know that one bottle hadn't been cracked yet, and that another bottle was half full. He pulled out his cell phone and said,

"Wussup Ug, round two?"
And I replied,
"Aliyah and Domonique?"

"You already know. Im'ma tell dem to bring somebody for Yella Boy too." Toni jumped in saying.

"Y'all too much... Well fellas, I'm in for tha night. I'm tired as hell. I'll get up wit'chall tomorrow." That was when Yella Boy and I grabbed the cooler and we all cleared the block.

Chapter 11

I woke up Sunday morning and went through my ritual of exercise, shower, prayer, and affirmation. I threw on some jeans, a white t-shirt, and a pair of Air Force One's. I made myself a bowl of Cap'n Crunch and a bologna sandwich, then sat on the couch and watched a religious sermon on the Christian channel. The pastor preached about making the right life decisions, and it raised a question. What *are* the right life choices when you feel you have no positive options? It just made me think.

Once the sermon was over, I turned the T.V. off and walked to my room to grab my hat. When I reached for it I saw Brittany's phone number on the dresser. I picked the number up and looked at it, then thought about her words. 'Don't make me wait'. As much as I wanted to call, I didn't want to come off as being too eager. So, I decided to call her this afternoon. Besides it wasn't even ten o'clock yet.

On the block, business was as usual. By twelve o'clock the whole crew was out on the grind. Candice was even out there enjoying her day off. She had on a tank top, pajama pants and house shoes. She had nothing exquisite on, yet she was still very pretty, in a Gabrielle Union sort of way. She asked me how I had been doing since the Friday incident, and what have I been up to since then. About a minute later she said,

"So that's how we roll now Ug?" I was sort of confused.
"Wut'chu mean Candice?"
"So, you ain't gone tell me about Miss Thang you met last night, huh?"

I chuckled about the comment that Candice had made. If I hadn't know any better I'd say she was a little jealous, but I quickly dismissed that thought. I knew she just wanted to hear the juicy details straight from the horse's mouth and not the big mouth that had told her. I honestly wish she hadn't brought it up, because now I was wondering what Brittany was doing. But Candice fucked all of my thoughts up when she broke me out of my thoughts saying,

"So Ug, wut'chu plan on doing for your birthday? I know you didn't think a bitch forgot did you?"
"I don't know, I thought about a party, but it all depends."
"On what?"
"On wut my money lookin' like. I'm trying to have a certain amount by my b-day."
"Boy stop! We havin' a party. I don't wanna hear nothin' else about it."
"Ok, party it is then."

After deciding to have the party on the block and panning out a few details, I asked Nassir to let me use his cell phone. I didn't want to wait any longer, I wanted to hear Brittany's soft sexy voice.

When the phone rang, she picked up on the second ring and said,
"What took you so long? I thought I told you not to make me wait."
"Hol'up. How you know it was me?"
"Call it women's intuition. Now spill it Mr."

Brittany was witty, charismatic, sassy and damn sure assertive. I liked it! So when I answered her question, I kept it all the way real.

"Well if I would'a called you at nine this morning like I started to, you would'a thought I was a stalker."
"Not true. Did it ever occur to you Adonis that waking up to your voice might have started my day off right?"

Damn, I'm glad we were on the phone because I had the biggest and goofiest smile on my face, like a fat kid in a cake factory, until she said, "Ok you can stop smiling now.... So what'chu doin' today?"

I took the phone away from my ear and looked at both sides like what the hell kind of technology they got out here now. Then I put the phone back to my ear and said,

"Uhhh, nothin' really, I was hopin' I could see you."

"Wish granted. What time you talking? You know what, never mind just tell your hoes to get lost, I'll be out there in a couple hours."

"Aight, cool." We said our goodbyes and I gave Nassir his phone back. Curiosity was eating at me, so I asked Nassir could the person on the other end of his phone see me. And he said,

"Ummmm Ug, If you want to continue being my friend, lay off the crack, ok?"

I laughed and said,

"Right, got'cha."

Around three thirty Brittany pulled up and parked. She got out of a dark green Dodge Neon, closed the door, turned her alarm on and started walking our way. Nassir spoke in a hushed tone and said,

"Man, do she see that big ass Hummer right there sittin' on dem thangs? Ain't nobody gone steal her piece o'shit." Then Candice laughed and said,

"Nassir you stupid as hell, but Ug she is pretty though. You ole' pimp you."

When Brittany got over to the maple tree, Candice made it her business to introduce herself. They shook hands and exchanged pleasantries, then we all just kicked back. When Candice and Toni started playing grab ass, Brittany just stared with a look of shock. I tapped her arm and said,

"You aight?"
And she said,
"Uh yeah, I'm cool."
I laughed and said,
"I think that's the same look I had on my face when I came home."
"Naw, It's all good, some of my good friends are gay. It don't bother me. Y'all both just so pretty. I just knew y'all had all the niggas." Then Candice said,
"The only niggas we got are these goofballs right here." Then she cut Nassir a look and said. "And you bet not start, it's too early for that shit."

A few more hours had rolled past and I completely sold out. Candice suggested we go to the lakefront and Brittany agreed with enthusiasm.

"Yeah Adonis, com'on, let's go." I hesitated at first. The last time I left the block I became part of a triple homicide, but I took this as a good time for us to get to get better acquainted. So, I said,

"Fuck it, let's do it."

Toni had Candice run to the store and grab some liquor to roll out with. Nassir and Yella Boy declined, which made it a llittle easier. I was trying to read Brittany's mind, and the less distraction the better.

While we prepared to leave, Nassir took a look back at Brittany's car and decided to let us use the Hummer for the night, and we accepted. I don't know what he had against her car but it was all good with me.

On the way to the lakefront, I watched Brittany as she grooved to the music. She was so full of life and I was just starting mine all over again. I wondered how she would react once I told her I was recently released from prison. Brothers coming home from the joint already had the odds stacked against them. But I figured that if she can accept my features and the fact that I hustled, I still had a fighting chance with being an ex-convict.

We pulled up to the lakefront off Jeffrey and Lakeshore Drive right behind Laribida Children's Hospital. The Jamaicans were out playing the bongos, which made the perfect ambience for a first date. Brittany grabbed my hand and led me toward the water. We found a spot on the huge boulders that separated the water from the shore, and Toni and Candice found a boulder about ten feet away. They wanted to have their privacy *and* be close, just in case something happened.

Once we were comfortable, I poured Brittany a drink. We stared out at the Chicago skyline as the lights twinkled across the water. Damn I missed the city. The Chicago skyline was one of the most beautiful sights to see, so I took it in and embraced the moment. Then Brittany finally spoke,

"Back on your block you said, 'when you came home'. What did you mean by that?"
I took a deep breath and said, "I just got out the joint."
"When?"
"Tuesday."
Then in a shocked and amazed tone she said, "This past Tuesday!?"
"Yup."
"Damn, ok. So how old are you?"
"I'm 26, I'll be 27 in a couple weeks on July 12th."

I went on to let Brittany know what I had done time for. She assured me that it didn't bother her, and that she'd just hoped I had a plan for myself. She also made me feel good by letting me know that she felt I had a great deal of potential. I learned that she was 25 with no kids and worked as a waitress at Red Lobster. She also told me that she lived in Blue Island, which was the next town over that bordered the City of Chicago. We talked about everything from failed love quests, to our favorite color and T.V. shows. We were definitely vibin'.

Chicago Police came around twelve o'clock and let everyone know that the lake was now closed and we had to leave.

On the way back to the block we stopped at the White Castle on 79th & Stony Island to get something to eat. It was just like I remembered, only the players were playing harder as the fly whips lined up South Chicago Rd. Hell it took us an hour just to get our food it was so packed. But it was good to see that the city was still alive.

When we got back to the block Brittany asked if I wanted her to stay with me. I walked closer to her, kissed her on the forehead and said,

"Let's just take our time. I ain't goin' nowhere."
She smiled and replied, "Ok, I'm good with that."
She got in her car, started the engine and rolled her window down. "You know Adonis, you keep scoring brownie points with me, you won't be able to keep me off you for long."

Then she drove away as I watched her leave the block.

Once I got in the house, I went to my room, grabbed the Nike shoe box from my closet and started counting my money. I still had forty-three hundred left from the ten thousand Nassir gave me. I doubled back on a re-up. So that made fifty-four hundred in profit, plus the forty- five hundred to go back to the store with. All together I had fourteen thousand and two hundred dollars. I was trying to hit twenty by my birthday. I just need to stay focused.

As I sat there thinking about where I stood, I remembered something my old celly told me. He said a fool can have all the money in the world, go broke and have nothing, but a wise man can have just a little bit of knowledge and die with it. He was always dropping deep shit on me. He told me he saw a bright future ahead of me, I just had to want it.

I got up from my bed and stripped down to my boxers. I put my money away and jumped in the bed, but before I closed my eyes I told myself that it was official. Tomorrow I would go to the local junior college and sign up for some classes. I closed my eyes, said a prayer for my mother's soul and then got me some much needed rest.

Chapter 12

After a six hour flight, Carlos arrived in Bogota Monday evening. He was greeted by his personal assistant slash lieutenant, Gustavo. Gustavo wore fatigues and combat boots. He was lean and fit with a bald head and beard— no mustache. Carlos however, was a bit more westernized. He looked extremely dapper in an all-black Armani suit, loafers with a white button up shirt and gold cuff links. At forty-one years of age Carlos still looked young with his short, well-groomed hair and thin mustache. He also appeared to still be in shape with his broad chest and wide shoulders. He had an overwhelming look of confidence and power, which made him appealing to many women.

Gustavo escorted Carlos to an all-black Executive Lincoln Continental, where they both sat in the back seat. Gustavo poured Carlos a drink then spoke.

"Your brother is waiting for us at the café. He is very happy you are home and so am I."

"Thank you Gus. I am very happy to be home."

"Carlos, you will be very happy to know that we are stronger now than we have ever been. Even stronger than when your father led the rebels."

"Yes, that has been the intention Gustavo… that has been the intention."

Once the driver pulled on the block of the café, Carlos noticed the rebel soldiers posted everywhere. The car stopped in front of the café and a rebel soldier immediately opened the door for Carlos. The rebels led Carlos and Gustavo into the empty café where Carlos' brother Estavan was sitting and watching television. As soon as he saw the two he turned the television off and stood to greet Carlos. Once they sat and got comfortable Estavan smiled and got right down to business.

"Carlos, we are about to re-establish history. Caquetá is strong, very strong. We have roughly forty thousand rebel soldiers guarding the growing fields, and they are producing beautifully. We have five thousand in Puerto Heath, Bolivia; fifteen thousand in Puerto Leguizamo, Peru and twenty thousand in Latagua."

Latagua was their main growing field. It was located at the southern end of Caquetá. Latagua was the city, Caquetá was the state, and Colombia was the country.

Estavan went on to fill Carlos in on how they'd taken over three other states in Colombia that bordered Panama, right off the coast of the Caribbean Sea. Those three states took for a total of twenty two major cities where they had warehouses set for shipping. The majority of the people in these cities were shipped to one of the three growing fields for labor.

Carlos was extremely happy. Their mission in Bolivia, Peru, and Colombia had been a success and their fields were flourishing. Carlos was now excited from the news as he leaned back in his chair and said,

"So, what about Panama?" Estavan chuckled and said.
"Panama is set, we have rebel soldiers posted in two cities bordering the Panama Canal, Cristóbal and Colón.

Colón was a major port where many international countries did their import and export trading. Many of those nations anchored their merchant ships in Cristóbal. Which made the perfect spot for shipping their product all over the world.

Estavan also told Carlos that they had rebel soldiers on guard in their warehouses located in Belize, Cuba and Half Moon Island. They also had rebels in Merida and Metamoroso, Mexico. That was when the conversation turned and Estavan said,

"Carlos, coming from Cuba and Half Moon Island into the U.S through Mississippi is not our problem, but coming from Belize to Mexico into the U.S., is. The Mexicans are ready to fight us over territory. A war that close to the U.S. will raise a lot of red flags."

And Carlos said,

"Brother, out of eleven Colombian cartels, we have subdued seven of them. If the others want to keep supplying the Mexicans, then let them. Will we lose if we decide not to use Mexico as a gateway?" Then Estavan replied,

"You're missing the point. This is what I meant by our associates in Chicago being unmanageable. Chicago is supposed to be our explosion point, hard flood to the middle of the U.S. and let the wave take over, our metropolis. And right now the only way to see this plan through correctly is being able to utilize the Mexican ports and using our Mexican associates. The issue now is they don't want to move our product because the other cartels have put pressure on them about their loyalty."

"Yes, I see, somehow I knew it would come to this. Don't worry brother this will not be a broken mission. Our Chicago associates have a great deal to learn when it comes to loyalty, I'll see to that. I will fix this, I promise brother.

"What do you have in mind Carlos?"

"I have an idea… just give me some time. Before you know it, the Mexicans will be begging for our product; and that's when we say, fuck you!" Estavan then chuckled and ordered Gustavo to get them some drinks.

Carlos and Estavan spent the rest of evening catching up on more personal matters. It wasn't long before Estavan left for Caquetá and Carlos prepared for his return to the U.S.

After Estavan left the cafe, Carlos pulled out his cell phone. It was time to put the next phase of his plan into motion. He called the one person who was going to see that his plan in the U.S. was successful.

Carlos dialed a number and the phone rang several times. A man answered the phone and said,

"Hello?"
Then Carlos spoke,
"Andre?"
"Yeah, this is Andre."
"Good, everything is set. Show up in the morning and talk to the person in charge, he'll be waiting. Give me a call and let me know how it all works out. Remember, you report to me directly, but never over the phone. We will meet when necessary, got it?"
"I got it."
"Ok, I'll be talking to you soon." Due to the heavy accent Carlos had, Andre knew exactly who he was speaking with and he was ready to give Carlos his money's worth.

Chapter 13

Back in Robbins; Ug, Toni, Nassir, and Yella Boy were up early Tuesday morning putting their packs together. Toni and Nassir sat at the kitchen table with the dope while Yella Boy cooked more. Ug sat on the couch bagging up weed on the small table in the front of the television. Ug had the channel 9 news on catching up on his current events as he called it. He was stuffing weed in huge plastic seal bags when a breaking news story came over the channel. Ug listened as the reporter said,

"In breaking news, seventeen men were arrested today in Robbins, Il." Ug's head popped up as he frantically called the crew to the television set as the reporter continued. "In a pre-dawn sweep all seventeen men were taken into custody this morning in connection to the murder of Christopher Bennet, Rashad Lewis and Jerome Baker." And all tree victim's pictures popped up on the screen. "Three other men are suspected to be in connection to the triple homicide. If you have any information that will lead authorities to their arrest, please call the Robbins Police Department.

After Nassir, Toni, and Yella Boy went back to the kitchen, Ug sat there on the couch feeling sorry for Racks. I mean damn, he just watched his brother lose his life and now he was going to lose his too. It was fucked up, but hey, it is what it is. What can you do? Some things are just meant to be.

Ug cleared his head, finished bagging up, and hit the block. When he came out of the house he saw a dude on a bike in the middle of the street serving a customer. The first thing that went through Ug's head was 'this is our block, our money, and this motherfucker just took food off our table'. Ug walked up to the guy and stared him down. The guy tried to play the roll and asked

Ug for a few bags of weed. The first thing Ug did was confront him about what he had just seen, and the guy said,

"Com'on Jo stop trippin', I'm shoppin' wit'chu anyway." Ug was past pissed off when he said,
"Head or gut!?" The guy looked at Ug as if he was confused, then said
"Head?" Head was the first word Ug heard, so before he could get another word out, Ug hit him in the face and knocked his ass off the bike. He then shook the guy down and went in his pockets. He took his money *and* his dope then stuffed the two bags of weed he asked for in his front pocket. He then left him lying there in the middle of the street.

What the fuck was he thinking? Did he think they were spending all of that time pumping up their spot just so he could waltz up and make money? Nah, I don't think so. So Ug had to set the tone and send a message to let other motherfuckers know that their spot wasn't going to take any losses, and they weren going to stand on it.

A minute or two later Nassir, Toni, and Yella Boy came out of the house. They all stared at the dude laying on the ground. Nassir looked at Ug and said,
"Ug, wut tha fuck going on out here? Wut tha fuck dude doin' in tha street?" They all walked over to him to get him up until they noticed the side of his face was swollen. Nassir looked over at Ug.
Then Ug said,
"I caught his ass servin'. Wut tha fuck was I suppose to do, shake his hand? Who tha fuck is he anyway?"
And Nassir replied,
"He one of tha Lords from tha next block. Hey Yella Boy, help me get dis nigga up."
Then Ug said,
"Y'all strapped?"

And Yella Boy replied,
"We always strapped my nigga."
"Well let's not fuck around, let's get straight to it. Put his ass in tha truck. Yella Boy, ride tha bike over on tha next block, we gone meet'chu over there."

When they pulled up on the Lords block, a handful of them were posted up. When Yella Boy came riding up the block on the guy's bike they all hopped out of the truck. Ug grabbed him by the shirt, snatched him out of the truck and said,

"He one of y'all?" One of the guys spoke up and said.
"Yeah he's one of ours, wussup?"
"Wussup is, I just knocked his ass out for servin' on our block. We don't step on nobody toes and we want the same respect!"

Ug reached in his pocket and tossed his work on the ground then pulled his gun out. Once he did that Nassir, Toni, and Yella Boy pulled theirs too.
Then Ug said,

"Next time dat shit mine! We all good here?" The guy stared at his man with a serious and pissed off look and said,
"Yeah famo ayathang love, we got him."
At that point Ug and the crew jumped back in the truck and rolled back to their spot.

Back on the block under the maple tree, Nassir cracked a smile. He knew Ug's hands were crucial, it had just been awhile since he seen him in action. Nassir walked up to Ug and put his hand on Ug's shoulder and said,

"Yo Ug, you aight fam, you need some pussy? Cause if you need some pussy, I'll get'chu some pussy my nigga."

"I don't need no pussy you damn fool. I need mufukas to respect our hustle! This is our shit, if we don't stand for sumt'n, we gone fall for anythang, feel me?"

And Yella Boy said,

"Hell yeah, I feel you Ug. I respect dat shit famo, real talk."

While they were discussing block ethics, Nassir's phone rang. He answered, then handed the phone to me. I looked at the phone suspiciously then said,

"Who dat?"

Then Nassir replied by saying,

"Fuck I know nigga? I ain't no mufukin secretary, it's a female."

When Ug took the call, he found out it wasn't a female at all, but he was excited all the same. It was his old celly, Carlos. So many people getting out of prison promise to stay in touch. But he saw that Carlos was a man of his word, and that was good enough for him.

They didn't talk on the phone for long at all. Carlos simply told Ug that he wanted to meet with him in the morning for breakfast at the Trump Tower, and Ug accepted. After they agreed upon a time, Ug showed his gratitude by saying,

"Hey Carlos, it was good hearing from you man, thanks for calling. I'll see you in tha morning."

Just as quick as that bum ass dude from the next block pissed me off, the call from Carlos put him back in his mode. So, before Ug gave Nassir his phone back, he called Brittany. She told him she was on her way to work, and wanted him to keep her company over the phone until she got there. Once she arrived she told Ug that she'd call him when she got off. They said their goodbyes and Ug got back to chasing the money.

Around six that evening, the dude from the next block Ug spoke to earlier pulled up on their block. When Ug noticed who it was, he told the crew to keep their hands on their pistols. When the guy noticed their moves, he stuck his head out of the window and said,

"Don't shoot famo, I came bearing gifts– my nigga." And he held up a fifth of Hennessy.

He parked and got out of the car carrying the bottle, then seconds later him and Ug got acquainted. He introduced himself as Rico, and Ug shook his hand and said,

"Wus good? I'm Ug." He sort of found Ug's name amusing, but he never questioned it. He came to the block with the drink to show them that there was really no hard feelings. He said he couldn't speak for the dude Ug knocked out, but assured him that he wouldn't be a problem.

Rico was a cool dude, and Ug felt it was decent of him to come through on the page that he did, but Ug still knew to keep his eyes open for the under play. Motherfuckers will butter you up then bake you, and it wasn't going to happen to them.

As Rico was getting up to leave, a Robbins police car rolled past them. It stopped quickly and they tossed their pistols in the bushes. The car stopped then backed up, and two officers got out and walked over. One of them– they all knew very well, Officer Ross. This was the dick head that sent Ug to prison. The other officer seemed familiar to Ug but he was almost sure he'd never seen him before. Nevertheless, Ross walked up to Ug with his arm out waiting for Ug to shake it. And when he didn't he just shook his head and said,

"Mr. Stuffy, welcome home." Ug looked at his hand then stared him dead in the eyes, but didn't say a word, then Ross said.

"It's ok, I see prison didn't teach you no respect for authority. Rico, wut'chu doin' over here, you buyin' crack mufuka? Come here nigga, let me pat you down."

He searched Rico's pockets and frisked him down, he then told him to get lost. He looked to his partner and said,

"Search those two, I got these two… Ahh yeah, Adonis Stuffy, the old gun slanger. You out here slangin' dope now? You ain't gotta answer that, if you is, I'm gone catch you… Fellas, oh and lady, this is my new partner Officer Watts, and we out here. If we catch you slangin' dope ya ass is out… Them two straight Watts?"

And his partner replied,
"Good to go."
Then Officer dick head spoke again,
"Ok lady and gentlemen, y'all be safe out here."
They got in their car and drove off.

If Ug never had to see Ross ever again, he wouldn't be mad. Ross had a hard on for Ug and wanted to see him in jail for the rest of his life. Ug knew that this was a problem in the making. So, unless he jobs for Ug and the crew, they were going to be out there too.

Chapter 14

It was about eight-fortyfive when I arrived at the Trump Towers, and Carlos was outside waiting near the door. He was leaning against the wall with one leg up fidgeting with his phone when I called out his name. He looked up and smiled. He waved me over toward the door and said, "Adonis, come with me, I have breakfast waiting for us upstairs." He put his arm around my shoulder in a father and son type manner. He smiled and said, "You're going to love the view, it's magnificent."

We got into the double door elevator and Carlos pressed the button labeled twenty B. When we arrived on the twentieth floor a screen with a blue hand lit up. Carlos placed his palm on the blue hand and the elevator doors opened. There was no hallway and there were no neighbors. Carlos' suite took up half the twentieth floor.

Once we entered, he directed me to a dining table in front of a huge picture window that overlooked the City of Chicago. There was a huge bowl of fresh fruit on the table, a platter full of pastries, and a pitcher of orange juice. He pointed toward a chair and told me to have a seat and get comfortable. He then pressed a button on an intercom box that sat on the table and said, "Maria, you can bring us our breakfast now."

I stared out of the window looking out into the city, and I thought to myself, this is the shit! That's when I was distracted from my thoughts by the sound of heels clicking. I turned to see Maria walking toward us and I was caught off guard. She was naked, and I do mean ass… hole… naked! Her arms were up, holding two platters in the palms of her hands. I instantly looked at Carlos and he was casually smiling. He slowly shook his head up and down and said, "I told you the view was magnificent." Once she reached the table, she looked at me and said, "Buenos dias señor."

I didn't know what the fuck she had just said, but it sounded sexy as hell and my dick got hard. When Carlos was done watching my reaction he told her thank you and gave her a light tap on the ass. She did a curtsy and smiled, then walked away.

The food looked delicious. Maria had prepared us both a T-bone steak and a three cheese omelet. As we ate our food, we did a lot of small talk about Maria and the view of the city. When I asked him what he'd been up to, he told me about some land development plan he was working on. When he asked me, what had I been up to, I told him about me signing up for school and just hanging out with friends. Once he finished his steak he pushed his platter away, leaned forward, clasped his hands together and said, "Adonis, I want you to be able to talk to me as a confidant, a friend. Friends don't bullshit each other. I want the core values of our friendship to be based on trust, loyalty, and respect. So, with that being said, what have you really been up to?"

Carlos didn't strike me as the type that wanted to hear about the hood, but then again, he had an asshole naked maid. Who knew what type of thrills he was seeking. I thought about what he had just said, and it dawned on me that Carlos was trying to establish a deeper bond with me. Carlos was a wealthy man, and if I wanted to get anywhere near his level, I needed to start creating that deeper bond right now.

I leaned back in my chair and relaxed a little more. I then told Carlos about my last seven days in its entirety. I told him about the triple homicide, Brittany, and even the bum ass dude I knocked off the bike yesterday. I also let him know about my weed hustle. Maybe I shouldn't have told him everything, but for some strange reason it felt like *that* was the type of shit he wanted to hear. Then he just got deep on me and said, "Adonis, pain alone is simply just pain. It's what you feel. But the experience and the memories of pain serve a worthy purpose. Those memories remind you of where you've been. It relives what you saw, and it creates a threshold that lets you know what you can and cannot take in life. Adonis, if a man is shot in the chest and is rushed to the hospital, he is not focused on the pain, he is focused on living. Now, you've been through a lot in life and you've experienced pain. I remember from the stories you told me. So, my question is, what are *you* focused on?

    Damn, he'd just hit me with a fist full of real life, my mind was still processing the shit, and I really didn't have an answer. I just pulled myself together and said, "I'm focused on gettin' dis money."
    Carlos then said, "Yes, but at what lengths and by what means?"
    "By any means necessary."
    Carlos smiled and shook his head up and down then said, "I like that. Confidence, determination, ambition! That is what's going to make you a wealthy man Adonis. I see a bright future ahead of you. Now, let's do some shopping."
    Carlos pressed the intercom button again and spoke to Maria. This time he spoke in Spanish. The only word I understood was dinero. He asked me if I was ready to hit the Magnificent Mile, and I told him, hell yeah! So we left his suite and headed for Michigan Avenue, better known as the Magnificent Mile.

    Shopping with Carlos made me feel some kind of way. It made me feel like a kid again, but not in a bad way. See my father got killed when I was fourteen, so it kind of filled an empty space I've had for years. It's funny how a man you hardly know can come along and make you wish he was your father. I guess deep down inside we all craved love and acceptance, and today Carlos was showing *mad* love.

Carlos told me to get whatever I wanted, but to make sure I picked out enough formal and casual wear. He told me that when we were together, I should look the part. He also said that over time he would introduce me to a lot of important people and he wanted them to respect me as much as they respected him. I took it that he wanted that respect to begin with my appearance.

It was three in the afternoon when we finished shopping and we loaded all the bags in the back of the black Executive Escalade limo we were riding in. Carlos leaned over to the mini bar and offered me a drink. Without waiting for an answer he poured liquor into two glasses and passed one to me. I asked him what type of liquor it was and he said it was scotch. He told me not to sip it, just throw it back. So, I tilted my head and tossed the scotch down my throat... That shit had to be the truth, cause I swear I could feel chest hair growing right now. It was definitely good shit and when I looked at Carlos, he started laughing at the face I was making as I adjusted to the scotch. He patted me on my shoulder and said, "I'm hungry again, let's get something to eat."

We spent the rest of that afternoon and early evening at the Taste of Chicago. If you've ever been to Chicago in the summer, then you'd know that the Taste of Chicago was one of the city's biggest outdoor events. Blocks and blocks of restaurant vendors showing tourist's what Chicago style food is made of. Oh yea!

We made it back to Carlos' suite around seven-thirty that evening. I followed Carlos to a sitting room with soft lighting that again had a view to die for. Carlos looked at his watch and said,

"Ah, seven-thirtyeight, we made it on time. Relax Adonis, the fireworks are going to start soon. Make yourself comfortable, I'll be back in a moment."

I walked toward the window and leaned against the metal frame with my forearm. Being that high up in the sky looking over the city made me feel like Scarface. I know that sounds a little silly, but I just couldn't help myself. I held my hands up like I was holding a machine gun, and with my best Al Paccino impression, I said, "Ok, I'm re-loaded! Aye aye aye, fuck you mane. I'm still standin'. I'm... still... standin'!" Carlos scared the shit out of me when out of nowhere he yelled out with *his* best Scarface impression.

"The world is mine! All mine!"

First of all, I felt like a complete idiot. Secondly, I felt confused as hell, cause when I turned around Carlos was standing there with his arms stretched out in the air with boxers and a robe on. Now, the last time I saw a man in boxers and a robe it was Nassir, and we had girls. I nervously looked around and scanned the room... there were no girls. There was nobody else in the room but Carlos and I. And when he walked a little closer, he smiled and said, "Scarface! I love that movie, it's a classic." Then he looked at me and said, "Adonis you seem a little uptight. Relax, take your shirt off..." Take my shirt off? Uhh what the fuck?! I started to think about all the clothes he had bought and the good time he showed me today, and I calmly said, "Hey Carlos, real talk? I don't do the homosexual thang. I'm not sure wut kind of signals you picked up on when we was behind tha wall, but I ain't on that fam."

The smile on Carlos' face went away quickly, and he just stared at me. Then all of a sudden he just exploded with laughter. He leaned on the sofa and held his stomach as he laughed himself silly and after he calmed down he said,

"I'm sorry I gave you that impression Adonis, but I was simply being hospitable, making you feel at home."

Phew! I'm glad we got that shit out the way, cause I didn't want to have to fuck Carlos up... He was still giggling when he walked over to the intercom, pressed a button and said, "Rosa, would you come to the living area please." A minute or two later Maria came walking into the room still naked. Carlos spoke to her in Spanish and they both smiled then looked at me. Maria then said, "¡Si Señor, uno momento." When she walked away I asked, "Wut did she just say?"

    Then Carlos said, "She'll be back in one moment.

It was nothing major, but curiosity was killing me and I wanted to know why Carlos had called Maria, Rosa. So, I asked, "Is Maria's first name Rosa?"

    "What do you mean Adonis?"

    "Well, when you talked into tha intercom, you said Rosa, then Maria came out." Carlos chuckled and said,

    "I think you should have your eyes checked Adonis."

    "Why you say dat?" Carlos pointed toward the door and said, "Because that's Maria… and that's Rosa. The other one right there is Juliana." He walked closer to me and whispered near my ear and saying, "Maria likes to shave and Rosa likes to leave a little." He then smiled and bumped elbows with me.

    Maria and Rosa were twins! Could my day get any better? Maria sashayed across the room holding a tray with cigars on it and Rosa was right with her holding a tray with champagne glasses on it. Juliana strolled behind them pushing a cart with a bottle of Scotch and an ice bucket chilling three bottles of Cristal. They were all looking sexy, I guess because they were all naked!

    Once they made it over to the sofa where we were, they sat everything down on the living room table. Carlos then said, "Have a seat ladies." He put his arm around my shoulder, smiled and said, "I'm doing well for a gay man, don't you agree Adonis?" I was embarrassed as hell, all I could do was smile and say, "My bad Carlos man. I just wanted to make sure we was on tha same page."

    "It's ok Adonis, I understand. Here, have a cigar, their Cuban, the best in the world." While he was handing me the cigar

I said, "Wait a minute, hol'up." I stepped back, gave the ladies a wink of the eye and I took my shirt off.

Carlos and I smoked Cuban cigars, sipped Cristal and threw back shots of twenty-five hundred dollars a bottle scotch while the ladies simply enjoyed the Cristal. The ladies were naked and Carlos and I were halfway there, yet the vibe in the room wasn't sexual. We were all just having a good time watching the fireworks at Grant Park from Carlos' Trump Tower suite. Living!

The fireworks were starting to calm down now and I was sitting back in a zone enjoying the moment. Carlos spoke something in Spanish and the ladies giggled, then Maria and Rosa got up and walked toward me. Maria stood between my legs and started kissing me. It was drunkenly seductive and I felt myself instantly get hard. Rosa watched for a few seconds as she bit her bottom lip, growing hornier by the second. As she ran her hand through Maria's hair, Maria looked at Rosa, then they both started kissing each other. They were so into it, I thought they forgot I was there. Juliana looked away and grabbed Carlos' hand and smiled as they left the room. I guess one was all Carlos needed tonight.

When Maria and Rosa stopped kissing, they gave a seductive giggle then pushed me backward. They unbuttoned my jeans, grabbed hold of my boxers and pulled both my boxers and jeans off at the same time. Maria messaged my joint while Rosa ran her hands up and down my chest and abs. Maria then slowly put me in her mouth as I threw my head back in ecstasy. That's when Rosa stood up on the sofa and positioned her legs on both sides of my head and slowly squatted down. She then held my head as my tongue gravitated toward her pleasure spot. I could feel her shaking as she gyrated on my face. The wilder Maria got with the head, the deeper I stuck my tongue down Rosa's tunnel.

When Maria stopped sucking, I stopped licking. I began to grab on their ass a little just for giggles then we changed positions.

Rosa leaned back into the sofa with her legs open and Maria planted her face in Rosa's sweet spot. While Maria was bent over with her face between Rosa's legs, I mounted Maria from the back and rubbed my joint up and down her wet spot. Seconds later, I gently went into Maria with deep slow strokes that made her gasp in between licking Rosa's sweet spot. The girls had crazy energy and they kept me sexing all night until the early morning. We all tapped out around 3am, that's when I went to sleep thinking, damn! My first threesome, and it happen with a pair of bad ass Latina twins.

Chapter 15

Carlos met with his Mexican associate. He arrived at the Trump Towers around eight that morning and Carlos greeted him in the lobby. He took him upstairs to his suite and escorted him into the dining area where Carlos initiated the conversation.

"Hector, we have a serious issue."
Hector knew exactly what Carlos was talking about, so he began to explain his position. He took a deep breath and said, "Carlos, the decision was out of my control."
Carlos got upset and said, "But you were fully in control when we made our arrangement, am I right?"
Then Hector said, "I was almost finished with the last ton I received from you. Moving your product made our Cartel Associates in Mexico wonder why we were so slow with *their* payment. They sent word to check our stamps, and when they saw the scorpion instead of the dolphin, they sent word back to Mexico that I was dealing with another cartel. The Ortega's threatened to kill my family back in Mexico Carlos, I had no other choice. I had to cease all contact with Caquetá."
"So, they know it's Caquetá?"
"Yes, they wanted to know what cartel the scorpion represented."

Carlos thought for a second. He felt like he'd been muscled. He felt like Caquetá had been muscled. It took every nerve in his body to stay calm when he said,

"Hector, we made an arrangement. You gave me your word that you would be able to distribute our product. We've put in a lot of work from Bolivia to the U.S. based on your commitment to Caquetá."
"I know Carlos, I'm very sorry, but I'm sure you understand."

"I understand that I sent you five tons of cocaine at ten million a ton, where is it?"

"Forty-nine million has already been shipped back to Latagua."

"Forty-nine is not fifty. You're fucking with my patience Hector. Where's the rest of my money."

"Like I said, I was almost finished. I hid the last one hundred kilos in a storage unit off Archer & Ashland."

Hector reached in his pocket and pulled out the key to the storage unit along with a gate code and storage number written on a small piece of paper. He sat it on the table then leaned back and said, "Carlos, I came prepared with peace offering of a million dollars. I wasn't sure how this meeting would turn out, so I left it in my car. I'm parked in the garage downstairs. This is my own personal money. I just want to try and make this right."

Carlos called Rosa to the dining area. He told Hector to give her the keys to his car and asked him what stall was he parked in. Hector asked if she would be able to carry the bag by herself. That's when Carlos said,

"Rosa, wake Señor Adonis and take him with you. There's a bag in the trunk, bring it back." Rosa left the room and did as she was told.

Ug was still in the living room ass naked and sleep. Rosa walked over and shook Ug a few times and called out his name. Once he opened his eyes, she said. "Hurry Señor Adonis, dress please, yes?"

Ug threw his clothes on and followed Rosa to the garage. They took the elevator all the way to the underground parking.

Once they were there, Rosa found the car and popped the trunk where they both stared at a black duffel bag. Rosa looked at Ug and said,

"You carry." Ug grabbed the bag and they took off toward the elevator and went back up to Carlos' suite.

Carlos and Hector were still deeply conversing. Carlos wanted to know exactly what cities in Mexico the Ortega's operated out of. He told Hector he wanted to contact their General to try and gain some understanding of business. Hector saw this as a good opportunity for the Ortega Cartel. So, he said,

"The Ortega's operate out of Loredo, Texas but their rebel army camp is located in Juarez." That was when Ug and Rosa walked into the dining area. When Carlos noticed Ug and Rosa standing at the entrance, he said,
"That would be all Rosa." Rosa gave Carlos a head nod and left the room, then Carlos said, "Come Adonis, sit the bag down, have a seat."

Carlos didn't bother introducing Hector and Ug to each other. He simply smiled, stood up, buttoned his suit jacket and walked to the window. He stood there silently as he looked out into the city. He then held his head down when he said, "Hector, I respect your loyalty to the Ortega's. It shows principle, faithfulness and devotion. It's quite honorable."

Carlos walked from the window to a desk on the near right of the room. He reached in the drawer then turned around. He was facing Hector's back but could see Ug's face. He then walked back over, stood next to Ug and stared at Hector and said, "Adonis, there's a great deal to learn from my friend Hector here. Loyalty solidifies the respect and trust level you have for a person. It creates a forever bond. Loyalty is based on personal and moral choice. Choice being the key word here." Carlos then pulled a gun from his waist and aimed it at Hector. Hector just stared at the gun with a serene look in his face. Somehow, he expected it. You can't ride two waves coming at each other and expect not to wipe out… Carlos looked at Ug and said. "Adonis, are you ready to make the money? You said by any means right? ... Make a choice." Then he nodded his head toward Hector and said, "Shoot him."

Ug stood up somewhat hesitantly. He stared at the gun for a brief second, then looked at Carlos. The look on Carlos' face pretty much told Ug that he wasn't taking no for an answer. Ug then took the gun as he left it pointed at Hector's head. Hector then tried one more act of rationale and said, "Carlos we can work this out."
Then Carlos erupted, "Shut up! You fucking coward! Caquetá is strong! We would have fought for you!" Then he stood behind Ug, put his hand on Ug's shoulders, and spoke closely into his right ear and said, "Relax Adonis it's ok, just aim for his chest."

Ug stood there staring into Hectors eyes. He didn't have a clue of why this was happening. He only heard Carlos' words flowing through his head, 'are you ready to make the money' and 'by any means necessary'. Hector could feel the moment building up. Then Ug saw a glitch. It was a quick and precise response to movement. Hector was making a move, and without hesitation Ug let off a shot.

A look of surprise stretched across Ug's face. He still had the gun pointed at Hector as he watched him gasp for air. Carlos took the gun from Ug's hand and walked closer to Hector. He leaned into Hector's ear and said, "You've made the wrong choice Hector, Caquetá lives." Carlos took a step back and said, "See Adonis, he's not worried about the pain, he just wants to live." Then he fired two more shots into Hector's chest.

Carlos walked to the near right of the room and put the gun back in the drawer. When he turned around he saw Ug still standing there staring at Hector's dead body. Carlos told Ug to have a seat and he pulled up a chair next to him. Ug didn't seem to be scared or worried, he simply just looked out of place. Carlos sat down and took a deep breath then said, "Adonis, was this your first time shooting someone?" Ug shook his head yes, then Carlos finish speaking. "Well, you did good. And despite how you feel right now, you made a decision that's going to last you a lifetime, if you let it. Let's not waste time dwelling on the past." Then he nodded toward Hector. "It's time to start looking toward the future, things are going to start moving very fast and I need you focused. Are we on the same page Adonis?" Ug shook his head again, then Carlos finished. "Adonis, look at me. I've had respect for you long before I ever met you. I've trusted you enough to bring you into my home, but right here and right now, this is where your loyalty begins. There's a million dollars in the bag, take it. Sometime today before it gets too late, I'm going to be sending you a package. Take your time, there's no rush. I'll be leaving out of town in a few days, I'll contact you when I'm back… Oh and Adonis? Don't fuck me." Then he looked over at Hector again to make his message clear, then said, "Now, go home, take a nice hot shower and enjoy your holiday, it's the 4th of July. I'll have the limo drop you off." Then Ug left the room to gather his things.

Carlos checked his watch, it was only 9:45am. He got on the intercom and called the girls to the dining room. While he waited for them, he got on the phone and called his appliance store. He told them to load a deep freezer onto one of their moving trucks and wait for Maria to show up, then hung up the phone.

When the girls appeared in the dining room they took a look at Hector and acted as if they hadn't seen a thing. Then Carlos spoke, "Maria go to the appliance store, they have a deep freezer on one of the trucks waiting for you. Take it to the storage unit at this address, this is the key, the storage number is on it. Take this also, it's the gate code. There are kilo's in the storage. Load them inside the freezer then call me. Go now. Rosa, make sure Señor Adonis makes it home safe with a clear head. Juliana, you stay here with me and help me with this piece of shit." And they all did as they were told.

Chapter 16

I was gathering all my shopping bags at the elevator door. I moved sort of fast cause truth be told, I wanted to get the hell out of Trump Towers. When I finished grabbing my bags, I was met at the door by one of the twins. Without them being naked, I couldn't tell them apart, so I asked. "How I know which one you are?"

She girlishly giggled and said, "Me Rosa. I like my hair long. Maria like her hair together."

Then I chuckled and said, "You mean ponytail?"

"Ponytail, yes!" We were quiet for a brief moment then she spoke again in her heavy broken English. "Well, are you ready Señor Adonis?"

"Yeah. I'm ready."

"Well come, the driver is waiting."

When we got all the bags into the limo, I got in and relaxed. Surprisingly, Rosa hopped in too. I gave the driver my address and Rosa told him to drive slow.

Once we were on the road, Rosa poured a glass of scotch and told me to drink it, so I did. And believe me it was much needed. Rosa was looking out of the window and holding her glare when she spoke to me saying, "Señor Adonis, you are very lucky to be in your position. You should embrace it."

I looked at Rosa long and hard and I thought to myself, damn this girl is fine as hell, but I didn't have a clue of what the fuck she was talking about. Maybe it was the money, or maybe even me knowing Carlos, but something told me that she was saying something far more than what she lead on.

****

Around nine forty-five, Maria showed up at the appliance store and met with the driver. After a short greeting, he took her around the back of the store where the truck was located. Maria reached in her purse and took out a small scanning device and brushed it across the driver's body. She then took her time inspecting the truck for tracking devices. Once she was satisfied, Maria gave the driver the address and they both jumped in the cab of the truck and took off. Maria wasted no time.

The truck pulled up in front of the storage unit around 10:30am. Maria leaned out of the window and pressed the four digit code for the gate to open. Once in, they found the storage garage with no problem and Maria said,

"Stay put, leave the truck on."

Maria turned the mirror on the passenger door inward so the driver couldn't see to the back of the truck, then she told the driver to do the same. She then walked to the garage door that matched the key number, unlocked the lock, and then heaved the garage door open. She saw four large boxes sitting in the middle of the floor. She looked in all four boxes and saw that they were all filled with the kilos of cocaine that Carlos mentioned. Satisfied, she closed the boxes and went back to the cab of the truck and told the driver to put the boxes onto the truck.

Once he finished, Maria told the driver to cut the engine and don't get out. She jumped onto the back of the truck and started loading the kilos into the deep freezer.

Fifteen minutes later, Maria hopped back into the cab of the truck, pulled out her phone and called Carlos. Once she connected, she told him she was finished. Carlos told her to stay put and hung up.

Three minutes later, Carlos called back and gave her an address then told her to deliver the freezer. Immediately, Maria gave the address to the driver. As he was putting the address into the GPS, Maria pulled a gun from her purse and nudged it into the side of the driver's stomach and said,

"Drive carefully. If this truck is pulled over, I'll blow your fucking head off, now drive!"

****

The expressway was jammed packed coming from the Downtown area and traffic was moving at a 20 mile per hour creep. Ug and Rosa were conversing, trying to get better acquainted. Overall, Rosa just wanted to keep Ug talking, until she decided to turn things up a bit.

There were two captain chairs and a bench seat in the limo with a bar in between. Rosa sat in one of the Captain chairs and Ug sat on the bench. Rosa reached under her skirt and pulled her panties off then balled them up in her left hand. She maneuvered her way across to Ug and kneeled down in front of him. She unbuckled his pants and pulled out his Mr., then they engaged in a heavily seductive kiss. Rosa sucked on his tongue until it came loose from her lips, she then put her panties in his mouth and giggled. When Ug tried to take the panties out she said,

"No! I want you to taste me Señor Adonis." Then she went down on him.

Rosa took Ug in her mouth slowly. She turned her head to the left as she came up then turned her head to the right as she went back down. When she came up, she held the tip of his shaft with her teeth, then tickled the tip with her tongue. It drove Ug crazy! She then softly grabbed his balls and messaged them as she went up and down, then stopped. Rosa reached up and opened the sunroof, then told Ug to stand up. When he stood up and stuck his body out of the sunroof, Rosa continued. This time she she got aggressive and went at him like a hungry woodpecker with her head bobbing from side to side. The only thing that kept Ug on his feet was him holding on to the roof of the limo.

Traffic was moving now, and Ug held his head back and let the wind brush past his face, to him it was surreal.

When Rosa stopped, she sat back down in the captain's chair and Ug came back down and sat on the bench. Rosa cocked her legs open and started masturbating. Ug sat and watched with his joint at attention. She sucked her finger slowly then smiled as she looked at her wet split and said,

"Hungry Señor Adonis?" Ug smiled then planted his face between her thighs. She wrapped her legs around his neck and rubbed his head while he ate.

Five minutes later, Ug leaned back in the bench seat and Rosa straddled him with her feet planted on the bench with her hands clasped behind his neck. She bounced up and down to his rhythm as she stared at the sky through the sunroof. Minutes later, Ug screamed out.

"I'm bout to cum!" Rosa hopped off and took him into her mouth and Ug erupted like a Hawaiian volcano.

Twenty minutes had passed when the limo pulled up on Ug's block. When Ug noticed no one was around he quickly grabbed the duffel bag and shot in the house. When he came back out, he saw that Rosa had sat some of the shopping bags on the front porch. He left those there and went to the limo to help with the others.

Ug was walking away with the last few shopping bags in his hand when Rosa came trotting behind him calling his name.

"Señor Adonis, wait!" Ug turned around and Rosa grabbed his face with both hands and leaned into his body with a kiss. She was still holding on to his face when she pulled her lips away and said, "Caquetá lives." She walked backward a few steps still looking into his eyes, then turned around and got back into the limo. Ug stood there for a minute and watched the limo drive away.

Ug got all the bags in the house then took them to his room. He grabbed the black duffel bag and sat it on the edge of the bed and opened it. He reached in the bag with both hands and pulled out bundles of money. He saw that all the bundles had money bands on them that said $10,000. Ug got excited and dumped all the money on the bed, leaving the bag empty. He figured that if it was to be a million dollars, there should be a hundred bundles. So, as he counted the bundles, he put them back into the duffel bag. He got up to eighty-seven bundles when the doorbell rang. He got paranoid and quickly took the edges of the blanket and covered the money, then ran off to see who was at the door.

When Ug answered the door, he saw a white guy in khakis and a Polo shirt, and without thinking he said,

"Ay, you mufuka's sho gettin' brave around here. Im'ma tell yo ass one time and one time only, don't bring yo funky ass to dis door no mo' lookin' fo no dope!" The guy quickly said,

"No wait! I have a delivery for Adonis, I just wanted to make sure someone was home." And he took off running toward the truck.

Ug stood at the door keeping his eye on the guy. He knew he didn't buy anything that needed delivering, so he was extremely leery.

Within a few seconds he saw the guy coming off the back of the truck with a medium sized deep freezer. His neck snapped back as he thought to himself 'I ain't bought no damn deep freezer.'

As the guy was walking toward the house, Maria hopped out of the truck with her ear to a cell phone. She walked up to Ug as the guy was wheeling the deep freezer through his front door. She walked in behind the guy and told him to go back to the truck and wait. Once he left, she looked at Ug and said,

"Don't worry about any payment. This is compliments of Señor Hector." Then she patted the side of the freezer and left. Ug went to the door and watched Maria get into the truck and leave, then he closed the door.

Ug stood there looking crazy. He was trying to figure out what he had said to make Carlos think he needed a damn deep freezer. Nevertheless, he didn't want to leave it just sitting in the middle of the floor, so he tilted the dolly and held the opposite side, then moved it to the right corner of the room. Ug brought the dolly down hard without holding the opposite side of the freezer and the freezer tilted over. When the side of the freezer hit the floor, the top door of the freezer opened and about 20 kilos came flooding out of the freezer onto the floor. Ug's eyes popped out of his head as he scurried to put the kilos back into the freezer and sat it upright. He instantly became paranoid and ran to the front window and looked around as if someone was watching him. Ug rubbed his chin as he paced the floor then said,

"Think Ug, think!" He ran to the linen closet and grabbed all the pillow cases he could find, then he went back to the freezer and started filling them with the cocaine. When he finished, he took the pillow cases filled with cocaine back to his room and tossed them in his closet. It wasn't even twelve yet and Ug was already having one hell of a day.

After Ug put the last thirteen bundles of money in the duffel bag, he tossed it in the closet along with the dope. Ug sat on the edge of his bed and tried to make sense out of what was happening. He thought long and hard until he came to a conclusion. Why try to make sense, when he had a million dollars in his closet. Ug smiled, then an overwhelming ease of calm came over him, then out of nowhere he just screamed out.

"Woooo!" He started stumping his feet and pounding his fist on his knees. All thoughts of Hector went clear out of his head as he started thinking about how he would get rid of all the coke. Even more so, how will he be able to keep it a secret? He just figured he would be more relaxed to think after a nice hot shower, so he stripped down to his boxers and headed for the bathroom.

Chapter 17

Back at Carlos' suite, Juliana was taking her time sharpening a machete. There was thick plastic sprawled over everything, and Hector's dead body still sat in the same chair he was shot in. Carlos was standing next to Hector with a cigar in his mouth as he rolled up his sleeves. Once he finished with his sleeves, he put the cigar down in the ashtray and said,

"Juliana, help me get him on the floor."

Carlos grabbed Hector by one arm as Juliana grabbed him by the other, then Carlos said,

"On the count of three. 1,2,3." And they lifted his heavy body and tossed him onto the plastic covered floor.

Once he was on the floor, Carlos stomped on his pelvis and his knees to straighten his body, then told Juliana to pass him the cutting board. Carlos rolled Hector on his back and placed the cutting board under his neck then reached for his phone. He got Maria on the line and said,

"Maria, get rid of the driver. No, don't kill him, just tell him to get lost and tell him that he'd see a bonus on his check. Bring the truck back to the Trump, and call me when you're in the garage." Then hung up.

Carlos sat his phone down and reached for the machete that was sitting on the table. Juliana had the machete razor sharp and ready to slice. She was ready for Carlos to make his statement.

Carlos grabbed the machete with a firm grip and admired the craftsmanship of the weapon. He then held the blade close to

Hector's neck to line up a good cutting spot. He lifted the blade high and got ready to bring it down when Juliana yelled out.

"Wait!" He looked at Juliana in a bewildered manner, then Juliana said, "Please, let me."
Carlos took a glance at the machete, smiled, and said,
"Well then, by all means." Then passed her the machete.

Juliana didn't bullshit around. She grabbed the machete, held it high, and brought it down quick and hard to Hector's neck. The head just flopped to its side like an apple that had been split in half. Juliana showed no fear of the dead. She grabbed Hector's head by his hair, and held it up high for Carlos to see. Carlos took Hector's head and sat it back on the floor. He then grabbed a hammer and a one inch nail from the table and got down on one knee. Subsequently, he positioned Hector's head and centered the nail in the middle of his forehead then brought the hammer down hard, nailing a vivid image into Hector's skull. Carlos stood up, lit his cigar, and smiled at Hector's head as if it were a grand prize.

Juliana took some plastic and tied it to the stub of Hector's neck. She then picked the head up, placed it in a box and sat it on the table. Next, Carlos and Juliana moved to a clear part of the plastic where there was no blood. They stripped down to nothing, then stepped off of the plastic onto the carpet. They then left the room to put on another change of clothes.

Once Carlos and Juliana returned, they started rolling the bloody plastic until it centered in on Hector's body. Juliana then reached for a fresh roll of plastic and unrolled about three feet. They then flipped the bloody plastic with Hector's body onto the freshly unrolled plastic. Carlos pushed the plastic roll out and they both rolled Hector's body over and over into a human cocoon. Carlos then lifted the feet of Hector's body and Juliana wrapped it in duct tape, then he grabbed the other end and she did the same.

They both grabbed the feet and pulled him to the elevator and waited for Maria.

Twenty minutes later, Maria called and said she was down in the garage and Carlos said,
"Good, pull the truck up to the elevator and lift the rear door, we're coming down now."

Ten minutes later they had Hector's body on the back of the truck. Carlos reached in his pocket and took out an address, then handed the piece of paper to Maria saying,

"Here, deliver the body to the funeral home at that address, they're already expecting you, they'll know what to do."

Carlos was feeling relaxed now. He was having Hector's body cremated, and now it was time to show the Ortega Cartel that Caquetá was not to be fucked with.

Chapter 18

I was fresh out of the shower, and as I sat on my bed rubbing lotion into my skin, I began to think about Brittany. I wanted to find out what her plans were for the 4th of July. Hell, I wanted to know what everybody's plans were, but everybody was M.I.A.

I looked at the clock and saw it was 12:45 pm. I went and grabbed the cordless phone and came back to my room and called Nassir first, there was no telling what he had lined up, and as soon as I got him on the line, he said,

"Nigga where tha fuck you at?! We out here ridin' around wit tha bangas lookin' fo you! We thinkin' somebody den kidnapped'chu or sumt'n."
"Damn straight up?!"
Then his fool ass started laughing saying,
"Naw, I'm just fuckin' wit' chu my nigga. We on our way back from Indiana gettin' some fireworks, we bout to light tha mufukin sky up tonight my nigga. We spent about fo' G's, we got dat big shit!"
"Damn ain't nobody bar b que'n?"
"Yeah we finna start gettin' it poppin' as soon as we get there. We hit tha meat market early dis morning."
"Ok ok, wut about da drinks?"
"Shiiiit, we was just gone wait til' later."
"Well shit, I'll get da drinks. Wut we sippin'?"
"It don't matter, wuteva you buy."
"Aight bet, I'm on it."
"Aight, one." And we both hung up.

Once I got off the phone with Nassir, I called Brittany. She told me she was at her mother's house helping her cook. When I asked her what she was doing for the night, she told me that she really didn't have any other plans besides eating with her family, so I said,

"Come through tha block later, I miss you and I wanna see yo pretty face." And she replied.
"Sounds like a plan, I'll call you when I'm ready to come that way."

Once I hung up with Brittany, I started putting all my new clothes on hangers while deciding what to wear. A lot of the clothes I bought weren't really made for the hood, and I didn't want to stunt on my people, so I kept it player. I set aside a pair of white Ralph Lauren cargo shorts and a turquoise Polo shirt, then I started putting the rest of the clothes up. I took a second and thought about the white cargo shorts. I figured that barbeque sauce and dust from sitting down would ruin my fit, but I smiled and said fuck it. At the same time I have to remember to stay humble. Even when you're shining, you have to act as if the shit means nothing. And in order to do that, I can't place any value on these materialistic items.

When I finished putting all my clothes away I tossed on some pants and a t-shirt, then jumped in the Maxima and headed to Trogan's to get the liquor.

When I got back to the block, the crew was on deck. Toni and Nassir where taking all of the fireworks into the house and Yella Boy and Candice were wheeling a couple of grills over to the maple tree. It must have been a lot of meat, cause the grills were huge, like the garbage cans you see at a park.

I took all the hard liquor in the house and filled the coolers with Corona's. When I finished, I started helping Candice and Yella Boy, while serving the weed heads. Everybody in the town was trying to get situated for the night, which made it a good day for the weed man, me!

Candice went into the house to start making spaghetti and potato salad. The rest of us sat under the maple tree and kept an eye on the meat. After a few minutes of thought I raised up in my seat and said,

"Ay, how much work y'all got left?"
And of course Nassir had to clown and say,
"Why wussup, you bout to start smokin' crack my nigga?"
Everybody giggled, then I said,
"Yeah aight mufuka. But for real doe, what y'all got left?"
Toni said,
"I got about a 63 left."
And Yella Boy said,
"I got about an ounce left."
Then Nassir said,
"I got a couple onions left, why wussup?"
I sat for a few more seconds thinking, then I said,
"I want y'all to do some crazy shit, but I need y'all to trust me on this." They all looked at me then I said, "I want y'all to give y'all shit away." Nassir looked at me crazy saying,
"Wut'chu mean? You want us to do giveaways to tha fiends to pump tha block harder?"
"No, I want y'all to think of somebody to put on and give it to dem as a blessing, right now today."
Then Nassir said,
"Aw hell naw, let me count my pack, cuz I know dis nigga must be smokin'. Wut da fuck you on Ug?"
I looked at them with a look as serious as cancer, and said,
"Like I said, I just need y'all to trust me on dis. I'm on some real shit y'all, some other level shit."

They sat there pondering over what I had just asked. I know it sounded crazy but I didn't want different work on the block. I wanted it all to be exactly the same. Yella Boy was in deep thought as he squinted his eyes. But soon after his face relaxed he responded by saying,

"Ug, I don't know what tha fuck you on, but sumt'n tells me you ain't on no bullshit, so wuteva it is, I'm wit'chu fam." Then Yella Boy took out his cell phone and walked away.

Toni then said,

"Yeah ok, but this betta be good Ug."

Then Toni walked off to make her call also.

Nassir sat there staring at me. I could tell he was trying to read me, trying to see what I was up too and with all the sincerity he could muster, he simply said,

"Ug, wusup fam? You know, I'm wit'chu no matter wut bro, and I don't give a fuck if I fall off behind dis shit." Then he looked over at Yella Boy and Toni then said,"T and Yella been grindin' hard to get on they feet. Toni got bills and Yella Boy tryin' to get tha fuck out of dat house, so alls I'm sayin' is, don't let *them* down. Aight?" Then Nassir pulled out his cell and looked at me real serious, then made his call.

After they all made their calls, Toni and I checked on the meat, then sat back under the maple tree. I had one more crazy request to ask of the crew, so I said,

"Now, how much money y'all got put up?"

Again, Yella Boy spoke first.

"I got forty-five hunnid put up."

Then Toni said,

"I got about ten racks."

And last but not in the least, Nassir laughed and said,

"Y'all need to get'chall weight up, I'm sittin' on a quarter. Wut'chu know bout dat Ug?"

I just giggled and held my hands up and said,

"Hey, you dat dude fam, you dat dude." Then I dropped the bomb on them when I said, "Gone grab y'all money and sit it on tha table in our front room."

Then Toni asked,

"Right now?"
"Yeah, right now is as good as any." And they all took off, that's when I smiled and I stepped to the grills to checked the meat again.

When the crew came back, I went into the house, sat in front of the tv and counted all the money. The total came to $39,500. I split the money three ways making three bundles of $13,166. I wrapped each bundle in a rubber band then tossed them in a shopping bag and took it to my room and tossed it under my bed. I then went back outside to the tree and joined the crew.

Once I stepped back under the tree, some girls pulled up looking for some weed, so I served them. When I turned back around Toni said,

"Really Ug? So we give all our dope away and hand over all our money and you stand there and serve customers in our face!?" I held my palms out and said,
"Toni relax, trust me aight."
Then Nassir said,
"So wut tha fuck we supposed to do now?" I reached in my bag and pulled out a hand full of weed sacks and put them in Nassir's hand and said,
"Roll up and enjoy the holiday."

Five o'clock that evening came around and all the meat was done. Me, Nassir and Yella Boy started setting up tables for the food and chairs for the people who would end up flocking to the block. See, in Robbins you didn't need an invite, cause when you had drinks and food, everybody would find their way, eventually.

Once we finished setting everything up, we all disappeared to make calls to our special guests and to get ourselves together for the evening.

Six-thirty rolled around and we were back on the block bringing out all the food. We rolled the flood light out to the curb and Nassir let the tailgate down on Hummer so the sounds could bump. Yella Boy and I went back in the house to start bringing out the liquor.

One by one cars started lining up the block, some of the people we didn't even know. It did it matter to us though, we were out to have fun, and before we knew it, we had ourselves a Fourth of July party!

Once it got dark, Yella Boy and Nassir started setting off the fireworks. Nas wasn't bullshitin' when he said they spent four grand. For about an hour and forty-five minutes they went hard as hell, and once people in the neighborhood saw that it was coming from our block, more people came.

By ten o'clock the fireworks finally stopped and we turned the flood light on. Everybody was kickin' it! I was standing in a huddle talking with some people I hadn't seen in a while, until someone grabbed my ass. I turned around to see Brittany standing there smiling. She was looking sexy as hell. I leaned over and gave her a tight hug and she reciprocated. I offered to get her something to eat, but she said she was fine. When I asked if she wanted a drink, she said yes. I then asked her what would she like and she said,
"Can you squeeze yourself in a glass?" She made my cheeks hurt I smiled so hard, but I managed to say,
"Why you always tryin' to mac me down?"
"Why you always lookin' so sexy Adonis?"

Instead of giving Brittany some of the hard liquor, I opened up one of the six packs of Moët Rosé. I gave one to Toni, Yella Boy, Nassir and Candice. Brittany and I just shared mine.

After that, I pulled Brittany out into the street close to Nassir's truck and started busting a few moves. She seemed surprised that a guy my height had moves, but it didn't bother her at all. She just turned around and started backing that thing up. Everybody around us caught on and started dancing with us. It was a great feeling just having pure fun. It was one of freedom's best benefits.

After a while I got tired, so I grabbed Brittany's hand and began walking back over by the tree. The closer I got, the more I could hear Toni yelling at someone. I looked through the crowd to see Toni arguing with some dude while Candice stood in the middle trying to break it up. When I walked up Toni pushed Candice out of the way and swung the Rosé bottle at the guy's head. I quickly reached out and grabbed her arm before she made contact. Then the guy said,

"Bitch, you was gone bust me in my head wit dat bottle?!" Then I jumped in his face and said,
"Ay, watch yo mufukin mouth! Now get da fuck on and walk dat shit off!" The guy looked up into my face then peeped my size and did exactly what I said, he walked that shit off. I later found out that he was one of the guys from the New Projects named Nukie. It didn't matter though, I think he got the message, and just in case he didn't, we all strapped up and stayed close to one another for the rest of the night.

Around twelve-thirty, we started clearing the block. Everybody went home alive, so I'd say it was a good holiday. I asked Nassir what he was about to get into for the rest of the night and he said,

"Shit! I'm drunk as hell, I'm broke as fuck and ain't got no dope, and to top it off all tha bitches I fuck wit on they period. Fuck kinda shit is dat? I'm going to sleep." Then he walked in the house. I laughed, then I pulled Brittany closer to me and said.

"You should stay wit me tonight, I need somebody to cuddle wit." She said ok, but she had to leave by 10am to get ready for work, so I said, "Perfect!" I held my arm out said, "After you my lady." Then we went in the house to end our night.

As Brittany and I cuddled in the bed, we talked a lot about our relationship. She told me she needed a man who could support her mentally, emotionally and physically. I told her, I needed a woman who can love me unconditionally, a woman that's goal driven with ambition, a woman with honest principles, and most of all one who's secure enough to handle a man like me. Her response to my list of requirements was.

"Damn, you just jumped all intelligent on me… I think it's cute on you." Then I asked her,
"Wussup, do you want to make me happy or smart?" She raised up, looked at me confusedly and said,
"Huh? Is that a trick question?" I pulled her close to me and told her,
"I read somewhere that if you get a good woman, she'll make you happy. But if you get a bad one, you'll become a philosopher. That's why I asked do you want to make me happy or smart."
"I still think it's a trick question, but I think I wanna make you happy."
"Then that's all I need to know baby girl." I was still talking when I heard a light snore. I just smiled and started thinking about the dope I had in the closet. I eventually closed my eyes ready to fall asleep until I heard a sound. I snapped my head back then out of nowhere I was attacked!... Ok, maybe I'm exaggerating a bit, but I wanted to push Brittany's ass out of the bed. The damn girl farted and stunk up my room.

I got out of the bed and started spraying cologne everywhere. I stood at the foot of the bed and stared at her thinking. How could someone so pretty smell so dangerous? I suddenly lost my urge to cuddle, so I waited until the smell went away then crawled back in bed and *tried* to cuddle some more. I looked at Brittany again and shook my head then I slowly fell asleep.

CHAPTER 19

I woke up around eight the next morning. I rolled out of the bed then walked over to the window and stretched. My window view was nothing compared to Carlos' Trump Tower view. All I could see was a boarded up bungalow style home. From the outside, it didn't look like it needed much work, but that wasn't what I was interested in. To the rear of the bungalow I saw a huge three flat apartment building that was also boarded up. All of a sudden, I had a light bulb moment. I grabbed the cordless phone and gave Carlos a call. When he picked up, I let the lightbulb speak.

"Carlos, hey this is Adonis. Listen, I got my eyes on some property. How do I go about seein' if somebody own it?"
"Adonis! I see you're in good spirit, I'm glad you called. Come out to my suite around three this afternoon and I'll get you situated on that information." I told him I'd be there, then I hung up.

After the phone call, I walked over to the bed and shook Brittany a few times to wake her up. When she opened her eyes I kissed her on her forehead and told her good morning. She sat up and cleared her eyes then asked what time it was. After I told her, she got out of bed and put her pants on. As she pulled them up, I looked at her big ass booty then asked,

"Brittany, wut' chu eat yesterday?"
"Ummm I don't know; some ribs, spaghetti, macaroni & cheese, potato salad.... why?" I chuckled a little saying,
"Cause I think you need to lay off of tha macaroni & cheese." Then I held my nose and waved my hand. Brittany smacked her lips and said,
"Wut eva boy." She smiled then walked over to me and gave me a tight hug.

I explained to her that I had some things to do and she told me no problem. I hated to have rushed her off, but I had to get my day going. Truth of the matter was, we both had shit to do.

After I watched Brittany drive off, I looked to see Candice pulling her garbage can to the curb so I went to lend her a hand. I asked her if she had to work and she told me she was off for two days. So, I asked her if she would run to the phone store and buy me a cell phone and she agreed. I told her I didn't need anything fancy, I just wanted to make and take calls. I then went in my pocket and gave her a hundred dollar bill.

When I stepped back into the house, I checked the clock. It was 8:45am. I walked to Nassir's room and peeked in on him. He was curled up like a little baby. I started to feel real mischievous, so I opened the door really wide then slammed it hard. When I opened the door again, Nassir was sitting up with his eye's buck wide looking around the room like he'd seen a ghost. I walked in his room and said,

"Wussup bro, I didn't know you was woke." He then spoke in a panicked tone saying.
"Ay, wut was dat noise?!"
"Wut noise? I ain't heard nuttin'." He relaxed a little bit and said,
"Aight Ug, Im'ma knock yo sea serpent lookin' ass out." I laughed and said,
"Get up, come to my room let me show you sumtn."

I hurried out of Nassir's room and ran to mine. I opened my closet and grabbed one of the pillow cases and emptied it on the floor. I hurried up and stacked 18 kilos neatly next to my bed away from the door. When Nassir walked in the room he looked around and started sniffing the air.

"Ug, why it smell like a mufukin cologne factory in here?" I didn't want to go into the whole ordeal about Brittany farting, so I just dismissed his question and said,

"I got sumt'n I wanna show you, but' chu can't tell nobody. This gotta stay between me and you." I gave him a real serious face and told him, "For real Nas, you can't tell nobody!" Nassir looked at me sincere-like and said,

"Check it out, if you squeeze it and puss come out, she burnt' chu, now I'm going back to sleep.

I back slapped him in the chest and said,

"Shut up! You damn fool, ain't nobody burn me." I walked over to the side of my bed and said, "Check it out."

Nassir walked around the bed and looked down at the floor. I snatched the pillow case off of the dope and Nassir just stared at it. He swore up and down that we had to kill whoever I had robbed, but I assured him that I didn't rob anyone. However, I was reluctant to tell him what my last 24hours had been like. I knew he wouldn't believe me, hell I didn't believe me.

I sat Nassir down and explained to him that I had a connect that was willing to front me the dope. I also let him know that if we were going to make this happen, we had to do it my way. I told him first and foremost, I didn't want anybody serving dope on the block until I give the word. Nassir shook his head up and down then said,

"Ok, so how do you want to do it?" And I told him,

"I wanna move around, reach out to dudes outside the town. Let's try to keep this on the hush hush until I get shit a little more situated. But when the time is right, we gone rock dis mufuka silly."

Then Nassir asked,
"So wuts da ticket?"
"Dudes still charging 30 grand right?"
"Yup." Then I looked at Nassir and said,

"Well, we gone go 25." Nassir didn't even think twice, he took his phone out of his pocket and started dialing numbers, until I said,

"No no no! Not over tha phone. Get up and get out! Move around and start lining dudes up, and don't let' em rush you. If they can't wait, then fuck'em. Get Yella Boy over here, I wanna see wut dis shit do, and get Toni over here too so she can get up to speed."

By 9:30a I had the crew on deck. I told Nassir to find a basehead and have him on point so we can test the work, so he left in search of a clucker.

While Nas took care of that, I filled Toni and Yella Boy in on the scoop. Once we got an understanding, I went to my room and grabbed a kilo and took it to the kitchen. When I sat the brick on the table, the doorbell rang and I got paranoid as shit as I whispered saying,

"Ay, Toni go check dat out," she walked over to the door and checked the peep hole then said.

"It's just Candice." In the midst of everything, I forgot I asked her to go buy me a phone.

While Candice was showing me how to work the phone, I told Yella Boy to just cook an ounce so we can see what it will take, then Yella Boy asked,

"How much soda you wanna put on it?"

"Let's start wit a full 35 grams."

"Thirty-five grams of soda on twenty-eight grams of coke?"

"Hell yea, I want to see how strong it is."

Yella Boy unwrapped the brick and we both stared at it like, what the fuck is that! The dope was white, but it had a pinkish gray tone with a scorpion in the middle. Yella Boy grabbed a corner of the kilo and broke it off the block of coke like a piece of butter.

The smell was strong, and the inside of the chunk was shiny, showing all the colors of the rainbow. Now, I wasn't a coke-ologist or anything, but despite the color, I was confident that this was some damn good coke.

Yella Boy began to do his thing, but before he mixed the baking soda with the coke he said,

"You sure you wanna go 35 to 28?"
"Yup, I wanna see if it double up. If it's shitty, we keep droppin' it until it get right."

Thirty minutes later, Yella Boy was finished. I went to the front window and saw Nas on the porch talking to Party Marty, one of the local smokers. I tapped on the window and waved him in, then ran to the kitchen and told Yella Boy to break me off a tester piece.

Yella Boy was trying his hardest to cut the dope with a razor blade, but the shit was rock fucking solid. So, I tossed the dope in a zip lock bag and smacked it with a hammer. When the dope shattered into pieces I gave Nassir a crumb to give to Marty so he could do his thing.

Nassir and I took Party Marty out the back door and gave him the piece of crack. Party Marty got his missile together and prepared for takeoff. He hit it one time and just stood there, then Nassir asked,

"So wussup, wut it do?" Then Marty said,
"Hol' up, it's kickin' in now... Yup yup, I hear fire bells! We got us a batch!" Then I asked him,
"You sure?"
"Oh yeah, dats gone be tha best shit in tha town, I'm tellin' you right now…. Now com'on nephew, let me get sumt'n to roll out wit." Fuck it why not? I ran back into the house and told Yella Boy to give me another piece, then I ran back outside and gave it

to Marty. He was damn happy too, he started snapping his fingers as he rolled out dancing and singing!

When Party Marty left, Nassir stared at the dope in a confused manner and said,

"Why dat shit look like dat?" And I told him,
"Fuck do it matter? As long as dat shit some fire it can be green for all I care."

I broke off a couple more pieces and told Nassir to lean on a few more smokers and see what they say. I didn't want to trust just one smoker's word, he might have been geek'n, and when a clucker trying to get high he'll tell you anything.

Twenty minutes later, Nassir came in the house smiling from ear to ear. He said the cluckers told him that the dope was the best crack that they'd ever smoked... Now, I knew we were onto something, so I sat the crew down and said,

"I gotta dip out fo a minute, but start lining shit up. Today is Friday, so line mufukas up for Sunday morning. Ay Yella Boy, break dat shit down in 8 balls. Y'all split it up and give it to the mufukas y'all holla at so they can sample it. Tell'em twenty-five for a brick, and twenty-three five if they want three or better. We ain't doin' no pieces, whole or nuttin', and don't serve nobody in tha town. *Nobody!*

The plan was clear and we all set out to do our thang. I gave Carlos a call and asked him if I could come right now. I wanted to get shit on the ball as soon as possible. He said yeah and I was out the door. Nassir took the Maxima, so I jumped in the Hummer, then I took off for the Trump Towers.

Chapter 20

Everything was serene in Carlos' suite. It was super spotless and reeked of cleaning agents. Carlos walked me into the living area and told me to have a seat. He sat next to me on the sofa and said,

"Adonis, I hope you're finding good use of the deep freezer." And he smiled saying. "Listen, don't worry about any money, the freezer is yours, just know that there will be more. I have my lawyer on his way to help with the property situation, but until then, let's talk. Adonis, this is just the beginning. The duffel bag and the freezer? Use it to build a cocoon." I was confused so I asked,

"Wut'nchu mean cocoon?"
"Adonis, do you ever go to any of the Latin communities?"
"Hell naw!"
"Why not?"
"Cause the Mexicans be bangin' like a mufuka!" Then Carlos said,
"Exactly! Do you have any idea how much coke is stored in those communities where the Mexicans bang? Well you call it banging, but they consider it protecting. You have to see to it that everyone around you is on the same page. People can't think it's cool to come in your neighborhood and set up shop or scheme to rob you. You have to make *that* neighborhood *your* neighborhood, Adonis."

I was hearing what he was saying, but it was easier said than done. Dudes in my town were too damn ignorant to be on the same page, so I told him.

"I don't know Carlos, but–" He cut me off saying,

"No buts Adonis. Never second guess yourself. The common factor in this, is the coke. The coke holds the power and the power makes shit happen. Did you have it tested?" I told him yes and I also told him they loved it. "Good, because this next shipment is going to turn them into beast. The coke you have now is only 85% pure, the next load will be 95% percent. You're going to end up with a healthy supply Adonis, the coke is coming whether you like it or not, and you have to protect it. If you need weapons, I'll get you weapons. I'll get you whatever you want, just move the fucking coke."

Carlos' phone rang and he answered. He sat the phone down and said,

"The lawyer is here, stay put. I'll be right back."

I listened to what Carlos had to say and I had no complaints. Just like I wanted my crew to do things my way, Carlos wanted me to do certain things his way. I didn't give a fuck, I was on my way to becoming a millionaire.

Carlos walked back into the room with his lawyer and introduced us.

"Adonis, this is Leonard Shultz. Leonard, this is Adonis Stuffy." We shook hands and Carlos said, "Adonis if you have any problems that involve legal action, give Leonard here a call right away." Then Leonard spoke,

"Nice to have finally met you Mr. Stuffy. How could I be of service to you today?" I reached in my pocket and took out the piece of paper with the addresses on it.
"I'm interested in buying these two properties. How do I go about that?" Leonard instantly started making phone calls. He wrote my phone number down and gave me his business card with all his info on it. He told me that it would take a little while to

gather all the info and that he would contact me as soon as he had word. I was feeling like my work here was done, so I started heading out, but before I left, Carlos stopped me.

"Adonis, remember what I said. If you come across *any* legal matters or run into *any* trouble, don't say *anything*. Call Leonard first." I told him no problem, then left the Trump Towers to get back on my hustle.

Twenty minutes later after I left the Trump. I pulled up at the projects on 39th & King Drive, known as the Wells. This was where my mother was originally from. The majority of my family was from the Low End of Chicago, but my older cousin Skeezo was the only family I was actually familiar with over the years.

Once I parked the truck, a dude ran up to the side of the truck holding a pistol. I didn't freak out, it was routine security. The guy holding the gun said,

"Who is you, and who you lookin' fo'?"
"I'm Ug, I'm here to see Skeezo." He responded by saying,
"Hol'up Jo, stay right there." Then he yelled out, "Ay, tell Skeezo a nigga name Ug out here." He didn't pose a threat, he just stood his ground, and it started to dawn on me what Carlos meant by building a cocoon. Minutes later I heard my name being called, it was Skeezo.

"Lil Ug, wusup cuzzo! Ay, hop out Jo, ain't nobody gone fuck wit' cho shit nigga, we got dis."

Skeezo and I chopped it up for a bit and caught up on old times. Now it was time to see what was poppin' in his hood.

"Ay cuz, how the money flowin' out here?"
"Which way? We got dat white, brown, *and* tha green. Wut' chu talkin' bout?"

"I'm talkin' bout dat white. Wuts tha ticket out dis way fo' a whole slab?"

"I can probably make it happen fo' you fo' about 28, 29, or 30, somewhere up in there." I sat there for a few seconds to let the anticipation build up, then I said,

"Check me out cuz, I'm tryin' to dump some work. I got a solid plug wit some good coke and betta numbas."

"Wuts a betta numba?"

"Fo' you cuz, twenty three-five fo' tha whole thang, no pieces."

"And you say da work good?" I just simply said.

"I did a double up on an oz. and tha cluckers loved it." He chuckled and said,

"Get tha fuck outta here, straight up?"

I told him to grab one of his best customers and follow me out to the town. I could show him better than I could tell him. He told me that if it was what I pumped it up to be, he knew at least five guys right now that would buy one or two kilos off the muscle. So, we hopped in our whips and headed for Robbins.

Chapter 21

It was two in the afternoon when Skeezo and I hit the block. We stepped in the house and the crew was there playing video games and chillin'. When Nassir saw Skeezo, he jumped up yelling,

"Aw shit, Skeezo wus good my nigga! I ain't seen you in a minute. Wussup wit dat Low End pussy?" And Skeezo said with a grin.

"It still get wet my nigga. Wussup wit'chu Nassir?"

I quickly broke up the reunion and got down to business. I looked at Yella Boy and said,

"How much of dat sample left?"
"It's still about a ounce left."
"Aight, break off a piece and take Skeezo out back so his customer can check it out. Nassir let me holla at'chu and Toni while they handle dat."

Once they left, I asked Toni and Nassir what they'd come up with. They told me as of right now, they had a total of fifteen kilos ready to be sold, but it would more than likely increase over the next couple of days. I told them that fifteen was cool for now, that's when Yella Boy and Skeezo came back in. Skeezo was smiling from ear to ear when he said,

"Cuzzo, we finna get dis money. Im'ma show you how the Low End get down." And he started twisting up a blunt. After he smoked with my crew, I told Yella Boy to give Skeezo half of the leftover sample. He told me he'd give me a call later, then he rolled out.

Yella Boy and Nassir went back to playing the video game, so I asked Toni to hit some blocks with me. I told her to drive cause I wanted to look around and get a better feel for what I was up against. First thing I *did* notice was that you weren't making it into Robbins unless you went over some railroad tracks, a bridge, or under an overpass. This was good, it gave me useful information in factoring on how to deal with the gangs in Robbins. My mission just became slightly clearer. There was only ten ways you could get into Robbins, and those same ten ways in, were the only ways out. Robbins sat directly in the middle of five bordering neighborhoods. The GD's in the New Projects and the Trailers bordered three entrances coming from Blue Island, IL. The GD's from the Old Projects bordered two entrances coming from Blue Island and Posen, IL. You had the Vice Lord's on Maxie Court that bordered Midlothian, IL and the BD's on the Bay bordering one entrance from Crestwood, IL, South Park bordered two entrances, one from Crestwood, IL, and one from Alsip, IL. The last entrance into Robbins was bordered by a national Guard base coming from Midlothian, IL.

Taking all of this information into consideration made me realize that our block sat right in the middle of Robbins. Our area was in the heart of the town. I thought about that for a second and smiled, then asked myself, *'How's that for a cocoon?'*

Out of the ten entrances, two of them were unmanned by the hood. South Park was still out of commission and the National Guard base bordered the other. I realized that eventually we would have to get a crew in the South Park area. Once we settled that, the South Park crew and the Mo's off the 9 would be able to patrol the National Guard base. Carlos told me that the coke carried the power, I just hoped he was right.

Around three thirty that afternoon, I was in the house sitting in the front of the television, bored as hell. With the block being dead, the crew was bored as hell too. I wanted them to relax and get as much rest as possible. The coke was going to come no matter what, so I needed them alert and on their feet.

　　Earlier today I programmed Leonard's number into my phone, so when my phone rang, I knew it was him. He was calling with the info I requested. He took a deep breath and said,

　　"Ok, Adonis, I have good news and bad news. Which would you like first?"
　　I then told him.
　　"Just give it to me straight Leonard." So, he said,
　　"Well, the bank owns both properties, but the two properties you requested info on, are part of a portfolio."
　　I was confused, so I said,
　　"So wut dat mean?"
　　"It means that you would have to purchase the entire portfolio."
　　"So wut's a portfolio?"
　　"It's a cluster of properties a bank wants to dump in a package deal. Which in this case isn't a bad deal. There's twenty properties in this portfolio and the bank is asking for $275,000, which actually breaks each property down to about $13,750 dollars." This sounded interesting, so I asked him.
　　"Where tha other properties at?"
　　"Well five of them are on the same block as the properties you requested. The other fifteen are spread around Robbins."
　　I was sold, so I said,
　　"I want it! I want the portfolio."
　　"I figured you would, so I had the bank draw up the contract and fax it to me. We're going to purchase the portfolio in the company's name so nothing ties back to you right now. I let the bank know that this is a cash deal and we want to rush the sale, so I should hear from the bank in a day or two with a closing date. Just have the 275k ready for me by Monday, so I can make it look good."

I hung up my phone thinking to myself like, damn! This motherfucker had his shit together. I was glad he was part of my team. But how did he know I was paying for the portfolio in cash, and what did he mean by putting the portfolio in "the company's name?" I just figured Carlos was behind everything, so I left those questions alone and started thinking about how I was going to control *my* town.

****

Carlos sat in his suite smoking a cigar, sipping scotch and listening to some jazz. He felt his plan coming together now. Leonard explained to him that the ground breaking on the development plan was a success, and construction crews were already working non-stop. The plan was originally for six towns, but Carlos thanked God for greed. The greedy mayor of one of the towns wouldn't sign off on the development plan in fear of losing his kickbacks. In the beginning, this situation made him mad because his old partner's passion for this plan was motivated by this town. Instead, the development plan was only signed off by the five towns that surrounded the one opposing town. This made Carlos want to indulge in that same greed as the mayor of the opposing town. Not only did Carlos want to indulge in the greed, but he began to embrace it. That same greed elevated his plan, and when his franchise businesses had their grand openings this fall, there would be no stopping the Caquetá Cartel.

Chapter 22

I was feeling myself dozing off. As I looked around the room I could tell that the crew was going through withdrawal. They were ready to get back to the hustle and I admired that, but the block wasn't going to start pumping again until I was left with ten kilos.

I got up from the couch and walked to the kitchen. When I returned to the front room, I told the crew I'd just got in contact with my connect and he was ready. I reached in my pocket and took out a couple of one hundred dollar bills then looked at the crew and said

"Ay, why don't y'all go to Applebee's or sumt'n, sit down and eat. Im'ma go get up wit my man. Get on tha phone wit'chall people and let'em know we gone be ready in a couple of hours. Y'all meet me back here in about an hour."

We all left the block going in separate directions. As soon as they were out of sight, I turned around and headed back to the block.

When I pulled up to the house, I backed the Maxima up to the side door and just looked around. I got out, went into the house and shot straight to my bedroom. I sat on the bed and gave Skeezo a call. I wanted to see if he'd found anyone that wanted to spend some money. Once I got him on the line, I got straight to the point.
"Skeezo, wus tha word fam? Mufukas wanna get down or wut? I'm ready to bust deez moves." He told me he'd call me back in about ten minutes, so I hit Nassir's line.
"Ay Nas, get me a tally on wut everybody got lined up, den hit me back." A few minutes later, Nassir called back saying,
"Check it out, altogether we need twenty bricks." Then I said,
"Aight bet." Soon after, Skeezo called back saying,

"Ay cuzzo let me owe you 17 on 22 of'em." I told him to just come through and we would work everything out later.

Once I got a tally, I went to the kitchen and grabbed a roll of garbage bags then shot back to my room. I counted out fifty kilos, stuffed them into a pillow case along with the garbage bags then sat them against the wall near the front door.

Forty-five minutes later, the crew returned from eating. Toni looked to me and asked if all was good, and as soon as I gave her the thumbs up, they all started making calls to see how long it would take their people to get to Robbins. When Yella Boy hung his phone up, he let me know his guy from Markham was on his way right now. Toni and Nassir both said that their people would be here within an hour. That's when I opened the front door, looked back at Nas and said,

"Go grab tha tek, hurry up." He took off and returned with a tek-9. I tossed it in the pillow case and told him to run out to the street and make sure the coast was clear. As he stood there in the street, he looked around then yelled,

"It's good famo, everythang clear!"

When Nassir gave me the word, I shot toward the maple tree carrying two pillow cases full of coke. When I ran pass Nassir, I said,

"Ay, come wit me!" I ran into the bushes and Nassir followed. I reached in the bag, grabbed the tek and passed it to Nassir. He tucked the gun in the waist of his jeans then I said, "Stay here and keep an eye on dis shit." When I ran back to the house, Yella Boy and Toni were standing on the porch. I looked at them and said,

"If y'all ain't strapped, then hurry up and get heated." I shot to my room, grabbed the 40 cal and tucked it in my waist, then ran back to the tree and posted up.

We were all standing by the tree getting our game plan together. That's when we noticed the first car pull up. Yella Boy noticed it was his guy from Markham and said,

"That's my man right there." I looked at the car again then started barking orders.

"Yella Boy, Toni, get on security. Post up at the curb and show dem pistols. Nassir stand up and let dat tek be seen." Then I walked toward the car with a confident stride.

I stepped to the vehicle and leaned into the window just enough to check everything out. When I was satisfied, I asked him,

"You Yella Boy's man, right?"

He replied with a yes and I jumped in the car and asked, "So wut'chu workin' wit?"

He reached behind my seat and grabbed a plastic shopping bag then passed it to me. I opened it and thumbed through the money, then he said,

"Dats 50 thousand right there, ten stacks five thousand a piece."

I continued to go through the money but didn't count it. I wasn't concerned with the amount. I was more impressed with how neat the money was. I looked at him for a second and figured he couldn't have been more than 19 or 20 years old. So, I asked him if all the money was his, and he said no. He told me him and a few of his guys put their money together. I smiled at him and asked,

"How old are you shorty?"

"I'm 18." Damn, he was younger than I thought, so I had to go a little deeper on him.

"Shorty, you know wut'chu gettin' into?

And he replied,

"I know how to get dis money and keep my mufukin mouth shut. Wut more do I need to know?" I chuckled.

Young and ready, I was diggin' shorty style, so I gave him back the bag of money and said,

"Take tha battery out'cho phone and step out the car. Leave the money on the seat."

When I stepped out of the car, I told him to raise his shirt up all the way past his chest and turn around. I didn't see any wires, but I *did* see a pistol. I told him to pull his shirt down, then I said,

"Dis how we gone do dis. Rule numba one, don't bring us no heat. Rule numba two, don't ever come back on dis block wit dat gun again. When you come to dis block, we yo security, and you ain't gotta worry bout shit. When you leave here today, take your time and come back wit as much money as you can. Im'ma fuck wit'chu hard, aight shorty?"

He smiled saying,

"Bet my dude."

I gave him some dap then said,

"Now count out 3 thousand of dat money in tha bag and put it in yo pocket. Honk tha horn when you finish. When I wave you over, pull up on the grass by dat tree where my man standin'."

He got back in his car and I walked back to tha tree and waited.

When I heard the honk of the horn, I waved him over and he parked on the grass. I took his money then disappeared into the bushes. I tossed four kilos into an empty garbage bag, then tossed his bag of money into another empty garbage bag. I came out of the bushes with four kilos and told him to pop his trunk, then I tossed the bag in and closed it. After placing the dope in his trunk, I leaned into his window and said,

"Wut'chu go by shorty, wuts ya name?"
"They call me Nitty."
"Aight then Nitty, trust and loyalty starts today. It's four bricks in tha bag, you owe me 47 G's, get at me." I tapped the roof of the car, then I walked away.

For the next hour, shit went pretty much the same way, only I didn't front the other guys any dope, but I did let them know that it would get greater later.

My cousin Skeezo pulled up an hour later, and I have to tell you, I wasn't diggin' *his* style. First off, he pulled up in a car with three other dudes. Secondly, the fuckin' car he was in had a big ass pair of rims on it! Really?

He got out of the car with one of those traveling cases with the wheels on it, and a blunt in his mouth. He walked toward me with this goofy ass pimp strut pulling the traveling case by the hand. I got heated, so I walked up to him like, cuz what's up? He smiled and started singing.

"It's all about tha Benjamins baby." When he started singing, I got a whiff of his breath then I snapped.
"Mufuka you gettin' high *and* you been drinkin'?!" I just stared at him in disbelief and said, "Cuz dis ain't finna happen."
"Com'on cuzzo, I got dis. Stop trippin'."
Then I told him,
"Skeezo, ain't no mufukin way I'm bout to let'chu ride out of here four deep in a car wit some big ass rims, drunk and high

wit 22 bricks! It ain't gone happen. Matter of fact.... gimme dat mufukin money cuz.!"

I snatched the carrying case and took it in the bushes. When I walked back out to the tree I went straight up to the car Skeezo was riding in and said,
"Who all gettin' work?"
They all said"me", so I told them,
"Look fam, we gone take care of y'all no doubt, but I aint bout to let Skeezo leave up out of here in this car wit all dat work. So wussup, y'all still tryin' to do dis or wut?"
One of the guys said,
"Hell yeah! I need dat!"
Then I said,
"Aight, check it out. Won't chall gone and take off. Im'ma have shorty over there drop him off. They'll be right behind y'all."
They hesitated for a second then one of them said,
"Aight, it's all good, but don't be on no bullshit tho fam." I let the dude get that last comment off only because I had about $500,000 of their money. I wouldn't want to be separated from my money either.

I was one hundred percent disgusted. I pulled the Maxima up to the tree, then went into the bushes and counted out 22 bricks and tossed them into a garbage bag. When I finished, I tossed the garbage bag in the trunk of the Maxima then looked at Toni and said,

"Baby girl, I need you."
Toni exhaled a frustrated breath, then looked at Skeezo and said,
"Com'on nigga!" I know she didn't want to do it, but a female driving would make for a safer trip.

I leaned into the window of the Maxima. I couldn't fix my mouth to say *shit* to Skeezo. I just looked at Toni and said,

"Thanks T, gimme a call as soon as you touchdown, so I know you made it." She shook her head yes then took off for the Low End.

I couldn't believe Skeezo. He was lucky to have even *made* it into the town with all that money. I mean, was he really that much of a clown? Truth be told, I really didn't want to answer that question. I just took a deep breath and tried my hardest to relax.

Chapter 23

Trying to calm my nerves wasn't easy. I was deep in my thoughts until my ears tuned into the sound of an engine accelerating. I quickly stepped to the curb and saw a Crown Victoria coming up the block, so I stepped back and yelled,

"Five-O!" Yella Boy and I tossed our pistols to Nassir and he ran in the bushes and ducked down.

The Crown Vic finally came to a stop and two officers hopped out fast with their guns drawn. As they walked close, one of the officers yelled out,

"Don't move motherfucker, let me see them hands." It was Officer Ross and Watts.

Just as the pain in my ass was going away, here comes officer's Dick and Balls. They put us on the squad car and searched us. I didn't trip though, it was part of the game. However, I never appreciated officer Ross' demeanor. He either wanted to see me break or he was begging for me to kick his ass. As he searched us, he started talking slick saying.

"Y'all was doin' it real big for the holidays. How much did y'all spend on fireworks?"
Yella Boy and I just looked at each other but didn't say a word, So, officer Ross kept talking. "You know what Stuffy, you a real disrespectful motherfucker, but Imma teach how to have some respect for authorities."
That's when I felt like I needed to stand on a little principle, so I said,
"Fuck you! You ain't my daddy, bum mufuka!" He got real ignorant and said,

"How you know I ain't yo daddy?" Then gave me a slick ass grin. I stepped to Ross and looked him square in his eyes and told him,

"One of these days you ain't gone have dat badge on, and dats gone be tha day I knock yo ass out." Officer Watts stepped to his partner and whispered something in his ear then Ross said,

"You know what Stuffy, one of these *days* I'm gone find something in yo pocket that don't belong to you, then it's back to a jail cell, you tough motherfucker." As Ross was walking back to the squad car, Watts stepped to me and said,

"Y'all gone and get'chall self a drink or something and relax, I got him." He gave me a head nod then got in their squad car and drove away.

As soon as they left the block, I told Yella Boy to look out. I then ran into the bushes with Nassir and we grabbed the bags *and* that fucking carrying case. I asked Yella Boy if the coast was clear and he gave me thumbs up. That's when we took off toward the house, made it through the door, and locked it down.

Toni finally called and told me everything was good. *Now* I was able to relax. By this time, we had emptied all the bags of money onto the floor and prepared to start counting.

An hour and a half later. Toni called back and told me to open the door. After I let her in, I went back to the piles of money. I looked at her then pointed toward two piles and told her.

"Dats yo people's money right there, count it ya self." Toni took a deep breath and said,

"Damn, where da weed at? Somebody roll up, I gotta get high for dis shit." Toni then flopped on the floor and began to count.

Ten o'clock came around and we were still counting. I never thought I'd see the day when I would say that I'm tired of counting money. My hands kept cramping and my back was killing me! I knew right then I would have to invest in a money counter, cause this counting by hand shit was *not* cool.

    I took a break and called Brittany. Her soft and sexy voice always brings me back to life. We talked for a little bit, but I let her know I had to finish up a few things and that I would call her later. After talking with Brittany, I noticed that everyone had finished counting. I was hoping that they still had energy, cause now I needed help counting the money in this *damn* carrying case.

    Around 11:30pm we finally finished. Yella Boy counted $47,000. Toni counted $188,000. Nassir counted $235,000, and there was $500,000 in the case. Altogether we'd counted $970,000. That's when I told Yella Boy I fronted his little buddy two kilos and he owed $47,000. Toni stood up and looked at all the money. I could tell her brain was at work. She had one of those curious but confused looks on her face, so she looks at me and says,

    "Wait a minute Ug. I got 8 sold, Nassir had 10 sold, Yella Boy had 2 sold and you hit is man wit 2. That's 22 bricks. How many did Skeezo get? I let her know that Skeezo bought 22 kilos, then she said, "That's 44 bricks! How much of dis shit you got Ug?"

    I looked around at my crew and saw that everyone was waiting for an answer. I figured trust was a twoway street, so decided to tell them.

    "My man hit me wit a hunnid of'em." Toni's eyes got huge when she said,

    "Damn! So wut'chu gone do for us?"

    I wanted the crew to know that this was part of that trust I asked for, so I took a deep breath and said,

    "Look y'all, we on. And when I say we on– I mean *we on*! I just need y'all to help me move these last forty-six bricks and we good."

    Once again Toni's mathematical brain started going to work.

"Hol'up, forty-six and forty-four is ninety. Wut about the other ten bricks Ug?"

"I'm savin' tha last ten fo y'all. Im'ma have Yella Boy cook it up and y'all can break bread. Y'all should end up wit about six and a half bricks apiece, and ain't nobody gone owe me nothin'. Dats when we gone open tha block back up and kill. These other dudes still gone be movin' dat 30,000 dollar bullshit and we gone come wit dat fire! Y'all gone sell 3.5's fo 80 bucks, and since 8 balls goin' fo 80. Y'all gone bust down eight big ass bags off tha 3.5 and murda deez fools, but ain't nuttin shakin' on tha block til tha other forty-six bricks is gone."

Nassir leaned back on the sofa and just stared into midair. He couldn't believe that we were sitting on that much work, all he could say was,

"Ug, how tha fuck you pull dis off? I mean, you just got out tha joint and you got a mufuka hittin' you wit a hunnid of them thangs?! You lucky as fuck my nigga, wit'cho turtle lookin' ass."

I just looked at him, smiled and I told him,

"Naw fam, I ain't lucky… we lucky."

Chapter 24

The sun was going down in Juarez, Mexico. Juliana had just crossed the U.S. border looking for any signs of the Ortega Cartel. Luckily for her, she didn't have to look very far. As she drove through the city of Juarez, she could see the Ortega rebels scattered everywhere carrying assault rifles. She paid very close attention to her surroundings until she noticed a group of them leave a bar. That's when she made a quick right and parked in an alley across the street from the bar, and when she pulled over she checked her weapon, secured her vehicle and walked toward the bar entrance.

Julianna looked around the dimly lit bar, then walked toward the counter where a short fat Mexican man stood wiping glasses dry. The man smiled at Juliana and asked her what she would like to drink. Juliana asked for a bottle of water and the man said with confusion.

"Water?"
"Yes please, I am very thirsty." As Juliana drank her bottle of water, she asked the bartender if the rebels in town came into the bar frequently and he said,
"Oh, the Ortega's? They are always here, they are my best customers." After Juliana finished the water, she walked out of the bar and returned to her car where she calmly sat waiting for any signs of the rebels to return to the bar.

Once the darkness entered the sky, Juliana saw a large group of the rebels entering the bar. That's when she got out of the car, opened the trunk and retrieved a box. She sat the box on the hood of her vehicle, then grabbed a piece of paper from the backseat of the car. She then grabbed a pen from her purse and wrote a message on the paper. After she finished, she took a wad of chewing gum from her mouth and stuck the message to the box. Juliana looked at the box, smiled and said,

"Come on Hector, time to go see some old friends."

Juliana reached the front of the bar and sat the box on the ground near the door. She ran back to the alley and checked her surroundings then stared at the door. Juliana decided to speed up the process, so she took out her gun and fired two shots into the air.

Seconds later, a few rebels came running out of the bar with their rifles drawn and looking around. One of the rebels noticed the box sitting on the ground, so he picked it up, inspected it and saw that there was a message attached. The rebel held the box in the light and read what was written on the piece of paper then began to bark orders. After he was done ranting, he took off into the bar carrying the box, while the others took slow steps backward with their rifles up scanning the area. When Juliana saw them go into the bar, she went back to her vehicle and started the engine. She took out her cell phone and called Carlos. Once he answered, she kept her conversation brief saying,

"It's done, I'm coming back." She then hung up the phone and took off into the night.

The Ortega rebels took the box to their lieutenant. He looked at the box strangley and read the message, and it said.

To The Ortega Cartel
We will not be muscled. Chicago no longer
desires your services. Pull your Brazers out NOW!
Or we will deliver them all to you like this!
Open the box

When he opened the box, they all turned their heads in horror of the first sight, but once the lieutenant looked again, he noticed the picture hammered into the skull. It was a picture of a scorpion, just like the scorpion he saw imprinted in the kilos of cocaine that he'd inspected in Chicago. The same kilos that Hector had. Immediately he thought, Hector! He looked at the head again and quickly put one and one together and instantly notified his General of their situation at hand.

Chapter 25

Six days had passed and a lot had been accomplished. I got the $275,000 to Leonard for the property portfolio, and the bank was eager to close, so they set a closing date for next Friday. Now as for my crew, they had their hustle in full go. Nassir dumped twenty more kilos and that made me extremely happy. I had to give it to him, he was silly as fuck, but he was one hell of a hustler. Toni? Well what can I say, she wasn't far behind. She kept it rolling by dumping ten more kilos, and even my clown ass cousin Skeezo came through and hit me with the cash he owed, plus he bought the last sixteen kilos.

While Nassir and Toni took a break from the hustle, Yella Boy and I had our own thing going on. I kept him busy by cooking up the last ten kilos I saved for them. And when he finished, we broke them down into 8 balls. It took us five whole days to bust that shit down. In the process of handling that, I put Candice to work by sending her shopping. I gave her a few thousand and told her to spend it all on food. I gave Toni and Nassir five thousand and told them to hit Kenwood liquor store and load up. I told them to make sure that they bought the good shit cause I wanted to see to it that I did it right, cause tomorrow was my birthday!

For the rest of the day me, Nassir and Yella Boy drove around the hood visiting some of the major players in town to invite them to my party. Some of them said they would come and others said they didn't do house parties. Oh well, I wasn't going to beg them. If they came, they came, but regardless of their decision, I was going to enjoy myself no matter what.

While we drove around I called Brittany and told her to stop by after work. My plan was to give her a few dollars so she could buy herself something nice to wear for the party. I was going to be fly, so I wanted my woman to match my swag.

Riding around the town in the summer heat made us thirsty, so we stopped at Trogan's for some beer. When we walked into the store, you would never believe who was at the counter making a purchase. It was Racks, and when I saw him I thought, damn! I was sure I would never see him again, at least not in this lifetime. Once he looked up and saw me, I asked him how he'd been doing and most of all how the hell did he get out of jail. He told me that the police didn't have enough evidence to indict him on the murder and that they found none of his fingerprints on any shell casings. I told him that was a blessing and I was sorry he didn't make it to his brother's funeral. I in turn invited him to my party tomorrow. I wanted to show my man a good time after all the bullshit he'd been through, but he wasn't feeling my invite. He said he would think about it, but that was translation for"I'm good". Nevertheless, I let him know that he was more than welcome. I gave him a manly hug and carried on. The situation with Racks and his brother made me think, so while I was in the store buying the beer, I bought a fifth of Patron. I then told Nassir to ride down on Rico so we could see what the Vice Lords were up to.

When we hit the Vice Lord's block I was sure that a few of them thought we were on bullshit, but when I hopped out with the fifth in my hand, they knew it was all good.

Rico walked up and shook hands with me, then we copped a spot and just simply kicked it a little bit while we sipped on tequila. I asked him about his position with the Vice Lord's and he told me he had the head spot for all the Lord's in Robbins. I went on to ask him how did they run their block and if all the Vice Lord's bought work from him. He told me that they sort of all did their own thing when it came to buying coke. So I said,

"Can you make them all buy dope from you?"
And he said,
"Shit, I don't know. Maybe, if I had a better price than these other niggas out here."

We kept sipping the tequila while my mind went to work. I told Rico I might have something up his alley, a real sweet proposition for him if he was interested. I then asked him how many members he had on count and he told me that he had about 100 or so guys that he governed over. I thought to myself that 100 guys just might work. So, I said,

"Listen, I can tune you in on sumt'n you want, if you can provide me wit sumtn' I need."
And he replied,
"Shiiit… wut'chu need?"
Then I told him,
"Security! 135th is the Vice Lord's strip, all throughout dis area, including our block. I want'chu to stand on it wit everythang you got."

I explained to Rico that I wasn't looking for him to start a war, I just wanted this area secure. I wanted my block to become Fort Knox. I tried to get a little personal with Rico so I pulled him to the side and said,

"Check it out fam, tomorrow is my birthday and I'm having a party. Come through and kick it, have a good time. Saturday when you get up, come through the block. Im'ma have a lil sumtn fo you. Just a lil sumt'n to show you I ain't on no bullshit. Wussup, you game?"
"Let's just see wut it do and we gone go from there."
To me that was fair enough, cause I knew I could show Rico better than I could tell him. After me and Rico's conversation, me and my crew jumped in the truck and took off for our block to continue chilling.

Later that night we all hit Adriana's, one of the hottest clubs in the South Suburbs, and we took Rico with us. I was basically putting our lives in Rico's hands, so I needed to pull him a little closer. I needed to know that he had our backs and I needed him to feel like he was a part of our team.

Adriana's was already poppin' when we walked through the door. A celebrity singer did a guest appearance and had the V.I.P section right next to us. We were kickin' it hard amongst ourselves, but Nassir complained about not getting enough action from the ladies. Honestly, I wasn't feeling how the females were acting myself but I knew one thing, they weren't flocking to the celebrity because they thought he was cute. They were flocking to him because the motherfucker was rich! As I pulled my thoughts together I sat back, looked around then waved the waitress over and said,

"Wut tha superstar over there drinkin'?"
"Oh him? He drinkin' champagne, Ace of Spade."
I shook my head up and down as if I were impressed then said.
"Aight bet, send him over four bottles of dat and tell'em it's from me, then bring me four cases of tha same thang. Put some of those sparklers on the bottles for me, make me feel special, it's my birthday I just turned 27. Oh and by the way I'm Ug." Then I extended my hand for a shake.

It wasn't long before the waitress came back with the four bottles I'd ordered for the superstar. When she served them to him she pointed in my direction, that's when he looked over at me and gave me a head nod that acknowledged my playerism.

Fifteen minutes later, six waitresses came walking through the crowd pushing carts of Ace of Spade. The sparklers on the bottles lit the club up like the 4th of July. As the waitresses made their way, the D.J came over the speakers saying,
"I'd like to wish tha big homie Ug a happy birthday. He just turned 27 today, so show him some love."

Now, I'm no superstar, but when the ladies in the club seen all those bottles coming our way, they came right along with them.

As the ladies began to flock, I pulled Nassir and Yella Boy to the side and gave them both $5000 dollars bundled in rubber bands. I then told them to split up and go to both bars and have the bartender give away whatever drink special they had for the night until the money ran out. Me and Rico walked toward the banister and looked down at the party people as the club partied. I wanted to make this a night that my crew would never forget, so I turned around and waved Candice over. Once she made it over to me I said,

"Gimme five more of dem bundles." Candice reached in her big ass purse and started pulling the bundles out, all were $5000 apiece. By this time Nassir and Yella Boy made their way over to us and I began to pass out a bundle a piece to all my crew, even Rico. They all looked at the money then Nassir asked,

"Wus dis fo' ?"
I smiled like a boss and told them,
"Make dis muthafuka rain!"
When I said those magic words, we all took the rubber bands off of the money and started tossing it over the banister and into the air. We watched the money float down over the dance floor like confetti, and the club went bananas! It was epic, and after we finished, we pimped away from the banister like real motherfucking players and went back to our V.I.P section.

On the way back to our section I locked eyes with Mr. Superstar, that's when he stood up, removed his hat and took a bow. When he raised back up, he saluted me and held his bottle up and finished partying. With that gesture alone he had now earned my respect and from his actions, I believe I earned his too.

When we sat back down, there were women everywhere in our section. The bartenders kept pointing our way. I figured they were letting everyone know who paid for the drinks. Many of them came by the section and wished me happy birthday, others just simply wanted to show their gratitude for the drinks. Either way, it was all love.

As I looked out into the crowd, I noticed a familiar face squeezing through the crowd and coming our way, so I yelled his name out.

"Ay Nitty!" It was Yella Boy's little homie from Markham.
I waved him over and shoved a bottle in his hand, then spoke to him in his ear saying, "Everythang all good fam?"
He smiled and said yes. Then I said,
"Well say no more, enjoy yaself." Then, I turned to Nassir and said, "Is this enough action fo' you fam?" He gave me a thumbs up then started dancing with the ladies.

I was now satisfied and enjoying myself, so I went and sat back down and took in my scenery. I was feeling good and my people were enjoying themselves to the fullest. I looked at Nassir, Yella Boy, Toni, Rico, and Nitty, then just smiled. Candice flopped down next to me and curled up under me like a sister would and said,

"Which one of these broads you starin' at with that big ass kool-aide smile?"
I giggled and said,
"None of 'em, I was just checkin' sumt'n out."
"What?"
I put my arm around her shoulder, then looked back at the crew and said,
"The future baby girl, the mufukin' future."

Chapter 26

I woke up the next morning to my cellphone blaring in my ear. I looked at the time and saw that it was 7:30am. I looked back at my cellphone's caller ID and saw it was Brittany. When I answered all I heard was,

"Happy birthday baby! Why you still sleep? You supposed to be up trying to get stuff together."

I was tired as hell, but she was right. We had to get all the meat cooked. Luckily, she said that she'd help with everything as soon as she finished shopping for something to wear.

After I hung up with Brittany, I jumped out of the bed and banged on Nassir's door as I passed his room. I then headed for the living room couch where Yella Boy was sleeping and sprinkled some water in his face. He popped up and wiped his face as he stretched and yawned. My next move was calling Toni, but to my surprise she and Candice were already up getting started on the side dishes. After I hung up the phone, I went to the bathroom, washed my face and brushed my teeth. Then I stepped outside and began to fire up the grills.

It wasn't long after firing up the grills my phone rang. This time it was Rico, and as soon as I said hello, he replied.

"Yo, I smell charcoal burnin'. Y'all bout to start cookin'?"
"Yea, we gotta start early. We got a shit load of meat, but we only got three grills."
Then Rico said,
"Don't trip, let me see wut I can do." Then he hung up.

Just as the coals were getting red hot, I heard a lot of loud music coming up the block. I stepped to the curb to see four cars and two pick-ups parking. A smile instantly found my face. I was happy as hell to see bar-b-q grills on the back of those pick-ups. While I stood there smiling and watching guys pull grills off the back of the trucks, Rico got out of his car with a few guys and waved his hand. 12 females piled out of the cars and stood next to Rico. Rico smiled then said,

"Ay Ug, I brought you a lil help fam. Ladies say wusup to tha birthday boy." He walked up to me then said,"I brought some of tha Vice Lord sister's to help with tha cookin'. They get down on them grills bro, so now you can relax a lil mo' on yo birthday." Man… you just don't know how relieved I was. Rico's guys had taken three huge grills and five smaller grills off the trucks and set them up, then the girls went to work.

By early afternoon all the meat was finished cooking and everything was setup and good to go. The D.J wasn't scheduled to be here until eight tonight, so we all just chilled out. I eventually decided to take a nap until it was time to party.

The night had finally come and the evening was running smoothly. Everyone was eating, dancing, and enjoying themselves until Candice ran up to me in a panic saying,

"Ug hurry up! Sumt'n wrong wit Brittany. She in yo room!"

I dashed into the house and ran straight for my room yelling Brittany's name. When I opened my bedroom door, she was just standing there with nothing on but black stilettos and a red bow tied around her waist. I was so distracted by her body that I forgot to close the door. So, I quickly turned around and slammed it, then locked it down. When I turned back around, Brittany was looking at me with her hands on her hip standing in a seductive pose. I was all smiles! She kicked her heels off real sexy like one by one. Then softly sat on the edge of the bed and leaned back on her arms and said,

"So, you just gone stare at me all night, or are you gonna open me up?" Then she pointed toward the bow and said, "You *do* wanna open your gift, don't'chu?"

I could hardly control myself. I walked to the edge of the bed and pulled her to her feet. I took a step back and tugged at the bow and it dropped to the floor. Next, I pushed her onto the bed, grabbed her legs and yanked her toward me. I stood over her and kissed her lips. I then raised up and smiled at her. I was trying to be smooth, but I really wanted to beat that shit up. I held my composure and flipped her onto her stomach. Her body was amazing! I couldn't help but to touch and feel her skin. I slowly and lightly brushed my hands down her body from her neck to her ankles. I could now hear her panting.

When I reached her ankles, I leaned into the left leg and started licking circles all the way up to her thigh as I grabbed and massaged her ass. Once I reached her inner thigh, I switched legs and licked circles all the way down to her right ankle.

I was really feeling Brittany and I truly believe she felt me too, so I didn't just want to *fuck* her. I wanted to enjoy every single minute of her.

I took my sweet time licking and tasting her entire body. That's when she grabbed my head and started kissing me wild and passionately. When she stopped kissing, she looked me in the eyes and said,

"Quit playin' wit me Adonis, I been waitin' too long for this."

She was right, I had made her wait long enough. So, I entered her slow. When I did this, she threw her head back and opened her mouth as she arched her back. As I began to stroke, we looked into each other's eyes as we found each other's tempo. She gripped my back for dear life. She felt so good I couldn't help myself. I whispered her name as I nibbled on her lobe. It was something about me saying her name that drove her wild, so I said it a few more times. She became so hot that she somehow maneuvered and flipped *me* over. She then got on top of me and said,

"Now it's my turn. Tonight, Im'ma make you believe that I'm that one." And that she did! I'm not embarrassed to say that I liked slow grinding with Brittany, but she was dead set on fucking my brains out.

An hour later, we tightened ourselves up and returned to the party. Once we got back outside, I swear I saw the entire hood out there. Nassir came straight up to me and said,

"You straight fam?"
I laughed then said,
"Oh yea, I'm straight den a mufuka ya feel me."
"Cool, cause I got a lil sumt'n fo' you."

Nassir took off into the crowd and left me standing there curious as to what he had planned. The next thing I heard was Nassir on the microphone saying,

"Yo! I want to wish my big brother Ug a supa happy birthday. I love you big bro, real talk baby. Ay Ug, where ever you at, look up."

When I looked up, the sky turned full of color. The crew had managed to find fireworks that spelled my name in honor of my birthday. And as the firework blazed, all the crew gathered around showering me with hugs and birthday wishes. Now I have to admit, I had enough money to be anywhere in the world right now, but there's nowhere else I'd rather be than right here in Robbins with my people. Real talk!

Chapter 27

The next morning while Yella Boy and Nassir were still sleep, I started getting everything ready for the crew. I brought three duffel bags out to the front room where Yella Boy was sleeping and lined them up on the floor. I sat a separate zip lock bag on the table in front of the television. Once I finished situating that, I got on the phone and called Toni to tell her to come over right away.

Once Toni got over to the house, I woke the guys up and gathered everyone in the front room. Everybody was looking beat from the night before, but when I started to sling duffel bags their way they all perked up. Now that I had their undivided attention I said,

"Check tha bag, all y'all got two color zip locks. The clear bags is all 8 balls, 1728 of 'em. Dats six bricks altogether. Tha blue zip locks is all dime bags broke down into packs of 144 a piece, dats a half a brick. Each of y'all should have a bundle of money in tha bags, 13,166 dollars to be exact. Dats the money y'all gave me, I put it together then split it three ways. Y'all got any questions so far?"

They all shook their heads no, so I continued. "I want y'all to sell all tha bags first. If these dudes want an 8 ball, tell 'em eight of deez bags is a whole 3.5 and they can buy as many as they want. If they don't wanna bite den fuck 'em, let 'em starve. We gotta juice our clientele first before we let them eat."

I looked at all of them for a second. They all had this different look of thirst in their eyes. It was somewhat a cross between I'm rich and I wish a motherfucker would. It was the look I was anticipating. So I said, "Now com'on, let's get dis mufukin' money!"

Nas, Toni and Yella Boy were like hungry lions and wasted no time. So, while they were occupied with getting the block back together, I decided I'd go get them some breakfast, but I had to make one stop first. I had to go get Rico's ass out of the bed.

I pulled up in front of Rico's crib and called his phone. I told him to throw something on and step outside and when he did, he walked up to the car and I said,

"Jump in famo. Take a ride wit me." Rico hopped in and I took off.

As I drove, I elaborated to Rico on the fact that I did indeed need him on the team. I also let him know that a wave was about to hit Robbins and I was going to be the only dude with a surf board.

When I pulled up to the Mc Donald's drive-thru, I just started ordering shit. It didn't even matter, I just ordered about fifty dollar worth of breakfast food, and after I placed the order I looked at Rico and said,

"I want'chu on the winning team bro, but I gotta keep it real wit'chu. Dis ain't bout to be no pre-school shit. We bout to go hard as hell, and I need you in full control of your guys."
Rico cocked a smile and said,
"Ug, I been checkin' you out for the last couple of days and I see you on some real shit. You ain't gotta convince me fam, I'm all in. I got *my* guys, and if any of 'em get out of line, on tha fin fam, they gone get dealt wit."

When we got back to the block, Rico and I carried a picnic table over to the tree and we all ate breakfast as a team. Once we finished, I took Rico in the house so I could get him situated.

Once we got in the house I told Rico to have a seat. I reached on the side of the sofa and grabbed the blue zip lock bag and tossed it on the table and said,

"Rico my man, dats all you. Its 1152 dime bags, a half of brick exactly. You don't owe me shit, dats your jump start. Work tha block wit Nassir and nem. Try to stay low key. When my next load come in, we gone go from there."
And Rico said,

"Bet! I knew you was serious but damn. You sure all you need is security? You know a half a key goin' fo' $15,000 right? Shit at that price you can get a mufuka brains blown out tha back of they shit."
I looked at Rico and said,

"Man Rico, shit just might have to come to dat, you still in?" Rico stared at the bag then smiled saying.
"Fuck yeah my nigga! Real recognize real and you been showin' me crazy love Ug. So wuteva you need, I got'chu." After our little meeting, I took Rico outside and showed him a spot in the bushes to hide his pack, then he posted up with the crew. Rico seemed pretty official, and for his sake, he better be.

It didn't take long at all for the town to start buzzing. The work was good and the bags were huge. The smokers were taking our bags and breaking them down into three dimes a piece. They would smoke two and sell one, then come back to buy another. The hustlers were doing something somewhat similar. They would buy our bags and sell them to their customers for 20 bucks a piece. They figured if they bought all of our bags, we wouldn't have a chance to serve any smokers. It didn't matter to us who bought the bags, as long as all the money came our way.

As the block picked up, Robbins finest became curious. The good thing about Robbins police was that their job was simply a pay check, but when the shift change happened, Ross and Watts came sniffing around like the dogs they were. This time, instead of searching us, they would just run customers off. It slowed down the hustle, but as soon as Ross and Watts drove off, the block went back to doing numbers. You know, the average cat and mouse chase. It seemed as though Ross was only interested in a shake down when he saw my face, and boy did he get pissed every time he came up with nothing. I loved it! It was like watching him rub dog shit all over his face. The more he searched and found nothing, the more of a problem he became.

Later that night around 11pm, I bumped into Watts at the local gas station. He was by himself, so I took the liberty of trying to gain an ally. I stepped to Watts and said,

"Hey Watts, can I holla at'chu fo' a second?"
"Speak your mind."
I rubbed my head in frustration and spoke saying,
"Man, wut tha fuck is up wit ya man? Why he always ridin' my ass?"
"Maybe he don't like drug dealers."
I felt like we were getting off to a bad start so I decided to come at him with a different language.
"How much you make as a police officer?" He looked at me sort of confused, then laughed and said,
"Well, I see you got glue in your eyes, so let me help you out. Number one, tryin' to bribe a police officer is against the law. Number two, when I punch the clock at 3pm and clock out at 11pm, my shift is done. Your job is to sell dope, my job is to catch you. So, what does that tell you?"
"Shit, it sound to me like you don't give a fuck what I do."
He smiled at me again and said,
"Exactly! So just do your fuckin' job and stop askin' questions about mine." Then he got in his car and drove away.

A few days had passed and I believe we had a solution to our problem. Between the hours of 3pm and 11pm we shut the block down, but from 11pm to 2pm we had it poppin'. The graveyard officers hardly came out of the station, and the daytime officers mostly patrolled the school zones. Problem solved. Now the other hustlers in the town had a chance to get a little money while we played it safe by saying fuck Ross. There you go, win for everybody.

Chapter 28

When Friday morning came around I was awakened by my cellphone. It was Leonard, my attorney. He told me we were meeting with the bank today for the closing on my properties at 12 o'clock this afternoon. I looked at the time and saw it was 9:45am, so I hopped out of bed and started getting myself together.

After going through my wardrobe, I decided to put on an all-black John Varvatos suit with a white button up shirt, black tie, and Coach Loafers. I had to admit, I looked pretty damn confident in my business attire. I could get used to this.

When we arrived at the bank we began to go over the paperwork and deeds to the properties. It took quite a while to go through all that paperwork, but by 4 o'clock I was the proud owner of my first twenty properties.

After leaving the bank, I drove around the town checking out the properties I had just bought, but I just did drive-by's. To be honest, I was more concerned with the properties on our block, so I headed to the house and changed clothes so I could check those properties out to see how much work was actually needed.

While checking out the properties on our block I became excited. The best part of this deal was that the three flat apartment building I originally had my eye on wasn't quite what I expected. From the outside of the apartment it appeared to be three large apartments, one on each floor, but the paperwork stated that there was an east and west side of the structure. Meaning there was actually six apartments throughout the building.

Once I got an idea of what was needed, I gave Leonard a call and he gave me a number to a rehab company that he was familiar with. I called them immediately. Luckily, I was able to get them to come out in the morning to give me an estimate on the work. I needed this shit to be done quick and fast so I can put the next phase of my plan in motion. I can definitely say that everything was flowing my way.

The next morning when I met with the guy from the rehab company, he checked out all five properties on our block and gave me what I considered to be a fair estimate. I wasn't concerned with the price, I just wanted to know how fast he could get the job done. So, I said,

"How long will it take to get all five properties move in ready?"
"I figure it will take us about a month."
"A month?!"
"Yup, I only have one crew available right now. Most of the work needed is cosmetic, but the building is gonna need some tuck pointing, plumbing and electrical. You're gonna need permits."
"Well listen, can an extra 10,000 get it done in two weeks?" He laughed seriously hard and said.
"I just can't pull my crews in the middle of other jobs buddy."
"Ok fuck it, I'll pay you an extra 50,000 *and* lock you in for fifteen other properties I need work on, wusup?" It's funny how money changes everything, because all he did was stick his arm out, shake my hand and said,
"We'll be here 7am Monday morning. How's that?"
"Perfect, can you start with the building first?"
And he said,
"No problem Mr. Stuffy. I'll have you move in ready in two weeks. First day may go a little slow because I have to get all the permits, but we'll make deadline."

Well what do ya know? First my name was buddy, $50,000 dollars later I'm Mr. Stuffy, and he didn't even have to think twice about it. I guess it's true when they say money is one of the three ultimate motivators.

Chapter 29

Later that night it was time to open up shop. Ug, Nassir, Yella Boy, Toni and Rico sat under the tree trying their hardest to catch a breeze. Ug suggested that Nassir go and get something cold to drink, So Nassir took off to Trogan's to make that happen.

After Nassir made his purchase, he walked out of the store and ran into Racks. Soon after a little small talk, Racks humbly asked Nassir to put him back in the game. He told Nassir that he spent a nice amount of his money on the lawyer that represented him in his murder charge, and that he needed to get back on the grind. Nassir was familiar with dealing with Racks, so he said,

"Uhhh… all I got right now is just some bags I'm moving, but holla at me in about two or three days and I'll see wussup."

Although he was familiar with dealing with Racks, Nassir was still a little leery about doing business with him again. First off, he wasn't sure how Racks actually made it out of that murder charge, and second, it was just something really different about him. Nassir tried to give him the benefit of the doubt that it was just everything that happened with his brother. But regardless of the reason, Nassir wasn't prepared to take that risk. So, he ended the conversation and headed back to the block.

As Nassir was coming back from the store, he saw a couple of dudes talking with a small group of females on the corner of their block. When he turned the corner, he stopped and stuck his head out of the window then said,

"Ay, y'all can't post up on dis corner like dat. Y'all gotta move around."

The guys hesitated a little bit. I guess to put on a front for the females, but Nassir sat there until they made a move. An hour later one of the smokers from the area came on the block and said,

"I see y'all got a little competition tonight." Ug snapped his neck back and said,
"Competition? Wut tha fuck you talkin' bout?"
"Some niggas on top of tha block was flaggin' me down when I turned the corner." Instantly Rico said,
"Ug, I got dis famo." And he started walking off until Toni said,
"Hol'up Rico, I'm comin' wit'chu."

Once Toni and Rico got to the top of the block, they spotted the two dudes fraternizing with the young females. Toni didn't like what she was seeing at all. Thats when Toni stepped to the girls and said,

"Ay, y'all bitches beat it!" The females sensed the tension in the air and took off. That's when Rico spoke up and said,
"Where tha fuck y'all niggas come from?" One of the guys got brave and said,
"Wut tha fuck do it matter where we come from?" Toni stepped closer and intervened.
"Nigga I see you got heart. But if you want to keep dat mufika beatin', I suggest y'all get tha fuck on."
"Bitch we ain't goin' nowhere, dis my mufukin crib right there!" Then he turned and pointed toward a house behind him then said," Y'all down tha block, don't come tellin' me I can't get money in front of my own shit! Dis me right here so fuck y'all!"
Toni became seriously pissed, and without even second guessing she pulled out her pistol and shot the guy in both of his feet. She then quickly turned and aimed the pistol at his friends head and said,

"Gimme tha dope mufuka. Hurry up before I kill yo ass." The guy then reached in his pocket and gave her his pack. "Get his shit too! I'm ain't playin' wit'chu niggas."

As soon as he gave up all of their dope, Toni stood over the guy while he squirmed on the ground and said, "Now you ain't standin' on shit you bum ass nigga!" Then she kicked him in the face and said, "That's for callin' me a bitch, you weak ass nigga!" Rico just looked at the friend and laughed, then said,

"Hey, I tried to be a playa about dis shit, but yo man had to get stupid." He hunched his shoulders up and down then hurried to catch up with Toni.

As they were walking *back* down the block Nassir, Ug, and Yella Boy came speeding *up* the block in the Hummer. When the truck stopped, Toni and Rico jumped in, then Nassir hit the gas.

Once they drove away, Rico started cracking up laughing and saying,

"Toni you wild as hell! Ug wut tha fuck you need security for?"

"Wut happened?" Ug asked.

"Dat nigga tried to get tough and call me a bitch, so I popped his ass in his feet. He lucky I ain't kill his ass." Toni replied.

Toni was a hot head, a real live wire, and she didn't give a fuck. She would react first and think about the consequences second, but no matter what, Toni was never scared of anyone or anything.

As the crew sat in the truck a block away, they watched the paramedics put the guy Toni shot into the ambulance. After the paramedics loaded him in, Ug turned in his seat and started asking Toni and Rico questions about the guys on the corner, and Toni said,

"I don't know, we were trying to figure all that shit out before dude started poppin' off at the mouth."

"Yea Ug, I don't know who tha fuck dem niggas is. I ain't never seen dem before."

Ug began to get a little annoyed. Not for what had happened, but because of what they did not know. So he said,

"Rico, dis is what I'm talkin' about when I said security. We need to know wut tha fuck is going on in dis area. Deez mufukas just pop up out of nowhere and set up shop on tha corner of our fuckin' block, and *you* don't know shit? If mufukas start thinkin' we sweet, we gone be shootin' at mufukas every night." Ug held his head back and rubbed his face. He then looked back at Toni and Rico again and spoke calmly,

"Look, I ain't mad. T, you handled yo business and dats wusup, but we gotta get on tha ball and learn dis area. I wanna know about every car, evey person, every fuckin' ant dat crawl around dis bitch."

Ug took a deep breath and began to relax. he even started to laugh a little and said,"Ay, wut he do when you shot him T?"

"Aww shit, dat nigga hit tha ground and curled up like a bitch. Then he started cryin' and talkin' bout ' my feet, my feet, oh shit my feet!"

The situation tickled them all to death as they sat there laughing. As a matter of fact, they made jokes about the shooting all the way back to the block where they continued to get their grind on as if nothing ever happened.

****

I got up early Sunday morning so I could catch the Sunday religious service on television. Being locked up had me accustomed to staying in tune with my spirituality. So, I sat in front of the TV with a bowl of Capn' Crunch and prepared for God's word. I always felt like it was meant for me to watch this channel on Sunday's. I also felt like God was trying to tell me something.

      I sat there watching the choir sing songs, the pastor get fat off the collections and shake a thousand hands before he got ready to preach. All while I sat there smashing the hell out of that bowl of Capn' Crunch because I love that shit.

      The preacher stood at the alter and wiped sweat from his head and mouth, then he looked out into crowd. As I watched, the crowd turned silent and the pastor told his congregation to turn to the book of Mark, the thirteenth chapter and seventh verse, then he read:

  'When you hear of wars and reports of wars do not be alarmed; these things must take place, but the end is not yet.'

      What the pastor had just said struck me in the head like a flying baseball, and I thought for a second...These things must happen huh? Like I said, I always felt like God was talking to me, and he was right. A war *was* coming, and it had to happen. These guys weren't going to respect our hustle how we gave it, so we were going to have to make them respect it by force. I just hope Carlos hurries up with those guns before this shit gets too real, because it was time to shift my hustle into the next phase and take out the trash.

Chapter 30

Since I've been back in Robbins, I've learned that there were four major players in the town that you could buy weight from. There was Moony, Chino, Hundo, and Gacy.

For the past week or so while the crew worked the block. I took the liberty of doing a little homework. I learned that Moony served his customers straight out of his barber shop and kept all his dope at his girlfriend's house a block away. Moony and Chino were best friends *and* partners, but Moony held the connect. Hundo hung out at the Cozy Corner lounge all day until someone hit his line for dope. He was a flashy stud, plus he liked to trick on the ladies. He'd make money all day and spend it on the women all night. And despite of how he spent his money, he made sure he kept his hustle tight. Gacy on the other hand stayed posted on his block. Unlike Moony, Chino and Hundo, he actually worked his block and controlled his area.

The next morning after I woke up, I went and rented a van. I drove it back to the hood and parked it at the Robbins Community center, which was two lots down from where Moony's girlfriend lived. I sat there for a second checking out the flow of the block just to make sure that my plan would be effective. Once I felt confident that no one was watching me, I got out of the van and began to walk away leaving the van behind.

Later that night after waking up from a nap, I put on some blue jeans and a navy blue t-shirt and left the house headed for Moony's barber shop. It was almost closing time and I needed to catch up with him before he left.

When I reached Moony's barber shop, I came up on the building from the rear and noticed Moony's gray Mercedes still parked in the lot on the side of the building. I took a few more steps then I stopped. I stood there as I noticed the area was dimly lit by a single fluorescent flood lamp that only gave light to where his car was parked, leaving the rest of the lot pretty much dark. After checking out the scenery, I began to walk toward the door of the shop.

As I was passing the Mercedes, I could hear Moony locking the shop down. When I heard his footsteps, I hurried up and ducked down by the front passenger tire so he couldn't see me. Here I was trying to be on some gangsta shit, and this motherfucker came around the corner singing bootyliscious! I tried my hardest not to bust up laughing, so I took a couple of deep breaths until the humor subsided.

Moony finally tuned his lyrics down to a whistle as he got into his car, started the engine and let the windows down. As he did this I reached in the small of my back and pulled out my black forty cal. I leaned against the tire and took a deep breath then jumped up and stuck the gun through the window and aimed for Moony's head. When I looked him in his face, I couldn't resist. I started laughing all over again then said,
"For real my dude, bootyliscious?"
Then I chuckled a little more. That's when Moony closed his eyes, turned his head straight and said,
"It's ten thousand in the glove box, take it and let's both leave here happy."

The humor had now definitely subsided. Motherfuckers always assume it's all about the money. I didn't want Moony's punk ass money, I came here for his life. And at this point there was no reason to keep bullshittin' around, so I fired two shots into the side of Moony's face and left his body slumped over the steering wheel. I then used my t-shirt to open the door and pick up the shell casings off of the passenger floor. I frantically turned to walk away but stopped. I then turned back around and reach in the glove box and grabbed the ten thousand. I didn't want the money, but since he was promoting it, I thought I should take it as a souvenir.

After I grabbed the money, I took off running. Once I made it over to the next block I brought my sprint to a halt then casually walked over to where I parked the van. As I got closer to the driver's door I heard nothing but sirens. So, I quickly got in and made my way to the back of the van and sat down. I sat there breathing hard as hell, I was still pumped up. The energy was running through my veins at 100 miles per hour and it felt hood.

Thirty minutes later, I saw Moony's girlfriend shoot out of the house, jump in her car, and take off flying. She must have gotten word about her man and wanted to see if it was all true for herself. I just sat right there and continued to watch the house. I figure it was only a matter of time before Chino came around to make sure all their dope was still there.

An hour after the girlfriend left I watched a black BMW ride past the van and pull into the girlfriend's driveway. A brief moment later, I saw Chino get out and walk toward the front door of the house. All of a sudden, he instinctively stopped then looked around. He must have felt something, because he turned toward the van and stared for a second. I swear it felt like he was looking right at me. Suddenly, Chino took his gun out and started walking toward the van. He had only taken a few steps before he stopped and looked back at the house. He had to have heard something near the house because he looked back at the van for another brief moment then took off walking toward the back of the house.

Once Chino was out of sight, I got out of the van. I left the door open and ran to the side of the community center and leaned against the wall. I peeked around the corner a few times keeping an eye out on Chino, and when I saw him coming I pushed the automatic start button on the key chain controller and started the van's engine. Chino heard the engine start and looked at the open door, then started walking toward the van with his gun drawn.

Once he got closer to the van, he aimed his gun through the open door then looked in the driver's seat and saw nothing. He slowly leaned in and looked around, that's when I crept up on him from behind and put my gun to his head and said,

"Drop tha pistol and don't move! Play games if you want, I'mma knock yo shit back."
He dropped the gun on the floor of the van then I said, "Look, I don't wanna have to hurt 'chu, I just want tha dope. Tell me where it's at."
"It's in tha house across the street, just be cool."
"Is it anybody in dat house? Who all lived there?"
"Shawty live there by herself and she gone right now, ain't nobody else there."
"If you wanna live to see tomorrow you gone do wut I tell you right?"
"Yeah, yeah!"
"Cool, bring yo ass on, and you bet not be bullshittin' me around."
"I ain't bullshittin' dog, it's in tha crib." I reached in the van and grabbed Chino's gun off of the floor and we started walking toward the house.

Once Chino unlocked the door to the house I advised him not to move to fast. I wanted to see everything in slow motion, that way I can easily notice any quick moves. When we got in, he took me to a room in the back of the house that looked like a baby nursery. I quickly shoved the gun into the back of Chino's head and said,

"Mufuka you told me she lived here by herself, you ain't say shit about no baby!"

"I'm for real my nigga, she stay by herself, the room is just a front, it's just a front!"

As we walked through the door of the nursery we moved slowly across the room until we got to the middle of the floor. Chino kneeled down and began to take boards out of the floor. A few seconds after, he reached in the hole in the floor and pulled out a big blue gym bag and tossed it on the floor by my foot. I didn't open it, I just looked at it and said,

"Is that everythang? Wus all in there?"
"It should be about three or four bricks."
"Three or four bricks?!... You fuckin' wit me Chino?"
"Naw man straight up, we loaded up earlier dis week, dis just the bottom of tha load." I was so ready to do Chino's ass in, I just had to ask him one more question.
"Chino listen close. You wit me?"
"I'm wit'chu I'm wit'chu"
"Chino, who y'all gettin y'all dope from?"
Chino paused for a moment, he didn't want to give up the name, but he thought that bit of information would keep him alive so he said,
"Black Pooh, tha nigga name is Black Pooh."

I stood there thinking for a moment. I was wrecking my brain trying to figure out who the fuck Black Pooh was, but for the life of me I couldn't figure it out. Instantly I began to think that Chino was playing with my intelligence so I smacked him across the head with my pistol and said,
"Quit fucking wit me Chino, who tha fuck is Black Pooh?!"
Chino got scared and started to cry saying.
"I ain't fuckin' wit'chu fam, for real his name is Black Pooh, he from Harvey! Com'on man don't kill me, I gave you all the dope and I told you wut you wanted to know."

Although the information was useful, I was going to kill Chino no matter what he told me. He just proved to me that he was just as useless as he was a rat, so I cocked my gun and shoved it in the back of Chino's head. He was on his knees breathing hard and crying hysterically, the shit was starting to bother me so I put him to sleep with one single shot to the head at point blank range.

Immediately, I grabbed the bag and ran toward the front door, and as I got closer I frantically heard a pair of keys trying to open the door. It was Moony's girlfriend so I had to think fast.

As the door began to open I ducked myself behind the front door and stood there as she yelled out Chino's name. When she rushed in, I jumped from behind the door and came down hard on the back of her head with the handle of the gun. She hit the floor like a sack of potatoes. I then stepped over her body, made my way out of the house to the van and casually drove away like I was delivering pizza. Now that I handled the trash, I could go home and start putting the next phase of my plan together.

Chapter 31

A week later the town was in a panic. Nobody knew what happened to Moony and Chino, but there was minor speculation about what had happened to Hundo. Word was, he was seen leaving the Cozy Corner with some girl, but no one could tell who she was. Either way, none of the crew was implicated, so fuck'em. Besides, I don't think it even mattered that they were dead. I believe the panic came from the people in the town not knowing where they would get their dope from.

As I stood on the block drowning in thought, I watched the rehab company bust their ass to make their deadline. While I watched, Nassir walked up and stood next to me. He looked around shaking his head as if he were impressed, but at the same time I could tell he had something on his mind. So I asked,

"Nas, you all good bro?" He paused for a second then said. "Ug, sumt'n don't feel right fam. Moony, Chino, *and* Hundo in the same week? I just don't think dats no coincidence."

This wasn't the time or place to go into specifics about what happened with the murders. When the time was right I'd tell him everything. But for now, the less he knew the more natural it would appear if people started asking questions.

I put my arm around Nassir's shoulder as we walked into some shade. I made sure no one was in listening range, then said,

"Nas relax man, you got'cho emotions mixed up. Fuck dem chumps, this a good thang for us. Wit dem mufukas out tha way deez streets finna dry up like tha Sierra Desert. Now instead of sellin' eight balls for eighty bucks, y'all can jam dem mufukas for the whole hunnid and kill'em easy. So instead of making 23 g's a brick, you make 28 and some change, and we do it wit less chance of going to war." Nassir smiled and said,

"Yeah, I ain't even think of it like dat. My mind was somewhere else fam."

"Don't even trip bro, Im'ma keep you focused on dis money. Y'all still got a lot of bags left?"

"Naw, everybody bout down to their last."

"Cool, when y'all tap out let me know. Don't start selling balls just yet."

****

Almost a month had passed and I still haven't heard from Carlos yet, so figured I'd give him a call to see what was up, but when I dialed his number I got no answer. I didn't even make it an issue because we still had dope left.

Later that night Brittany and I sat on the couch watching a movie. Being with her made me feel much more relaxed. Every time we were together I thanked God that he put her in my path. She never bugged me about going places and spending money. She was simply content with just being in my presence and I felt the same about her.

Thirty minutes into the movie my phone rang. I looked at the screen to see it was Carlos, so I excused myself to answer the call. The call didn't last long at all, he just told me to come see him tomorrow and we hung up. When I returned to the couch Brittany asked if everything was ok and I assured her it was. It was Brittany's genuine concern and level of compassion she had when she dealt with me that made me want to be with her and only her.

As we continued to watch the movie, I just sort of stared at Brittany in awe. I felt like either this woman was the truth or she could bullshit with the best of them. Either way, I had to know what was on her mind for real. Before I could get the first word out of my mouth she looked at me and said,

"Why are you just staring at me." I had all of these thoughts and questions running though my mind, but when I looked into Brittany's eyes, all I could do was stare. I mean I was at a complete loss of words. Brittany put her hand on the side of my face and said. "Baby what's wrong?" I paused for a moment then took a deep breath and said.

"Brittany, why you wit me? I mean for real, cause I need to know. You can have any man you want I'm sure, so why me?" It took her no thought at all, she came straight out and said.

"Adonis, I'm with you because I'm with you. I'm not one of these superficial chics that's out for money or status or whatever else these hoodrat hoes be into. I never asked you for anything but just a little bit of your time Adonis, and yea there are a lot of cute guys out there I could have my choice of, and baby I choose you. When I first met you your aura was just so strong, like you were above being petty, like a king. Now, I will admit, I said to myself 'Brittany, he ain't all that cute... but damn he sexy'."
She giggled a little then said, "Baby I'm not worried about your looks. Beauty fades away, but royalty is forever and I wanna be your queen."

When Brittany said that I just froze and started to think about my mother. She used to always tell me that exact saying. I couldn't help but to asked her where she'd gotten it from. And she said,"I don't know, it was just from the heart I guess."

After she made that last comment I looked her in the eyes and I shed a single tear. I never mentioned that saying to her, and hearing her say it made me sort of emotional. Brittany then leaned into me and wiped the tear away and said,

"Aww baby, see this is why I'm with you. You're not ashamed to leave all the streets at the door when we're together.

Come here, lay your head on my lap." And when I did, she rubbed my head and sang this song. I couldn't tell you the name of it, but the girl could sing her ass off. As I laid there listening I closed my eyes and lived in that moment. It was definitely one of those moments where I was saying, damn I'm feeling her.

The next day I met with Carlos at the Trump Towers. He seemed a little tired and burned out. I guess that will happen when you have three butt naked maids.

As I settled in, Carlos asked how everything had been going and I told him I'd been taking care of business. He gave me a slight chuckle and went on to ask me about the property I had just bought. I let him know that the renovation on the first five properties would be done in a week, and that everything was going just as planned.

After a series of questions, he finally got to the one question I was ready to hear. And he said,

"So are you ready for the next load?" I smiled and told him,
"Hell yeah!"
"Do you have your security worked out?"
"I got a few kinks to straighten out, but I'm cool."
"What kind of kinks."
"I got my guys in order, I'm just working on job assignments."
"And you are sure that this is no problem?"
"I'm positive."
Carlos thought for a second then said,
"Ok, give me some time, but expect the next load at any moment, after that I'm going to load you up hard and heavy, but this next load will be five tons. I'm going to charge you ten million a ton. Oh, I will have those guns for you as well." I didn't know how to respond, he just spoke clear over my head so I said,

"Five tons?! How many kilos is dat exactly?"

Carlos smiled confidently and said,

"Five tons is exactly 5,600 kilos. I know that sounds like a lot but trust me, this shit sells itself. So, don't get overwhelmed."

After we got the business out of the way, we discussed more personal issues that pretty much gravitated around my life. He wanted to know when I was going to start school and if I had anyone special in my life. You know, the father and son type of stuff, and that was cool with me. Carlos always made me feel like he had my best interests at heart, and for that reason, I wanted to make sure I didn't disappoint him.

Chapter 32

It was still early in the day when I got back to the house. I went to my room and grabbed the black gym bag I took from Chino out of my closet. With everything going on and my lack of interest in the bag, I never even looked inside to see what was in it. I figured now was a good time to do just that.

I sat on the couch and opened the bag, and just like Chino said, there were four kilos in the bag along with three guns and a nice amount of cash. I took all of the cash out and zipped the bag back up, then woke Nassir up so we could chat a little bit while things were still fresh in my mind.

Nassir came out of his room and plopped down on the couch and I gave him an excited smile and he said,

"Comon Ug wit dat goofy ass smile. Wusup?"
"Ay, remember when I told you we was on?"
"Yea ok, I already know dat."
"Listen bro. When I came home you blessed me hard fam, now it's my turn to bless you, but I need to know where you stand."
"Wut'chu mean *where* I stand?"
"Look, I want you to oversee the operation, be the face of tha mob. I want you to be our go to man and make sure everything is running smoov with the business. Wussup wut you wanna do?"

Nassir thought for a moment then said.
"So you want me to run shit, but you still gone be in charge, right?"
"Just like dat. All the work go through you, so you gone profit off every brick sold. So all you gotta do is fill orders, make sure everybody on they shit and be the man." Nassir didn't even question it, he just said.
"I'm wit it. So when the next load comin'?"

"Soon, but check it out, this shit gone be different. My man said it's way better than the last shit and it ain't gone be a hunnid bricks this time."

"So how many we gettin', 50?"

I looked Nassir square in the eyes and said,

"He gone hit me off wit 5 tons."

Nassir's eyes grew big as hell as he replied with nervousness and excitement,

"5 tons? Nigga dats-"

"Five thousand six hunnid bricks, I already know."

"Man, who tha fuck you den bumped into, Noreaga?"

After giving Nassir the run down, I let him know that the price of the dope was dropping to 19 thousand a brick for him and the crew. I also let him know that regardless of the price dropping, the kilos were still to be sold at 23 thousand a brick. I then went on to explain to him that he would earn an extra 1,000 dollar commission off of every kilo on the back end, and that we had a shipment of guns coming too. Now that Nassir and I had this understanding, it was time to tune in with the crew to explain their jobs.

After speaking with Nassir, I called Toni, Rico, and Yella Boy over so we could talk. When they all arrived, I sat them down and everyone got quiet. I instantly opened up the meeting by saying,

"Next load gone be comin' soon, so it's time to tighten up. Nassir is gone be our go to man. When y'all got orders to fill you holla at Nas. If somebody ain't on they job you holla at Nas. Toni you gone handle tha money. Im'ma get wit 'chu one on one and show you how I want dat ran, but I don't want 'chu takin' money from nobody else's hands but Nassir, so plug all yo customers directly wit him. Yella Boy, once Toni count tha money she gone tell you how many bricks to give to Nas. Im'ma give you a count sheet. If we got a hunnid bricks, the count sheet gone have a hunnid numbas; one to one hunnid on it. I want 'chu to slash out the numbas as the bricks go out. Each kilo *gotta* be accounted for. Last but not least, Rico. Yo job is tha most important."

I picked up the gym bag I took from Chino and tossed it into Rico's lap then told him to look in it. When he opened the bag, he smiled. I then went on to explain his job.

"Rico I want 'chu to think long and hard, cause I want 'chu to give me your best twenty guys. They gotta be solid and they gotta be riders. Them twenty guys gone work security on dis block, ten at a time in rotating shifts.
"How do you want tha shifts rotated?'
"Six hours on, six hours off. They gone be on payroll, $1500 a week. I'm payin' good money so I want tha best you got. Take that dope in tha bag and dump it. Take it outside of the town and get rid of it wholesale. Sell it for wuteva, I don't give a fuck, it's yours. Keep tha guns, the more we got the betta off we are. Make it a priority to always keep your ears and eyes open for anybody selling pistols." I stood up and told them all to take a walk with me. I took them outside and told them to take a good look around, then said. "I want y'all to know dis block. Pay attention to tha neighbors and the cars they drive. Rico you see these four houses getting worked on? Three of them gone be security posts. I want two of yo guys on each porch strapped at all times. I want tha other four in sniper mode on the top floor of dat apartment building. Dats gone be tha main stash house, so I want all tha focus on protecting *that* mufuka. I want two of your guys workin' tha front and two workin' tha back. You can see everything on yo block *and* ours from those four spots. Everythang outside tha block is all on you Rico. Yo people gotta stand on tha area fam. Hit these blocks, pay attention to who parked or standing around dat don't belong. I want a security clearance for two blocks every which way from dis building. If we ain't expectin' a mufuka, jam they ass up and call Nas, then we gone take it from there. Now, as time go on we gone adjust to wut works betta, but dis where we at

for now. Oh and one mo' thang, if you get caught up in these streets don't say *shit*! Just shut tha fuck up and call Candice. Do not and I repeat, *do not* call anybody you lookin' at right now. Candice gone get wit me and Im'ma get wit tha lawyer, everybody good?" I looked at them all as they acknowledged my orders and then I said, "Cool, Rico get started on them security measures asap. I wanna see those twenty guys by tomorrow morning and I wanna see yo people circulating dis area today, non-stop."

Rico took off while the rest of us chilled. We sat and discussed ins and outs of the operation until it was time to open up shop. There was still a lot to do, but I had faith in my crew that they would pull it together.

CHAPTER 33

Word had gotten back to Colombia about the threat and demand made to the Ortega Cartel. Estavan was extremely furious when he heard of the situation. He clearly remembered telling Carlos that he didn't want to raise any red flags, and now he was forced to make a decision about going to war with the Ortega Cartel.

The Ortega Cartel was not backing down. They continued to send threats to Colombia and this infuriated Estavan even more.

Once Carlos arrived in Colombia, he tried his hardest to make Estavan believe that his actions were well within reason, but Estavan wasn't buying into it.

Months ago, war wasn't an option for Estavan, but now that it was inevitable, Carlos decided to come clean with his true intentions. He took a deep breath and said,
"Brother, I did what I did because it had to happen. The Ortega's tried to stop our distribution in Chicago, and that would have set our plans backwards if not destroyed them. Now even though we've created a different transport pipeline, the Ortega's will eventually make it difficult for us."
"How so Carlos?"
"My resources tell me that the Ortega's have strong political ties with the Americans. That's how they get their product in with no problems, but if we begin to bring in better quality of cocaine at a better price, we will dismantle them financially. That alone will make them tip off American authorities and shut us down. At that point brother, it would have all been for nothing."
Then Estavan said,
"I believe I'm beginning to understand, but how will this war benefit our product if the Americans are allied with the

Ortega's? If you try to create this force, it will destroy your diplomatic position and discredit our franchise business."

"I know Estavan that is why I need *you* to create that ally force. All we have to do is disable the Ortega Cartel, and the Americans will be looking to see who steps up. Estavan, the Americans are greedy, you just have to present the opportunity. In the end this will position us for high political influence and illegal political power.

"I see, I see."

"Good because we need our rebels on Mexican soil invading Juarez now! In the meantime, I'm sending 50 rebels into the U.S. to work the Chicago warehouse, along with five tons of cocaine. I'll send the shipment through Mississippi as a test run while all the attention is on Mexico."

Carlos finally got Estavan on board, and now it was time for him to return to the U.S. He had to put his ear to the ground and put his political influence to work.

****

It was an early Wednesday morning, the last day of July to be exact. I sat on the front porch thinking and watching the sunrise. In prison, watching the sun break the horizon became my favorite pastime, but since I've been free, I think I've started taking the natural elements in life for granted. I guess I've been so busy, I haven't even payed it much attention.

I may not have been paying the sunrise that much attention lately, but I was watching these streets like a hawk. As the days went by, the streets began to dry up even more, and as the streets dried up the guys in the town became a bit more aggressive, but it's what I expected, it was the response I was looking for.

Later that morning Nassir informed me that the crew had finished up on all the dime bags they had. He also let me know everybody's phone was constantly ringing with customers wanting dope. So, I told Nassir get the crew together and tell them to start feeding their customers the eight balls. Nassir seemed a little uneasy about my statement and said,

"Ug my people want weight. What tha fuck they gone do with an eight ball?"

"Look, I feel you, I just aint ready to put no work out on *these* streets yet."

"Why not?! Wut 'chu waiting on Ug?"

"Why *you* so in a rush? Nas deez mufukas ain't going nowhere. Deez tha same mufukas dat used to play *us* shady in a drought, charging us 150 dollars for an eight ball. Tha same mufukas dat used to spoon feed us so we hustled at they pace. Fuck dem Nas, focus on us."

"I'm just saying Ug, its crazy money out here."

"And its crazy money out there Nassir."

I was trying to get Naair to understand that if we move prematurely we'd kill ourselves, and that was in more ways than one. The City of Chicago was huge, and we needed to gain more trustworthy allies before we just started slanging dope everywhere. At the same time, I didn't want him to think I didn't give a fuck about the town. I *did* want to see these guys get money, and when the time was right they would.

Later that afternoon Nassir and the rest of the crew realized that they didn't have to persuade their people into buying anything. It just so happen that Robbins wasn't the only street drying up. The crew was hooking up with guys all over the city of Chicago and they weren't just buying a couple, they were buying 50-100 at a time. Even Skeezo came through and spent some decent money, so I'd have to say that this was far better than I expected.

Before Skeezo left, he pulled me to the side and said, "Aye Jo, is yo connect Mexican?" I was unsure why this question had relevance, so I said,

"Why yo ask dat?"

"Cause the Mexicans we was fuckin wit came to me tryin to see if I could get *them* some dope. He was sayin dat dis drought shit was for real. He also said some shit about it being a war in Mexico and that it was going to be a while before they get some more dope.

"How long yo people talking?"

"Well shit, my people talkin about a week or two, but I guess we'll see."

After Skeezo left, I spoke to the crew about what he had told me. They weren't surprised about the talk of a drought because the word drought itself had spread clear across Cook County like a lightning bolt. What had them worried was the look on my face, and what had me so uneasy was the fact of not knowing if this war would affect us. Honestly, I didn't know if Carlos was Mexican or not, I just know he never brung up any talk about a war *or* drought. So as far as I was concerned, Carlos was going to deliver as promised, and that would be soon.

Three days had passed and I must say, this drought *was* real. The first of the month had come and gone, and left the crew completely tapped out. This was a beautiful thing, and I could feel this playing out in our favor as long as Carlos was on point.

That night, I sat on the couch and watched CNN news. I wanted to see if I could catch any reports of this Mexican war, but nothing crossed the screen. I flicked through some more news channels and still no reports. I started to question if this talk of war was even true.

Eventually, I got bored and stepped outside to get some air and saw Yella Boy and Toni sitting under the tree smoking weed.

The ambience of the night was extremely creepy. Usually you would hear sounds bumping, sirens blaring or even some lonely ass dog barking. But as I listened, all I heard was a dead silence.

Minutes later, Nassir and Rico returned to the block. Nassir hopped out of the truck and just started reporting the neighborhood news. He walked over to the tree real animated like and said,
"Niggas out here wild jo. Mufukas den pulled off three kick doors tonight." And Rico said,
"Ug, don't even trip, I got the brothas circulatin' tha area hard right now, so mufukas betta be right if they thinkin about tryin us."

This didn't surprise me at all. It was the ultimate thirst move when you weren't making any money. If you're one of those types that stack your money, then chances are you're somewhere laid up under some pussy, and if you're a petty hustler, then chances are you were somewhere trying to figure out how you were going to eat tomorrow. Nevertheless, I told the crew not to leave the block alone, and *stay* strapped all the time.

As the night continued on, I finally started hearing the familiar sounds I became accustomed to, only because people began to come outside. With no dope in the town, there was a lot of mingling going and a lot of sets clashing. All it took was a little bit of liquor and a whole lot of stress, and before you knew it somebody was going to get their head busted.

By the time Monday morning came around, the jail cells in Robbins Police Department were full, and Robbins was now dealing with a war of its own. One of the GD's in town was killed in a home invasion and the madness hasn't stopped since.

Despite all the uproar in the town, I had a smile on my face. As promised, all five of the properties on my block were finished being rehabbed. The extra fifty- thousand I spent seemed well worth it, because in so short of time, they did an amazing job.

No sooner than the rehab crew left the block, I hit Yella Boy on the phone and told him to come to the block.

Once he got there, I took him over to the house that I had prepared for him. It wasn't a big house, just it a simple 800 sq ft. ranch style home, but I made sure they hooked it up real nice. Yella Boy didn't care anyway, just the thought of being in his own shit made him happy, I thought I even seen him tearing up a little.

I was in the front room of Yella Boy's house, leaning on the wall texting Brittany when Yella Boy came and stood next to me. He seemed as though he had something on his mind, but he was a little hesitant to speak. I put my phone in my pocket, then crossed my arms and said,

"Wussup, wuts on yo mine lil bro." Yella Boy cleared his throat when he spoke in the utmost humble manner saying.
"Thanks Ug, dis tha most anybody ever did for me, and I just want'cha to know, if its anything you need me to do just let me know." Yella Boy put his hand on Ug's shoulder and looked him in the eyes and said. "Ug, I do mean *anything*... I gotchu"

I looked at Yella Boy and just smiled for a moment. I couldn't even find the right words to say. It was an emotional moment for the both of us. He was overwhelmed with what I had done for him, and I was happy to be in a position to be *able* to do something for someone I had grown love for. I mean shorty was my little man, and when I looked at him the words finally came to me.

"Yella Boy, you got yo high school diploma?"
"Yeah I graduated."

"Ok well check it out. After Labor Day, I start night school at the junior college."

"Why don't you sign up and come to school with me." He hesitated for a second then I said,

"Ay, you said anything, right?"

"Yeah, I *did* say anything."

"Well dis wut I want. Take a business class or sumt'n, figure out wut 'chu gone do wit all dat money you finna make. Don' trip, I'm gone pay for everything."

It didn't take Yell Boy long to realize that he wasn't just doing something for me, but he was taking a step to make something happen for himself. Besides that, I wanted to keep Yella Boy close to me and away from as much bullshit as possible. Yella Boy was still young and with the right guidance he could be the face of our future.

Chapter 34

While Ug and the crew helped Yella Boy get settled into his new home, Ross and Watts were at the Robbins police station working Moony and Chino's case.

There were a few things that confused them about both cases, but one thing they knew for sure was that the same gun was used in both murders. They had disregarded Moony's death as a robbery gone wrong due to the fact that the Mercedes wasn't taken and he still had on jewelry.

Chino's death was however written up as a robbery/homocide. Ross and Watts were unsure of what was taken, but they knew by the whole in the floor something was missing. They wanted to get more answers from Moony's girlfriend that fatal night, but due to her severe head injury, she just wasn't in the mood to talk. Now it was time for them to back track and cover all bases so that they could close their case and bring a murderer to justice.

The first thing they did was call the girlfriend and have her come in to answer some questions, and once she got there, Ross started the interview by asking the woman one simple question that got their ball rolling in a good direction. Ross leaned into her and said,

"Ma'am, how did you know the deceased found in your home?"

She let him know that Chino was Moony's best friend, and that Moony was in fact her boyfriend. Now things were starting to connect, so he went on with his next question.

"What did your boyfriend and his friend have hid inside the floor? We noticed some boards taken up where the body was found."

"I don't know." She responded.

"Ma'am listen, you're not going to get in any trouble, but in order for us to find their killer, we need to know what was there."

She sat there for a moment fidgeting her thumbs. She remained silent as she contemplated on answering the question truthfully. Then she finally spoke,

"Can I smoke in here, please? I need a cigarette bad." Ross let her light her cigarette then said,

"Ok, now what was in the floor?"

"Like I said, I don't know. Maybe some guns or something I'm not sure."

"Guns, ok that's good. Do you have any idea of how many?"

"Nope." The officers didn't feel like they were getting anywhere, so they decided to switch their line of questioning.

"Did you see the person that hit you in the head?"

"Nope."

"Ok Ma'am, can you think of anything that seemed strange that day? Anything unusual or out of place? Anything that just stood out to you? Please take your time." She took a couple of puffs from her cigarette and thought hard. Seconds later her eyes lit up as she said,

"You know wut, come to think about it, it *was* this van that sat at the Center all day. I thought that was strange cause the Center been closed for the last few weeks. It was still there when I got home, but when the paramedics was puttin' me in the ambulance it was gone."

She went on to describe the van to the officers, but couldn't recall the license plate number. However, she did say she remembered seeing an Enterprise rental sticker on the rear window.

The officers figured that was enough to get them started, so they told the woman that she could leave. Their next task was canvassing the block and questioning neighbors, hoping they would stumble across any signs of a motive.

The next morning Ross and Watts arrived early to their shift. They wanted to canvas the girlfriend's block before they started contacting the Enterprise Rental companies.

Once they got to the girlfriend's block they realized that there were only four other houses on the block. There were three houses on the corner of the block, and one house on the other corner, leaving the girlfriend's house and the community center in the middle of the block, singled out.

The lady that lived in the first house they went to said that she *did* notice the van but didn't know anything else. She also made it clear that she wasn't home around the time of the murder.

When they got to the second house, the man wouldn't even open the door. He cracked the window and said,

"I ain't seen shit, I ain't heard shit, and I don't know shit, so don't come back." Then he slammed the window closed and walked away.

There was an old man in the third house that pretty much said the same as the lady in the first house. He said he saw the van, but it *didn't* seem unusual to *him*. He said people parked there all the time.

When Ross and Watts walked up to the fourth house they noticed a little old lady sitting on an enclosed porch with mesh windows. The porch seemed like a nice spot to sit and it made the officers wonder if she was sitting there at the time of the murder.

As they walked toward the porch, they found out that the little old lady had questions of her own. Before they could even get a word out the old lady said,

"So, did you catch'em?"
"Uhh no Ma'am, not yet. We were hoping you saw something that might help us out."
"Well I was sleep bout time that boy got himself killed, so I ain't see nothin."
"Well what about the van that sat at the center all that day?"
"Now that there van is different. I seen when the boy pulled up, got out, and walked away. Thought it was strange, but I just mind my own business. You don't live this long being all up in people's business, but I knew it wasn't gone be long before sumt'n happened over there at that house. Them boys was always comin and goin carryin' big ole bags and actin sneaky."
"Ma'am you say you saw the guy get out of the van and walk away? Did you have a chance to see what he looked like?"
"Well he was tall and dark skinned, but I couldn't really see his face."
"Can you remember anything else?"
"Nope, that's all I remember."
"Well, we appreciate your time, if you happen to remember anything else please give us a call, ok?" Ross gave the old lady one of his business cards and they left to go explore some of their investigative leads.

Once they returned to the station, they sat in front of a computer and pulled up the Enterprise rental car website. They then pulled up every facility within a twenty mile radius then printed out the results. When they saw that the results reported fifty facilities, they knew this would take up a chunk of their day, so they split the results in half and started contacting all the facilities to see who rented out vans in the past three weeks.

After the first few calls Ross and Watts realized that they'd hit a brick wall. The rental facilities did not want to give up any information without a warrant, so Ross and Watts took off for Markham court house to find a judge that would sign off on the court order.

By three o'clock that afternoon, Ross and Watts left the court building smiling. They had their court order, and they were confident that they were on the tail of a killer.

****

Toni had just left the used car lot driving in what she considered to be her new toy. Although she had the money to buy any car she wanted, she chose to buy a 96' Chevy Impala. Toni was a speed freak. She just loved a car with a strong engine. So to her the Impala was perfect, cause it was quick but yet stylish. Her plan was to come out on parade day and show the town that Nassir and Ug wasn't the only ones that could ride a clean Impala.

As Toni was about to turn onto the Block, she looked to her left and saw the dude that she shot in the feet sitting on his porch. The guy didn't recognize the Impala, so he continued to talk to his friend that was standing next to him. The situation itself tickled Toni a bit, not just because she was admiring her handy work, but because the guy she shot was sitting in a wheelchair.

When Toni made her turn she stopped at the corner and smiled at the guy in the wheelchair. Buddy was not happy at all, in fact he mean mugged Toni and gave her a cold hard stare. It didn't bother Toni one bit. To her, he was just some punk that was still trying his hardest to be tough. Either way, Toni decided to mess with him a little, so she leaned out the car window and said.

"Awww boo, don't look so mean. You makin' me think you don't like me... don't worry, you a be up and runnning in no time." Then Toni gave him a real girly like smile, blew him a kiss and drove away.

When Toni drove off, buddy's face scowled as he said,

"Man I swear to God!!... On my momma...I'm gone kill dat bitch!" And he kept watching her as she moved up the block.

****

Once Ross and Watts returned to the police station, they realized it was too late to follow up with their court order. All of the Enterprise facilities were closed for the day, so they decided to hit the streets for an early patrol.

As Ross and Watts were about to leave the station, the Chief walked up and slapped a manila folder in Ross' chest and told him good luck. When Ross opened the folder he quickly scanned the contents saying,

"Aww com'on chief we were just gettin' started on this one." The chief replied.
"Death has no priority Ross. You got three dead bodies, they ain't goin nowhere. Take ya time, work it at your own pace, just bring me some killers."

Ross and Watts had just been handed Hundo's murder file. The chief theorized the situation and told them that all three murders happened in less than seventy-two hours, so there *could* be a connection somewhere. Nevertheless, they briefly scanned the file, then hit the streets hoping to come across some leads.

When Ross and Watts were out and about, they noticed the town was dead. With all the shootings and robberies going on no one wanted to be the next statistic, so the majority of the people moved cautiously from point A to point B, *if* they moved at all.

By the end of their shift they had absolutely nothing. This had been the first time that Ross actually wished there *was* dope in the streets, that way he could arrest somebody on a petty drug charge and press them for info. He knew snitches came a dime a dozen, he just had to create the perfect circumstance, but with no dope on the street it was a fucked up day for a crack dealer and a boring day for a police officer.

Chapter 35

The town was at a standstill, so the crew decided to get with their significant others and head to the theatre to catch a movie.

When they returned to the block everybody noticed Toni and Candice's door to their home wide open. Toni's heart dropped as she thought about all the money she had stashed away in the house. She looked at the door with a blank stare, then took off running into the house like a bat out of hell. All of the guys followed right behind her to make sure no one was still in the house.

After making sure no one was there, they continued to look around to see if they noticed anything missing. Every room in the house was pretty much intact except for their bedroom. The drawers were pulled out, clothes were all on the floor, and the bed had been flipped over. Toni shot to her closet where she kept her stash and noticed her safe was missing.

Toni flopped on the edge of the bed with her elbows in her knees and hands covering her face. Ug walked in the room and saw her sitting there with a look of defeated, so he walked up to her and said,

"Wussup T, wut they take baby girl?"
"They took my safe Ug."
"Don't worry bout no money, I'll get'chu back right."
"Naw Ug, I had…" And before she said another word, she jumped up quickly and closed the door. She turned to Ug and whispered,
"Ug, I had dat gun in there, the one I popped Hundo wit!"
"Oh shit Toni! I thought you stashed it wit the 40 cal?"
"I never got around to it."

"Toni, you shoulda handled dat shit. If a mufuka get caught wit dat gun they ain't gone have no problem wit confessing to a robbery, but a mufuka ain't gone go down fo no murda."

"No shit Ug! Tell me sumt'n a bitch don't already know. Fuck!... Ug, you gotta help me, we gotta find dat pistol, and we gotta find dat mufuka fast!"

****

The next morning, Ross and Watts came in early again to get started on the van lead. As they contacted each facility, they faxed over a copy of the court order and waited for the hits to roll in.

After all the calls were made, Ross decided to go through Hundo's murder file. It was taking a little time for the rental car facilities to respond, so he wanted to become a bit more familiar with the case.

Ross soon learned that Hundo was a big timer in the hood and wasn't even on his radar, and since Ross didn't believe in coincidences, he did in fact find some connection between both incidents. He started to think, how does three key suppliers in an area get killed in less than 72 hours?

Ross wasn't liking how this situation was beginning to look. If he didn't know any better, he'd say that someone new was trying to corner the drug market in Robbins.

As Ross pondered on his thoughts, reports of the recently rented vehicles started pouring in, and Ross and Watts jumped right in and started going through all the records.

Two hours had passed before the fax machine became silent. Watts looked at all the records, rubbed his bald head and said,

"This shit is gonna take forever. We asked for van rentals and they give us every fuckin vehicle they rented in the last three weeks." Then Ross replied,
"Don't pay attention to every hit. Just look in the vehicle type section and look for any style of van."

This became tedious work for the officers and by mid-afternoon Watts stood up and stretched his neck, then suggested they take a break to get something to eat, and Ross agreed.

By one o'clock they were back at the station going through more files. They were half way through the paperwork when Ross said,
"Oh, fuckin shit! You have got to be fuckin kiddin me!" Then he stood up and looked closer at the piece of paper and said, "Watts look at this!"

Watts took the piece of paper and read through it. Once he saw what Ross saw, his face froze and his eyes got big, then he said,

"Adonis Stuffy, you dumb muthafuka." Then Ross said.
"I told you that kid was bad news, and now I finally got his ass right where I want it." Ross grabbed his car keys and radio then stepped toward the door when Watts said,

"Where you goin?"
"We're about to bring this bastard in and question him!" Watts grabbed Ross by the arm saying,
"Wait a minute, what if this is all a coincidence."
"Listen, the old lady said the guy was tall and dark skinned. That's him, that's Stuffy!"
"Ok ok, just think for a second. If Stuffy is our guy we want a for sure conviction. We need to first get a picture of the van rented in his name, then take a photo lineup and re-interview the neighbors. Let's see if they can I.D. Stuffy or the van. Then we

take everything to the S.A. and have him draw up an arrest warrant. He's already killed two maybe three, so if we tip him off prematurely he may go back and start tying up loose ends." Ross knew Watts was right, so they set out to get the picture of the van so they could re-interview the neighbors before it got too late.

An hour and a half later they had their picture of the van, mug shots of Ug, and their photo line-up. Since the old lady was the most helpful, they went to see her first.

Once they got to the old lady's house they were let in and offered a seat. Ross wasted no time, he was hungry for this conviction. He took out the picture of the van and said,

"Ma'am, I want you to look carefully at this picture. Is this the van you saw parked at the center?" She looked at the picture and without hesitation, she said,
"Yup, that look like the one." Ross gave a sigh of relief then finished.
"Ok ma'am one more time. I want you to look at this photo line-up and tell me if one of these guys are the one you seen walking away from the van." This time she looked long and hard, then said,
"This the one right here." The old lady pointed directly at Ug's picture then said. "Hell, he so ugly I thought I just wasn't seeing too well, but that's him, ugly as a catfish. That's him!"

Ross left the old lady's house feeling energized. Watts however felt like he was moving too fast. All they had was Ug walking away from the van, but they still could not place him at the scene of either murder. Watts explained to Ross that everything they had was all circumstantial, and a state's attorney would not award an arrest warrant with circumstantial evidence. Ross sat in silence and thought about what Watts had just said. Then he spoke,
"Watts, we need to search that house again for clues. Killers always fuck up, and I think we're missing something."

After several attempts to reach Moony's girlfriend, they were finally able to get her on the line, and by four o'clock they were back in the house searching for clues. As Moony's girlfriend stood close to the door watching the officer's she said,

"I been staying wit my sista since everything happened, so everything is left the same way."

Ross and Watts went into the room where Chino was killed and just looked around. The room was decorated with a teddy bear theme and there was a baby bed in the corner with baby toys on the floor. Watts looked at all the toys and said,

"Why would they hide dope in they kid's room?" Ross stuck his head out of the door and yelled out to Moony's girl.
"Why was you lettin them hide dope in your baby's room?" The girl snapped her neck back and said,
"Kids!? I ain't got no damn kids!" Ross seemed confused, so he asked,
"When was the last time you been in this room?"
"Never, I ain't get in they business. Besides, they kept it locked all the time anyway."

Ross examined the door and saw a key hole in the handle, which was unusual for a room made for a kid, and when he turned around to scan the room something else caught his eye. He walked toward a shelf that sat on the wall above the whole in the floor where Chino and Moony hid their dope. He stood by the shelf and stared at this cute little teddy bear. When Ross tried to grab it he noticed that it was stuck to the platform, so he yanked on it, and when it came loose Ross saw wires hanging from the back of the bear and yelled,

"Hot damn! Jackpot, we got us a nanny cam!"

He stood back and looked at the wires coming from the wall and wondered where they led to. There was no closet, so Ross got on his knees and flashed some light into the hole in the floor and saw a video recorder. Ross got down on his knees and reached in the hole and pulled the recorder from out of the floor and said,

"How the fuck did we miss this! Can you believe this shit? They knew somebody would've tried to rob them. This is some smart shit," And all Watts could say was,
"Dumb... mutha...fucka!"

When Ross and Watts returned to the station they rushed into an interview room and watched the video. They couldn't believe they had the entire murder caught on tape. The only thing that frustrated them was the fact that the video had no audio, but nevertheless they had what they needed.

After they finished watching the tape, Ross started writing up the report for the state's attorney while Watts stepped out of the room. He said he wanted to call his girlfriend and see what her Friday night plans were looking like.

When Watts stepped back in the room, he asked Ross how long it would be before he finished the report. Ross told him it would take him at least two hours. So Watts said,

"Hey listen, I'm gonna take off for a minute. I'll be back before you finish."
"Ok cool, see you in a minute partner."

Chapter 36

I sat on the couch in a daze. I couldn't believe how a good plan began to turn to shit. I wanted to be mad at Toni and I wanted to be mad at Rico, but I felt like it was nobody's fault but my own. I should have had security on the block that night. Instead, I felt like since the load hadn't come, there really wasn't a need for the block security. Damn was I wrong!

I stood up, grabbed my glass of tequila, and walked to the window. As I looked out at the block I gathered my thoughts to figure out what was the next best move. I needed to talk to Toni to see what was on her mind, so I called her and told her to come through, and once she made it over, I told her to relax and make herself a drink. We sat in silence for a second until I said,
"So wus tha plan T?"
"I don't know Ug, I ain't heard shit in tha streets yet, but I know one thing. We gotta keep dis block on lock." I couldn't argue with her, she was right, so I took a sip from my glass and called Nassir. I told him I needed him at the house ASAP, and after I hung up I looked at Toni and said.
"Check it out Toni, these mufickas thirsty as hell right now, so put the word out that you got 5,000 for anybody dat got info about yo house gettin' robbed. Somebody know something, and for a easy five G's they gone tell it." Toni stood up and downed her liquor and replied,
"Ug, I swear when I find out who robbed me Im'ma," I cut her off saying.
"Hey, don't even trip. Wus already understood don't need to be explained." Then she left the house to put the word in the streets.

As Toni was walking out of the house, Nassir was walking in. I urgently told Nassir to get with Rico and tell him to get his guys back on the block and lock it down. I expressed to him that we couldn't afford anymore mishaps, so I told him to stand on Rico and make sure he's on it. Nassir didn't ask any questions, he just gave me a fist bump and said,

"I'm on it my nigga." Then he left to handle the task.

Chapter 37

An hour and a half had passed when Watts walked back in the squad room. Ross was now typing up the last page to the report when Watts said.

"Hey wut'cha got goin on tonight, let's celebrate. I'm taking my girl out tonight and her sista could use a date. What'cha wanna do?" Ross cocked his head and thought for a second.
"Sister huh? ... Hmmm. On a scale of 1-10, and ten being the hottest, what would you rate her?"
"She's a 12, I promise. I wish I would've met her first but hey. Com'on, you'll thank me tomorrow, I swear."
"A 12 huh? Well in that case, I'm all in."
"That's what I'm talking about. I'll call my girl back and set it all up."

Later that night Ross, Watts and the two women sat in a booth at a bar n' grill outside of Robbins. They'd just finished eating their meals and now they were enjoying the music, having drinks, and engaging in some interesting conversation.

After a while, the evening started to get a little more personal as Watts and his girl became more involved with each other. This didn't bother Ross because it too gave him some time to get better acquainted with the sister. Ross was glad that he agreed to the double date. He needed a break from all of the monotony that occurred in his life due to the job, and Watts knew this, so he kept the drinks coming.

After many rounds of liquor and deep conversation, the sister leaned in and whispered in Ross' ear saying,

"Let's get out of here." And Ross replied,
"Are you sure?"

"Very!" Ross stood up and leaned against the table for balance then said,

"Well partner, I appreciate you gettin' me out tonight, but I think we're gonna take off. You know what I'm saying?" Ross gave Watts a devilish grin then the sister clung to Ross' elbow saying,

"I'll call you in the morning sis." Then they both left the bar as if they'd known each other for years.

Once they got in Ross' car the sister became relentless as she started to grind against him. She started licking at his neck and ear as she massaged his joint until it became rock solid. As they began to kiss, she pulled his joint out and rubbed it up and down. She didn't care that they were in a wide open parking lot, she wanted to suck his dick right then and there. So, she put her mouth on him and went to work. Ross leaned his head back and closed his eyes. Her warm mouth reminded him of some of the best pussy he ever had. Then out of nowhere, a man with a bandanna across his face snatched Ross' door open and the sister screamed. He stuck the gun in Ross' face then disguise his voice with a deep tone saying,

"Shut up bitch! And you, give me yo wallet nigga! Don't make me kill yo dumb ass!" Ross then said,

"Just be easy, I'm a police officer. I'm gonna reach and give you my wallet, ok? Just don't shoot." Then the man said,

"Hurry up muthafuka!"

Ross moved cautiously because he could tell that the man was becoming impatient. He grabbed his wallet and shoved it toward the robber without looking at him. Ross was so nervous that he made the mistake of dropping the wallet, and the robber didn't wait for another move. He clenched the trigger of the gun and let off eight shots. Ross never stood a chance. His body was left slumped over the steering wheel with the horn blaring out into the night, while the sister just screamed her head off.

Seconds later the sister came running into the bar screaming for help. Watt's girlfriend ran up to her asking her what happened. She could see all of the blood splattered across her face and clothes. She was trying her best to calm her sister down so she could find out what had happened.

A minute or two later Watts came out of the bathroom and saw the sister all bloody and instantly asked where his partner was. She was still in shock, but managed to let them know that he was still outside.

Watts took off running for the parking lot. As he got closer to Ross' car he could see his partner's body leaning over the steering wheel with gun smoke still rising from his back. The loud horn began to draw a crowd as it screamed through the night and all Watts could do was helplessly turn around and walk away to call the incident in.

By the time the police and coroner arrived, Watts was moving around the parking lot asking questions, but nobody seemed to know anything. Watts identified himself to the other officers at the scene, then gave them the rundown on what he knew. He let them know he was already dead by the time he'd gotten to the parking lot, then pointed toward the sister and let them know she was with him when it all happened.

The officers questioned the sister extensively before they exonerated her from being a suspect in the shooting. They also let her know that her statement was important and that they may need to ask her some more questions later, but nevertheless she was free to leave. Watts got in his car and the sisters got in another. Then they all left the parking lot leaving the officers to finish processing the homicide scene.

Chapter 38

I woke up late Saturday morning still cuddled with Brittany. I never liked sleeping this late, but since I had nothing else on my agenda and Brittany was off today, I decided to give her all of my time.

I snuck out of the bed in an attempt to surprise her with breakfast and made my way out of the room without waking her up. On the way to the kitchen I saw Nassir sitting on the couch eating a sandwich and watching CNN News. I had to say I was definitely shocked. I never seen Nassir watch anything besides rap videos, so I said,

"Wut tha fuck?! You watchin tha news fam?"
"Hey, a wise man once told me ya gotta keep up wit'cho current events." I just smiled saying,
"Check you out. Be careful na, you just might learn sumt'n." I giggled a little then carried on to the kitchen.

After contemplating on what to cook, I decided to keep it simple and make ham and cheese omlettes, so I grabbed all the ingridients and started whipping the eggs. Just as I was chopping up little peices of ham, Nassir yelled out my name.

"Ug! Ug!! Come here my nigga, check dis shit out!"

When I got in front of the television, I read the caption and it read: *'Live footage from Juarez, Mexico.'* You saw shit blowing up, dead bodies sprawled all throughout the streets and motherfuckers running around with assault rifles like it was nothing. Oh yeah, I'd say it was a war alright. The reporter said that the war was becoming more intense as the days passed, and this was now starting to make me nervous, because Carlos still hadn't came through with the load yet.

I checked my watch and saw it was almost twelve. So, I told Nassir to turn to the local news channel to see if they were going to report anything on the War of Mexico. I told Nassir to turn the volume up so I could hear the television from the kitchen, then I left to finish chopping up the ham for the omelets.

No sooner than I reached the kitchen, I heard the news reporter say.

"In breaking news, Robbin's police officer shot and killed last night."

I instantly dropped the knife and ran to the television to see which cop from the town had been killed. When I looked at the screen, I almost shit myself. It was Ross! Tough ass, dick in the booty ass Ross! I couldn't control myself. I started yelling at the screen as if he could hear me, saying,

"See, I wasn't the only mufka you pissed off! That's wutcha get, wit'cho punk ass!"

After I saw that, I was one hundred percent satisfied for the day, maybe even the year. Oh, what the hell, who am I kidding? For the rest of my fucking life! I just turned with a smile and went on to finish making my baby something to eat. Hot damn! What a hell of a way to start a day!

Chapter 39

While Ug spent the day with Brittany, Toni and Rico beat the streets still looking for any info on the break in. They hit up every part of the town and no one knew anything– or so they say. Rico took one look at Toni and somehow knew that this day was not going to play out well for somebody.

As Rico continued to turn corners, Toni blurted out,

"Rico, dis shit anit workin."
"Com on T, wuts on yo mind? You got dat look in yo eye."
"Who is tha first mufuka dat pop in yo mind when it comes to stealin?" Rico went into deep thought when Toni asked the question, then he finally blurted out,
"Peanut." Toni then smiled and said,
"Peanut it is, let's pay him a visit."
"Whoa Toni, You do know Peanut stay in the Old Projects right?"
"Yup."
"So you know it's gone be niggas everywhere, right?"
"I sho hope so, that's wut I want." Rico looked at Toni again then shook his head and said,
"Damn Toni, I don't know how I be letting you get me into shit, but fuck it, let's do it."

Toni and Rico rode through the Old Projects as if they lived there. Seeing as this being an all GD set, Rico got a few ugly mugs, but Toni was well respected around the town.

The summer heat had every soul throughout the projects outside, so it was somewhat hard for Rico to spot Peanut, but not Toni. She scanned the whole projects from left to right then locked her sights in and said,

"There he goes right there. Call him over, then get out and holla at him."

Rico did exactly what Toni requested. He leaned against his truck and started asking Peanut questions about the break in. He actually took offense to the questions, and instantly got aggressive. He tried hard to defend himself as he swelled up and said,

"Wut tha fuck you askin me fo? I ain't do it and I don't know shit!"

This was Toni's que to intervene. She got out of the truck on the passenger side then opened the back door and grabbed a small bat off the seat and casually made her way over to where Peanut and Rico were standing. Peanut was so busy ranting on about his innocence, that he didn't see or hear Toni walking up. All he heard was Toni voice say,

"Hey Peanut."

As soon as he turned around Toni caught him off guard with a swift swing to the face. His body stood still for a second, then his legs gave out and he hit the ground. Toni stood over Peanut's unconscious body and brung the club down on his back several times saying,

"I. Want. My. Shit. Back!"

Now that Toni had everyone's attention, she looked around the crowd then said,

"Somebody, broke in my crib and took sumt'n dat belong to me. So, until I get my shit back, I'm goin in on anybody dat got sticky hands around dis bitch." Then she kicked him in his stomach and said, "Five G's to tha mufuka dat got info about my shit." Then Toni and Rico got in the truck and drove away.

Everybody in the town knew Peanut was a thief, so she wanted to send a message saying that there are consequences when you fuck with her or her people, and she hoped they heard it loud and clear.

Chapter 40

Around five thirty, I stepped outside while Brittany took an early evening nap. The whole crew sat under the tree discussing what took place while I was laid up. They all thought I was going to get pissed off by Toni's actions, but right now it was just what we needed. Right now, I pretty much figured the chances of us getting that gun or Toni's money back were slim. But as long as people understood that we weren't just going to accept that shit, I was fine.

While the crew caught me up on the day, I heard one of the guys from the apartment building yell out.

"Top of tha block! Top of tha block!"

When we stepped to the curb, we saw three cars and a van hit the block simultaneously and Nassir yelled,

"Fall back and wait for my signal!"

When the vehicles stopped and parked, there was a certain humbleness about the ensemble, but when they all got out I was like, oh shit! It was the area Governor for the GD's, Bino G. I'd seen Bino G in the hood for years as I grew up and never had I been this close to him. He was one of those legends in the hood, I just hated we had to meet like this. I just wasn't sure what this was, but whatever it was, it didn't stop Nassir from holding down his spot.

As soon as they all got out, Nassir threw his arm in the air and moved it in a swooping motion, and the block security came off their posts guns drawn. As the security moved closer Nassir locked eyes with Bino G then pointed toward the upstairs windows of the apartment building. He wanted to make sure Bino G saw the snipers. He wanted to make sure they had fair warning.

Bino G looked around and watched the block security circle them in. When he turned his head back to Nassir he said,

"I see you all growed up now. I can respect that, but see if I was on some bullshit, I would've just sent every gansta out tha new projects, old projects, and the trailers to come rock dis mufuka out. Four vehicles just say I wanna talk." That's when I jumped in and said,

"Ok, cool. Let's talk. Won't 'chu grab four of yo guys and have everybody else get back in the ride and wait." One dude got jazzy and said,

"Nigga was he talkin to you? Yo name Nassir nigga?". Bino G stuck his arm out and stepped in between us saying,

"Who whoa whoa, it's all god... See, my niggas ride or die too, but it's all good. Tron, Red, Bobbo, Rell y'all stay wit me, the rest of yall go back to the cars."

Once they got back in the cars, Nassir told the block security to fall back to their post's, then we all stepped under the tree to see what was on Bino G mind. As soon as we all huddled up, Nassir said,

"So wussup Bino?"

"Ok, check it out. I just spent the last hour in an emergency meeting wit my guys. Toni, we been knowin each other for years, but baby girl, ain't none of my guys got nothing to do wit yo shit gettin robbed. I just wanted to personally deliver dat info so dat you know its official. Besides dat, Toni I can't have you runnin down on my spots shakin mufukas down. It sends tha wrong message to tha otha oppositions in tha town, know wut I'm sayin? If you got a problem hit my line, you got my numba. That way we'a both get it handled tha right way. Now, Toni I got love fo ya like a sista, but if you come through tha land like dat again, Im'ma have the GD sisters touch you up. Now I don't want'chu to take dat as no threat, but dis business. I'm sure you can understand dat wit all dis fine security around here."

Bino G said what he had to say. There was no negotiating, no misunderstandings, and he didn't need feedback. He simply turned and started walking away and his guys followed suit. I couldn't do anything but respect him, to me, he came correct and respectful. I wouldn't have handled the situation any different. Now this was the kind of guy I wouldn't mind doing business with. I wanted Bino G at the table. Not to be a part of my crew, but to be a key player in our hierarchy. So, before he got any further I called out his name. When he turned around he stopped and looked at my hands, then he studied by face and said,

"Ugly, right? Yeah, I remember you. You kinda nice wit'cha hands." Then he did a few shadow boxing moves. "You used to come to the boxing classes at the C.Y.C. So wussup youngsta?"
"Man Bino, me and you need to have a sit down. I might have sumt'n that'll interest you."
"Interest me? How you figure? As a matter of fact, who you plugged wit?" I looked Bino G in the eyes with confidence and said,
"I'm plugged wit Benjamin, Grant and Jefferson. Do I need to keep going?" And Bino said,
"Oooh, my kind of gansters! Well, in dat case holla at me when you ready. Toni got my numba." Then they all got in the vehicles and left the block.

Once the last car turned off the block, I looked at Toni as she exploded with excitement. She ran up to me and said,
"Ug, did you see dat shit? Nas did you see dat shit?! When a mufukin Gov come to give you a message personally, dat mean you on sumt'n. I'm. Dat.Bitch!"
Nassir started laughing and said,

"Toni you aint on shit, wit'cho Rocky and Bullwinkle lookin ass."

"You just a hater Nassir." Toni replied. I had to giggle a little bit myself, then I said,

"But for real, Toni got a point. Bino G could have sent anyone of his guys down here wit dat message, but he came his self. Dat says a whole lot. Dat says dat these mufuka's is startin to respect our movement. Like I said before, we were going to have to make this town respect us by force, and that we did."

Chapter 41

Shortly after Bino G left the block. I sat down with the crew and explained to them what our next move was. Now that we have the attention of the GD's, it was time to make our alliance stronger. I had Rico contact Big Moe who represented the Stones, and I had Nassir contact Gacy who represented the Bd's. I told them to arrange a meeting for tomorrow at noon right here on the block and to assure them that this was no bullshit. Ten minutes later Rico confirmed Big Moe's attendance. Nassir however was getting burned by 101 questions from Gacy.
When he hung up his phone he said,

"Ug, Gacy want us to come through his block and holla at him."

Down on the Bay, Gacy was standing in the middle of the set like a third world General. Nassir looked around and said,

"Wut tha fuck! Sumt'n aint right Ug. I see some of tha guys from a few different sets. Wut all dis extra security about?"
And I said to Nassir,
"Same reason Bino G hit tha block, we shakin shit up."

Once Nassir and I stepped out of the Hummer, Gacy waved us over. He didn't waste time or sugar coat his words, he went clean in saying.
"So wut, y'all niggas wanna kill me too?" Instantly Nassir said,
"Wut tha fuck you talkin bout BD, we just got a proposition for you. Sumtn dats gone get us all paid."
"Yea yall probably had a proposition for Moony, Chino and Hundo too. They turn yall down?" Now it was time for me to step in.

"Gacy, you takin shit to tha extreme fam. We don't know shit about no murdas, so why is we even talkin about shit dat aint got nuthin to do wit none of us? Check it out, we tryin to bring you in to tha table. I got sumt'n you want and you got wut I need."

"And wus that?"

"Trust, loyalty and this." I held my arms out and looked around letting Gacy know I was interested in his area. Then I said, "Gacy, how much you pay for a brick?"

"Shit, I usually pay about 27 or 28."

"And about how many you go through a month?"

"Probably about eighty in a month, it depends."

"Gacy when I came home you showed me love, let me return dat favor. Come to tha meeting tomorrow and hear us out, dats all I'm askin for now. If you trust me on this, I promise you, we gone make history." Gacy pondered over what I had just said and he was extremely hesitant, but ultimately he came around.

"Aight Ug, but I aint comin alone. I still gotta protect myself fam." I looked Gacy in the eyes then bumped fists and told him,

"I wouldn't have it any otha way fam. Twelve o'clock, our block. See you then." Then we headed back to our block.

Back on the block, I had Toni contact Bino G and let him know that we were on for tomorrow at noon on our block, and Bino G agreed to be there. I truly had to say that this felt good. We were on to some hood shit and it felt gangsta. I was on my way to accomplishing something that no man in this hood was ever able to do. This was huge! This was major! I just hope those guys see this as I do, and for their sake, they'd better hope they do too.

Chapter 42

As darkness filled the sky, we rode around the hood just scoping out the land until I received a text message on my cell phone. I didn't recognize the number, so I was somewhat reluctant to read the message, until a second message from the same number appeared. I hit the read button on my phone and the message read:

+7083596720: We need to talk. URGNET! Meet me at the Comfort Inn in Crestwood. Room 307.

+7083596720: Come now and come alone. Don't make me wait, or your fate will be in the hands of the wrong people by the morning.

The message disturbed the shit out of me. I didn't want to take the chance on anyone making good on a threat, so I told Rico to drop me off on the block.

Around eleven thirty I stepped into the elevator of the Comfort Inn and pressed the number for the third floor. As the elevator started to move, I took the 9 millimeter out of the small of my back, and checked it one more time. Everything was good, so I tucked the gun back in the waist of my jeans and exited the elevator once the doors opened.

When I got to room 307, I stood at the door and checked my surroundings. I wanted to see if I would catch an eerie feeling and I didn't, so I took a deep breath and knocked on the door.

A few seconds had passed and the door opened, but I saw no one. I stood in the doorway peeking around the room until I heard a voice say,

"Come in and hold your arms out, let me see your hands."

When I stepped in the room, I heard the door close and felt a gun in my ribs. The first thing that went through my mind was bust a move, that's when I heard the voice say,

"Be cool, everything all good. You got anything on you?" Then he felt around my waist and grabbed the gun I was carrying.

He then felt around my ankles then told me to raise my shirt, so I did. Next, he asked me was I alone and I assured him that I was. Then he said,

"Ok, now turn around slow with your shirt still up."

When I turned around I almost shit in my pants. I froze dead in my tracks and locked eyes with officer Watts! We both just stood there looking at each other and it started to get a little creepy.

Watts finally put his gun away and told me to have a seat. He reached in a shopping bag and pulled out a six pack of beer and a bag of popcorn. I just sat in silence wondering what the hell was going on. He passed me a beer and I declined. Then he said,

"Trust me, you're gonna want this." So, I took it.

He opened the bag of popcorn and took a swig of his beer then turned the television on. Then I asked,
"You got me up here to watch a movie wit 'chu?"

Watts smiled at me and took another swig of his beer then pressed the play buton on the remote. What I saw next was about to change the whole dynamics of my plans. I just sat there feeling empty and hollow, exposed and vulnerable. Watts sat there chomping down on popcorn, then finally spoke,

"See that guy right there? That's you! Now that poor guy right there on his knees is Chino. Ooh Ooh, watch this! This is my favorite part…Wait a minute…BAM!! Oh shit!" He took another swig of his beer and said, "I gotta give it to you, that shit was gangsta. But you wanna know what ain't gangsta? You having the entire funckin' murder on tape! Now that shit is just plain fuckin' stupid!"

Watts had me by the balls, all I could do was sit there and take it. How did I let this happen? Where was that fucking camera hiding at? How many copies of this tape did he have?

Then I just stop thinking all together and took a deep breath, then asked the *real* million dollar question.

"So wut'chu want man?"
"You can start by telling me the truth, and don't bullshit me. Right now, I'm the only thing that's standing between you and freedom. Now, the gun used to kill Chino was the same gun used to kill Moony, this I know. Now tell me what I need to know about Hundo."
"I want a Lawyer."
"Adonis, I see you still got that glue in your eyes. If we were in a police station I'd respect that request, but we in a fuckin hotel room! So, I'm gonna say it again. Tell me what I *need* to know about Hundo, I can't help you if you're fuckin around."

I felt trapped. I couldn't understand Watts' motive as to why he would want to help me. He had me cold blooded on Chino's murder and he knew the same gun was used on Moony. Now he wanted me to confess to Hundo? I just gathered my thoughts and said,
"I aint kill Hundo."
"I don't give a shit *who* killed him. Did you have anything to do with the murder?"

I looked away from Watts and stared at the wall. Overall, I kept my fucking mouth shut. Watts sat there still staring at me and waited for a response, until he got up.

"Ok. That look on your face tells me everything I need to know right now. Stand up.

I stood to my feet with my chest out and head up. There was no need to bitch up. I'm a man before anything, so I was ready to accept the fact that I was going back to jail. Until Watts said,

"Go, get the fuck outta here."

I stood there for a brief moment trying to understand if I heard him right. Watts sensed my hesitation, so he reiterated what he'd just said,

"Go! Hurry up before I change my mind."

While the getting was good, I took his advice and started walking toward the door. Once I reached for the door handle, Watts called my name. When I turned around Watts tossed me my gun back and said,

"Hey! We're on the same team Adonis. Be careful, I'll be in touch."

Chapter 43

When I made it back to the house Yella Boy and Nassir were there entertaining a few females. I was so deep in thought I probably resembled a zombie by the way I walked to my room.

When I got to my bed, I plopped down and fell backward like an angel. Just when I thought I had all the answers, a motherfucker comes along with a new test. There was no way out of this shit. If I hadn't recognized it then, I recognize it now. I was way in over my head and in too deep.

My body was exhausted and my nerves were bad. My thoughts consumed my entire mind until I drifted off into deep sleep, and it soon became a nightmare.

I ended up somewhere dark, maybe a tunnel or a cave. The smell of the place was horrid and the ground was mushy, like walking on jello. As I navigated through the dark I kept hearing voices whisper.

"Help me, Help me."

I followed the voices until they got stronger, and it sounded like we were in the same room. All of a sudden, lantern lights lit up along the wall and I instantly look down at my feet. The entire floor was covered in bloody guts. I was about ready to freak out until I heard those voices again. This time they were screaming so loud I had to cover my ears. It got so bad that I dropped down to my knees and started begging for the voices to stop. Out of nowhere a Latino man appeared next to me and helped me to my feet. He gave me a towel to wipe my hands clean, then he whispered in my ear and said,

"The whole world is lying in the power of the wicked." Then I asked,
"Wut do dat mean?"

The man didn't answer my question, he simply smiled then pushed me. When I turned around, he was gone. Then I felt hands grabbing on me. When I turned *back* around, I saw Hector, Moony, Chino and Hundo all clawing at me. They were all chained to the wall and had limited reach, so I fought my way loose and just stared at them while they screamed out.

"Help me, Help me!"

When I turned to run away I bumped into the Latino man again. He just appeared out of nowhere, this time I asked *him* to help *me*. He grabbed me by the hand and we started running. As we ran, I could hear him mumbling something, but couldn't quit make it out. Whatever he was saying he kept repeating it. We ran until I was out of breath and I became irritated by the mumbling. So, I finally asked,

"Wut tha fuck is you sayin?!"

He instantly stopped in place, and didn't move. For a brief moment, everything went dead silent. Then, with the speed of lightening, he turned and stared at me with the face of a demon! Then in a monstrous tone he said,

"We are not punished for our sins; we are punished by them." He gave me a demonic grin then started laughing like the devil himself. Then out of nowhere, he raised a gun and shot me in the face.

I instantly woke up in a cold sweat and breathing hard. I looked at my watch to see it was one 1:45 in the morning. I ran to the bathroom and splashed water in my face then went to the kitchen and poured myself a shot of tequila. I was trippin, and I was trippin hard. I took another shot of tequila then went back to my room and laid down. I stared at the ceiling and thought about the one positive thing I had in my favor right now, and that was freedom. So as far as I'm concerned tonight never existed. I got too many people depending on me, so Watts can just kiss my ass. Like he said, my job is to sell dope, so that's exactly what the fuck I'm gonna do. And if Watts tries to stop me, he'll be the next motherfucker clawing at me in my dreams!

Chapter 44

The next morning, I hopped out of the bed like I was late for school. I didn't intend to sleep that long, but I swear it was much, much needed.

First thing I did was get Toni on the line and told her to order a pan of combo fish, and a pan of chicken wings from Sharks. I wanted to make the fellas feel comfortable while we laid our proposition out. I was having a meeting with all the gang leaders in the town, who knows? A little food just might ease the tension.

After getting dressed, I sat down with Nassir and went over a few things, just to keep him on point. After that we stepped outside where we were greeted by Rico and a few of his guys, then walked across the steet to the apartment building, and hung out around the entrance until the other guys showed up.

The first person to pull up on the block was Gacy. He got out of his truck with three *big* motherfuckers! They didn't look like they were affiliated. They looked like they were hired. Anyhow, I waved him over, and they all walked over to the apartment building. That was about the time Bino G and his goons pulled up. Of course the O.G. had his four car caravan going on, but it was all good. Whatever makes a man feel safe.

While we were all outside of the apartment building, fraternizing, Big Moe pulled up two cars deep. Now, when I say there's always atleast one ignorant motherfucker, I believe I was speaking about Big Moe. When he walked up amongst the crowd, he looked around and said,

"Rico, you aint tell me dis was gone be a mufukin folk meeting. Wut tha fuck kind of shit you on Lord, cause yo star lookin a lil blue right now."

Rico stepped to Big Moe and tried to rationalize a little. He tried to make light of the situation, and whatever he told him seemed to calm him down. So Nassir said,

"Ok fellas, let's get dis goin. First and second command only. Everybody else stay outside."

When we walked inside the building Nassir asked all the second in commands to wait in the hallway for a second. I closed the door and Nassir said,
"It's gone be some real sensitive shit discussed here, and it might be some shit only *you* want or need to know right now, but its yo call."

Bino G opened the door and told his second in command to stay by the door. Rico and Gacy followed suit. Big Moe, however said,
"Naw fuck dat. Ay star, step in here wit me." Then I closed the door and everybody took a seat, except for Big Moe's second in command. There were only eight chairs, so he had to stand.

Before Nassir got down to business, he offered everybody food and beverages then told them to make themselves comfortable. He waited until everyone was situated then began to speak,

"First I want to thank y'all fa comin'. I know y'all lookin around tha room like wut tha fuck is dis, but I promise you, y'all play a major part in wuts about to happen. It's a new day my niggas, and we about to flip tha whole mufukin script. Bino, Rico, Big Moe, Gacy, y'all hold tha power to control y'all areas, me and my people hold tha motivation for new structure."

Nassir was holding his ground *and* everyone's attention, but Bino G was a little confused as to where Nassir was taking this. I could tell by the look on his face. So Bino's response was,

"Nassir, what make you think dis town need new structure? I'm sayin, if it ain't broke don't fix it."

Then Nassir said,

"Check it out Bino, y'all tha heads out here. So why is so many niggas spending all they money wit mufuckas dat ain't in position? We want to put y'all in total control of y'all positions, make y'all tha only niggas movin *major* weight. Push all tha otha hustlers dat ain't on our page out tha way, and out of dis town. We want to give y'all tha motivation to tighten up in y'all areas and have a systematic order of business."

Then Gacy said,

"So wus dis motivation? I mean, shit *sound* good, but tha shit'chu talkin bout I can do on my own. So where *y'all* at in all of dis?"

And Nasir said,

"I'm glad you asked. There's a smart and strategic way to do shit, and there's an extreme and violent way to do shit, and we gone do it both ways.... We ready to flood dis town wit a shit load of work and we wanna share tha wealth."

Then Big Moe said,

"I got my own connect fam. Fuck make you think I need yall?" Then Nassir said,

"Big Moe, wut'chu pay for a brick?"

And Big Moe replied,

"27"

"Just like I figured. Tha average brick right now goin fo anywhere from 27 to 32, and tha quality barely reachin 75 percent. We offering better and cheaper."

Bino G and Gacy raised up in their seats. I could tell that Nassir had their undivided attention. However, Big Moe stood up and said,

"I appreciate tha invite, but we aint sittin at tha table wit no brick ass niggas! Ay star we out."

I learned back in my seat and clasped my hands together. I took a few breaths to even my anger, then spoke,

"Big Moe! You sure you wanna do it like dat?" Big Moe didn't even turn around he just kept on walking saying,
"Yup, but yall gone do yall, we straight!"
Then I stood up and said,
"Well before you leave, I want'chu to deliver a message fo me. Tell Black Pooh if he keep tryin' to push dat weak ass dope in dis town Im'ma find him, then Im'ma blow his fuckin head off."
Big Moe stopped then turned around. Everybody looked at me in shock, even my own guys. Big Moe walked back to the table and said,
"Wut tha fuck you say to me nigga?!"
"Com'on man, drop tha act. You might pump fear in tha mufukas dat follow you, but I can tell you all talk."
Big Moe came closer and I stepped to him as we stood face to face. I studied his eyes and body language, then smiled at him and said,
"Yeah, there it go, there's dat twinkle in your eye I was looking for. I knew from tha first time you opened yo mouth you was a bitch."

Big Moe's second in command stood there in disbelief. He couldn't believe I just called Big Moe out like that. Right then and there, I knew I had him. So, I just finished playin my cards and said, "See, I was trying to be a gentleman and ask you to sit at dis table. I was tryin to be a playa and put mo money in yo pocket than yo chump ass could count. But you just wanna be a tough guy. You disrespect my food by not eatin wit me, and you start talkin like you got bodies under yo belt! ... Look, check it out. Dis shit right here is gone happen wit or without'chu, so Im'ma give you one mo chance to sit'cho weak ass down at dis table and play yo fuckin part."

Big Moe was heated and for damn sure embarrassed. I actually respected the fact that he was standing on a principle he believed in, but the tough guys act made me want to expose his ass. The one thing he didn't take into consideration when he was talking shit, was that the only principle to a dollar bill, was a hundred-dollar bill. Meaning, for every man that won't, there's at least one that will.

After me and Big Moe's stare down, he looked at his man and said,

"Let's go!"
I shook my head saying,
"One man's trash is another man's treasure!"
And Big Moe replied,
"Fuck you nigga, see me in deez streets!"
And I said,
"Oh, trust me, I was planning on it."

After the door closed, I turned around and looked at the remaining group. I walked back to the table, took a swallow of juice and then spoke,

"Anybody else wanna leave, or do ya'll wanna finish hearing dis out?" And Bino G said,
"Do yo thang youngsta. I'm enjonin the show."
Then Gacy replied by saying,
"Yeah Ug, lets talk some numbas."
I quickly gathered my composure and sat back down. I leaned forward with my elbows on the table and finished spittin the lick.

"A month ago, we did a test run. We took an ounce of coke and put 35 grams of soda on it and brung it back to 56 grams of crack. Customers told us it was tha best shit they den smoked in years. Dat load we had was 85% pure. Dis next load is gone be

95% pure." I shook my head up and down and said, "Yeah, tha mufuckin beast! Yall numba gone be 23 apiece, and we givin you a hunnid at a time. After every load we finish, we givin' out bonuses. How much, gone depend on how fast we move tha load. So wut'chall wanna do?"

Gacy frantically said,

"Hell yeah! Hell yeah! Im all in!" Bino G got up then went and opened the door and spoke to his second in command saying,

"Tron, run to the liquor store and grab us a couple bottles of Cristal." Bino G then closed the door and returned to his seat and said, "You got it boss, its yo world."

Gacy jumped back in saying,

"Hey Ug, you offering a lot. What exactly do you want from us?"

I looked at them as a matter of factly, and I told them straight up,

"I want dis town on lock! It ain't all gone happen overnight, so we gone make it happen in phases. First and foremost, meet wit yo guys and let'em know it's gone be some changes, but stop layin in tha cut! Make you presence known in yo area and around tha hood. Show mufukas who in control. Tighten up yo area! From dis point on, all problems get handled and settled at dis table. However we gone handle it, it's gone be decided right here. When you get called to tha table, everything get put on hold and we make it our business to be here. Most importantly let it be known that dis block is off limits. If we not expecting you, *Do Not* come to dis block unless you call first."

Gacy sat in his seat looking confused. I could tell that it was something he wasn't getting. So I asked,

"Gacy wussup bro? Did I lose you somewhere?"

"Ug I still don't get it. You givin out all dat work and givin cash bonuses just for us to pretty much do what we been already been doing."

"I'm putting out all dat work because yo loyalty is worth dat to me. Over time, Robbins is gone become one big ass stash house. The strength of yo area is wuts gonna protect this big ass stash house. If your spot is weak, then the security of the stash house becomes vulnerable in dat area. Am I startin to make sense?"

Then Bino G replied,

"Like the change from a dollar? Ug, you busted a pipeline didn't you? Wut is he, Mexican, Columbia, Peruvian, what?"

Gacy then intervened,

"Ug, when we gone touchdown?"

"Soon! I can't tell you exactly when, but any day. Now as far as wut tha connect is, dat don't matter. Just gimme wut I need and lock dis town down, and Im'ma keep you flooded wit tha best dope dat ever touched dis land."

I took a brief moment and scanned everyone at the table, then said, "It's only gone get betta fellas, and we gone ride dis mufuka til tha wheels fall off!"

After the meeting, I was still a little bent out of shape over the Big Moe situation. Everyone had left the room, but I was sitting there in deep contemplation. The exchange of words Big Moe and I had where critical, and those words only let me know one thing. I had to kill him! He thought he could come into my spot, throw his size around, and talk like a gangster. Obviously, he didn't realize he was dealing with the wrong motherfucker. I was on a mission, and I wasn't going to let him *or* anybody else stand in my way. My hands were already covered in blood. One more body wouldn't have made a bit of a difference to me. None at all!

Minutes later, Toni, Rico, Yella Boy and Nassir walked back in the room. Yella Boy stood next to me and asked if I was all good. I guess they all could sense I was still pissed off. Nassir chimed in saying,

"Yeah Ug, you seem a little tense. Especially how you went in on Big Moe. Ay, did yall see dat boy face when Ug called him a bitch?! I swear to God dat nigga looked like he wanted to cry, and his man just stood there like daaamn!"

Everybody laughed, even me, but I took this time to let my crew know where I stood. So, after all the laughing I said,
"Shit changin yall, and it's time fo us to take tha gloves off. If we can't show mufukas we for real, den mufukas gone take us fo a joke. I'm lettin it be known right na dat I'm serious as a mufukin heart attack. It's time to take shit to tha next level, by any means necessary."
That was when Nassir jumped in,
"So how we gone handle Big Moe?"
Rico cut me off by saying, "Let me holla at him Ug. If nothin else, I can try to fill him out and see what page he on."
"Naw, fuck dat chump! Holla at his second in command and let him know I said to either come on in, or strap the fuck up!"

Chapter 45

Shortly after everyone left the apartment building, Ug received a phone call and took off to handle some business. Rico took this as the perfect time to pay Big Moe a visit. Although he heard what Ug said, he was still going to try and convince Big Moe to get on board.

When Rico pulled up on the 9 where the stones hung out, him, Yella Boy and Toni hopped out of his truck and approached the group of Blackstones brothers, looking for Big Moe.

When Big Moe saw them walking up, he approached them aggressively saying,

"Rico, I aint tryin to hear all dat bullshit, so wut tha fuck you want?" Rico remained calm and tried to explain the benefits of sitting at the table. He also stressed what was most likely to happen if he didn't. Big Moe hunched his shoulders and replied, "Well, it is wut it is. We ready for wuteva!"

Rico looked at Big Moe and said,

"Brotha, you sure about dat? Mo man, open yo eyes! You talkin bout standin on principles, when all you standin on his hate. Dis should've been a decision based on tha well being of yo people. Did you think about dem? Did you think about they kids and they families? Did you think about the financial growth of tha Black P Stones? Look, you hate tha folks, I get it, but hatin tha folks ain't gone bring dat bitch back to you. Dats folk'nem ole lady now, so let it go nigga and get rich!"

Big Moe had gotten into it with one of the G'D's some months ago because he couldn't accept that fact that his girl didn't want to be with him anymore. Ever since then, he'd been carrying a huge grudge against the folks that only festered over time.

Listening to Rico throw it in his face only pissed him off even more, so he said,

"Get'cho sell out ass off my spot!"
"Sellout?! You know wut, my man wus right, I'm startin to see dat twinkle in yo eyes too."
Big Moe pulled his gun and aimed it at Rico saying,
"Next time any one of yall come on my spot…" Rico stepped closer to Big Moe's gun and said,
"You gone wut?! You gone kill me nigga?!" Rico walked even closer to the gun until the gun was poking him in the chess saying, "Why tha fuck you gotta wait for a next time? Kill me right now nigga!"

Rico and Big Moe just looked at each other, but Big Moe wouldn't pull the trigger. Rico simply chuckled then whispered to Big Moe, "You know you den fucked up right?"

Rico then took a couple of steps backward then turned his back on Big Moe and started walking away. Toni and Yella Boy followed. As they stepped away, Rico walked past Big Moe's second in command and gave him a wink of the eye and whispered,

"Get at me."

Then Rico yelled out, "When tha rest of yall ready to get dis money, send ya'll *strongest* member to come holla at me!"

Then they got in the truck and drove away.

By early evening, the town started to recognize something different. The pressure the gangs were putting on the streets had everyone on egg shells. All the areas were reinforcing security, standing on law and violating anyone who acted outside of it. People in the town thought some major war was about to kick-off between nations until Bino G was seen with Rico, Gacy was seen with Bino G and all of them at one point was seen with Nassir, Yella Boy and Toni.

A few hours later, Lil Stone, Big Moe's second in command went over on the Vice Lord's block to pay Rico a visit. While Lil stone waited for Rico, he noticed how strong they were. There was only about forty stones in the town, and even though they had love for each other, he never saw that dignified unity he was looking at right now.

When Rico pulled up, he got out of his truck and gave Lil Stone a formal greeting by saying,

"All is well, Mo?"

The two shook hands and Rico led him to a quiet spot where they could speak in private. As soon as they were alone, Rico initiated the conversation by saying,

"So, I take it you tha strongest member, huh?"
"Ay Lord, we just tryin to get dis money, ya feel me? My kids gotta eat. I don't give a fuck wut flag a nigga ridin, as long as it ain't disrespectin' mine."
"Fam, you think I would be a part of dis shit if it was about disrespectin' Vice Lords? We respect each other enough to know it's about dis money, and tha nigga Ug gone take us to the promise land. You ever been to tha promise land nigga?"
"Hell naw!"
"Me either my dude, but I'm sho tryin to see wut dat be like……So how yo guys feel about dis?"
"You know, they feel like Big Moe on some bullshit. We aint had no work since Chino got popped and we thirsty as hell right now."
"How thirsty are yall… Look, Im'ma keep it one hunnid witc'hu. We gotta chair at our table wit'cho name on it. We gone hit'chu wit a hunnid of dem thangs off tha muscle at twenty-three apiece. You can't beat dat, plus bonuses after every load, but'chu gotta decide right now how bad you want it."
"So, I take it ya'll want me to kill Big Moe… huh?"

"Hey, if you don't, another one of yo guys will. Might as well be you on top, right?"

"Man Rico, just gim'me some time to think dis out."

"Aight cool, but'chu betta think fast. You got about two days, after dat every GD, BD and Vice Lord in dis town gone be on y'all block ready to wipe all y'all out the whole equation. I don't wanna see dat happen, but'chu need to realize dat dis here ain't gang related no more my nigga. Dis here dat mob shit."

Lil Stone finally understood what was going on. He also understood that the Stone's couldn't take on the entire Robbins by themselves, and since the pros out-weigh the cons, he knew what had to be done. He was going to have to kill Big Moe.

CHAPTER 46

I spent a chunk of my day at some campaign fundraiser with Carlos. Although I found it boring at first, he told me I needed to make and meet new friends, so I did. I met all types of politicians, doctors, lawyers, and community activist. I even met a handful of U.S. Attorney's and Federal Judges. Carlos introduced me as a board member of his corporation. I can't remember the name, but everyone thanked me for my generous contributions. I didn't know what the hell they were talking about, I just smiled and said,

"My pleasure."

Whatever amount I contributed *had* to be generous, because it had me dancing with the mayor of Chicago's wife, and I could've sworn I was being flirted with by one of the U.S. Attorneys. Overall, I ended up having a decent time partying with the rich folks. By the end of the night I had a pocket full of business cards and a stomach full of champagne.

As Carlos and I were about to leave, that sexy ass U.S. Attorney chick walked extra close and slid her card in the inside pocket of my blazer and said,
"Mr. Stuffy if you ever need to be informed of your rights, give me a call." Then she winked at me and walked away.

I stood there for a second and admired her curvy shape. She had the sway of a model and the grace of a cat. She was bad! So bad in fact that Carlos stood next to me and blurted out.

"Great ass! Boy boy boy, I'll tell you Adonis, if you don't I will." He chuckled and bumped elbows with me saying, "Com'on its been a long day, let's get out of here."

We made it to the garage at the Trump Towers all tired out. Carlos asked if I enjoyed myself, and I told him it was different. He laughed a little and said,

"Adonis, sorry for the hold up, but there's a lot happening on my end of business, bureaucratic bullshit. Nevertheless, the shipment is here in the U.S. Once I get it here in Chicago you'll hear from me. Until then, take this number. I want you to contact this person ASAP. He's a very good person to know, his name is Andre. Give him a call tonight. This should help you get things in better order, ok?" I shook his hand in a confirming manner and he said,"Ok, I'll talk with you soon."
Carlos then went up to his beautiful suite. I jumped in the Maxima and took off for the land of no return.

When I got back to the town the first person I saw was Rico. He was on the block making sure his guys where on point with security. As soon as I got out, he approached me with the Big Moe situation. He was telling me how Big Moe's second in command came to talk to him. I wasn't surprised. I saw it all in his face. He'd lost all respect for his fearless leader, or should I say cowardly. Anyhow, he said he believed that the situation was going to be handled soon. I looked at Rico inquisitively and asked,

"Handled soon? So wut dat mean?"
"I let him know dat tha only thing dat stood in tha way of him sittin at tha table wit us was Big Moe. And well, he got tha message."
"You think he good for it?"
"Tha spot?"
"Naw, tha hit? I'm saying, we aint sendin no little boy to do a grown man's job is we? You gotta be sure Rico, we can't fuck dis up."
"He want tha spot Ug. I think he gone make it happen, but I'll fuck wit'em tomorrow and see where his head at."

"Naw Rico, fuck wit him right now. By dis time tomorrow, I want Big Moe's bitch ass on a slab. Remember wut I said fam, its time to take tha gloves off, so take'em off."

"Aight, aight, don't even trip, I got'chu." Rico grabbed a couple of the Lords and took off. When he left, I got on the phone and made a call to see what's up with this Andre. I was eager to see what kind of help he really was.

I gave Andre's number a call, but I got no answer, so I tried it again and still got no answer. After a few minutes, I received a text message asking who I was. I told him I was a friend of Carlos, and the message stopped. Twenty minutes later, a message popped up from Andre saying.

+7734455090: Meet me by the oil refinery in Blue Island in 20 minutes.

Close to thirty minutes later, I arrived on the block along the oil refinery. The area was secluded and dark as hell, I could hardly see a thing. I drove up and down the block a couple of times til finally I saw a car flash its headlights, then I pulled over. The guy stepped out of his car and leaned against the hood. It was so dark, that I could only see the silhouette of his body.

I parked about twenty feet away from the guy and yelled out to him from my passenger side window.

"Andre?" He said yeah, and told me to pull up and hop out.

As I was walking toward Andre he was saying,

"I thought you wasn't comin, I was about to take off."
And as I moved close to shake his hand, I said,
"My bad, it's dark as fuck over here, I almost didn't…"
And I froze. I was looking at his face in confusion, anger and ultimately relief. I couldn't believe that Andre was actually Watts!

I grabbed my head with both hands and walked in circles trying to subdue the anger. I then took a few breaths and finally said,

"Damn Watts, why you ain't been told me you was fuckin wit Carlos man?!"

And he said,

"Adonis, that wasn't my place to tell. When you came to me at the gas station that night I knew Carlos hadn't told you about me, so I just left it at that. I figured if he didn't tell you, maybe you didn't need to know, but I guess *now* you needed to know."

"Man…Man I was gone kill yo ass my dude. I thought you was gone bank me on dat double murder. Maybe try to extort me or sumt'n. I don't know!"

"Adonis, be cool. You ain't gotta worry about Moony and Chino. I already took care of that, but what I *need* is for you to tell me about Hundo, so I can figure out how to fix that.

This time when he asked, I had no problem giving him what he wanted. I turned around and leaned on his car then said,

"Aight, check it out. I couldn't get to Hundo as easy as I could get to Moony and Chino. So, since he was a sucker for tha girls, I put Toni on him."

"And Toni is the girl you hang with right?"

"Yup."

"Alright, keep going."

"I sent her to the cozy corner to flirt wit'em a little, get his dick hard. Once she got him going she lured him out tha lounge and over on tha back streets where I was waitin in a basehead car. A few seconds later, Hundo was noodle soup. She got out, jumped in tha car wit me and we took off. Dat's it."

"Please tell me you still got the guns you used."

"I buried tha one I used on Moony and Chino. The one used on Hundo was stolen."

"Ok, this is good. I can make this work. Get with me tomorrow and bring me the gun you do have. Trust me, the other one will pop up, and when it does, I would hate to be the person holding it. Other than that, all I can tell you is, get that money. I got'cha back."

Talk about relief. I left Watts feeling like a brand new man. I literally felt as if someone had just blown air into my lungs and gave me the breath of life. This was an absolute game changer. Having a police officer on the team gave us that extra room to mark our territory with authority and impunity. Eyes on the other side of the law is exactly what we needed. This wasn't just going to give us order. This was going to make us untouchable!

On my way back to the block, I called Rico to see where he was. He told me he was on the block talking with Lil Stone, so I told him to stay put and don't move, I was on my way.

Once I got there, I stood in front of Lil Stone and looked him up and down. Then said,
"You ready for dis shit famo?"
"As ready as I'm eva gone be big homie."
"Ok, get Big Moe on tha line. See if he'll give you a ride to Harvey. Tell'em you wanna go check out some work.

After Lil Stone made the call, he let me know that Big Moe was game. I rubbed my hands together like a mad scientist saying,

"Bet! Rico, snatch Toni up and yall work out a spot to meet up at in Harvey." Then I looked at Lil Stone and said,"Take him to a dark block somewhere and just do his ass. Make it quick and sweet, den jump in the ride wit Toni and Rico and get tha fuck up outta there. Toni, Rico, yall just make sure everything go smoov, Aight?"
Rico gave me a fist bump and said,

"Quick and sweet. You got it my nigga." And they left to handle the task at hand.

Chapter 47

Toni and Rico sat on a dark secluded block in Harvey waiting on Lil Stone's call. While they waited, they conversated about what they wanted to do with their money once they had enough saved. Rico talked about starting a tow trucking business, while Toni raved about taking a trip to Paris. Rico found that funny and said,

"Toni, wut yo ghetto ass gone do in Paris?"

"I am *not* ghetto sweetie. I am a lady. I just standz on my shit."

In the course of them going back and forth, Rico's phone rang. When he answered the call he said,

"Yo, wussup?"

And Lil Stone replied,

"I'm turnin' on yo block right now. I'm in a black Cadillac."

"Pull up by tha light pole, we already here." Then they both hung up.

The phone call was simply a diversion to let Rico and Toni know what they were riding in and when they were pulling up.

As soon as Rico hung up, he reached in his middle console and pulled out a pair of binoculars. When Toni saw him pull the binoculars out she said,

"Stop playin! Did you really just pull out some binoculars nigga?!"

"Hell yeah, dats why I told him to pull up by the light pole, so I can see they ass through the windshield."

As soon as Big Moe pulled over and parked, he looked around scoping the scene. Something to him didn't feel right, so he asked Lil Stone how long was his guy was going to be. Lil Stone told him a few minutes, then reached for the door handle. That's when Big Moe got paranoid saying,

"Where you goin Star?!"
"Be cool, I'm just finna take a piss." And once Toni seen him get out she said,
"Wut tha fuck he doin'? Why he ain't shoot'em when he was in tha car?"

When Lil Stone went to the rear of the Cadillac to take his so-called piss, Big Moe was watching him through the rear-view mirror and saw him pull a gun from his waist.

Once Lil Stone got it all together he turned around to open the door. Once he did, Big Moe fired a shot at him piercing him in the side. Toni and Rico watched him hit the ground, and that's when they made their way straight for the Caddy.

Big Moe had extreme tunnel vision when he hopped out of the car, he was moving around to the passenger side to finish Lil Stone off, when out of the corner of his eye he saw the two figures coming at him. He quickly stopped in his tracks and turned around letting off about four more shots, one hitting Toni in the shoulder blade. When Toni hit the ground, Rico ducked behind a car for cover. Big Moe kept letting off shots at them as he moved closer to Lil Stone and when he walked up on him, Lil Stone let off three shots in his chest. Simultaneously, Rico ran up on Big Moe from the side and hit him once in the head.

Instantly Rico grabbed all the guns and tossed them in his truck, then ran to check on Toni as he called for an ambulance. Toni was in complete agony. She kept saying,
"I'm gone die! I'm gone die!"
Rico tried to calm her by saying, "Shorty you gone be aight. Tha ambulance comin' right now."

Toni was still hysterical. She grabbed on to Rico's shirt and said,

"Rico, please don't let me die."
"You hear tha sirens T? They comin' to get'chu now."
"Rico, I…I feel light headed." That's when Toni said,
"Rico…Tell Ug…I love him." And then her eyes closed.

Rico dropped his head for a brief moment, then went to check on Lil Stone. He was on the side of the car squirming and crying, but nevertheless he was still alive.

When the ambulance finally arrived, they rushed Toni and Lil Stone to the hospital. They took one look at Big Moe and knew it was only one place he was going, and that was to a morgue. When the police started questioning Rico, he told him everybody was outside chillin when some guys came out of the gang way shooting. He also told them that he didn't know who they were, why they were shooting or who they were shooting at. The cop looked at Rico and said,

"So, I guess you the lucky one huh?"
And Rico said,
"Lucky?! Fuck naw, I'm tha smart one. When I heard that first gun shot I got my black ass up under that car!"

After a few more questions the cop let Rico go and they started wrapping the scene up. Rico then casually walked away from the police and prepared himself to call Ug and tell him what happened.

Chapter 48

I was chillin on the block with Yella Boy, and Nassir just kickin it like we used to. You know, sipping a few beers, cracking a few jokes. Just acting silly. With all that had been going on lately, we really hadn't had that down time like we were accustomed to. So, I made a mental note to put together a vacation for the crew once we finished this next load. I think it would do them some good. Hell, I think it would do me even better.

As we sat there laughing, my phone began to ring. When I checked the screen, I saw it was Rico. I answered with enthusiasm and said,

"Rico, tell me sumt'n good fam." He hesitated for a second then said,
"Ug, Toni got hit fam. I'm at the emergency room at Ingalls..."

I didn't even let him get the next word out. I just took off running toward the ride. That was when Nassir yelled,
"Ug, wussup?!"
And I said,
"Toni got shot, they at Ingalls Hospital."

Nassir volunteered to drive, which was good, cause I was in a straight panic. What the fuck had happened? This was supposed to be an in and out hit. I knew I should have just handled the shit myself. What the fuck was I thinking!

We arrived at the hospital around twelve in the morning. When Rico saw us walk in the emergency room, he got up and walked toward us. The first and only words I could get out was,
"How she doing?"
And Rico said,

"They're operating on her right now, so I aint sure."
"So, where Lil Stone at?"
"They patchin' him up too."
"Damn! He got popped too? ... Ay step outside, let's talk."

As soon as we got outside of the emergency room doors, the first thing I asked was,
"Wus tha word on Big Moe?"
And Rico said.
"He outta there."
"You sue?"
"I'm positive."
I looked at Nassir and said, "Ay Nas, you got a Black n Mild? My fuckin nerves bad as hell."

Nassir passed me a Black n' Mild cigar and I started freaking it. While I did that, I asked him what did he tell the police. He explained to me that he told the police that they were out in Harvey kickin it with a friend, when all of a sudden some dudes just started shooting. Then I said,
"Did they buy it?"
"As far as I kow."
Once I finished freaking the Black n' Mild, I lit it and took a deep pull, then said,
"So wut tha fuck happened out there?"

Rico spent the next fifteen minutes telling me all the details of what happened. I didn't know if I should be upset or pissed off. I just didn't like the fact that one of mine was laying in some hospital bed probably clinging on to her life. As far as Lil Stone went, I was having a hard time deciding if I was going to let him keep his. Rico however stood there looking at me sort of strange and curious. When I asked what was on his mind, I kept seeing his eyes dart toward Yella Boy and Nassir. So I said,

"Ay yall, let me holla at Rico in private for a minute." And they went back in the hospital. Once they were out of sight, I looked at Rico and said, "So wussup Rico, wus on yo mind?"

Rico hesitated for a second while he rubbed his chin then he said,

"Ug, you and Toni fuckin around fam?"

Shocked as hell I said,

"Wut make you say dat?!"

"Cause Toni said, and deez are *her* words not mine, 'Tell Ug I Love Him'."

I couldn't believe what Rico had just told me. So, I smacked my lips and said,

"Never! Get tha fuck outta here!"

Rico chucked a little and said, "On tha fin nigga, I ain't bullshitten! She said 'Tell Ug I love him' right before she passed out. My guess is, and this just me 'thinkin' out loud, but I think she thought she was gone die and she wanted you to know how she felt before she left this earth."

Damn! Naw, double damn!! Rico had just fucked my head up with that one. Toni?! Not pussy eatin' Toni! That's crazy, maybe she meant to say Candice and my name just slipped. I don't know, I just looked at Rico and said,

"Ay fam, don't tell dat to nobody else… aight. Don't even tell her you told me. Let's just keep dis between us, aight."

And Rico said, "Cool, but hey. If you and Toni hook up, let me get at Brittany."

And I said,

"Be easy Rico, you doin' to much."

We both just smiled at each other, then went back in the hospital to check on Toni and Lil Stone.

After a while, Candice showed up to the hospital hysterical and crying. I tried my best to calm her down, but she only ended up crying herself to sleep on my shoulder.

Around three in the morning, a doctor stepped out and asked for the family of Antoinette Simmons and Candice jumped to her feet. I took it that was Toni's full name. So, we all walked over to the doctor to hear the news. He waited until we all gathered together then said,

"Ok, bad news is, Antoinette lost a lot of blood and we had to run a transfusion. We also had to repair some major veins and nerves then ultimately reset the ball joint in the shoulder blade. Good news is, the bullet just missed damaging a major artery, so she's going to be fine. She's going to need a lot of rest and a little while to heal, but she'll be good as new in no time. We're going to track her vitals for a day, and if everything pans out well, we'll release her by tomorrow morning."

I was glad to hear Toni was going to be fine. Now that I'm calm and my adrenaline rush is coming down, I was getting sleepy as hell. I told Yella Boy to stick around and keep an eye on Candice and to listen out for any word on Lil Sone, while the rest of us went home.

I laid in my bed just staring at the ceiling thinking, all this bullshit drama behind one person's stupid decision. I never asked Big Moe to be best friends with the folks. I just simply wanted him to be cordial enough to maintain an operation. I mean, how do you get to that point in your life when you're willing to die over *not* wanting money, you know? True enough, money isn't everything and it can't buy you happiness, but I've seen it put one *hell* of a smile on a person's face, real talk!

Later that morning after getting a little rest, I made my way back to the hospital to check on Toni and Lil Stone. When I made it to Toni's room, I found her, Candice and Yella Boy sound asleep. I tapped Yella boy and woke him up then waved him out into the hallway.

"Everything all good?"
"Yeah, she doin aight. She woke up a few times, but fell right back to sleep."
"You heard anything on Lil Stone?"
"Yeah, he stopped by here about a hour and a half ago. He said it was a straight through shot, didn't hurt nothin but a little flesh, so they patched him up and let him go."
"Aight bet. Imma wake Candice up. Y'all gone back to the block and get cleaned up and shit. I'll sit here wit Toni til yall get back."

After Yella Boy and Candice left, I went and stood over Toni while looking down in her face. I was amazed to see that even after hours of surgery and her hair looking a mess. Toni remained to be a beautiful woman.

While I stood there falling deep into my thoughts I saw Toni's eyes started to blink, a few seconds later she opened her eyes and I said,

"Ah, sleeping beauty finally awakes." She looked at me and smiled then said
"Hey Ug...Ug!! Oh shit! Where Rico at?!"
And I told her,
"He back on tha block. Why wussup shorty?"
"I ummm...just...I just need to see him."
"Ok, don't trip, I'll have him come see you in a little bit. So, how you feelin?"
"I feel like shit. My arm is fuckin killin me and I know my hair is a mess."

Toni tried to slick her hair back and fix herself up. I had to laugh. That's when Toni giggled herself and said,

"Wut'chu laughin at Ug?!"
"I'm laughin at'chu. All shot up and shit and still tryin' to look good. Who you tryin to look good fo?"
And just in those simple words, the room grew silent.

Somehow in the moment I believe Toni knew that Rico had told me what she said. Her face flushed red and she tried to appear tired, so I gave her some room to save face and I said,

"You still look tired T. Go ahead and get'cho self some more rest. I'll be right here chillin til Candice come back." Then I dearly kissed her on the forehead and let her get some more rest. I needed my road dog back on the block, well and focused.

Chapter 49

Hours later, Yella Boy and Candice retuned to the hospital with Rico and Nassir. They all sat around cracking jokes trying to help Toni get her mind off the pain, and it seemed as though it was working. Toni kept a smile on her face the whole time the crew was there visiting. Ug however, left to go handle a few matters, but promised he'd be back later.

Once Ug left, Toni gave Rico a "I need to talk to you look," so Toni asked everyone if they would give her and Rico a moment in private.

When they all left, Toni looked over her shoulder to make sure no one was listening and said.

"Rico! Please, please, please tell me you didn't tell Ug what I said."

Rico felt stuck between a rock and a hard place. He didn't want to be dishonest to Toni, but he had already committed to Ug. What was he supposed to say?

Rico felt bad for what he was about to do, but he looked Toni square in her eyes and said,

"Naw, I ain't said nothin T."
Toni's head flopped back on the pillow.
"Good, cause I was definitely trippin. I ain't mean to..."
"Ay T, it is what it is. Fuck it, yo secret safe wit me, mufuka can't tell you wut to feel or wut not to feel, right?"
"Yeah, I guess you right."
Then an awkward silence fell between them, before Toni said, "Thanks Rico, for everything. Now, tell everybody to come back in before they think *we* messing around."

While everyone sat in the room reminiscing about old times, Toni laid there feeling stupid. She couldn't believe that she had let her true feelings out of the bag. Toni still loved Candice dearly, but she couldn't deny the fact that she was falling *in* love with Ug. She was confused about her emotions, but she was clear in her thinking, and she didn't want Candice to find out about her true feelings.

Chapter 50

Later that night, Brittany and I sat cuddled together watching the local evening news. I always loved Brittany's company without a doubt, but tonight I strangely found myself reveled in the thought of Toni's feelings toward me. Although I found this situation to be a huge conflict of interest, I was oddly flattered. I mean, I was even trying to picture myself being with her until Brittany squirmed in my arms and I looked at her. I instantly thought to myself ' What am I doing'? How could I've let those thoughts invade the one on one time I was spending with my ole lady? Most of all, how could I forget that Toni was my best friend's girl. Damn, damn, damn! This is fucked up.

Lucky for me, the local headlines stopped me in my thoughts and caught my full attention. Headline after headline, the Chicago news was saturated with home invasions, grand larceny, car theft and identity fraud. You would think that with the absence of cocaine in our out our way the communities would be better off, but it was actually turning people into monsters. But when the world headlines popped up, it showed that the black folks weren't the only savages in this world.

The war in Mexico was still going strong and the body count was consistently getting higher. Every time they showed footage, you would see men being shot down in cold blood with assault rifles. Bodies laying in the streets with no regard. Even the paramedics in Juarez were scared to tend to the injured. You know, it's crazy cause as I sit here looking at the news and hearing about the home invasions, robbery, and homicides we were dealing with in our own communities. I was glad I stayed in the hood and not Juarez, Mexico.

Around five thirty the next morning I heard my phone ring. I was tired as hell. Brittany and I had been up all night doing some intense fucking. Or should I say love making? No, no, no, we were definitely fucking! Anyway, the ringing stopped. My body relaxed and I began drifting back off to sleep. Not even ten seconds later the fucking phone started ringing again. This time I grabbed my phone and looked at the screen but I was so tired I couldn't focus my vision to see the name. So, I pressed what appeared to be the ignore button and the ringing stopped, then I laid my head back down. Would you believe that no sooner than my head touched the pillow, that fucking phone started ringing again?! This time I went into a tantrum. I snatched the covers off of me and started kicking and swinging at the air like a little kid. I grabbed the phone, pressed the answer button and said,

"Wut tha fuck?! Who is dis?!"
And the voice said,
"Ug dis Rico. We got a problem on tha block! I'm on my way over there right now!"

I jumped out of the bed and ran to the window. It was still sort of dark outside and all I could see were bodies and guns, that's when I quickly tossed my jeans and shirt on. As I was putting my shoes on, my phone rang again. I didn't even look at the screen I just answered, and all I heard was,

"Adonis, get your ass outside, *now*!"

As I was walking out of my room. I bumped into Nassir. He'd also received early morning calls, so we both walked out on the block together.

When we stepped outside, I realized we were in the middle of a standoff. Maria and five guala goons stood posted around a furniture truck with sub machine guns, while being surrounded by the block security. When I realized it was Maria, I quickly jumped in the middle screaming.

"It's all good, It's all good, fall back!"

When our guys lowered their guns, Maria and the guala goons did the same. Maria didn't speak at all, she just smiled at me and tapped the side of the truck twice then they all hopped into the Escalade limo and drove off. She didn't have to tell me what was in the truck. I knew that smile, so I had Nassir back the truck up to the apartment building, so we could start loading the coke into the stash house.

As Nassir backed the truck up, Rico was walking up the driveway to the apartment building. When he said,

"Ug, wuts going on out here?"
And I told him,
"Get Yella Boy on tha line and tell'em to get out here. We got work to do."

Nassir got out and walked around to the rear of the truck where Rico and I were standing right around the time Yella Boy came running up all out of breath saying,

"Wuts goin on? Wuts tha word?" He looked at the truck and said, "Fo'real Ug? You got us out here at five sumt'n in tha morning to unload some furniture?"

Yella Boy and Rico looked at me with the same annoyance and confusion. That's when I started to undo the latch on the rear door of the truck and heaved it open. We all stood there looking at a truck full of boxes and Rico said,

"Wut tha fuck is dis?"
And I said,
"That right there my dudes is five mufukin tons of 95 percent pure cocaine!" They all looked at me like damn, and I just smiled.

We started unloading the boxes and taking them to one of the second floor apartments. It took us almost two hours before we got to the last wall of boxes, and once we started moving them, I noticed some coffin sized military chest stacked on top of each other. Six of them to be exact. I called out to Rico so he could help me grab the top one and pull it down. I was eager to see what was inside. When Rico and I grabbed the ends of the chest, Rico said,
"Oh shit, hol'up. Dis mufuka heavy as hell Ug!" That's when I called Nassir and Yella Boy, then said,
"Help us wit dis box, dis mufuka heavy as fuck. Be careful."

Once we got the box down, I opened it. Rico, Yella Boy and Nassir's eyes popped out their head as they looked at me. The chest was filled to the top with what looked like AK-47 assault rifles. I instantly closed the chest and said to the guys,

"Let's hurry up and finish getting deez boxes upstairs."

Once we finished moving, the boxes, we took all the chests out of the truck and placed them on the ground, *then* we carried them all into the first-floor apartment across from where we have our meetings.

When we got them all inside the apartment, we opened them all up. I swear all I could say was, I wish a motherfucker would! Two of them were full of AK-47's, two filled with SMG submachine guns, two packed with brand new 9 millimeters and .380 glocks still in the boxes. The room was beginning to reek of the fresh factory scent of new metal. I picked up one of the uzi's and smelled the muzzle, then I did the same with the AK and said, "Deez mufukas brand new! They aint never been bust before." Then I placed the the AK back in the chest, then looked to Nassir and said,
"How many boxes we move?"
And Nassir said,
"A hundred and thirty-two."

After I broke the math down in my head I said, "Ok, sumt'n aint right. It should be 5600 bricks. So, if it's 132 boxes, that would put close to 42 and a half bricks in each box. That's kinda odd. Yella Boy, you stay here and get an inventory of dem guns. Yall two come wit me, help me bust deez boxes open.

Sure enough, after opening all 132 boxes, 20 of them were full of ammunition for the guns. I looked at Rico and Nassir then said,

"Start countin dem bricks. If my math is right it should be 50 in each box, Im'ma go help Yella Boy."

By the time Yella Boy and I finished counting the guns, we were looking at: 75 AK-47 assault rifles, 75 SKS assault rifles, 250 SMG submachine uzi's, 100 9 millimeters and 100 .380 glocks. We had enough artillery to take over any spot, any project and any hood. We also had enough man power to stand on it!

Once we got the artillery squared away, Rico and Nassir were about finished. Rico looked at me and said,

"We on the last two boxes right now, so hol'up." They took a few minutes to finish their count, then Rico said,"Yup Ug, you was bout right, 112 boxes, 50 bricks each box. So wut now?"
And I said,
"Let's take all dem bullets back downstairs and put'em wit tha guns." And we did. I then looked at the time and saw it was two thirty in the afternoon. That was when I said,"Let tha other guys know we meetin at 7 tonight. Y'all gone and get'chall self together and get a little rest. We gone meet back here at 6. Oh and Rico, make sure Lil Stone got his ass here. Wit bells on!

Chapter 51

I popped back up at the apartment building around five thirty. Nassir, Yella Boy, and Rico were already sitting at the table watching the new flat screen television that sat on the wall at the end of the large oval cherry wood office table. There were eight soft leather executive's chairs that surrounded the table and a name plate sat on the table in front of seven of the chairs. I guess you can tell that our meeting apartment had a makeover. Since the last meeting I've been having Nassir spruce the place up a bit, making it look business like, so the guys and girl would feel presidential when sitting in this room. And it had that feeling as soon as you walked through the door. From the carpet on the floor, to the pictures on the wall, this apartment felt like an executive office.

When I sat down at the table, Rico hit the power button on the remote and turned the television off, then all three of them turned and looked at me. I then checked my watch and said,

"Yall could've kept watchin TV, we still got time."
And Nassir said,
"Naw, we good. wut's tha word?"
I sat down in my seat then said,
"Aight bet, this how we gone do dis. Yall already know dat tha goin price is 23. Y'all gone get paid for every brick. Y'all price is gone be 19, but yall gone get paid on tha back end. I know it sounds fucked up, but you come out better in tha end. See if it's all about who you serve, den one of y'all can make a million and the other can make 300,000. You know what dat brings? Jealousy! And dats when all that extra bullshit get tossed in tha game. Dis way you three plus Toni come out of dis load wit 5.6 million plus you still get your even cut bonuses. All yall gotta do is run tha operation. I'll take Toni's place til she gets straight and we just play our parts."

The plan was clear. Rico, Yella Boy and Nassir were in full cooperation and they were more than ready. I leaned back in my seat and started to think, until I was taken from my thoughts by a knock at the door.

Rico went to the door and looked through the peep hole and said,

"Awww shit! Then he opened the door and said, "It's Toni ya'll!
The rest of us got out of our seats and hurried to the door to greet her.
Toni stood there in the doorway with her good arm on her hip and the bad one in a sling and said,
"Damn y'all was just gone leave me out here huh?" We rushed her with gentle hugs and welcome backs. When she stepped in and looked around, she said, "Damn y'all hooked dis mufuka up! This shit is fly as hell." She walked up to the table and saw her name plate then took a seat and said, "Oooh this chair feel so good. So, what did I miss?"

Damn! That was just like Toni, always on business, so I spent the next twenty-minutes filling her in on what was new. Before I knew it, Bino G, Gracy and Lil Stone showed up and took their seat. Before I discussed any busy I addressed the elephant in the room and said,

"Lil Stone, we set you to handle some grown man business. So wut tha fuck happened?"
And Lil Stone said,
"And I handled dat grown man business Ug. Shit just got fucked up out there."
"Yeah and dat shit almost got Toni killed!"
"Look, I don't mean no disrespect Ug, but I almost got killed out there too! I lost blood just like Toni did!"

I felt where he was coming from. I just didn't like the fact that Toni got shot, so I opened the table for everyone's thoughts on the situation. Bino G chimed in and said,

"Hey Ug, cut younsta a little slack G. You know, when you out there in the field tha game can change at any time. He got tha job done and Toni still alive, so go easy on him."
I looked around the table and said,
"Who all feel tha same way Bino feel? Raise ya hand."

It was unanimous, everyone including Toni voted for Lil Stone. I told him to stand up as I walked over to him. I looked him up and down then stared him in the eyes. Then I reached in my back pocket and pulled out his name plate and sat it on the table. I shook his hand and said,
"Welcome to tha team. Now sit'cho ass down so we can get down to business."
Everybody walked up to him, shook his hand and congratulated him. I also took that time to formally congratulate Bino G and Gacy as well. Then we all sat down as I took the floor and said,

"Lil Stone, Bino, Gacy, Nassir gone square yall way today wit a hunnid bricks, 23 a piece like we discussed." I watched their faces light up, then I continued. "Like I said before, tha bonus is gonna depend on how fast y'all move. Keep tha gang bangin shit at bay. Keep your guys in they own area, so we don't have to deal wit territory issues. Use y'all status and move around to some of tha other areas and connect wit some of tha other heads. We need to touchdown out west, over east and all out south. Remember, we did a fire ass double up wit tha last shit we had. Dis shit right here 10% stronger, so you can re-rock it or cook it and stretch it. It don't matter, dis shit gone stand up like yo little man on Viagra." Everybody started laughing then I said, "Bino, I want seven of yo realest and most loyal members. You too Gacy, Lil Stone, you give me six of yours. We gone beef dis block security up a bit. Handle *dat* shit first before you do anything else. When you got'em together, call me. Im'ma have Nassir come pick'em up. We good?" Everybody gave me a head nod, then I said, "Bet, pull y'all whips back here so Nas can load y'all up. It's time to get dis money."

Chapter 52

Later that night, the hood was back in business. As we drove through the town checking out the blocks, all we saw were headlights and taillights. I don't think I've ever seen crackheads move this fast. I mean they were on the move, just a shucking and jiving trying to chase that beast. But when we stopped at Trogans to get something to drink, we noticed how dead it liked on that end of town. So, I asked Nassir what was up with Racks and had he seen him lately. Nassir just bunched his shoulders saying,

"Man, I don't know wussup wit Racks weird ass. I mean, he drove on me a minute ago tryin to get me to put him on, but I don't know."

And I said,

"Stop being petty, tha man saw his brotha get smoked bro. Dats some shit to deal wit. Besides we need somebody down here, dis shit left wide open, look at it. Gone throw'em a brick or sumt'n, see wut he do."

Then Nas said,

"Hey, I told you tha damn boy weird, now if he smoke dat whole brick up, Im'ma laugh at'cho hungry hippo lookin' ass."

I chuckled at Nassir's comment then said,

"You a fool bro, Im'ma grab dis drink then we gone ride down on him."

Once I got the drink, we pull on Racks' block. He was sitting on the hood of his car smoking a cigarette and staring into the sky. Nassir parked next to him and we all got out. While Yella Boy and Toni stepped to the side and started pouring drinks, Nassir and I stepped to Racks to see what was on his mind. But as we got closer we could see he had his cigarette in one hand and a gun in the other. So, I calmly said,

"Yo Racks, was been up famo. You maintainin'?" He never took his eyes off the sky. He just said,

"Man jo, dem mufukas took my brotha from me fam. I still can't get over dat shit."

I really didn't know how to reply to what he just said. All I could do at that moment was offer him a drink and he accepted.

After we both had a few sips, Nassir finally spoke,

"Ay Racks, you still tryin to jump down on tha hustle?"
He took another sip from his cup and said,
"I don't know Nassir." Then he got pumped and said, "Cause on tha real, I'm bout ready to start layin mufukas down!"
Then he looked back up at the sky and said, "You hear me little bro? I ain't finish wit deez niggas!"

Nassir stared at me with that 'I told you look' and just looked back at him. Racks *was* kinda bugging out, but I felt him. I just couldn't imagine. So, while he was still looking up in the sky, I nudged Nassir in the arm, nodded my head toward Racks and Nassir said,
"Ummm, so wussup Racks? You wanna get dis money or wut? Just say tha word and I'll gone and drop you a whole thang to work wit, know wut I'm saying, help you get on yo feet." Racks was still a little pumped up, but he said,
"Yeah, yeah, fuck it let's do it. Deez niggas aint tryin to see Racks come back. I'm wit it! That's when I asked,
"You out here by yoself bro? You ain't got nobody to help you hold it down?"
"Once I get dis money goin, deez little niggas gone start comin out from everywhere. So don't trip, I got dis."
While Nassir and I talked with Racks I had Yella Boy and Toni run to the block and grab a kilo for Racks. When they came back, Nassir gave him the brick and let him know the price. Racks got even more pumped and said,
"Get tha fuck outta here!"
I looked at Racks and said,

"Ay bro gone and take dat shit in tha crib. We gone get up wit'chu later."

When we got in the truck I leaned back in the seat and took a deep breath. Nassir looked at me and said,

"Yeah! I told you dat mufuka was weird. Dat nigga gone smoke dat whole brick fam. Watch, mark my words, dat nigga face had two for fifteen wrote all over it."

I told Nassir not to trip. Racks may never be a hustler again, but we won't know unless we give him a chance. Besides, after seeing what I saw, I was past looking for the hustler in Racks. I wanted to see what the killer inside of him was all about.

The next morning, Carlos called me over for breakfast, which in translation meant he wanted to talk. I didn't want to leave the area because there was shit I was trying to get accomplished. But whenever Carlos called me over "to eat breakfast," I had to go see what was on the menu, so to speak.

Once I made it to the suite, I kicked my shoes off and made myself comfortable. I followed Rosa to the ever so familiar living area to see what my man Carlos was up to.

When I walked in the room, Carlos was looking casual as usual in a pair of ripped up jeans and button up shirt. He wore a pair of glasses that sat on the edge of his nose while he read the morning paper. He never looked up, he just kept reading as he waved me over saying,

"Adonis, come. Have a seat. I'm starved, how about you?"

If I wasn't hungry before I got here, I was now. Something smelled good as hell. I couldn't resist asking what we were having to eat. Carlos took his glasses off and stood up. Then, he reached over and took the top off the supper tray and said,

"It's Halibut Milanese served with Spanish egg whites and hash browns! It's delicious, try it." Carlos was always trying to diversify my taste buds, so I sat down and dug into it to see what the hoopla was all about. Seconds later Carlos initiated the conversation by saying,

"How's everything going?"
And I said, "Its all good, It all good."
"You and Andre working things out?"
"Aw yeah, good ole Andre. We workin' it all out. Everything cool."
He stared at me curiously yet casually then said,
"Oh! Before I forget, Leonard wants you to give him a call. He's come across some other property in your area that's for sale. He said it may be a good business venture."

He went on to tell me about a chain of grocery stores and a few hotels he had opening soon and I immediately said,

"No shit, so dat been *you* wit all dat construction?"
"Yeah, trying to get it all done for a late September opening. This is going to get us where we need to be Adonis."
"How so?"
"Oh, you'll see, I guarantee it. Do you watch the news Adonis?"
"Yup, I sure do."
"So, you aware of the war in Mexico, Right?"
"Yeah. I been keeping up wit it."
"Well, when it's all over, we're going to flood the U.S. with so much coke that the president is going to want in."
"But den Im'ma have to compete wit tha Mexicans."
"There won't be any competition. The Mexicans can never produce the type of quality we have, even if they can they can't compete with the price."

"So, who else in Chicago you workin wit?"

"Just you and only you, no one else."

"So Imma be tha only one in Chicago movin dis work?"

"Chicago?! Adonis you'll be the only person in the entire fucking country, I will be giving this cocaine to. Every kilo we ship to the U.S. will be coming straight to you. Just get it all flowing and stay out of trouble. Speaking of trouble, have you called that sexy U.S. Attorney chic?"

"Naw, I ain't really interested."

"Not interested! To hell with your interests Adonis, she's a U.S. Attonery! You know, F.B.I., D.E.A., U.S. Marshalls? Look, just take her out a few times, for me. She's going to come in handy one day, trust me."

What am I getting myself into? The only woman I was trying to be involved with was Brittany, but Carlos had a way of laying the guilt on pretty thick. The right thing to do would be to just say no. So how come the right thing feels so wrong right now? I was going to hate myself in the end for this, but I collected my thoughts and took a sip of orange juice then said,

"Fuck it, I'll give her a call." That was all Carlos needed to hear, then he shut up about the situation and I finished eating my food.

Chapter 53

After Ug left the suite, Carlos made a call to his good friend Charles Parker, who once was the city councilman, but now happens to be the Chief of police in Robbins, IL. Carlos met Charles when he first began organizing his South Suburban development project. When Carlos proposed the project to the mayor of Robbins in a town hall meeting, Charles was all for it but community reform was not what the mayor of Robbins had in mind. The mayor was clear about not wanting to run the citizens of Robbins off with property tax increase, but the truth of the matter was, that the Mayor became comfortable in his underworld elements. He would use the State and Federal funding for his own selfish desires without putting anything back into the community. This left the village of Robbins povertized and disenfranchised. Charles didn't agree with what the mayor was doing because he knew the youth was being cheated out of opportunities. Carlos simply felt like, to each his own, but at some point give back. The mayor of Robbins never gave back, he was simply all take.

Carols left the phone ring about three times and was about to hang up until Charles answered,
"Hello?"
"Hey Chuck, what's up?!"
"Carlos? Hey what's up man, how's it hangin?"
"Ohhh a little to the left, but the younger women don't complain."
The both of them laughed for a second then Carlos spoke and said,
"Say Chuck, when ya gonna have some free time on your hands? I want to get together."
"If it's about that damn project, count me out. I need my job man. I ain't tryin to ruffle no feathers."

"Just here me out Chuck, give me a chance to tell you what's on my mind. Maybe I can spark something in you. Let's have a few drinks later."

"I don't know Carlos."

"Com'on Chuck. Worst case scenario, you'll go home drunk off good scotch. Wuduya say?"

"You know Carlos, the last time we tried to make this project happen, things didn't play out to well."

Carlos fell silent for a second then humbly spoke and said,

"Yes, I know, that's why I'm back Chuck. Things are different now."

"Different huh? Yeah… Ok… Uhhh what time you talking?"

"You still live in the same place?"

"Unfortunately."

"Great! I'll pick you up around seven tonight." Then they disconnected.

When Carlos hung up, he sat there for a second thinking of the vey incident that fueled his current motivations. Carlos was adamant about what he wanted to achieve and he was confident in believing that if he could get Charles on board, they could both achieve similar goals. Not that he necessarily needed Charles, but things could definitely go a lot smoother.

A little after seven, Carlos pulled in front of Charles' home and called him out to the limo. When he came out, he got in and Carlos told the driver to just drive.

First thing Calos did was make Charles that drink, and when Charles took the first sip he scrunched his face said,

"Good scotch."

"Yea I know, twenty-five hundred a bottle good!"

"Oh, shit Carlos, now I know what you have to say is no good." Carlos chuckled then said,

"What do you see the future of Robbins being?"

"To be completely honest Carlos, I can give a shit less. I'm just trying to make sure my pension is right so I can retire with a 'hey fuck you' smile. Nothing good can come from this town Carlos."

"That's a uhh, strong comment Chuck. Do you really feel that way?"

"The mayor ran this city in the ground years ago."

"So why don't you run for mayor and do something about it?" Charles exploded with laughter saying,

"Me, mayor?! You've got to be kidding me. That's a heavy position Carlos, I don't know if I have the energy for of all of that."

Carlos broke it all down for him. He let Charles know that he'd fund the campaign and provide a political assistant to guide him in all aspects of the position. Carlos also told him that he'd fund some community projects in good faith of his candidacy. It would show the community that he was serious about the position, and to top it off, Carlos assured him that he could get him the votes. When Carlos finished, Charles took a few more sips from his glass and said,

"Ok, let's by chance say you're serious. How can you assure the votes?" Charles quickly gasped and said, "You're not talking about rigging the polls are you!?"

"Hell no! I'm a shark Chuck, not a snake. Look I've done my homework. We do this simply by a majority ruling. The majority of the population in Robbins are people ranging from the ages of 18-28. That's 50%! Then you have another 30% aging 29 and up that will jump on board just from community deeds. The last 20% are kids that can't even vote yet. I can get you that majority ruling."

Charles thought long and hard before he said,

"So, what do you want from all of this? Oh, and please don't tell me you're just trying to be a good Samaritan."

Carlos gave Charles a cocky smile then said,

"What I want is not asking for much."

"Com'on Carlos, spit it out."

"Ok, I get to choose the Chief of police, any and everything else we can discuss along the way."

"So, who do you have in mind?"

"Well let's just cross that bridge once we get there, but I take it you're in."

"I take it that I'm something, but yea, im in… Hmm, mayor Parker, it does have a good ring to it. But hey, what about this piece of shit mayor we're dealing with now? You know he doesn't like going out without a fight."

Carlos leaned back in his seat and said,

"Let me worry about that. For now, just keep doing your job. I'll have the political assistant give you a call so you guys can start preparing for the campaign, but don't speak of this to anyone. I don't want to tip Mr. Mayor off about the election."

"Hey, you got it man."

Carlos extended his arm, shook Charles' hand and said,

"Welcome aboard Chuck. You're apart of a winning team now."

Chapter 54

Two weeks later August 23rd had come around and everything was still flowing pretty smoothly. Although Toni's arm was still in a sling, she was doing *and* feeling much better. It only took her one hand to work the money machine, and she did it like a pro.

Yella Boy remained solid while making sure the inventory stayed on point. There wasn't a kilo of cocaine being moved from that building unless Toni gave him the word and she wasn't giving the word unless that money was right.

Rico stayed in constant rotation of the area. He wasn't just sitting back playing the boss, he was out making sure his guys had the area protected. Not only did he keep tabs on our area, but he stayed in rotation of the town making sure the other areas played by the rules.

Nassir, well… Nassir was out simply being Nassir. He moved around town showing his face in *all* the areas. He'd even stop and chat with the other heads to solidify the fact that he was important. Everyone recognized his status and the heads would let it be known that he was not to be fucked with.

Me on the other hand, I'd been out of prison for two months now, and I couldn't believe how sixty days could change a persons' life so dramatically. Everything just kept moving so fast, but I was finally at a point where I could let the team handle things on their own. Besides, I wasn't trying to be the boss, I just wanted to make sure Carlos got his money. Fifty million dollars was the kind of money that said, 'I'll kill you, and everybody you know.'

As I was sitting back day dreaming and thinking, my phone rang. It was Yella Boy letting me know that his friend Nitty had given him a call saying he had the money he owed *and* that he was ready to buy more. Shit, with all that had been going on, I simply forgot about the forty-seven grand that Nitty owed. He could have gotten away without paying, but the fact that he got back with us lets me know that he *was* what I saw in him and that was a standup hustler.

On my way to go see Nitty, I stopped to see if Racks wanted to ride with me. For some odd reason, I was beginning to take a closer liking to him. Even though the other guys were moving major units, Racks still impressed me. First and foremost, he didn't smoke the shit up. As a matter of fact, he banged that motherfucker out in two days, and in the last two weeks he sold about twenty-five more. He was still sort of to himself, but I could tell that the hustler in him had resurfaced and I was digging it.

When I pulled on Racks' block I saw business flowing. He even had a few shorty's out there working. It was a good look for Racks, but an even better look for the area.

I pulled up next to Racks and told him to hop in and roll with me, he looked at me for a second and said,

"Ay Ug, I got dis banger on me fam. I'm just saying, I'll ride wit'chu but I ain't letting dis mufuka go."
I just waved him over and said, "Don't even trip, let's roll."
Once he got in he said, "Where we headed?"
And I told him, "To Markham. I gotta pick some money up."

When I pulled up on Nittys' block in Markham, I saw Nitty leaning on his car talking to a female. Once he saw my face, he said something to the girl and she kissed him on the cheek, then she got in her car and drove off. Nitty then walked up to the Maxima and said,

"Gone and pull up in front of my car fam." So, I did.

When I pulled over, Racks and I got out and stood by the car and peeped the scene. Nitty saw how we looked around and said,

"Relax bro, dis Country Air we all throughout dis mufuka. Ain't nobody gone fuck wit'chu while you wit me."
And Racks said, "Oh, you got it like dat around here?"
And Nitty replied, "I do now thanks to the big homie here."
We were beginning to do too much talking. So I said,

"Wus tha word, wut'chu got for me.?"

"I got'chu fam, in one second. As soon as shorty pull back up Im'ma get'chu right. Just kick tha bo bo wit me for a minute."

Since we were killing time I asked him how things were moving around here and he said, "Ug, I'm killin deez niggas out here. Dat shit'chu gave me was the truth. After I broke bread wit my guys, I had a half a brick and a little over an eigth, plus tha two you tossed me. Dat shit took damn near gram for gram! Man Ug I'm ready to get dis paper. I got'cho forty-seven, plus I got one twenty-five to work wit, all me!" Nitty stood up straight and poked his chest out hard.

I couldn't do anything but smile and say, "All you huh?"

"Hell yeah, I'm tryin to get in where I fit in. I got niggas dat want weight, I'm just tryin' to get my brick game tight. Tha only nigga dat come through here wit weight is dis nigga name Black Pooh from Harvey."
Instantly I said," Black Pooh?!"

"Yeah, wut'chu know him?"

"Naw, just heard of him."

I looked at the time on my phone then said, "If you had to guess, how much you think he be grabbin'?"
Nitty scratched his head and said, "Shit, I don't know fam, don't make me lie to you."
By that time, shorty pulled back up in a different car and Nitty said,

"Ay Ug, back seat or trunk Ug?"

I popped the trunk from the remote button and the trunk opened.

Nitty quickly grabbed a back pack from the back seat of the girls' car then tossed it in the trunk of the Maxima, and she drove away. I then closed the trunk, looked at Racks and said,

"You ready fam?" Racks nodded his head and I said, "Ay Nitty, dis shit we got now is wayyyy betta, so you gone be able to do yo thang, but check it out. I want'chu to try and dump some on yo boy Black Pooh. See if he bite."
"Cool, soon as you get me right I'm on it. So, when you talkin?"
"Right now, follow me."

When we got back to the block, Nitty and I pulled up to the apartment building. When we stepped out of the car, Nitty looked at the three guys standing on the back porch of the house in front of the apartment building, they were all holding assault rifles. One of the guys looked at Nitty and pointed up. When Nitty turned around and looked up and saw two guys looking back at him with assault rifles. Racks was a little caught off guard himself. Neither of them had been to the block since the new changes. I just smiled at them and said,

"Don't ever come to tha block unless you call first. These guys take dat personal." I looked at the guys on the back porch and said, "Don't let nuttin happen to my buddies aight. Nitty, Racks yall chill for a minute while I handle dis business."
When I stepped in the building, I went up to the second floor to see Toni. Once she let me in, I gave her the book bag and said,

"Wus good baby girl, how you feeling?"
"I'm cool, just bored as hell. Wut'cha got?"
"Ay dis dat money Yella Boy little homie owed me, so I need you to separate twenty-four grand and give it to me later. It should be one forty-eight left. Tell Yella Boy to put eleven of dem thangs together. I'll be downstairs in tha driveway.

"I thought he owed forty-seven grand? You just told me to separate twenty-four grand."

I snapped my neck back and said, "Damn T, yo arm might be fucked up, but' cho brain still sharp as a tack I see."

"Com'on Ug. Bitch ain't gone let nobody do you dirty. You should already know that."

"Yeah, yeah, I know. Shorty came correct tho. He got one twenty-five on five bricks. I'm frontin him another five, plus I'm buyin one for him so he could take care of sumt'n fo me. That's where the other twenty-three going."

"I was just sayin Ug, you ain't gotta explain yoself to me."

"Naw, I think I do. Besides I ain't tryin to get shot in my foot."

I went back downstairs with Racks and Nitty and waited for Yella Boy. They were in a deep conversation about mutual friends, mainly females. Me myself, I just really wasn't trying to hear all that bullshit, so I interrupted.
"Ay peep. Soon as you touchdown, hit dude up. Hopefully he bite, so I can get you right like I want to. I don't wanna load you up too hard and have you sittin' on tha shit, know wut I'm talkin' bout? So let's see how deep my man pockets is first."

"So wut if he aint tryin to shop wit me?"

"Den find out who all he be servin' and take his customers. He either gone knuckle up or fall in line."

Finally, Yella Boy came down with the same back pack Nitty gave me earlier. I grabbed it from him then he greeted Nitty saying,

"Wut up fooly, you good?!"

That's when I heard Nitty say in a loud whisper,

"Nigga! Why you aint been told me yo people was on like dis?!"

And Yella Boy said,

"Well, now you know. It's all good! But Ay, Im'ma get up wit'chu in a minute tho, Aight? Love."

Then Yella Boy walked back upstairs. I could tell by the look Nitty had, that his respect level for Yella Boy had just shot through the roof, but what I saw was a couple of youngsters on their way to becoming millionaires well before twenty-one.

I tossed Nitty the bag and told him to hit me up when he got Black Pooh to come through. I wanted to see what he looked like so I could match a name with a face. That would even the playing field for me and it would give me a chance to see how Nitty worked his magic. If he wanted to be one of the big boys he had to know how to *handle* the big boys and speaking of handling the big boys I said,

"Wut kind of heat you got Shorty?"

"I got a little .25 automatic, but it keep dem niggas off me."

I chuckled and shook my head my head saying,

"Put tha dope up and come wit me."

I took Nitty into the first floor apartment where the artillery was stored. I opened up the chest with the AK's in them and said,

"Grab one of those, and here take a couple of uzi's too."

Then I opened the chest with the nine mills and .380's and grabbed one of each then grabbed some ammo and said,

"You good?"

And he replied, "Hell fuckin yeah!"

"Good, let's go." After we tossed the guns in his trunk, I said,

"I got'chu eleven of dem thangs in tha bag, ten for you. You owe me a buck O five. The other brick is for Black Pooh, just give it to him as a tester. Show'em you a real playa. Matter of fact, hit his line right now and let him know you wanna holla at him."

It wasn't long before we were back on Nitty's block waiting for Black Pooh to show up. When all of a sudden, I heard the faint sounds of music bumping from afar. The music kept getting louder and louder until an all-white Escalade pulled up and parked. Nitty looked at me and said,

"Dats Black Pooh. Dat mufkin Escalade sick, ain't it?"

I didn't respond to Nitty's comment, I don't ride any other man's dick. I just kept my eyes on Black Pooh.

When he stepped out of the truck, I was like, damn! No wonder the motherfucker was getting money, he was ugly as shit, what else could he do besides sell dope. Now don't get me wrong, I know I'm not the cutest motherfucker but he was the type of ugly that made a person think he was still a virgin. Straight up, if I was a female, I wouldn't give his ass NO pussy. I mean, you couldn't even really tell if he was human or not, but hey, to each her own. Right?

Black Pooh walked up with a real flamboyant swag like he was the first and last motherfucker to get money. I was instantly turned off by the chump, but hey business is business.

He stepped to Nitty and gave him some dap then looked me and Racks up and down and said,

"Nitty, wus tha business fool? Wut'chall trying to do?"

And Nitty said, "Man, tha question is, wut *you* tryin' to do?"

Black Pooh chucked a little bit and said,

"Shorty, wut tha fuck is dis? You playin games?"

"Naw, never dat. I'm just sayin', I got dat work."

"Ay Shorty, I think you barking up tha wrong tree. I don't buy no mufukin happy meals. I eat from got damned smorgasbord, you feel me? So, unless you know Escobar or some mufukin body lil nigga, I'm out." Nitty instantly got offended, but he kept his cool and said,

"See, dats wus wrong wit'chu older nigga's. Y'all to blind to the fact dat times is changin'. Pooh, I'm tryin' to keep dis money in yo pocket fam. Now you can bar-b-que or mildew. If you bar-b-que we gone eat, but if you mildew, Im'ma clean tha whole mufukin South Suburbs up wit dis shit."

Black Pooh's face twisted up as he drowned himself in his own ignorance. Nitty simply stood there waiting for Black Pooh to give him an answer. Nitty finally became impatient and said,

"Check it out fam."

Then Nitty opened his car door and reached under the passenger's side seat and pulled the kilo of coke, and said, "Here, take dis. Dis just to show you I'm on some real shit. Check it out, den hit me up."

Black Pooh grabbed the kilo and stuffed it in the waist of his jeans and said,

"Ok lil Nitty, I see you. If dis shit good, Im'ma hit'chu right up. If it's some bullshit I'm bringin it right back."

Then Black Pooh and I locked eyes for a brief second then he turned to leave.

Black Pooh walked away as humble as a motherfucker begging for change. I think it killed his spirit to even consider buying dope from an eighteen year old, but like Nitty said, times were changing. I had to say I was proud of the little homie. He stood his ground like a man, firm and direct. Those were the qualities that were going to make him rich.

Chapter 55

Watts sat in the squad room finishing some paperwork from an arrest he made about an hour ago. He kept his eye on the clock because it was almost time to punch out. He was down to the last line of his statement until the phone rang. When he picked it up he said,

"Robbins P.D., homicide and narcotics unit. How can I help you?"

"Yeah uh, can I speak with officer Watts please?"

"Watts speaking."

"Officer Watts, this is detective Callahan, Chicago P.D. Listen, I gotta a guy in the box I've been holding for about forty-eight hours. Picked him up on a firearm possession. I was ready to process him out to County until the ballistics report came back, and well, report states that bullets pulled from a Terry Miller A.K.A Hundo, matches the gun I found on ole gang bang here. I thought you might want to take a shot at clearing a case."

"No shit, huh? Boy I tell ya, these criminals get smarter everyday. What precinct are you in?"

"51st and Wentworth. Just ask for Calahan."

"Great! I'm on my way."

An hour later, Watts was standing in the hallway of the Chicago Police Department waiting for Detective Callahan. Once he came out, he escorted Watts to the door of an interview room and said,

"Perp's name is David Wallace A.K.A Toughy. He claims the gun wasn't his. Go figure right? Who's gonna claim a pistol charge? Anyway, he doesn't know about the ballistics, so you sorta have an advantage." Watts stuck a piece of mint gum in his mouth and said,

"Advantage? Well let's see, wish me luck."

Then he entered the room.

Toughy sat a small table with his hands cuffed in front of him. Watts walked right in and sat down across from him. Watts just sat there chewing his gum with a real nonchalant gaze on his face until Toughy said,

"Wut tha fuck you starin at?"

"I'm staring at a man who's about to spend the rest of his life in prison."

"For a gun?!" Yeah right, fuck you nigga!"

"And I take it this is why they call you Toughy, right? Well Toughy, I have one question and listen to me closely, because I want you to understand my position here. You ready? Where's the money?"

Ug had met with Watts a few weeks ago to give him the gun used on Moony and Chino. In that meeting, Watts asked Ug more questions about the gun used on Hundo. Including how it came up missing. So, Watts took a shot at trying to get the money back also, but Toughy stood his ground.

"Money?! I don't wut tha fuck you talkin' bout."

"So, we gone do it like this after I just put myself out there like that? Ok, Toughy. That gun you were caught with was used in a homicide. So what's about to happen is, I'm gonna take you back to the Robbins Police Department and charge you with first degree murder."

"Murda?! I aint killed no mufukin body. Fuck dat shit!"

"Well if you know somethin' I need to know, say it right now, or forever hold your peace."

"Man, I ain't saying' shit cause I don't know shit. Matter of fact, I want a mufukin lawyer."

"Cool no problem, stand up. David Wallace you're under arrest for the murder of Terry Miller."

After he mirandized Toughy, he switched cuffs and led him out to the unmarked chevy caprice he was driving. Once they were in, they took off for the Robbins Police Department, so Toughy could formally be charged.

Chapter 56

It was deep into the evening and Nitty's day had done as smooth as leather. He was able to get Black Pooh to bite and buy the ten kilos he had at 25K a piece. Two hours later, Black Pooh came back and bought fifteen more.

Nitty was laying back in his room enjoying some nice slow head from his girl, until he started to hear some knocking at his front door. He tried his best to ignore it, but it just kept making his dick go limp. So he hopped up and stormed to the door yelling,

"You niggas gone have to start hittin' my line before y'all come through dis mufuka!"

As soon he snatched the door opened, Nitty was staring at two guys with bandannas covering their faces, holding guns. All in a split second, Nitty tried to close the door, but with house shoes on his feet, he began to lose traction.

One of the robbers managed to squeeze his hand in trying to aim his gun at Nitty. That's when Nitty let go of the door and grabbed the barrel of the gun, and slammed it hard against the wall. He saw it was a revolver, so he tried to get his finger around the trigger to let off the six shots the revolver was holding.

While Nitty tussled with one robber, the other one forced his way in and smacked Nitty across the head with his gun. Nitty instantly got woozy and a little disorientated from the blow and the robbers wrestled him down to the floor.

Once Nitty used all his energy trying to fight, he stopped resisting so he could try and regain his strength. Right then, was when one of the robbers got up and closed the door. After that, they grabbed him by his ankles and dragged him into the front room and ripped his pants off then went through his pockets.

Nitty's girl heard all the commotion and opened the bedroom door, only to see the two robbers standing over Nitty with their guns pointed at his head.

As soon as she saw them, she screamed and tried to run back in the room, but the robbers kicked the bedroom door open knocking her to the floor. He ran in and grabbed her by the hair and said,

"Bitch, where tha money at?!"
She started crying and saying, "I don't know nuttin' about no money!"

The robber then took her out into the front room and put his gun to *her* head and said,
"Tell me where tha money at before I kill dis bitch!"

Nitty was on his knees with his head down. In his mind they were going to kill him and his girl regardless of what he said. So Nitty raised his head and said,
"Fuck you nigga, I aint tellin' you shit!"
The robber got furious and smacked his girl in the face with the gun and she fell to the floor. When Nitty tried to get to her, the robber smacked him in the back of the head *again* with his gun and continued to do it consecutively. After about four blows to the head, Nitty raised up and looked both of the robbers in the face. One of them yelled out,
"Time! Time! Time!" And he took off running. The other robber paced around Nitty as he contemplated shooting him. He couldn't decide what his next move was. They were expecting Nitty to just bitch up and hand it all over but when they saw the realness in Nitty's eyes, it changed everything.

Nitty could feel death lingering in the air, so he looked at his girl and whispered "I love you" to her and closed his eyes. While he waited for that fatal moment, his mind qued in on the memories of his life. He was thinking so deep, that he couldn't hear a sound, but seconds later he felt his girl's arms around him as she started kissing him all over his face. The other robber took off running out the house. Empty handed!

When Nitty stood to his feet, he hugged his girl super tight. He thought he was never going to see her again, and she thought the same. In the midst of all the crying she was doing she managed to say,

"Baby, I know who it was! His mask was comin off and I saw his face!"
Nitty was still holding her when he menacingly said, "Shhhh Shhhhh Shhhhh. It's all good lil mama. I saw his mufukin face too. Don't even trip shorty, I got dis!" And he continued to embrace her so that she would know that she was safe.

After Nitty got his girl to calm down, he sent her home and hit the streets. He was so pissed with thoughts of laying a motherfucker down, that he couldn't even smoke the blunt he had rolled up. He just lit it and hit it then sat it down in the ashtray.

As Nitty kept hitting blocks around his neighborhood, he couldn't help but to replay the incident over and over in his mind. He felt so disrepected and embarrased that his girl had to see him in such a vurnerable state. He couldn't understand how the person he saw could do that to him, but you'd be shittin him if he wasn't about to find out.
He picked up his cell phone and dialed his right hand man, Niko. When Niko anserwed the phone, Nitty spoke,
"Aye, were u at my nigga?!"
And Niko replied, "We just out ridin around, wats good?!
"Man jo, sum niggas ran in my crib on me fam, who u wit?!"
"I'm wit Corey, we on our way to yo spot right now!"

Ten minutes later Niko and Corey pulled up in front of Nitty's house. Nitty was sitting on his porch smoking the same blunt he'd put out a while ago. When they walked up to Nitty, Niko instantly started asking questions.

"Damm fam, so wat tha fuck happend?!"
Nitty hit the weed again saying, "Aye, let's step in tha crib. I dont wanna be talkin all loud out here."
Once they stepped in the house, Niko asked again.
"So, wat happend famo? You know who it wuz? Cuz we can go lay dem niggas down right now, on errythang!"

Right then at that moment Nitty snapped out and punched Niko square in the mouth, then quickly pulled his pistol out on Niko. Once Corey witnessed the punch, he made a move to step in between them, but Nitty quickly pulled his other pistol from the small of his back then aimed it at Corey and yelled,
"Wuz dat' chu wit him nigga?!"
Corey looked at Nitty confusedly and said,
"Huh?! Wit em?! Wut tha fuck you talkin bout?!"
They both turned and stared at Niko and he just stood there with the stupidest look ever. That's when Corey said,
"Niko, wat tha fuck he talkin bout?!"
When Niko didnt answer, Corey said, "Aww com'on Niko. We supposed to be boys dog. How you gone try to buss a move on the hommie fam."
Nitty jumped in saying, "Fuck dat! Who tha fuck was dat wit'chu?! Niko still stood there speechless and it only pissed Nitty off even more, so Nitty jammed his gun into the side of Niko's head and said, "Nigga you think I'm playin wit'chu? You betta start talkin before I blow yo fuckin face off!"
Nitty looked in Niko's face as a few tears slid down off his cheek bone. Nitty became relentless and started smashing Niko in his face with his gun. As Niko laid there on the floor, Corey gave him a swift kick in the stomach and Niko balled up crying saying,

"I was wit Auto, one of Black Pooh's guys! I'm sorry bro, I'm sorry. Black Pooh promised to put me on his team if I got him his money back from you. I was salty cuz you aint tell me shit bout you havin no work and I thought you was tryin to play me. For real, wasnt nobody supposed to get hurt. I promise bro, we jus wanted tha money."

Nitty wasn't trying to hear all that bullshit. However, he did want to keep Niko alive for a while, but only because there stood a method to his madness. He told Niko to stand up then looked him the eyes and said,

"You owe me mufuka! Yo ass gone pay me back by puttin in some work."

Niko nodded his head and Nitty said, "Cool, cuz weneva I hit yo line up, yo ass betta be ready to put in that work. Now get tha fuck out my house before I change my mind."

The next night Niko met up with Auto at the Burger King in Canterbury Center. As soon as Auto saw his face he said,

"Damm fool! Who tha fuck u piss off?!"

"Aw dis ain't shit. I got into it wit dis nigga ova dis broad I was fuckin wit."

"Well you need to leave dat bitch alone, real talk! So, wats tha word?" Niko went on to explain to Auto that he had another way of getting Black Pooh's money back and Auto was all ears.

As the two sat there plotting against Nitty, Nitty was in the parking lot attaching a GPS tracking device to Auto's gas tank and once he was finished, he got in his girlfriend's car and left the parking lot. When Niko noticed the car leaving, he tied up his meeting with Auto and said,

"So soon as I get tha perfect chance, you gotta come ASAP. In and out and we good."

Auto nodded in aggreement and said, "Kool, I'm wit it, jus hit my line." Then the two went their seperate ways.

Chapter 57

Sunday afternoon came around and I was bored as hell. Brittney was at work and everybody was on the grind, so I decided to cave in to Carlos' wishes and call Ms. U.S attorney.

I went to my dresser and rummaged thru the stack of business cards until I found hers. I held it to a glare and said,
"Ok Alexis Robinson, I hope u ready for a thug."
Then I dialed her number. She answered the phone with a no nonsense tone and said, "Hello, U.S.A Robinson speaking."
Her voice was so business like and full of authority I didn't quite no how to respond. It kind of caught me off guard but I said,
"Hey, how u doing? Dis is Adonis Stuffy. Remember I met'chu at dat fund raiser a few weeks ago?"
"Ummmm, oh yea! I remember you! I didnt think you were going to call."
"Yea, I been sorta busy. But betta lata then neva, right?!"
"Noooo, its betta on time to prosper."
Then an uncomfortable pause fell between us then she said, "Ok, well, what are you doing today?"
"I was gonna ask u tha same thing, but I guess my answer is wateva you wana do."
"Well there's this jazz festival going on today in Grant Park. How does that sound?"
"I dont know much bout jazz, but dat sound kool wit me."
"Great, meet at Buckingham fountain at 3pm and don't be late. I dont like waiting."
"Well it looks like we already got sumt'n in common. I'll be there around 2:30. See you in a while."
When I met up with Alexis she was even more beautiful in her casual state then in her business attire. She wore some tight fitting jeans that accentuated her curves and a cute little button up blouse. She had her hair pulled back in a long silky ponytail that

made me question her ethnicity. When she saw me tilt my head and squint my eyes she said,

"African American and Armenian. My father is black. Don't worry, I get that look alot."

I sort of looked down in embarresment and said, "My bad I didn't mean to stare, its jus dat..... Damm your gorgeous!"

"Stop it Adonis, you're gonna make me blush... Come on, the music is about to start."

Spending the day with Alexis was cool. She was surely a different type of chick but hella down to earth for a United States Attorney. We listened to jazz and even danced a little. I have to say I was enjoying myself.
After the festival, Alexis and I enjoyed a quiet Mexican meal accompined by a Mariachi band. Talk about different! I was way out of my element, but not because I was struggling with culture shock but because I was there with Alexis and not Brittney.

As I poked around at my tostada platter, I heard Alexis say, "So, whats her name?"

My hand stopped moving and I quickly raised my head up and looked Alexis in the eyes and said, "Uhhhhh…"

"It's ok Adonis. I'm not going to prosecute you." Then she gave a sexy laugh and said,

"Listen, Im a 35 year old busy lawyer. I'm not looking for any commitment. I'm more into casual dating."

"So why you not out wit a judge or some CEO type?"

And that's when ole sista girl showed me her father's true blood and said, "Because good boys aint not fun."

Right then I knew for sure I was what she was looking for. The temptation had me geeked up, but the guilt was heavy as hell. So, I called a cab and ended our date.

Once I got in the cab the driver drove off and turned a corner and that's when I recieved a text on my phone from Alexis that read:

Alexis: Can't wait 2 c u again. Nite Nite bad boy!
I was drowning in flattery, but all in an instance I was suffacating in guilt. All I wanted to do was hurry back home and spend the rest of the night with my baby Brittney. So, I called her phone to let her know I was on my way.

Chapter 58

In the early hours of Sunday morning, Nitty and Niko pulled up on a quiet residential block that they assumed Auto's house sat on. They wasn't for sure if this was Auto's home but at 3am in the morning, this is were the GPS tracking led them.

While they were still in the car they both checked their guns then hopped out and made their way to the side of the house. Nitty took a peak in the window and saw nothing, so they worked their way around the house checking every window until they came upon the kitchen. If they had to guess, they'd probably say that Auto was drunk, because he stood there at the island counter smashing hot dogs straight out of the pack. Nitty looked at Niko as he counted to 3 then Niko kicked the back door in like a wild baboon. Auto was completely taken by shock as he dropped the hot dog and scrambled for his gun, but it was too late. Niko came rushing through the door gripping a 45 by the barrel cracking Auto across the bridge of his nose with the handle of the gun. Nitty came right behind Niko stomping Auto's head into the kitchen floor until he stopped and said,
"Nigga... wat tha fuck you jus standing there for? Go check tha house and dont forget the closets!"

While Auto was disorientated, Nitty tied his hands and feet together with some fishing rod. Then he jumped in the air and pounced down on Auto's legs with force. By the time Nitty was done having a fit, Niko came back in the kitchen with Auto's girl saying,
"Lookie lookie chocolate chip cookie." She was dark skinned and clad with some pink boy shorts and matching bra. Nitty looked at her, then looked at Auto and kicked him in the stomach saying,
"Nigga, I oughta fuck yo bitch! Come here bitch! Aye, you gone suck my dick to keep dat nigga alive?!" She was crying like

a baby when she shook her head yes and Nitty said, "Get on yo knees bitch!"

And when she did, Nitty gave Niko a head nod and Niko blew her brains all over the kitchen floor. That's when Nitty said,

"Hurry up and pop his ass too so we can get tha fuck outa here!" Niko stepped over the girl's dead body and gave Auto a matching head shot then they both tore ass up out of the house and got as far away from that neighboorhood as possible.

Chapter 59

A few days had passed and Watts was now sitting in an interview room at the Cook County jail waithing to see Toughy. Watts had a smile on his face and a confident attitude. Toughy however, walked into the room looking scruffy as hell. His hair was nappy and his beard started to ball up into little fist. Watts spoke up first then Toughy returned the greeting. Watts then exploded saying,

"Got damn! What the fuck they feeding y'all? Shit soup?! Here man take a couple of these mints. If not for you then for me pleeease!"

Toughy didn't take to light at the insults, so he declined on the mints and just sat there with a mug on his face.

Watts then said, "Ok fuck it, don't speak at all. It's better on my breathing anyway. So heres where we are. We raided your house yesterday morning and found two other guns and 50 grams of powder cocaine. Here's the chance to save yourself."

Watts slid some paper and a pen toward toughy and said, "Tell me who you were with when you robbed the house in Robbins, or at least tell me who put you on to it."
Toughy took the paper and pen and began writing and when he slid it back to Watts it read: 'Suck my dick.'
Watts looked at the paper and smiled. "Suck your dick huh?"

Watts stood up and chuckled while pointing his finger at Toughy and saying, "You a wild boy Toughy. Have fun fighting off the needle muthafuka. You do know we still put niggas like you to sleep in this state, right? Don't worry, see you in about a week when the ballistics come back. I'm sure we'll have lots to talk about then."
Watts then left the room leaving Toughy to ponder over the words he had just spoken. Toughy wasn't worried about the murder charge because he knew he didn't do it and he definitely wasn't worried about any drug charges because to him that was petty. He could do that time standing up, but what bothered him was the fact

of not knowing where the other two pistols came from. So, at this point Toughy didn't know what to expect, he just held his gansta and waited for the outcome.

Chapter 60

Me, Racks, and Nassir sat on the block in the cut while I waited for Nitty to come through and load up. The security guys were well aware of who Nitty was, mainly because he was one of the few that actually came to the block to do business. So, when a car none of us recognized pulled up and parked, security rushed the car with uzi's and AK's drawn like the U.S Marines. A few more of our guys walked up unarmed and said,

"Who tha fuck is you and who tha fuck you lookin fo`?"
All I heard was a voice getting loud saying,
"Fuck you nigga! I ain't gotta answer to you. I'm..."

And before he could get the next word out, the security guys snatched him out of his car through the window and slammed him on the ground. Nassir instantly looked at me in a shocked manner saying,

"Ug, that's Skeezo bro!" I smiled at Nassir and said,
"I know, but this shit funny as hell."
Me and Racks started laughing then Nassir said,
"Com'on Ug, dat's yo peeps fam."
"Aight, aight... Aye, let'em throug! It's all good."

Then I waved Skeezo over to where we were standing. As he got closer, he kept looking back at the security men saying,

"Damn Ug! Wut tha fuck cuz?! Man I almost fucked one of them niggas up cuz."

"Yea I saw. So wusup wit'cho phone? I been hittin' you up like crazy."

"Awww man. I lost dat mufuka, but it's all good, I got another one."

"Good, so don't ever come on dis block without calling first."

Skeezo finally took the time to follow the scope of the land. Once he realized how much security was out there he said,

"Yeah yeah, I feel you. So, check it out, everythang still good?"

"Yup, everythang beautiful cuz. Wut'chu tryin to do?"

"I got 550k, do sumt'n nice for me."

"I'll do you 25 and you owe me 25k."

"Com'on cuz, dis all me, nobody else. Lookout for me one time."

"Twenty-three my number cuz, plus tha work way better dis rip, so dat's tha best it's gone get for now."

Skeezo didn't bother trying to go into any further negotiating, besides he knew I wasn't budging anyway. He just chilled out until Toni counted the money and gave Yella Boy the word. Five minutes later Nitty pulled up. He hopped out and started walking our way. Skeezo looked at Nitty in a shocked manner and said,

"Why tha fuck niggas ain't snatch him all out his shit?"
Me, Racks, and Nassir said,
"Cause he called first!"

When Nitty walked up, I instantly saw the big ass knot on the side of his head and asked,

"Shorty, wut tha fuck happened to yo shit?!"
Nitty looked over at the guys and said,
"Aye, let me holla at'chu in private big homie."
I looked to my left and said,
"Aye Skeezo, chill over there in front of the building. Yella Boy gone be down in a minute to get'chu right."
Once Skeezo walked off, Racks and Nassir still remained standing there with me. I looked back at Nitty and said, "This is as private as its gone get lil bro. Wus tha word?"

He went on to tell me about him being robbed and how Black Pooh set it all in motion. Just listening to the story irked the fuck out of me. His boy Niko was a straight bitch! There's no explanation for disloyalty and furthermore the name Black Pooh had just began to leave a bad taste in my mouth. At the same time, I can't put myself in a position to fight everybody's battles. Nitty had to learn and understand that this is what comes with the territory so I asked him,

"So how you planning on handlin the situation wit Black Pooh?"
"I don't know yet. I'm still thinking about it."
"Well take yo time shorty, and make sure it feels right. Niggas dats been around for a minute got a lot tricks up they sleeve, so be careful. Now com'on let's get down to business."

Chapter 61

As our business hours came to an end for the day I ordered some pizzas and had Nassir contact the guys to have them report to the table. Within twenty minutes everybody was on deck. I was feeling that. It's nothing like good solid structure, that's what keeps an organization in tact.

While we sat there stuffing our faces with pizza, Nassir grabbed a napkin and wiped his mouth then said.

"So wus poppin' in tha hood? Errythang errythang?" Bino G spoke up first.
"Everything good wit tha folks. My areas lookin sweet." Then he brung three fingers together and kissed them like an Italian mob boss. Gacy still had a mouth full of pizza, so he just stuck his thumb up and gave us his confirmation. Lil Stone however, seemed a little conflicted. It was like he had something on his mind, but didn't want to speak on it. I looked him in the eyes, wiped my mouth, then took a sip of juice and said.
"Lil Stone, wus on yo mind brotha? Gone and speak on it." Lil Stone sat his slice of pizza down and wiped his hands then spoke.
"Well it ain't really nuttin'. I mean, nuttin we couldn't handle anyway, but dis nigga tried to rob one of my guys a few days ago. Dude thought Mo was by his self until some of tha other Stones jumped out tha back of tha truck. As soon as tha dude turned around and looked at the Mo's, star popped his ass. But like I said, it wasn't nuttin' we couldn't handle." I nodded in approval saying.
"Good shit ... Ay y'all gotta be on point, cause niggas out tough on dat jack boy shit right now. Matter of fact, Im'ma tighten everybody up wit some Uzi's and rifles before y'all leave, aight? But on anotha note, wus on y'all agenda for tha parade dis weekend?" Gacy instantly lit up and said.

"Ooooh, I'm bout to shit on tha land, on *errythang*!" Bino G rubbed his chin and smiled. He was real cool and nonchalant when he said.

"Well I'm just keepin' it simple know wut I'm sayin'. I ain't trying to do much." Which really meant, I'm trying to do the most. Toni jumped out there excitedly saying.

"Y'all niggas ain't on shit! Im'ma show y'all what sexy really look like." While everybody sat around feeling themselves, I interrupted.

"Ay, ay, ay, check it out, Nas got some news for y'all."

Everyone in the room turned their attention towards Nassir as he leaned back in his chair smiling, looking like a Don, and making everyone die from anticipation. After a few seconds of waiting, Toni couldn't take it anymore, so she said.

"Damn Nassir, spit it out already! A bitch gone start menapause fuckin' wit'chu."

"Ok ok ok! Clear yo plans for after tha parade mufukas, cause we got Squalay and Big Bandz performin' at the center." Yella Boy got super excited saying.

"Get tha fuck outta here! How y'all pull dat off?! Oh shit, I gotta hit tha mall again and find something super fly. All deez hoes gone be like, ' I wanna fuck you Yella Boy' , and Im'ma be like, I wanna fuck y'all hoes too!." I had never seen Yella Boy that excited before. He was so quiet that I'd forget he could talk sometimes, but that's my lil' dude so I was happy I could make his day.

A couple of days later, I was laying in the bed with Brittany. I couldn't quite put a finger on what or how I was feeling, and I really couldn't decide if I liked it. But as I laid there on my side with my arm around Brittany's waist, I thought of Alexis. Now, just a couple days ago I was with Alexis, and I couldn't think of anyone else but Brittany. Weird right? I don't know, call me crazy, but I actually felt like I was cheating on Brittany with my thoughts of Alexis. I thought about gripping Alexis' long black hair and straddling her from the back. I could almost feel how wet her pussy was, then out of nowhere, Toni entered my thoughts. She was standing there with her hand on her hip saying.

"Who is this *bitch* Ug? Do you even have a rubber on? I *know* you ain't fuckin her without a rubber on?" Instantly, my body tensed up as I yanked myself out of my subconscious thoughts, and I think Brittany felt it. She shifted her arm and placed her hand over mine and asked me if everything was ok. I pulled her tighter into my embrace, kissed her on the neck and said.

"Yeah, errythang cool. Why you say dat?"
"I don't know, it just felt like your whole body got stiff."
"I thought you liked it when I got stiff." She gave me a light and playful elbow to the gut and said.
"Whateva boy, I'm serious though Adonis. You can talk to me about anything. You know that right?" This was just like Brittany, always attentive to my needs. Always open, honest and able to express her emotions. Damn, if she keeps this up, one of these days I'm going to marry this girl.

Chapter 62

Early Sunday morning came around and we were out on the block chillin'. It was parade day, so the Vice Lord sista's were back throwin' down on the grills! It was only eight o'clock in the morning, but as soon as you stepped on your porch, the aroma of bar-b-que came together from every block and filled the whole town.

I walked over to Toni's driveway where she was wiping her Impala down then smiled and said.

"So, this is wut sexy look like huh?"

Toni had her Impala painted a funky ass pink chameleon that flipped teal, turquoise and purple when the sun hit it hard. She had the windows bubble wrapped the same hot pink as the base color chameleon, and her 26" rims were the same hot pink chameleon as the car. She had a chrome billet grille with dual exhaust flow master pipes, and a three stage moonroof. Toni smiled and said.

"I ain't playing wit'em Ug, watch this." Toni stepped back and pressed a button on her tiny remote and the driver side door open straight up lambo style. When the door opened an electric running board extended from the bottom so Toni could step right in. When she sat down she said.
"Check it out Ug!" When I walked closer I saw the entire inside was all white. Toni smiled at me saying. "I named her pussy. See, pink on the outside, all white on the inside. "I just shook my head and said.
"Toni, you terrible." All of a sudden I felt the ground vibrating as Bino G pulled up on the block in a brand new Mercedes G Wagon bumping Jay-z's 'Allure'. Right behind him was Rico in a charcoal gray Porche truck and Yella Boy in a silver

Range Rover. I walked away from Toni's car and greeted the caravan by saying,

"I see y'all big boyin' it huh?" Bino G hopped out of his G Wagon and said.

"Man Ug, we bosses, and bosses do big thangs!" Right then Gacy pulled up in the biggest fuckin' truck I had ever seen in my gotdam life. When he hopped out of the truck I said.

"Gacy, wut tha fuck is dat?!" Gacy stuck his chest out and said.

"Ths right here my nigga is a Ford F-650 baby!" I started walking around the big motherfucker and checking it out. I scratched my head saying.

"I ain't never seen no shit like dis befoe." And Gacy said.

"And you never will. I had this mufuka custom made! I bought it as a commercial flat bed and I had an Excursion body put on the back. Look in that mufuka Ug! I got stripper poles, a mini bar, 40 inch flat screen, $22,000 worth of sounds, 2 sunroofs, and one convertible roof in the back. Man dis bitch is loaded!" I just stared at the monstrous motherfucker and said.

"Well got damn! So y'all just conspired on me and all went big truckin' huh?" Then Rico said.
"Naw fam never dat. We just wanted to show Squalay and Big Bandz how we do it in Robbins." All of a sudden, I heard pipes. I looked to see a car coming up the block. When the car stopped, I looked at the crew and said.
"Now that's a mufukin car!" Lil Stone had pulled up in an all black Chevy Chevelle with all red interior sittin' on Ralley Racers and letter walls. One hundred percent all american muscle! When I asked him how much he paid for it, he said.

"I got it at a antique auction for $70,000. Everything original except the interior, I re-did it."

Now that they all had their whips out on the block, Nassir and I pulled our 73' Impalas out. The only thing different we did to them was convert them to drop tops which only made our shit look even more gansta. While they checked our whips out, Nassir and I went back to the garage to pull our 4-wheelers out. All their mouths dropped when they when they saw the 17' rims spinning. We were killin'em! But as soon as they saw th 4- wheelers, Rico said.

"See Ug, we already knew about y'all lil 4-wheelers. Stay right there, don't move." They all took off through a path that led to Rico's block. Minutes later, they all came out of the alley driving golf carts that resembled their new whips. I mean, same colors and all! I just looked at Nas and smiled, then said.
"On my mamma they petty as hell bro." Nassir and I just shook our heads, then went on to prepare for the rest of the day.

Aroound one o'clock everyone who was in the parade was all lined up waiting for the festivities to begin. There was our local little league football team and their cheerleaders, marching bands, dance troops, drill teams, and a host of businesses that were apart of the community. Oh, and of course us!

It was almost time to begin, so we started to set ourselves in position. We lined the golf carts up in the front which were driven by the crew. Next was Toni's Impala and Lil Stone's Chevelle side by side driven by Candice and Lil Stone's girlfriend. In the rear of our caravan were the trucks, driven by some of the security guys from off the block. All the doors were open on Gacy's truck as a group of strippers helped accessorize it. His sounds were so loud we all just cut our shit off. Lastly, smack dead in the middle were me and Nassir's Impala's. Nassir had a couple of females in the front seats while he sat up on the rear window ledge. Racks drove my Impala with one of his new little guys riding shotgun, while I sat up on the rear window ledge.

Once the parade was ready to begin, Nassir hopped off the back of his car and started to assemble our *on foot* security. Then he walked up to Bino G's Mercedes Wagon and opened the back door. When Squalay and Big Bandz got out people went ape nuts! Squalay rode with Nassir and Big Bandz rode with me. We never promoted the show, so no one knew they were coming to town. It was a private show for my hustlers, so if you weren't on count or had a pussy between your legs, you wasn't getting in.

After the parade, we all parked our whips in the car show parking lot and moved around on the golf carts. The streets were so full of people you could hardly move. Everywhere you went was a party, and occassionally you caught a few females fighting over some bum ass dude who thought the shit was funny, but all the guys in the town knew pumpkin heads were being distributed if any hood shit popped off.

Aside from this being parade day, this was also known as the beginning of "cuff'em season". On parade day, every chic wore something that said, 'I'm going home with you tonight', and every dude tried to floss their summer savings and cuff the best looking chic they could. Sometimes you came up, and sometimes you just settled, but either way, everybody in the town was going to be fucking by the end of the night, guaranteed!

By five o'clock that evening everybody had switched their swag up for the seven o'clock show and headed over to the center. Nassir and I stayed back for a second so we could make our killer arrival. I still couldn't believe how the crew tried to stunt on me and Nassir with their golf carts, but I know they didn't think *our* night was over. Me and Nassir was about to shut the land down, so I hope motherfuckers were ready.

When we pulled up on the block that the center was on, mouths dropped and pussys instantly got wet. Me and Nassir crawled up the block in matching black on black Bentley Arnage's. We pulled up to the center and parked right in front of the door. Racks and I got out of my car and started gathering the security together. Once everything was good, Nassir, Squalay, and Big

Biandz got out of Nassir's Bentley and walked inside. That was when Lil Stone, Bino G, Rico, and Gacy whipped out their list and started letting everyone in. I just stepped back in the cut and chopped it up with the owner while making sure everything ran smoothly.

Thirty minutes later I heard a lot of commotion at the door so I excused myself to see what the problem was. Once I made it to the door I instantly whispered in Lil Stone's ear and said.

"Go over by the stage and tell Nassir to come here asap! Hurry up!"

After giving Lil Stone the message, I stood straight up and let my size speak for me as Rico and Black Pooh went back and forth with words. Black Pooh was with about seven of his guys and tipsy as hell. He was ranting on about how if it wasn't for him guys in the town would have starved years ago. He was getting totally beside himself. He got in Rico's face saying.

"Nigga, do you know who tha fuck I am?" Rico stood his ground and said.
"Nigga, do it look like I give a shit. If ya name ain't on one of these lists, yo ass ain't gettin in."

Just then Nassir appeared at the door asking what was the problem. Black Pooh spoke up first and said.

"Ay, me and my niggas tryin to get up in dis bitch. Wussup?" Nas said.
"Who count you on?"
"Count?! I ain't on no mufukin count! I'm Black Pooh mufuka, I got my own count!" Nassir looked at Black Pooh with something of a smile saying.
"Ohhhhh, so you Black Pooh? I den heard a lot of stories bout'chu but I never met'chu. I'm Nassir." And he held his hand

out for Black Pooh to shake, but Black Pooh just looked at Nassir's hand and said.

"Mufuka do it look like I came here to meet'chu nigga? Wut tha fuck I need a mufukin friend fo' when I got deez killers wit me." Nassir felt disrespected to the fullest, but he maintained his composure and said.

"You know what? You ain't welcome here. Dis a private show Snow White, so why dont'chu grab ya seven dwarfs and get tha fuck outta my town!" Before Black Pooh could get another word in edgewise, I gave him a strong blow to the right side of his eye! Racks instanly pulled his pistol and put it to Black Pooh's head then looked at his guys and said

"I wish one of you mufukas would." That was when we surrounded Black Pooh's men and diarmed them. Once we had all of their guns, I gave Racks a look that said let him up, and he did. When Black Pooh stood to his feet he looked at Nassir and said.

"So, dis how it's gone be huh? It's all good, we gone leave, *for* now." As Black Pooh and his men began to walk away, Black Pooh held his eye saying.

"You gone see me again... You mufukas should've killed me." I wanted to send a strong message to Black Pooh, so I whispered in Nassirs's ear and Nassir yelled out.

"Ay, Black Pooh! Don't bring yo ass back to Robbins, dis yo first and final warning." Then he yelled out to all the guys standing in line waiting to get in. "Ay, listen up, I gotta half mill on Black Pooh head if you ever catch him in dis town again." Then he looked back to Black Pooh and said. "You been warned mufuka." Then Black Pooh and his men were escorted to their cars and out of the town by some of our security guys.

After we got that bullshit out of the way, the show went on. There were strippers in the crowd doing their thing, picture booths in overload and shit load of weed smoke in the air, all while Squalay and Big Bandz ripped the stage up. See, this is what gettin' money is all about. It's not about who has the flyest whip or whose rocking the freshest gear. It's about creating memories to last a lifetime, and I'm damn sure my guys will never forget this night.

Once the show was over and the crowd disbursted, we hung back for awhile to let the streets clear up. All the guys had snagged them something cute and thick to take home, well everybody but Toni, and Lil Stone, they were already there with there significant others. Me, I was on my way to Brittany's house. Yeah, I could've left the show with any of those chics, but my heart told me to do the right thing.

As I looked around at the small crowd of us left, I checked out the ladies who were chosen by my guys. You know, observing their taste. When I looked to check Rico out, all I saw was the back of his head. he was in a corner laying his game down super thick. When I got closer and called his name, he turned around and I got a clear view of the girl he was mac'n down. It was Moony's girl, or should I say EX-girl. I extended my arm out to shake her hand and said.

"Hey, how ya doin, I'm Ug." As our hands connected Rico cut in saying.
"Ug dis Erica, Erica dis my man Ug." Then she smiled, saying,
"Nice to meet'chu Ug." I could tell by her smile that she didn't recognize me, so I continued to speak.
"My man Rico ain't givin you no problems is he?"
"No, as a matter of fact he being a real gentleman."
"Well in that case, Im'mma leave y'all two be." Then I walked away feeling confident that she didn't notice me as being the guy in her home the night Moony and Chino was murdered. Good thing for her, cause I didn't want to have to knock Miss Pretty noodles back.

Chapter 63

Watts sat in the interview room at the Cook County jail waiting on Toughy. He had given Toughy multiple chances to make things easy for himself, but Toughy stuck to his guns.

As soon as Toughy was brought into the room, he sat down. Watts pulled out a mini recorder out of his pocket and sat it on the table. Toughy instantly jumped defensive saying.

"Nigga I told you I ain't got shit fo you. Wut tha fuck you keep comin' down here for?" Watts chuckled and said,
"Toughy, I think you got this visit confused. I ain't come here to ask you shit!" Watts then leaned into the mini recorder and pressed the record button, then read from some papers in his hand.
"On August 23rd a David Wallace a.k.a Toughy was charged with possesion of a firearm. Due to the ballistics report of the said firearm, Mr. Wallace was rendered to a search and seizure in which two more firearms were found along with 50 grams of crack cocaine. After recieving ballistics on the two recent firearms, evidence proves that these two firearms were also used in the murders of a Brian Flynn a.k.a Moony, Marcus Green a.k.a Chino, and a Sgt. Terril Ross of the Robbins police department. Mr. Wallace will be arraingned in court tommorrow morning for the additional murders of Brian Fly and Marcus Green. He will then be arraigned in front of a Federal judge for the murder of Terril Ross, a peace officer." Watts then stood up, grabbed the recorder and headed for the door, but before he left he stopped and looked back at toughy then said. "Fuck you very much Toughy. You just don't know how much of a help you've really been. See ya when they juice the needle up." And he left out of the room. As Watts walked away he could hear Toughy scream for him to come back, but Watts' work here was done. He had no more chances for old Toughy.

Chapter 64

I took a sip of Patron as I overlooked the city from the Trump Towers. I was completely stressed the fuck out. Yella Boy and I had just started school a week ago and Brittany and I had gotten into an argument over the Bentley. I didn't appreciate her questioning me about what I chose to do with my money, and she didn't like me being so secretive when we were supposed to be open and honest with each other. To top it off, Black Pooh was making the town hot by sending his minions to our town on drive-by missions. We didn't agree with drive-by's, that was coward shit, so we started serving him up the old fashion way, good ole pussy set-ups. No man can resist some good pussy, and even if they don't fall for it they'll at least know that we were about business.

While I stood there thinking of all the bullshit, my phone rang. It was Nassir checking in on me, making sure everything was all good. While I spoke to Nassir, Maria entered the room asking if I was hungry. Nassir heard the heavy spanish accent and said.

"Who is dat?! Ay, is dat that bad ass mexican bitch dat squared up with us wit that Uzi?!" My man Nassir, ole thirst bucket. I just took a deep breath and said,
"Yeah that's her bro."
"Oh shit, Ug you gotta hook me up bro. Straight up I think I love her."
"Lover her? What, fool you don't even know her!"
"I know, but if you put me on I *will* know her, and everything else gone happen like magic!" I just shook my head and said what the hell.
"Hey Maria, you busy tonight?" Maria put her hands on her hips as if I was up to something sneaky and replied.
"No, why do you ask?"
"Well my brother want to meet'chu and-"

"Brother?! I didn't know you had a brother Señor Adonis. Yes, I would love to meet him." I turned back towards the window and whispered into the phone.

"You owe me big time mufuka. Meet me at the Trump Tower and don't dress hood." Then I hung up. I took another sip of Patron, then spoke to myself say.

"Yo turn Ug." And I dialed Alexis' number to see if she was busy.

When I got up the next morning I was seriously hung over. We met Alexis at the House Of Blues and did Tequilla shots all night. I wasn't surprised that Nassir had the ladies laughing themselves silly. However, I was impressed with the maturity of his humor. I was so used to him kickin' it with the chics in the hood, I didn't think he knew how to switch his swag up. Nevertheless, Maria enjoyed his company and they exchanged numbers in an attempt to stay in contact.

Chapter 65

Over the pass few weeks Nitty had definitely made a statement in his hood. Black Pooh had sent some of his men to Nitty's hood to strong arm the guys into shopping with him and only him, but Nitty in turn sent those men back to Black Pooh in body bags, and the guys in his area gained crazy respect for him. That pissed Black Pooh off big time because not only was he loosing men, but he'd lost a chunk of money at the same time.

****

Black Pooh sat in the living room of his six bedroom home and contemplated his next move. He felt something had to be done, if not he would loose all control and respect in the streets.

Black Pooh grabbed his cellphone and dialed a number, and when a man on the other end answered, he said.

"Ay, check it out. I need you to take care of dis nigga name Nassir, he from out there in Robbins. Mufuka in tha streets doin too much."

"Ummmm, can you call me back, I'm in a meetin-"

"Nigga I don't give a shit about no fuckin meetin. Niggas out there is fuckin shit up, and if my boat crash, yo ass sink wit me!" Then Black Pooh disconnected his call. He then placed another call. When the person on the other end of *that* call answered, all you heard was,

"Nigga, wut tha fuck you want?!!" Black Pooh then said.

"Relax Nitty, I'm callin in peace. Look, let's meet up."

"Mufuka is you serious?"

"Hey, you a boos now, right? All this come with tha territory. Real talk no bullshit, let's bump heads. Name a place and time, anywhere public and I'm there."

Nitty sat silent for a second trying to figure out Black Pooh's motive. He couldn't understand why he would go through all the trouble of starting a war if he was just going to give in so easily. Then it hit him.

"Hmph, can't hang wit youngsta, can you?" Then Black Pooh said.
"It's like you said, times is changin, right?"

The next afternoon Nitty and Black Pooh met at Sabrina's Soul Food Kitchen for their meeting. Both of the men seemed leery of each other, but neither wanted shit to pop off in public.

Black Pooh sat at the table with a plate of smothered pork chops, scallopped potatoes, candied yams, and mac n cheese. He looked over at Nitty and said.

"You ain't gone eat shorty?"
"Naw I'm good. Gone and speak yo mind."
"Stright to tha point, I like that."
"Look, cut tha shit nigga! Wus tha bidness?!"
"Aight, peep. I see you about yo shit. Times change and it's a new day, I get it. I'm 38 years old, It's time for me to step out tha game anyway. Just let me leave like a playa. Dis wut I'm proposin, I'll buy 50 of them thangs from you at a time at $25,000 a peice. I'm guaranteed to re-up wit'chu at least twice a month, just let me keep dumpin in yo area. You gettin all tha money anyway, why should it matter who brings it."
"I ain't trying to fuck wit'chu, so Wut make you think my people gone fuck wit'chu?"
"For real fam? You think them niggas fuckin wit'chu because yo name Nitty? Niggas don't give a fuck about'chu bro. They gone follow tha money, and if you ain't got it, they gone go to where they can get it." Nitty thought for a second. He wasn't feeling the move. However, jumping on this opportunity gave him a chance to step his brick game up, so he said.

"Ok check it out. You gotta buy the whole hunnid bricks up front every moth at $26,000 a pop and I'll give you a six month run."

"Six months? You can't even buy liquor yet! You way ahead of yo time younsta. Gimme a year, help me to help you get us both right."

"Six months, take it or leave it."

Black Pooh accepted Nitty's deal because he figured six months would be more than enough time to get shit back in order. He never had intentions on leaving the game, he was trying to reclaim the game and take it to the next level, or so he thought.

Chapter 66

Yella Boy and I had just made it home from school when I recieved a text from Watts. Watts never hit me up unless it was something important, so I was wondering what the urgency was.

Later that night when I met up with Watts, he was nervously checking our surroundings when he said.

"Ok, here's the deal. Toughy, the guy I wrapped up with the guns? Well he finally gave up the name of the person he did the robbery with. Joint task picked *that* guy up two nights ago and he gave up Toni's name as the person who's house they got the gun from. He also named you and Nassir as major dealers. Now, he's working with the feds as their informant, and I can't get his name because he's active."

"Active? Wut tha fuck that mean?"

"It means the only people that know who he is are the agents he's working with."

"Fuck!"

"Yup, now I got good news, sad news, and bad news. Which first?"

"Awww com'on man! Fuck it, tell me sumtn good, cause dis shit fucked up."

"Ok, the feds ain't gone fuck wit Toni. The gun she's being accused of having is the state's problem, and they don't want to invest anymore time into it. They're comfortable with what they have, so Toni is good. Sad news is, the feds are investigating Nassir and Ug. All they know is your nick name, they don't have anything on you. Bad news is, the feds have had an open investigation on Nassir for the past eight months. He's been in contact with an informant and an FBI undercover agaent. Adonis, they already have enough to indict and convict him on. My guess is they're just trying to let him hang himself.

Watts' lips kept moving, but I heard nothing. I was stuck and momentarily paralyzed from the neck down. Everything Watts just told me, had slapped me in the face like a ton of bricks. My mind drifted way off somewhere until Watts clapped his hands in my face yelling my name saying.

"Earth to Adonis!" That's when I snapped out of it saying.
"Oh! Uhhhh w...wwut did you just say?"
"I said we gotta find out who this informant is and fast."
"We?! I thought that shit was yo job?"
"I'm saying, I'll do everything I can, but two heads are better than one. So just do what you can, ok?" Then he walked away from me still looking over his shoulders as if someone was watching us. Shit, this time when I saw him do it, I started doing it myself. I took two quick looks over my shoulder then hopped in the car and got the fuck away from that area, immediately!

As soon as I hit the block, I ran into the apartment building and found Nassir in the meeting room talking on his cell phone. He could tell by the look on my face that something was up. He held the phone close to his chest and said.

"Ug, wuts wrong bro?" I looked at his phone then said.
"Who you on tha phone wit?"
"It's Maria, wusup?"
"Tell her you'a call her back?!"

As soon as Nassir sat his phone on the table, I grabbed it, slammed it into the floor, then stomped on it until it crushed into tiny pieces. When I finished, Nassir just chuckled a little and said.

"Damn bro! If you ain't want me messin' wit shorty dats all you had to say, you ain't have to stomp my mufukin phone out! Wut tha fuck my phone do to you?

Nas, tha FEDS on you!" The smile on his face faded quicker than a Thriller jacket. The only word he could manage to squeeze out of his mouth was.

"FEDS?!" I sat down with Nassir and told him everything I knew. Nassir jumped out of his seat and yelled out. "It's dat bitch ass nigga Black Pooh, I bet'chu!"

"Nas, we don't know dat for sure bro. Right now it could be anybody, so I want'chu to lean back while I look into a few things. Matter fact, Im'ma have Maria reserve a suite downtown for you. Gone and lay up for a minute, let me see wut I can see."

Once I got Nassir off the block, I got Leonard on the phone and briefly explained to him the situation with Nassir. He told me the only thing we could do right now was wait it out until Nassir was formally charged. That bit of info wasn't helpful at all, but at least Nassir had his attorney on stand-by. My next call was to Alexis. I just hope she's willing to help me, cause right now, I'll take whatever I can get.

Chapter 67

I met Alexis at her condo off Lake Shore Dr. My nerves were bad and my mind wouldn't stop racing. As soon as she let me in, I gravitated towards the mini bar I spotted in the corner of her living room. I downed a glass of vodka then poured another. Alexis stood there with her hand on her hip and asked.

"What's wrong Adonis, trouble in couple's paradise?" She caught me off guard with the question, so I replied.
"Yeah, I meam no! I mean, dat ain't wuts on my mind."

Alexis walked towards me, grabbed my hand and led me to the couch. When I sat down, she sat next to me Indian style and put her hand on my leg then said.

"Now tell me, what's on your mind?" I looked into her soft gray eyes then let it all go.
"I need you Alexis, and you tha only person dat can help me." She had a disappointing look on her face when she said.
"I see, does this involve me breaking any laws."
"I'm not sure wut it involves, but I need to find out wuts tha word on Nassir."
"Nassir?! What's going on with Nassir?"
"I got word today dat tha FEDS got a open indictment on him and I'm trying to find out everything I can about tha investigation. His full name is Nassir Randall."
"Hold on Adonis! I need a little time to think about this. What you're asking not only goes against my better judgement, but it breaks a shit load of laws in the process."

Alexis stood up, put one hand on her hip and the other across her forehead then walked around the room. She stared at me periodically in disbelief until finally making *herself* a drink. She took one strong sip then said.

"Hypothetically speaking, suppose I do this for you. What's your overall intentions after finding out what you want to know?"

"I just want to be able to let him know who to stay away from. Wuteva tha FEDS got on him, I need it to stop right there. I don't want them stackin shit else on my man."

After a few drinks and some hard thinking, Alexis finally said ok. I got so excited, I jumped up off the couch, kissed her on the cheek and headed towards the door until Alexis yelled out.

"Uh uh brotha! This doesn't work like that! This type of info is gonna cost you."

"My bad baby girl, just say tha word and you got it."

She sat in the corner of the couch, put her arm on the armrest, crossed her legs and pointed her finger at me saying,

"You can start by taking all of *that* off." I looked down at the clothes I was wearing then looked back at Alexis. She was staring at me with this devilish grin shaking her head up and down. For the first time in my life, I felt like a piece of meat, and that shit kind of turned me on!

All of a sudden, I started walking back towards Alexis with a slight seductive smile, until I got into a 'Look but don't touch' range. I lifted my shirt over my head so my muscular upper body would grab her full undivided attention, and it did! So much, that Alexis sunk in the couch, put her hand down her pants and started pleasuring herself. So, you alread know what I did. I pulled this motherfucker out slow enough for her to catch every inch by inch and said under my breath.

"Dis one fo you Nas." Once I got it out, I just stood there like a carpenter with a brand new hammer ready to build a house, then I just let it flop down over my jeans. I grabbed a hold of my jeans and boxers at the same time and shoved them off of my hips and onto the floor. As I stepped out of the jeans, Alexis began to quickly take her clothes off, and I mean her body was bangin!!

I reached out and grabbed her arm and pulled her into me. Alexis jumped up and wrapped her arms around my neck and her legs around my waist as we began to kiss like wild savages. Once I found that spot, I slowly eased into her as I watched her head lean back and her mouth opened. After a few deep strokes, her entire body started shaking like it was twenty below in the room. That's when we found our rythm, and that's when I got deep into that U.S pussy!

I threw her up against the wall and started going strong. Her body was responding like she'd never been fucked like this before, and if I did't know any better, I'd say she probably came about three times already. The wet walls of her sweet pot gripped my manhood for dear life as I slid in and out of her hot sex tunnel. She moaned my name as if she'd been practicing it for weeks! It sounded so sexy, that it only made me want her even more.

I eased her down onto the floor and onto her back as I held her legs up in a V shape. We stared at each other in the eyes as I grinded her tunnel in a circular motion. Her hips started to gyrate to my rythm as I Spread her legs wider and wider until her body started shaking again. Then Alexis turned into a wild beast!

Alexis pushed me up off of her as she scooted back and stood to her feet. We still held each other's gaze as I kneeled in front of her like a helpless sex slave. She pushed me onto my back and stood over me as she slowly eagled down on my manhood. Her feet were flat on the floor as she dug her hands into my chest and bounnced around in a figure eight motion. The girl was official and it wasn't long before I said those magic words.

"I'm bout to cum!!"

Alexis hopped off of me and started stroking my manhood with her hands, and right before I came, she put me in her mouth as I exploded like a taliban bomb! My body jerked three quick times until all my muscles went limp. Alexis looked at me and smiled then stuck her tongue out to show me that there was nothing left. That's when I flopped my head back and laid in the middle of the floor like a drunken snow angle. Damn, that pussy was grrrrrreat!

Chapter 68

A week had passed and I still wasn't able to get any info from Alexis. She told me these things take time. She was trying to get the information I needed without breaking any laws, and it could possibly take up to six weeks. All that good fuckin' I just did, and the best she could come up with was six weeks? This whole situation was becoming more and more frustrating by the minute, so I grabbed my jacket and went outside to get some fresh air.

When I stepped out on the porch, I began to look up at the telephone poles. I even mean mugged the garbage men as they picked up the trash. Everything and everybody was suspect, so I started paying close attention to every little detail so I could focus in on what I wasn't seeing.

As I scanned the block in a panoramic view, the first thing that stood out to me was my Bentley. Looking at the car made me release a miserable sigh. Not only did the car alone say to much, but it had me and Brittany all fucked up. Just looking at it made me realize how foolish I've been, so I pulled my cell out and dialed Brittany's number. When she answered she immediately went in on me.

"What do you want Adonid, cause I don't have time to be arguing wit'chu today." I jumped in super quick and said,
"Baby I'm sorry." A moment of silence came over the line, then I finished speaking. "Did you hear me? I said I'm sorry."
"Adonis, I..."
"Hol'up let me finish. You were right Brittany, about everything and I'm gettin rid of tha Bentley. I miss you baby and I don't wanna loose you."

"I miss you too Adonis, but if we're gonna make *us* work, you gone have to stop being so damn stubborn." I just smiled and said,

"Stop being stubborn huh? Ok, yeah, I can handle that." And I knew right then, Brittany and I were going to be alright.

A couple of weeks after Brittany and I made up, I could feel more bullshit coming down. I'd just recieved a call from Watts and he didn't sound like he had good news. When I met up with him, he was still in his paranoid mode, wearing a hooded sweatshirt and a ball cap pulled all the way down. I stepped out of the Grand Prix I had just bought and Watts said.

"Look, let's be quick about this. Ya boy Nassir has got more heat. This time the complaint came straight down from the mayor's office."

"Mayor?!"

"Yeah, that's what I said. I don't know who he's pissing off, but he's definitely got his self in some shit." All of a sudden Watts tensed up and looked me in the eyes and said, "How much do you really know about Nassir? I'm saying, does he know about me?"

"Naw, he don't know shit about'chu, and for real, *I* don't know shit about'chu!"

"Does he know about Carlos?"

"Fuck naw, and I don't appreciate wut'chu thinkin about my man!"

"I don't mean any disrespect Adonis, but there were a lot of guys who were stand up guys until the FEDS came into play. You'd be amazed at who comes walking through those court room doors ready to testify against you. So, what I'm telling you is, don't ever underestimate these guys out here. Your life could never be more important than theirs."

As much as I wanted to fight it, I knew Watts was right. There has never been a gangsta to ever walk this earth who wasn't betrayed, but if there was anybody I would trust with my life, it was Nassir, and no one could ever convince me of anything different.

Chapter 69

Rico and Erica had just come from the movies and decided to spend the rest of the night doing what grown folks do. Rico had tried to be respectful of the fact that she'd lost her boyfriend Moony just months ago, but he was ready to spread her legs.

After they finished smoking a little weed and having a few drinks, Rico grabbed Erica by the waist and pulled her into him. Erica could feel Rico's gun buldging out of the waistline of his jeans so she backed away from him. Rico looked at her strangely and said.

"Wuts wrong lil' mama? It's only a dick."
"Naw, dat ain't no dick nigga! Wont'chu quit playing and put dat gun up."

Rico giggled as he went to his bedroom and put the gun up. He turned the lights out as he left trying to set the mood, then he went back into the living room and grabbed Erica by the hand and led her back to his bed, where they did what grown folks do.

After Rico and Erica finished doing their thing, Rico sat up and turned the light on. This was Erica's first time in Rico's bedroom. When she sat up, she scanned the the room trying to check out his taste, until her eyes rested on the gun sitting on Rico's night stand. When he noticed her staring at the gun, Rico said,

"Wut? Dat gun ain't gone hurt'chu shorty." Erica's whole demeanor changed. She stared at the gun long and hard until a single tear fell from her eye. Rico tried calming her by saying,
"Hey hey hey, ain't nuttin gone happen to you while you wit me." He tried to console her until she snatched away from him saying,

"Where you get dat gun from?" Rico looked over towards the pistol, then looked back at Erica and confusedly said,

"I bought it, why wusup?"

"From who?"

"Whoa whoa whoa! You doin a little too much shorty. Why you so mufukin worried bout my pistol?" When she noticed him starting to get aggressive, she softned up and tried to change the subject by saying,

"It's just .... I don't know, I'm still goin through it, you know what I'm saying?"

"I feel you, it's all good, come here." And he pulled her close in a tight embrace until they both dozed off.

Once Erica heard a light snore coming from Rico, she opened her eyes, looked at Rico then quietly slid out of bed. When she stood to her feet she looked back at Rico again and put her t-shirt and panties on. She then snuck out of the room and rushed to the bathroom.

Rico woke up to the squealing of hinges as Erica was closing the bedroom door. Rico laid there for about five minutes until he became curious as to what Erica was doing. Rico's curiosity was killing him so he got up, tossed on his jeans, tucked his gun in the small of his back waist line, and put his phone in his pocket, then went to see what was taking her so long. He figured, if she went to take a piss, she should've been back minutes ago.

When Rico stepped into the hallway, he looked towards the bathroom and saw that the door was cracked. As he got closer he could here her whispering, so he tip toed up to the cracked bathroom door at the same time Erica said,

"I ain't sure if he did it, but I promise you he got his gun... Yeah I'm sure, I bought tha mothafuka! Dont'chu think I'd know wut it look like. Oh shit! I think I hear sumtn, I gotta go." Then she quickly hung the phone up and flushed the toilette.

Erica nevously reached for the sink and turned the water on and started washing her hands. Rico knocked on the door, then pushed it open. When he walked in he went straight the toilette, looked at her, then pulled the seat up. Without unbuckling his pants, he just just unzipped them and pulled his joint out and started taking a piss. Erica turned the water off and walked behind Rico as he used the bathroom. When she walked past, she looked at the gun tucked in his jeans and saw the initials" BF" engraved on the handle. Right then she knew without a doubt, that was the gun she'd given Moony for his birthday three years ago.

When Rico finished using the washroom, he stuck his head out out in the hallway to make sure Erica wasn't in listening range. When he saw that she wasn't, he dialed Ug's number and told him to hurry up and come over. When Ug asked what was going on, Rico just said,

"Ug, I think shit just got real." When Rico went back in the room, Erica was in bed with her eyes closed. Rico turned on the telelvision and waited for Ug.

Twenty minutes later, Rico's phone started to vibrate. He checked his screen to see that it was Ug. When Rico answered the phone, Ug said,

"Ay, I'm at'cho door." Rico ended the call and left the bedroom to let him in.

When Rico opened the door, Ug and Racks stepped in and started looking around, until Ug said,

"Wusup Rico, wus tha biznis?"
"Ug, dat bag you gave me awhile back when we first hooked up. The black one wit tha dope and guns in it. Where did you get that from?"
"Wut tha fuck is dis Rico? Wut tha fuck is going on?!"

"Ug, I over heard Erica on tha phone tellin a mufuka dat dis here gun belongs to Moony." Then he showed Ug the 32 automatic handgun, and said, "Bro when she first saw tha mufuka, bitch started freakin' out and cryin and shit, then she asked me where I got it from!"

"So wut'chu tell her?"

"I ain't tell her shit!"

"So, where she at now?"

"She in tha room sleep."

"So, who she call?"

"Shit I don't know, I ain't ask her all that. First thing I did was hit'chu…" Rico's face froze and his eyes gave a slow blink. Then he looked Ug in the face and said, "Ug please, please tell me you didn't kill Moony bro." Ug stood there for a moment as he looked Rico square in the eyes and said,

"You been eating right? It ain't matter then, so why should it matter now. Fuck it! It is wut it is. We here now." Rico started freaking out and patting his head until Ug asked,"Wut tha fuck you trippin foe? You act like he was your best friend or some shit!"

"Dat was Moony bro! You know, Moony?!" Ug stood there with a confused look on his face trying to figure out what the hell Rico was hinting at. Then Ug nonchalantly hunched his shoulders saying,

"Fuck him, feed'em beans. Why tha fuck should I care?" Then Rico exploded and said,
"Cause Moony was tha mayor's mufukin son bro! I thought'chu knew dat shit!" Then racks jumped in,

"So Ug, if *you* killed Moony, then you kill…" Racks held his fist to his mouth as he gave a short gasp. Then he laughed and said, "Oh snap! Ug! You gansta as hell my nigga!" Then he held his fist out for some dap, but Rico smacked his fist saying,

"Man get tha fuck outta here wit dat bullshit. Ug, dis bad news bro. If dis shit get out, we gone have all kinda heat on our ass." Ug looked at Racks and said,

"Go get tha girl!" Then he looked at Rico and said, "We gone find out who tha fuck she called."

Not even two minutes later, Racks came out of the room with Erica in his grips. When he tossed her on the couch, she nervously looked up at all three men and somehow felt she was in the presence of Moony's killers. Rico sat down next to her and tried to take the calm approach by saying.

"Look, I aint gone let them hurt'chu aight, but'chu gotta tell me who you was on tha phone wit when you was in the bathroom." Erica sat there shaking like a leaf with nothing to say. She felt stuck between a rock and a hard place.

Racks began to get impatient and swung his arm back to smack her. As he released, Ug caught his arm and said,

"Hol'up dog!" Then Ug just gave it to Erica straight up and said, "Check it out. Dis shit gone end in one or two ways shorty. If you don't tell us wut we wanna know, you ain't gone live to see tommorrow. But if you act right, I'll let'chu get out of dis town wit enough money to relocate and never have to look back. So, it's all on you. Now, who did you call?" Erica was crying and sniffling when she said,

"I called Black Pooh." Ug sat thinking, why Black Pooh? So, he asked,
"Black Pooh? Wut tha fuck you call him foe?"
"Cause Black Pooh is Moony's uncle." Rico stared at Erica and said,
"You gotta be shittin' me. You mean to tell me Black Pooh and tha mayor is brothas?"
"They half Brothas, they got the same daddy." Racks started laughing again and said,
"Like I said, dis shit gangsta!"
Rico hopped up off the couch saying,
"I gotta get high. Dis shit way too crazy!" Then he walked away to go grab the blunts he had rolled in his bedroom.

Ug finally convinced Erica to talk, now he wanted to keep her going.

"So wut'chu tell him when you called?"
"I just told him I saw Moony's gun?"
"How you know it's Moony's gun?"
"Cause I saw Moony's initials on it. I bought it for his birthday three years ago."
"And dat's all you told him?"
"I told him dat I thought Rico might've been the one who killed him, but I wasn't sure. Then I heard Rico coming, so I hung up."

After Rico hit the blunt a few times, Ug held his hand out to hit it also. When Rico looked at Ug strange, Ug said,
"It's one of dem nights big dog." Then he passed Ug the weed.
Once Ug hit the weed a few times he tried to pass it to Erica and she shook her head no. Ug held it out to her insistantly and Erica said,

"I'm straight." Racks then swelled up and yelled.
"Bitch, hit dat mufukin weed foe I knock yo ass out!"
"Erica quickly grabbed the blunt and hit it like her life depended on it, cause by the looks of things, it did."

Once they were done smoking, Ug left the room. Erica sat there high as giraffe ass wondering if she would make it past morning. Ug came back in the living room and tossed Erica her phone saying.

"Call him back. Tell him you was trippin and you thought'chu saw Moony's gun, and you betta sound convincing." Erica took the phone and began to dial Pooh's number. When she reached to put the phone to her ear, Ug quickly said,

"Put it on speaker phone so we can hear it!" Then she pressed a button and they all heard two rings, then Black Pooh answered, "Erica wusup." Erica was still buzzing when she spoke slow saying,

"Heyyyy Pooh, wut'chu on?"
"I ain't on shit! Wus tha word on my nephew!"
"Awww man, I was trippin'. I thought the initials said BF, but it said 8T. I looked at it closer when he fell asleep."
"Bitch'u high?!" Erica giggled and said,
"Hell yeah, high as fuck!"
"Man, I'm out! You on dat bullshit! Don't be hit my mufukin line wit dat tweekin' shit!" Then Black Pooh hung up.

Ug snatched the phone out of Erica's hand and checked it to make sure the call was dead. He wanted to be a man of his word, but somehow he felt like letting Erica go would eventually come back to bite him in the ass, like it already had. Racks looked at Ug and said.

"Ug let's do dis bitch and get tha fuck on." Erica darted her eyes towards Racks with a look of horror, then looked at Ug and said with a panicked voice.
"No no no. Please! You said yo was gone let me go, Please! I promise I won't say nothin!" Racks intervened,
"Shut up bitch! Ug think bro, think. You really think she just gone disappear and don't say shit? Com'on man let's do dis!" Rico pulled Ug to the side and whispered to him saying,
"Look, our real problem right now is Black Pooh. We don't know wut he thinkin right now. Maybe we can use her to get to them." At that moment, Racks' reasoning was sounding a hell of a lot better than Rico's, so Ug gave racks the green light.

Instantly, Racks pulled his pistol from his waist line and snatched Erica off of the couch by her hair like a rag doll, and slung her into the middle of the floor. Then he stood over Erica taunting her with a look of terror as she scooted back in fear. Racks just smiled at her as she squirmed around on the floor, because he knew there was no where for her to go.

As the intensity of each second started to increase, Erica's instinct and will to live, became animalistic. That's when she gave Racks two swift kicks. One in the balls and the other in the hand, knocking the gun over his head and into the wall. When the gun smacked the surface, it went off, leaving Ug to duck behind the couch, and Rico taking a bullet in the leg. When Ug saw Rico go down, he instantly looked at Erica and saw her scanning the room for the gun. Once he saw her lock her sights in, they both scurried to get their hands on it, but Erica got to it first.

When Erica grabbed the gun, she aimed it at Ug's head as she stood to her feet, frantically looking amongst them trying to watch their movement. Still recovering from the kick to the nuts, Racks attempted to move closer to Rico until Erica fired a shot in Racks' direction telling him not to move. She then took a couple steps back with the gun at Ug's head saying.

"Let me see yo hands! Put'em out in front of you where I can see'em!" Ug had just spent five years in the jooint, survival tactics were nothing new. He just took a deep breath and waited to make his move.

All of a sudden, he grabbed Erica by the ankles and yanked her legs! This caused Erica to flip flat on her head and loose control of the gun. When Ug got on his feet, he grabbed the gun and looked to see Erica knocked out cold. He then told Racks to hurry up and get Rico to the hospital. Racks was pissed off and embarrassed about what had just happened and said,

"Naw fuck dat shit bro! You take fam to tha hospital, Im'ma finish dis bitch!" Ug stood in front of Racks defiantly saying,

"Dog, I got dis. Take fam to tha hospital! Im'mma get wit'chall in a minute." Racks took one last menacing look at Erica, then did as Ug requested and took Rico to the hospital.

After Ug got rid of Erica, he sat in his car thinking. As the wheels turned in his head, he realized that Nassir just may have been right and Black Pooh could be their snitch. Watts did tell Ug a complaint about Nassir came down from the Mayor's office, and if Black Pooh and the Mayor are brothers, then that would make perfect sense. But, if Black Pooh was the FBI informant, why would he need the mayor to put his local police dogs on Nassir if he already has the government behind him? It was just all too confusing, and the only thing Ug could say was,

"Damn!" He knew right then and there that they had more than one snitch, and if he had to guess, he'd say that person was staring him right in the fucking face. He just couldn't see it!

Chapter 70

A few weeks later, October came and made its presence loud and clear. The leaves began to fall from the trees, cool winds filled the air, and the females in the town started to put on what civilized people call clothes. It wouldn't be long before the winter sets in, and before it does, I want to be able to settle all the bullshit. First thing I did was pickup my phone and call the one person who I knew wanted to see Black Pooh dead as much as me, Nitty!

Once he got to the block, I led him to the building and into the meeting room. I didn't bullshit around with him, I got straight to the point.

"So wuts tha deal wit'chu and Black Pooh?" Nitty got super cocky.
"Shit, mufuka be all on my dick, but dat nigga don't want no smoke, know wut I'm sayin?" And that was the response I was expecting. So, I took it to the next level by saying.
"I want'chu to keep dis conversation between us, wut I'm bout to tell you my own people don't even know."
"Aight big homie, I got'chu, so wus good?"
"Ya boy Black Pooh is straight up bitch made." Nitty chuckled saying,
"Tell me sumtn' I don't know." So I leaned into him and said,
"Aight check it out, Black Pooh ratted Nassir out to dem peoples. Nitty smacked his lips and said,
"Swear to fuckin God bro!"
"It's real fam. My source is all the way official. Ain't no bullshit in between."
"Ok, so wuts tha move?"
"It's all up to you. If you put in dis work, I'll put'chu in tha game right where you want to be. So wusup, you game fo some gangsta shit?"

"Man, I ain't got no problem wit dat fam. I'm sayin', wut'chu tryin to do?" I broke it down to Nitty about how I had the complete lick on Black Pooh, stash houses and all. Not only that, but I also had the 411 on where he laid his head. Nitty sat there smiling like I was handing him an ice-cold glass of kool-aid, then he rubbed his hands together and said." Ok, so where exactly is you trying to put a nigga like myself, wuts in it for Nitty?" That's when I smiled like he'd given me the kool-aid back, and told him.

"I want to bring you in to take Nassir's spot. Fam gone have to leave and do some time soon, so I want'chu to hold dat down." Then, I looked him square in the eyes and said, "Nitty, dis dat real shit, I promise. By the time Christmas come, you'll be a fucking millionaire! That's when Nitty sat straight up and said,

"Wus dat nigga address? I'm ready right now!"

After my conversation with Nitty, I sent him home and told him I'd be on touch with all the details. Now it was time to sit down with the family and come clean about what was going on, but first I had to get up with Racks and put him up on the scheme.

I made it over to Racks' block and scooped him up to go grab something to eat. I figured I could have my talk with Racks, fill my stomach, and surprise my baby with a visit all in one mission.

On our way to the restaurant we rode in silence. Racks and I had that kind of relationship. Somehow our minds always stayed on the same level. When we stopped at a red light, Racks opened up.

"Ug, we gotta get our hands on dat nigga Black Pooh bro. Not even because of dat shit wit ole girl Erica, but just on G.P. fam. Dat nigga gone be a problem fo us as long as he alive." As I drove away at the sight of the green light, I started to smile. Racks looked at me and said, "Ug, wusup? I know yo ass bro, and any time I see dat goofy ass grin, I know you up to sumtn', wus good?"

"Racks I'm already two steps ahead of you. I got tha low down on where he lay his head and both of his stash houses."

"So, you wanna rob dat nigga? Shit, I was talkin' bout murkin' that nigga!"

"I feel you, but killin' him just gone take him out tha equation. If he still got money and work left, the next mufuka can come up behind him tryin' to be the boss. Now if we hit him *and* his spots, we take him out the equation and kill his financial source. Bum mufukas ain't gone be left wit a leg to stand on. Not to mention, if we do dis right, we ought'ta be able to take out a few of his key playas at tha same time." Racks simply looked at me shaking his head.

"Ug, you ain't tha cutest mufuka, but'chu sharp as a tack my nigga, I'll give you dat. So, when we gone bag his bitch ass?"

"Hol'up, there's one more thing."

"Wusup?"

"I'm pullin' Nitty in on dis."

"Nitty? Man, Ug I mean, shorty cool and shit, but wut tha fuck we need him fo?"

"It's a test of loyalty. Plus, I need dat leverage. I need blood on his hands."

"English dog, cause I ain't followin' you bro."

"Don't worry, I'll explain everything later on tonight. Now, let's go in here and get our eat on."

When we stepped inside the Red Lobster, I scanned the joint for my baby Brittany, but I didn't see her. Instead, some skinny chic with a Prince hair doo walks up and asks if we want a table or a booth. I told her to just give us a booth, and while she escorted us to our seat, I kept looking around for Brittany until the waitress asked.

"Is you supposed to be meetin' somebody or sumtn' ?"

"Naw naw, I was just tryin' to see if my girl was workin'"

"Wus her name?"

"Her name is Brittany. Brittany Jamerson." The waitress stood there thinking long and hard with an extra confused look on her face, then finally she said,

"Naw, I don't think no Brittany work here. You sure she supposed to work at this one? I been been workin' here for almost two weeks, and I don't know no Brittany. Maybe she go by another name or sumtn. I'll ask the manager when I go in the back."

She laid down a couple of menu's and said she'll be back in five minutes to take our order. *Ten* minutes later, a heavy set black lady with some big ass titties came to our table smiling and smelling like a thousand dollars worth of cheap perfume. She stood there with her hands on her hips and said,

"Ok, which one of y'all lookin' for Brittany?" I really wasn't in the mood for all the bullshit, I just slightly raised my hand and said,
"I am."
"Alright, well Brittany got transferred to another location about three weeks ago. I just called the other location a second ago, she's at work right now. She should be off in a few hours, maybe you should give her a call." She must have recognized the anger in my face, cause she took a deep breath and said,
"I'll tell you what, since you're already here, order whatever you want, it's on the house. I'll have the waitress come out and take your order, ok? Enjoy your meal."

Ain't that about a bitch! Brittany came at me hard as hell about trust and honesty and all that other bullshit! Now here I am sitting here looking like a fucking fool! Man I ought'a…

"Ug!..." Racks snatched me out of my ranting thoughts and said,. "Relax bro, you was lookin like your head was about to whistle. Com'on, say it wit me, wooooosah." Racks thought that shit was funny. He sat there laughing himself to death, until he said, "For real tho fam. Brittany ain't goin nowhere bro. Dat girl love yo ugly ass." I lightened up a bit then said,

"Wuteva mufuka. Look, Nassir and nem gone be on tha block in a little bit, I don't wanna keep dem waitin'. Let's just eat and get tha fuck out of here."

On the way back to the block, I received a few text messages from Brittany, but I ignored them. Now wasn't the time to be dealing with my relationship problems. I had to put my emotions to the side and deal with my *real* issues. Besides, I just got clowned by Racks with that woosah shit. The last thing I wanted to do was let him catch me all in my feelings, again!

When we made it back to the block and entered the building, Toni, Yella Boy, and Rico were at the table watching television. Fifteen minutes later, Nassir walked through the door with Maria right behind him. Toni just couldn't resist being Toni. She took one look at Maria and said,

"So, wut Ug? We can bring our bitches to the meetings now? Let me know cause I can call Candice right now."

Maria took one step towards Toni and Nassir grabbed her by the arm. That's when Maria snatched her arm away from Nassir and walked straight towards Toni. She didn't walk fast or aggressive, she simply sashayed her way across the floor like a runway model, then stopped right in front of Toni and said,

"I am going to let that slide because you are Señor Adonis' friend, but I would like for you to know, that I am no one's bitch! So, whenever I am in your presence, I demand some fucking respect!" Toni hopped out of her seat and I instantly yelled out,
"Toni!... Let it go!" Toni tried to explain herself.
"But this…"

"Toni, I said let it go!" Toni just stood there staring Maria in the eyes. Maria didn't flinch or budge, she just simply tilted her head and smiled. That's when I said,

"Everybody just relax and sit down. Maria here, you can take my seat. I want all y'all to meet Maria. She probably tha closest person to my connect y'all gone ever meet. So, like she said, whenever she around I want'chall to give her tha same respect y'all give me. Do I make myself clear, Toni?" Then, Toni said,

"Hmph! Yea, whateva you say. You tha boss, boss!"

Toni was pissed off and I could tell, but I had to put her in her place. Toni had to learn that she couldn't just pop off at whoever she wants whenever she wants. What if something would have happened to Maria? What the fuck was I going to tell Rosa? What the fuck was I going to tell Carlos? Toni was just going to have to charge this one to the game and suck it up, cause the end of the day, we had millions to make.

I started the meeting by asking Yella Boy where we stood on the work, and he let me know that we were down to a hundred bricks. I then attempted to calm Toni's anger by asking her how her arm was doing, and she replied,

"I'm all good, boss!" I wasn't going to win this battle right now, so I just decided to go into the matter at hand.

"Ok y'all listen up. I know y'all den noticed that Nassir ain't been around lately, so Im'ma give it to y'all stright. We stumbled across a few FED problems and in a minute Nassir gone have to leave to do some time." Toni gasped and put her hand to her mouth, while Yella Boy just simply dropped his head. Racks and Rico's eyes got big as hell as they stared at Nassir in disbelief, and when Rico shook off the shock he said,

"So, is they comin' fo tha rest of us? I need to know! I gotta at least be able to set my kids straight fam.". The whole room just broke out in a panic. So I stood up and held my hands in the air and yelled,

"Whoa, whoa, whoa, everybody be cool!" Once I got their attention I finished, "As of right now the only person in tha mix is Nassir. Tha investigation been goin' on for about eight or nine months and they haven't been able to pick up on anything lately. So right now, tha only person standin' between us and prison is Nassir." Nassir quickly jumped in and said,

"And I ain't sayin' shit! Y'all just keep gettin' dis mufukin money and make sure I'm straight. Im'ma do dis time like a real nigga. Y'all just gotta hold me down like my real people."

As I looked around the room I noticed a single tear fall from Toni's eye. Right then at that moment she couldn't hold back. Toni jumped out of her chair, ran towards Nassir and hugged him super tight. Nassir hugged her back and said,

"It's all good Toni deez hoe ass niggas can't break me. I'm comin back." Rico then said,

"So how long you gone be gone fo fam?" I intervened saying,

"Right now, we not sure. The indictment ain't even been issued yet." Rico then said,

"So, he ain't been picked up and ain't no indictment been issued. So how you know dis shit even real?"

"Let's just say I got freinds in high places, and as of right now, Black Pooh one of tha rats." Racks shook his head and said,

"See Ug, you should'a let me push dat nigga wig back on parade day."

"Oh, don't worry, he gone get exactly wut he deserve. First, we gotta make sure we keep dis business flowin, so I'm bringing somebody else in to take Nassir's place. Now before y'all start trippin, let me explain. First and foremost, y'all my family and I need y'all. Y'all positions are important and I can't afford to lose no more of y'all. Tha next time tha heat come down, all tha attention gone be on him." Rico then asked,

"So, who you got in mind?" Then, Racks blurted out,

"Yella Boy lil homie Nitty." Then, Rico said,

"So how you know he ain't gone rat none of us out?" Then Yella Boy said,

"It ain't gone happen. My man ain't cut like dat. I guarantee it wit my life!"

I explained to them that Nitty knew exactly what this was, and that he was willing to accept all the consequences that landed on his doorstep. For the most part they all trusted my judgement. Toni sat there with a mug on her face when she said,

"So wut tha fuck we gone do about dat rat ass nigga Black Pooh?" Instantly, I said,

"We?! Ohhhh no! Not dis time shorty bang bang. Me and Racks gone handle dis one. I just want'chall to finish gettin' rid of tha work. Toni, I want'chu to count out fifty-mill and set it to tha side fo tha re-up. After dat, get wit me so I can tell you how to chop up payroll. Yella Boy, when all tha work gone, let me know asap. Cause once we clean house we gone fuck Black Pooh whole world up then sip champagne on tha beach, ya feel me?"

Everybody left the room with an understanding of where we were, and where we were headed. We were about to dismantle Black Pooh's entire ooperation and it felt hood! It felt ... gangsta!

On our way out of the building, I caught up with Toni. I didn't want what happened in the room to be left off on a bad note, so I said,

"Toni, I know you mad at me. I just want'chu to understand..."

"Understand wut Ug?! Ain't nothin' to understand, I'm straight, boss!"

"Toni, stop fuckin' playin' wit me wit all dat boss shit! You was way outta line, I had to speak on it!"

"Wuteva Ug! You embarrassed me in there! And for your information, I'm not mad, I'm fuckin hurt! I'm hurt dat'chu would even talk to me like dat! I just thought ... you know wut, never mind. I don't know wut tha fuck I was thinkin!" And Toni began to walk off. When I called out her name, she simply turned around and snapped at me saying,

"Kiss my ass Ug, ooops, I mean, boss!" This time she turned around and kept walking, so I gave Miss Attitude her space. Besides, we were never going to get anything settled with the way she was feeling, not right now.

Chapter 71

It was now time to confront more drama, so I pulled out my cell phone and called Brittany. I told her I was on my way to her apartment and to be looking out for me. It was time for me to get down to the bottom of that whole relocation shit and find out why she felt she had to hide that from me, because for real, I was definitely feeling some kind of way about the whole situation. I just couldn't wait to see what her excuse was.

When I pulled up in front of Brittany's apartment building, she was standing outside the door sipping on a wine cooler, waiting for me. Even though I was upset, I still managed to give her a hug and a kiss. After all, she was still my ole' lady. It wasn't like I was looking to break up with her or anything, I just wanted to get this off my chest.

Once we got into her apartment, she asked me if I wanted a cooler and I told her yes. When she came back from the kitchen, she handed me the cooler and I said,

"So dats wut we on now Brittany? When was you gone tell me you got switched to a different spot? What'chu hidin'? You had me sittin' in dat restaurant lookin' like a damn fool."

"Adonis, what is you talkin about? I told you a few weeks ago that I got transferred."

"So now you wanna play games Brittany?"

"Whoa, wait a minute mister! First off, I think you need to bring your tone down a few notches. Secondly, I did tell you. You called my phone two weeks ago at one in tha mornig talkin bout you missed me. Do you remember that?" I smacked my lips and said,

"I always call you late to tell you dat'chu been on my mind."

"So, you don't remember you sayin ummm and I quote Brittany let me come over so I can love you long time?" I held a confused look as I snickered and said,

"Love you long time?"

"Yeah! That's when I asked you if you were drunk, and you told me that you had just left Rico's house and y'all was smokin' some weed or wuteva. Do any of that ring a bell?"

Oh shit! That had to be the night when everything went down at Rico's crib. After I took care of Erica, I rushed to the hospital where Racks and I smoked another blunt in the parking lot. Brittany probably *did* tell me. I don't know, I was fried. Damn, well there's only one thing left for a playa like myself to do in a situation like this. So, I fixed my expression, looked Brittany in the face and said.

"Naw, don't none of dat ring a bell at all. I'm saying baby, I wanted to surprise you at your job and I ended up lookin like a fool." I gave her the saddest puppy dog look ever, and won! Brittany walked up to me and threw her arms around my waist and said,

"Awww baby, maybe I should have just told you again later. I should have figured." Then she stepped back and slapped me across the chest and said, "Yo ass don't need to be smokin no more weed. It's bad for your body." Then she grabbed a hold of my joint and said, "I need all of your body to stay workin'." And when she hugged me again, I just rolled my eyes and took a sigh of relief. Phew, glad I'm out of that jam!

As Brittany hugged me she pressed her face against my chest and said,

"Baby, can I ask you a question?" I held her tight and said, "Yeah go ahead, ask me wuteva you want."

"Ok, well who is Alexis?" Oh my God! I think I have take a shit. Did she just ask what I think she did? Com'on Ug, pull it together, think!

My mind was racing and I felt out of time. I needed to feel her out and get an idea of where all of this was coming from and exactly how much she knew, so I said,

"Alexis? Shit, I don't know, why you ask me dat?"
"Cause the other night I heard you say that name in your sleep." Ok, finally were getting somewhere. Now I was able to get my thoughts together and come up with something quick and slick, then I shot my shot.
"Baby you sure I said Alexis, and not tha Lexus? Cause ever since I got rid of tha Bentley I been having dreams of ridin' dat new Lexus I been seein on t.v." Brittany softly pulled away from me then looked me in the eyes and said,
"You know what, I'll buy that, but don't make me fuck you up Adonis."

Oh shit, two for two, a playa is on a roll! Phew, I gotta get my shit together, because this telling lies shit is not my forte. I *was* thinking about trying to get me some booty, but I think I'm going to just take my ass *home* and get some sleep before I do or say some more dumb shit. Cause this right here has been one *hell* of a day.

Chapter 72

It was a cool and rainy night, two days away from Halloween. Black Pooh showed up at the Mayors house trying to find out the status on Nassir and his crew. When the mayor answered his door, he stared at Black Pooh and shook his head, then let him in. The mayor spoke no words, he just walked over to his liquor cabinet and made himself a drink, and Black Pooh followed suite.

After Black Pooh took a seat on the sofa, the mayor downed his liquor, slammed the glass on the table, and said,

"Pooh, I want'chu to explain to me how tha fuck some young ass punks come out of nowhere and just start runnin shit!" Black Pooh wasn't intimidated by his brother by a long shot. He took a sip from his glass and nonchalantly said,

"I ain't tha mayor of Robbins nigga, you tell me. I told you dem niggas was out there fuckin shit up, but'cho ass was to busy holdin' meetin's and shit." The mayor began walking around the room and rubbing his chin, until Black Pooh said, "Look bro, all dis arguin' ain't gone solve our problem. We need to get rid of deez niggas!" The mayor pulled himself together and said,

"Look, for now just be patient. The FEDS all over them niggas. It's just a matter of time. Now what's goin on with the coke? Have you heard from Martinez?"

"Hell naw! I ain't heard from Martinez in months. I been just grabbin' little shit from dem niggas in Robbins through my little buddy in Markham."

"So, what about the heroin? Everything still good with Amer?"

"Yea we super tight on tha D. We just strugglin to stay afloat on tha coke."

"Well look, I don't want'chu gettin' caught up in that FED shit, so let the coke clientele die down, but keep your eyes and ears open for a new connect. Until then, just pump the heroin. Start buying more than usual and drop the prices a little. Try to lure in new clientele and take *that* shit to the next level. We gotta keep this money flowin' by all means. I got another election comin' up in the spring, so we need to keep all the bullshit at a minimum in Robbins. Let those motherfuckers sell all the coke they want, and let the FEDS do they job. Everything will work itself out in the end."

"And wut if it don't?"

"Hey, I can't figure out everything, can I? Just be creative. Now get the fuck out of my house, you pissing me off."

Black Pooh wasn't happy about leaving the coke alone. Even though he knew he could make more money selling the heroin, cocaine was like his first love, and just like any first love, he didn't want to let it go.

CHAPTER 73

On Halloween night me, Racks, and Nitty got together so I could give them the details on the lick. I let them know that both of Black Pooh's stash houses were a block apart. Money in one, and dope in the other. Racks rubbed his chin saying,

"So wut his security like?" I smiled and said,

"Weak as hell. Same setup on both spots. One camera on tha back door and one watchin' tha front." Nitty then asked,

"How many niggas we gotta worry about.?"

"As far as I know, two or three in each spot." Racks responded with,

"And dis nigga been gettin' money for how long?! Dis gone be like takin' candy from a baby. How much dope and money we lookin' at?"

"Dats wut I don't know. We just gotta come prepared. As a matter of fact, we gone need a extra head. Nitty wussup wit'cho man Niko?" And Nitty heatedly said,

"Niko?!... Man Ug I don't fuck wit dat nigga at all!" "Cool, bring him wit'chu."

Nitty looked at me strange and said,

"Ug, did you hear wut I just said fam? I don't think dat's gone be a good idea. Dat nigga a mufukin snake." Then I firmly told him,

"Did *you* hear wut *I* just said? Bring him *wit'chu*! Bum mufuka gotta be worth sumtn." Nitty just hunched his shoulders and said,

"Aight, it's yo call fam. I still don't think it's a good idea, but it's yo call."

I figured since this was up Niko's alley, he could be of some use. Besides, Black Pooh used Niko to try and rob Nitty, so I wanted to throw Niko right back in Black Pooh's face. Can you see the irony in that? To me it was my funny little fuck you message, and it was saying that I'm Ug, and I'm not going anywhere!

While still going through the game plan with Nitty and Racks, I got a text message from Watts saying he needed to see me asap, so I wrapped everything up and headed out.

When I met up with Watts, he was still looking over his shoulders, but this time he managed to smile as he handed me a large manila folder. I gave him a curious look and asked.

"Wuts dis?" Watts held a proud smile and excitedly said,
"Take a look! I went out with the joint surveillance taskforce a few days ago and I managed to get a shot of our informant with my cell phone. He was doing a hand to hand with some dude over east, but I got a good clear shot of him."

This was it, I was finally about to officially see who was trying to burn our operation down. As I took the photo out of the folder, Watts kept going on and on about some damn sting operation, like I was supposed to be happy I was hearing about some guy getting set up. The nerve of these motherfucking pigs. I just kept smiling and went ahead and looked at the photo, then my smile instantly faded. Watts finally stopped ranting about that fucking surveilance ride and said,

"So, do you recognize him?" Then I faintly said,
"Yeah, but I wish I didn't."

Once I left Watts, I didn't want to see or talk to anyone. I just went straight to my room, and strip down, then jumped in the shower. I let the water get as hot as I could take it and just leaned against the wall. As my mind wandered off, I thought, what the fuck part of the game is this? All I do is show love to motherfuckers! I don't cheat *or* try to get over. I just want to see all my people get it like real players. I want to see beautiful things happen in the lives of everybody I love, but it seems like no matter how hard I push, the ugly just keeps trying to present itself. Ha, my stupid ass, I'm out here living my life according to the loyalty of others. When was someone going to tell me that loyalty didn't carry any weight nowadays? When did motherfuckers stop standing on principles? Most of all, when did selling your soul and self preservation become a common interest and new way of living? Then it dawned on me, it's always been this way. That's when something my father told me when I was a kid, made all the sense in the world. He said son, tha game doesn't ever change, you just hear new names and see new faces. He said a doctor cant't be a doctor if he never studies medicine. A lawyer can't be a lawyer if he never studied law, and a motherfucking hustler will never live to tell his story if he doesn't pay attention to these streets. Any dumb ass can buy some dope and sell it, but it takes time and patience too learn the game. I just hate that I had to it learn like this!

Chapter 74

Brittany told me that I didn't need to smoke anymore weed. Obviously, she didn't understand what the fuck a brother was going through. So, after I got out of the shower, I went into my room, rolled me up some weed and cracked open a pint of Hennessy.

After I smoked a couple of blunts, I downed the rest of my drink and sat at the edge of my bed naked as the weed and liquor circulated throughout my body. Somewhere along the line I became numb from all emotions. I couldn't feel love, I couldn't feel anger, and I definitely couldn't feel any betrayal. I couldn't feel shit, and you know what? It felt good!

As I sat there breathing hard and thinking about the motherfuckers I wanted dead, the room started spinning. I tried to stand up from where I was sitting, but I blacked out. Next thing I knew, I was in my car speeding down the street. I kept looking side to side trying to recognize where I was when I heard a voice from behind me say,

"Slow down Adonis! You goin to fast!" When I turned around around and saw who it was, I said,
"Ma?! Mama wut'chu doin' here?!"
"What's the matter Adonis? You don't want to be seen with your mother?" Then, she screamed out, "Adonis look where you goin'!?" When I turned back around, I smashed into a brick wall and everything went black again.
When I came to, I was sitting in a chair holding a crying baby. I stood up confused as hell trying to figure out what the fuck was really going on. All of a sudden, Toni, came in the room shaking a baby bottle saying,

"Ug, you just gone let'cho son scream to tha top of his lungs?" All I could say was,

"Yo son?! Wut'chu mean yo son?"

"Damn ok, well *our* son if that makes you feel better." I was still holding the baby when I said,

"Toni, wut tha fuck is you talkin about? I ain't got no mufukin kids!" Toni put her hands on her hips and started rolling her neck saying,

"Ug, you betta quit playin' wit me. That's yo damn son! He look just like you!" When I actually looked at the kid, it was like staring at a cartoon character. The baby had *my* grown ass head, and an infant body. My eyes got big as hell as the baby said,

"Da-da da-da." I raised my head and looked at Toni with a blurred expression. She then stared at me and the baby with the proudest motherly smile ever. That's when I heard another voice in the room say,

"For real Adonis?! So, this is how you play me, huh?" I snapped my head towards the voice and said,

"Brittany! Baby look, it ain't wut'chu think!"

Brittany stood there with her arms folded saying,

"It ain't what I think? Adonis that baby look just like you!" Again, I looked at the kid, and all I heard was.

"Da-da da-da." When I looked back towards Toni, Alexis was standing next to her rubbing *her* stomach saying,

"What do you want to do girl? I'm a lawyer, we can hit his ass for child support and take *all of* his money!"

I started to freak out as I looked back and forth between the ladies and the baby. Brittany didn't wait for me to choose, she just grabbed me by the hand and we took off running towards the front door. When I turned around, It wasnt't Brittany's hand I was holding, It was Hector's! He grabbed me by the arm and smiled. His face was demonized as saliva dripped from his razor-sharp teeth. I kept trying to break free, but his grip was way too tight. He then whistled, and out of nowhere, more demons began to surround me. They all just stared at me like a fresh piece of meat, then they all started to grab at me. This time I began to yank my arm violently away from Hector's crucial grip, I went wild as I screamed out.

"Leave me alone! Get tha fuck off me!" I kept struggling to break free, and once I did I jumped out of my bed and stood in the middle of my bedroom floor like a WWF wrestler. I was still ass naked sweating like a Hebrew slave, and out of breath like I'd been in a real fight. I nervously looked around the room to make sure I was alone, and once I realized I was, I started to laugh. Not because the dream was funny, but because I had to find some humor in it. The nightmares weren't going to stop and I knew it, so I figured I might as well get used to it. I'd created my own after life fan club, and they just couldn't wait until I made my speacial appearance in hell!

When I woke up the next morning I was still a little fucked up, and I was still ass naked. I checked the time to see that it was 8:45 a.m. My stomach was growling and I felt like shit, so I went to the kitchen to find something to eat. As soon as I sat down to smash a bowl of Cap'n Crunch, my phone rang. It was Carlos, and when I answered the phone he said,

"Meet me at the new Sho-A-lot over here in Crestwood in an hour." Then, he hung up.

When I arrived at the Shop-A-Lot I was met by Rosa. She escorted me to the clerk's office in the warehouse where Watts and Carlos were talking. By the look on Carlos' face, I couldn't tell what he was feeling, but it didn't look good. Either way, Carlos and Watts stopped talking, then they both looked at me. Carlos didn't smile, he just stared at me saying,

"What's up Adonis? You look like shit. What's going on?"
"Awww man, it ain't nuttin I can't handle. I got everythang under control."

"Are you sure about that Adonis?"

"Yeah I'm sure. In tha next day or so all my problems gone be just anotha part of history."

"Good, cause we're there Adonis, and we can't afford any fuck ups. We have a lot of shit riding on this, and you're *the* major part of it."

"I'm good fam, I got'chu." Carlos walked up to me and put his arm around my shoulder and said,

"Come with me Adonis." Then, he looked at Watts and Rosa and said, "You two stay put, I'll be back."

Carlos took me to a room that was separated from the inventory warehouse, and when we stopped at the door he said,

"Adonis, you are the only person besides me who has access to this area of the warehouse." When he opened the door, I walked in. I looked around the room, then I looked at Carlos and he said," So, what do you think?" I don't know what kind of response he was looking for, but I said,

"Looks like you ain't gone need no coffee for awhile." Then I laughed. Carlos laughed also, but then he grabbed one of the wooden sealed crates and popped it open with a crowbar. He dusted the surface of coffee and we both stared at each other. I looked back across the room and said,

"Oh shit! All of this…"

"One hundred tons of coke Adonis, and it's all yours." If that couldn't lift my spirits I didn't know what would, but as I admired the product, Carlos leaned against the wall with one leg up and said,

"So, Adonis, this informant situation. Are you sure you have it under control?"

"I know who it is and I already got my plans in the works. Im on it. When I finish handling that, I'm takin' off for about a week. I think my people can use some down time, but as soon as I get back I'll be ready."

"So hows the money from the last load looking?"

"I got'chu all counted out. How you want to do it?"

"I have a delivery truck out back for you. Take it, load the money in it and drop it off to me in the morning here at the store. Just pull up in the dock area and park it, I'll take it from there. As soon as you come back from your vacation give me a call, I'll get you all loaded up. I don't want you to take all of it, just take five or ten tons at a time. That way yo don't have to run back and forth so frequently, ok?"

Carlos took me to the rear of the loading dock and showed me the delivery truck. I jumped in and took off, leaving him and Watts to whatever they were doing before I got there. I had a shit load of things I needed to get done before dark, because tonight I was going to make R.I.P Black Pooh's first name.

When I made it back to the block, I got with Toni and asked her if the fifty million was all boxed up and ready to go. She assured me that it was, so I told her to have Rico and a few of the security guys load it all in the truck and just leave it parked in front of the building. After that I had Yella Boy take me back to my car so I could handle the next thing on my agenda.

On the way to my car Yella Boy was silent. I know he's usually quiet, but not this quiet, so I asked him.

"Errythang all good my dude?" Yella Boy gave a casual smile.
"Yeah, I'm good bro, but'chu know you made dat girl cry, right?" I didn't have to ask who he was talking about, cause I knew it was Toni, I just didn't want to get into all that at the moment, I just said,
"Yeah, I know bro. She'll be aight tho."
"I feel you big bro, but all I'm sayin' is, just rememba who we is fam. Me, Toni and Nassir? We ain't gone ever do you dirty, and dat damn girl hold you up next to Jesus my nigga, so just know she mean well."

When I got in my car I sat there for a second thinking about what Yella Boy had just said to me, and he was absolutely right. I needed to start embracing and appreciating my *real* family a little more, so I grabbed my phone and gave Skeezo a call. As soon as I got him on the line, he said,

"Ug, wusup cuzzo?" He seemed a little down, so I asked,
"You all good cuz? You don't sound like ya self today. You usually live as hell."
"Man cuz, dis bitch I'm fuckin wit been stressin' a nigga out. Man, you know how deez project bitches get." I laughed at him a little then said,
"Fuck all dat cuz, I got just tha thing fo dat. Keep ya phone on."
"Aight bet!" Then I hung up to make my next call. When I dialed the next number, a female answered and said,
"Hey Ug, what's up?"
"I need you to do sumtn fo me, it's some real freaky hood shit"
"What'chu need, I gotcha."
"You got a pen and some paper?"
"Yea, what's good?"
"Write this number down, seven-seven-three-five-five-nine thirty-eight thirty-eight. You got it?"
"Yeah, I got it, what's up?"
"Give him a call. Hook up wit'em and give him a taste of that heaven. I really think he need it. Can you do dat?"
"Don't worry, I got'chu. When should I call him?"
"Gone and hit'em right now, and call me when you done so I can catch up wit'chu before we leave outta town tonight, aight?
"Don't even trip, I got'chu." I hung up the phone, started my engine, and got in motion to my next destination.

While I was driving, I made another call to Yella Boy. I had him get all the crew together including Nitty, so we could meet.

Two hours later after making my last stop I was back on the block ready to meet with the crew. I pulled up in front of the apartment building, parked next to the delivery truck and went in to get everything started.

When I walked in they were all watching Menace II Society and eating chicken wings. Toni got out her chair and walked over to me and said,

"Hey Ug, you hungry? Tha chicken still hot." I smiled dearly at her and said.
"Yeah T, I could use a lil' sumtn' to eat." She smiled back and replied.
"Cool, gone and sit down, I'll make you a plate. How many wings you want?"
"Uhhh, gimme six."
"Cola or rasberry tea?" I told her tea and said thanks, then I sat down.

After I smashed my food I checked my watch. It was 1:45p.m. I looked around and smiled at everybody then said,

"Aight y'all, tonight we rollin out." Gacy spoke first and asked.
"Where we goin'?"
"We goin' to Jamaica, you can bring one guest, so gone and get'chall self together and be back here ready to roll out by eleven tonight." Everything was set in motion, and so far everything was going as planned. I hope that tonight will be the end of all the bullshit and drama, because it was *our* time, no if's and's or but's.

Chapter 75

Around five o'clock, Racks and I were on the block standing next to the two U-haul vans I had a basehead rent. I *did* attempt to be a little smarter this time, and this was the best I could come up with. Ten minutes later, Nitty and Niko pulled up and joined us. It was time to make this shit happen, so I led them to my car and popped the trunk. I handed them all a nine millimeter and an Uzi, and as they held the guns, I said,

"Ay check it out." Then I held the Uzi in the air and let off a few shots, then did the same with the nine. Racks then said,
"Oh shit, you got deez mufukas silenced up! Aw dis finna be sweet!" and I replied,
"Ay, I just wanna do dis wit tha least attention possible, ya feel me? So just stick to tha plan. Now let's do dis."

When we got in the area of the stash houses, we pulled up on the block that the money house was on first. I parked the van I was driving at the end of the block, then jumped in the other van with Racks, Niko, and Nitty. We then rode over to the other stash house that kept the dope.

Once we made it over to the next block, I scanned the scene and noticed a guy sitting on the porch of the stash house smoking a cigarette. The area was illuminated by the street lights which made it easier to recognize him from the top of the block, so I told Racks to keep going and hit the alley, and once we were there I said,

"Nitty, take the wheel. Racks, Niko, come wit me." I hopped out of the van saying. "We gotta get him away from tha door so tha camera can't see us. Racks gimme a cigarette." Racks looked confused when he said.
"Huh?"

"Gimme a damn cigarette fool!" After he gave me the cigarette, I said, "Y'all stay in the dark and creep up tha side of tha house and get low. When dude get close to tha gate and away from tha door, up banga on him, aight?"

I jumped the fence to the yard next door and crept around to the far side of the house. When I got close to the front, I tucked the Uzi in the small of my back next to the 9 mil., then turned and walked across the front yard moving closer to the gate, dude stood up and moved his right hand close to his gun. I held both my hands up and showed him that All I had was a cigarette, then I said,

"My bad fam, I'm just trying to get a light." Dude stood there for a second starring at me, then he finally spoke,
"A light huh? Yea aight, you try some funny shit if you want to and Im'ma knock yo shit back." He then pulled his gun and started walking my way.

As soon as he got away from the door and got a little closer to the gate, Niko and Racks came off the side of the house with their guns up, that's when I pulled mine out too. The dude didn't even put up a fight, he just dropped his gun saying.

"You know you just fucked up, right? You know who spot dis is nigga?" What the fuck kind of question was that? I knew exactly what I was doing, and I knew *exactly* who spot this was. I just stared at him and said.
"How many in the house?" Now, I had to give him credit, cause he stuck his chest out and held his head high when he said,
"Fuck you nigga, I aint tellin' you shit!" Right then, Racks shot him in the neck and his body dropped. Niko then followed up with a few" for sure" shots to the face. As I jumped over the gate, Niko and Racks dragged his body to the side of the house where no one could see him, then Niko said,
"Wusup, we in dis bitch or wut?" I simply told him.
"Lead tha way killa."

Without saying another word, Niko twisted the door handle and crept in the spot with Racks and I right behind him. As soon as we got past the front door Niko spotted two other dudes sitting on the couch playing video games. They never stood a chance. Truth be told, Racks and I never had a chance. Niko just opened up the Uzi and ripped them boys apart! I'll tell ya, he might be a snake, but the boy was wicked! I then turned to Racks and told him,

"Search tha rest of tha house, make sure ain't nobody hidin' in no closets. We gone hit tha basement and look for tha dope." Ten minutes later, we were moving like bats outta hell trying to load all that dope in the van, but we got it done in a little less than thirty minutes. Now it was time to go get that money!

When we made it over to the next block, we switch vans and made our way up the block to the stash house. We parked across the street and just stared at the house for a second. This was going to take a little more finesse, cause no one was standing around outside to give us access, but after a few moments of silence, Racks finally said,

"So, I guess dis mean I'm up, huh?" He reached for the door handle and said, "Don't even trip Ug, I got dis."

Racks strolled across the street and headed straight for the house then knocked on the front door. A few second later, I saw the door open. I could see Racks talking to the guy through the thick steel screen door, when all of a sudden, I saw Racks begin to get a little animated. I cracked the window a little so I could hear what was being said, and all I heard was.

"Nigga I know she in there! Tamika! Bring yo ass out here bitch before I start wildin' out!" Instantly I seen the screen door open and the guy rushed out on the stoop and said,

"Ay, calm yo ass down nigga! I told you, you got tha wrong house! Ain't no fuckin' Tamika in here nigga!" Racks started walking closer to the guy saying,

"Fuck you nigga! You fuckin' my bitch?" The guy must have felt something about to happen, cause he reached for his pistol. Racks didn't even pull his pistol out, he just let off a shot from the center pocket of his hoodie, and the guy hit the ground. Me, Nitty, and Niko quickly hopped out the van with our guns aimed at the front door of the stash house. We ran across the street to where Racks stood over the guy saying. "Who else in there?!" And the guy responded by saying,

"No... body..." I wasn't about to go through another one of these epidodes, so I helped him out by simply puttung him out of his miseries with a shot to the head, then I said,

"Racks, Niko, check tha house. Nitty, help me move dis nigga.

Nitty and I quickly disposed of the guy and rushed into the house to find Racks and Niko running around looking for the money. Racks walked past me saying.

"Tha nigga wasn't lying Ug, ain't nobdy in dis mufuka." I then asked him.

"You ain't found tha money yet?

"I ain't seen shit, I can't find it." I thought back to Erica's house and how Moony and Chino had their stash spot in the floor, so I frantically said,

"Split up and start checkin' tha floors. Look for any loose boards or capert dat aint nailed down. Mufukas might be hindin' it in tha floor."

After fifteen minutes of stomping around on floors, we still didn't find the money. Frustrated, I walked into the kitchen and leaned against the counter trying to figure out where could it be until I noticed a garage out back. Instantly, I yelled out to Racks and they all came running. Once they entered the kitchen I said,

"Ay, Im'ma run out there and check dat garage, y'all keep checkin' tha house." Niko then replied,

"Fam, ain't shit in here!" I got pissed and yelled,

"Keep checkin'! We ain't leavin' dis mufuka wit'out dat bread!"

I was standing on the side of the garage staring at two heavy duty pad locks that secured the entrance. I stepped over to the window trying to get a look in, but it was covered by a sheet. It only intrigued my curiousity even more, so I centered myself with the door and gave it two hard kicks. Surprisingly the motherfucker didn't budge, so I aimed my nine at the door and said,

"Ok, plan B then." That's when I took a step back and blasted both locks. I then fired two more shots into the door handle. Once I unlatched the pad locks, the door practically opened on its own, and I peeked into the garage with my gun drawn waiting for anything to happen.

After I realized no one was in there, I hit the light and just looked around for a second. I saw nothing but an old Chevy van and a Mercedes. I was instantly drawn to the van until I saw an alarm light flashing. Immediately, I thought about the key hook I saw in the kitchen, so I ran back into the house to grab the keys to see if they worked.

As soon as the guys heard the back screen door open Nitty called out my name. He sounded excited, so I hit the hallway to see what was up, and as soon as I turned the corner Nitty was smiling from ear to ear saying,

"Ug, deez mufukas was hidin' tha shit in the attic!" I looked on the floor and saw five large duffel backs. While I stood there with a smile on my face, another bag dropped from the open space in the cieling. Racks looked down at me saying,

"Ug, his slick ass was hidin' it up here. Dis must of been his rainy day money cause it was all behind this wall they built. I noticed all the plaster around this piece of drywall then kicked it in, and what do ya know?"

"How much still up there?"

"It's about ten or so bags left." I looked at Nitty and Niko and asked,

"How tha fuck he get up there? And Niko said,

"We lifted him up."

"Niko go up there and help Racks wit dem bagas. Nitty help me lift him up." As we were helping Niko get up in the attic, I said, "Nitty, as soon as we get him up there I want'chu to go pull the van around to the alley, aight?" Nitty shook his head up and down, but my mind was still on that van in the garage, so as soon as we got him up I ran to the kitchen and grabbed the keys off the hook and shot back to the garage.

After I disarmed the alarm on the van I opened the passenger door and peeked in. I couldn't recognize what was back there, I could only tell it was bundled in plastic, so I opened the garage door and swung the rear door to the van open and got a better look. It was more dope! At that point I didn't even bother to trying to estimate it, I just closed the door then ran to the drivers side and started the engine. By that time Nitty pulled up behind me and I told him,

"Watch dat van! Im'ma go in here and start bringing dem bags out!"

Robbing folks was never my thing, but for real, I was excited! My adrenaline was pumping through the roof, and I swear my dick was getting hard. Had we found anymore dope or money, I just might have bust a nut!

Just as I was about to walk out of the garage, I heard a gunshot. Nitty hopped out of the van and I quickly said,

"Stay there! Keep yo eyes open!" Then I pulled the Uzi out and started moving towards the house. Right before I reached the back door a dude came running up the side of the house with his gun drawn, that's until he saw me and stopped. At that moment, we were both aiming at each other, but neither of us made a move or a sound. Then all of a sudden he said,

"So wut it gone be?" What? This fool had me fucked up for real. I just cocked a smile and said,

"Tell tha rest of dem mufukas in hell to stay tha fuck out my dreams!" Then I quickly dropped down low and let that Uzi rip. His arms opened up, and his body shook like he had the holy ghost, then his body simply fell to the ground. Instantly I made my way to the back door, but Racks and Niko were already running out of the back door with bags in their hand. Racks brushed pass me saying,

"Ug, all the bags in the hallway! We gotta hurry up my nigga!" Then him and Niko kept on moving towards the U-Haul van in the alley.

Once we got all the money I told Nitty to trail me over the other U-Haul van while i jumped in the van that was in garage. Once we made over to the other U-Haul Racks hopped out and got behind the wheel. We didn't speed off and we didn't panic, we just casually left the area like a family moving to a new neighborhood. We just happened to be a family with a lot of dope and money!

Chapter 76

It was about 7:45 pm when we got back to the block. As soon as we pulled up into the driveway of the apartment building, we all hopped out and and I stormed up to Racks yelling,

"Wut tha fuck happened back at dat house?!" Racks spoke up first saying,
"Man Ug, I was about to drop a bag of money from the ceiling, but when I looked down dude was standin there wit his gun pointed at me! Then dat mufuka bust a shot at me!"
"Wut happened afta dat?"
"I threw tha bag of money down in his face and he fell backwards, but as soon as he moved the bag out tha way, I hit'em. That's when we hurried up and tossed tha rest of the bags down and start movin'. I ain't wanna chance no more of dem niggas poppin' up." I gave Racks some dap and said,
"Good shit my dude, dat was good thinkin, dats why I fucks wit'chu." Yella Boy and Toni then came walking out of the building. Yella Boy took one look at the Chevy van and asked,
"Who peice of shit is dat?" I laughed and replied,
"It ain't who's it is, It's who sponsored it!" I opened the back door of the Chevy van up and let the light off the building shine in. I looked back at Toni and Yella Boy and said, "Compliments of Black Pooh lady and gentlemen." Toni walked up, smiled and rubbed the side of the huge plastic bundle and said,
"Ooooh pretty!" Then Racks said,
"Dat ain't all either." Then Racks and Nitty opened the rear doors of the U-Haul vans. Yella Boy then said,
"Ok, I see y'all wasn't bullshittin'." I then said with a little cockiness.
"You know how tha fuck we do, now y'all mufukas help me get deez bags." Once the U-Haul's were clear of money, I said,
"Toni, count dat bread. The rest of y'all count dat work and box it up. When y'all finish, load it back in tha vans. Niko, grab

dat gas can and come wit me." Niko instantly got nervous, I could tell and as soon as I started the van, Niko immediately said,

"Ay, if you gone kill me, I rather you do it right here." I chuckled saying,

"Relax killa, think happy thoughts."

"Well at least tell me where we goin'." Then I smiled and said,

"Relax, and just think happy thoughts." Twenty minutes later when we reached our destination in Harvey, Niko blurted out,

"Dis Black Pooh crib!"

"So, you been here before?"

"Yea, we met here one time."

"When, when y'all was plottin' on robbin' Nitty?"

"Man I..."

"Save dat shit! Right here and right now is yo only shot. If you can make it back to dis van wit him dead and you alive, me and you gone be on a whole notha level."

"And wut about Nitty? Fam ain't gone let dat stick-up shit go."

"Hey, you let me worry bout Nitty, I just want'chu to go in there and handle yo biznis!" As Niko turned to get out of the van I said, "Nicko! Remember, me and you, a whole notha level!" Then Niko got out, and started moving toward Black Pooh's house.

As Niko moved closer, Black opened his front door and Niko immediately took cover in front of one of the cars that sat in front of his house. Black Pooh closed his door, locked it, and began to walk toward his truck that was parked in his driveway. Niko kept sneaking peeks until he finally jumped out, and started bussin' shots. I couldn't hear the shots being fired, but I saw Black pooh take cover, Niko then tried to move up to the next car that sat in front of Black Pooh's house so he could get a better view of the spot Black Pooh was in, but as soon as Niko made his move, Black pooh let off four shots that echoed through the night like a world war cannon. When Niko peeked his head up again, Black Pooh let off two more loud ass shots, I looked at Niko ducked behind the car, and I could tell he was looking at me too. That's when Niko pointed at his head, then pointed at himself, then pointed at me. I knew what he was saying. He was saying remember, me and you. Then he took another peek, and saw Black pooh making a move for his truck. This time he jumped up, and started furiously letting go. I focused all my attention on Black pooh as his body jerked twice and his head snapped back. I was so pumped about seeing his body hit the ground that I wasn't even paying attention to the police sirens that kept getting louder by the second. Nitty didn't give a fuck, he was going in for the" for sure" shot until I yelled out and said,

"Ay! Fuck all dat, we outta here!" Niko stopped, and looked back toward me then again in Black Pooh's direction. The sirens *were* getting closer, so I yelled out again, "Lets go!! Com'on!!" Then Niko ran back to the van and hoped in, then we got the fuck off that block *asap*!

A few minutes later we made it to the other side of Harvey where I spotted an old Buick Regal. I pulled up next to it and asked,

"Can you peel it?" Niko then replied,

"Com'on Ug, dis what I do!" Then he took off his hoodie, wrapped it around his fist, then got out. I thought it was going to take him a second to get in, but he just ran up on the car and power punched the drivers side window and all the glass shattered. Not even a minute later Niko leaned out of the window and said, "Go ahead, lead the way!"

We drove two more blocks where I parked the van, doused it in gasoline, and set it on fire. I then hopped in the steamer with Niko, gave him some dap, and said, "A whole notha level my dude, a whole notha level." Then I leaned back in my seat, and took a deep breath, cause now I could finally say, good riddens to Black pooh. Mission accomplished!

A day passed, and I was now sitting under an umbrella on a Jamaican beach enjoying the view. The sun was beginning to set, the sounds of the ocean were calming, and I was witnessing one of the most beautiful skies I'd ever seen in my life. I guess this could be considered fruits of my labor, and boy do I love this fruit.

As the sun was going down, I couldn't stop wishing that Brittany was here with me, she would love this. Instead, I was stuck here with no companion.

While I was sitting there thinking about Brittany, Nassir, Maria and Erica walked up. Yes *Erica,* you heard me right when I said I got rid of her, but I never said I killed her!

That night after Racks took Rico to the hospital, I put her up in a hotel suite next to Nassir. Trust me, I was going to toss her ass in a river somewhere, but Erica had a way with words. In fact, the whole lick on Black pooh was all Erica's idea, and when I asked her why she was so forthcoming with the info, she said,

"My love was for Moony. Me and Black Pooh ain't never got along, so fuck him. If it's going to increase my chances of living, his black ass can die, straight up!". And from that moment on we started plotting and scheming.

As the three of them sat on the beach with me watching the sunset, Erica let out a breath saying,

"This sky is amazing, look at it." Maria jumped up and grabbed Nassir by the arm and said, "Come on sexy man let's take a romantic walk on the beach." Nassir replied,
"Maria, you know I ain't with dat soft shit." Maria took a step, and pressed her body against Nassir's frame then whispered something in his ear, all of a sudden, Nassir jumped, and said,
"Well y'all, romance it is, we out!" After they left, Erica and I sat in silence until the sun disappeared, then she said,
"So, I take it everything went good?" I smiled saying,
"Yyyyup"

"What y'all come off wit?" This time I giggled a little as I thought about what she'd had just asked me, then I told her,

"550 bricks of coke, 1,000 kilo's of heroine, and twenty million in cash, but don't trip Im'ma break you off wit some decent cash when we touch back down. I just don't know what what I'm gone do with all that fuckin heroine. We don't even fuck with dat shit." Erica paused, then said,

"Give it to me." This time I cracked up laughing. That was until I saw the look on Erica's face. I brung my laughter back to a smile, and said,

"Damn you dead serious ain't chu?"

"Hell yea! Don't think that just because Im'ma female I can't get down. If it wasn't for me, Moony and Pooh wouldn't even been fuckin wit tha heroine in the first place. I was the one who turned them on to my cousins out West, *and* over East. They been pumping blow spot for years." While I took in everything Erica just said, Niko and Racks walked up. Racks took one look at Erica and said,

"I see you out here slumming." Erica instantly got offended, and said,

"Yo bum ass! Fuck you nigga"

Racks, and Erica was still beefing from that night at Rico's spot. Racks didn't like her, because she embarrassed him in front of me, and she didn't like him, because he wanted to kill her that night. Niko however was just enjoying the show, and after listening to all the bickering, I finally yelled out,

"Would y'all *please* shut tha *fuck* up. Damn! Y'all two been bitchin at each other ever since we left the fuckin airport. Let that shit shit go! Matter of fact, Erica run back in the beach house, and get Nitty so I can holla at chall." Minutes later, I had all four of them in my presence, so I got straight to the point, and spoke my mind, saying. "If I was goin by tha opinions of others, wouldn't none of y'all be here, so I want'chall to start appreciatin' tha chance I done gave y'all. Nitty, Niko ... Erica, Racks, whateva tha fuck y'all feelin towards each other, charge dat shit to tha game, and come together like family. Y'all think this shit just gone be sweet cause we gettin good money? Fuck naw! If this gone be wut'chall on let me know right mufuckin now!" The four of them sat there looking back and forth at each other, but no one said a word, so I continued. "Good now Nitty, I'm given you 100 bricks from tha lick, Racks, Niko, I'm givin y'all 225 bricks a piece. Erica since you laid tha lick down, Im'ma give you wut'chu want, but we gone break bread 60/40 yo way. All tha money stay wit me, everybody good? Good! Nitty walk wit me."

I pulled Nitty away as we walked back towards the beach house, and said,

"Don't trip over dat 100 bricks dog, trust me. I told you that you'll be a millionaire before Christmas, dat 100 bricks just got' chu there, so hold on, we just getting started." Then we walked in the beach house, and joined the rest of the crew.

****

As the dark skies filled the night, the crew left the resort in search of some fun, and stumbled upon a hot night club in Kingston. As soon a they entered, the natives already pegged them as tourist, so the manager sought out the one in the group who had the most authoritive presence, and it was Ug. The manager and one of his waitresses made their way through the club, and approached Ug with a thick Jamaican accent saying.

"Wuta do Boi?" Ug looked back at the crew not understanding what he'd just said, so the waitress spoke in a light Jamaican accent, saying,
"He asked how you doin." Ug replied.
"Oh, my bad, we all good. Can we get a VIP room or sumtin?" The manager spoke to the waitress then looked back at Ug and the crew and the crew and said,

"Welcome to Kings-taan! Anjoy!" The waitress then led Ug, and the crew to a large table in the V.I.P section of the club, and began to take their orders. When she finally got around to Yella Boy, she looked up from her writing tab and froze in awe as if Yella Boy were someone famous. She moved closer to him with an inviting smile, and asked,

"Wuta want boi?" She watched yella Boy look down at her dark round titties, and said "Ain't nuttin down ner ta drink boi." Yella Boy smiled at her breast, and said,

"All of a sudden I got a taste for some coconut juice." The waitress blushed with a flirty smile, and said, "I got just ta ting for ya. I'll be back witcha orders." Gacy stopped her before she left and asked,

"Where dat weed at? Everybody in dis mufuka blowin, shit I wanna smoke sumtin too!" The waitress then replied,

"No worries eh, every ting irie." Nitty then said, "Wut tha fuck she just say?" And Gacy replied,

"I don't know, and I don't give a fuck. I just hope she come back with dat weed." Yella Boy watched her as she walked away. He was mesmerized by her natural beauty, and turned on by her thick thighs and fat ass. He wanted her, and he wanted her bad. Yella Boy's only problem was that he couldn't hide it. Nassir tapped him on his shoulder and said,

"Oooooh wee! You know you need to go wash your mind out wit some soap! Shawty gone need a cigarette afer wut'chu was just thinkin!" All Yella Boy could say was,

"Man Nas, dats wifey right there! On errthang!"

A little while later, most of the crew hit the dance floor while the others simply migrated throughout the club checking out the scenery. Yella Boy however sat at the table watching the waitress make her rounds. When she looked in Yella Boy's direction, they both locked eye's until she looked away to tend to a customer. The situation was mind blowing for Yella Boy. This had been the first time he'd ever felt this way about a female, especially when he didn't even know her name. As he continued to watch her he grabbed his drink, tilted his head, and downed the whole glass, and when he leveled his head, the waitress was standing there smiling at him. She stood there holding a tray saying,

"Why no dancin?" Yella Boy shrugged his shoulders, and said, "I don't know, maybe I'm just having more fun lookin at'chu." Then she asked,
"Wuts ya name?"
"Yella Boy."
"Yella Boi eh? I like tat. It fit'chu puuurfect." then she held her hand out and said." Hi I'm Nala." After their formal greeting Nala said." Wuta doin afta da club."
"Whateva you want."
"Good, eer's my numba, let's hook up." She leaned on the table, and wrote her name and number on a napkin, then moved in and gave Yella Boy a soft kiss on the lips, she stood back up with a seductive grin, and said." I'll be waitin." Then she took off into the crowd. After the club, they all made their way back to the beach house where they sat around a bond Fire unwinding. Toni was enjoying Candice's company, Nassir was enjoying Maria's Company, and Lil Stone, and Nitty were enjoying their girls company. Ug, Bino G, Gacy, Racks, Niko, Rico, and Erica simply just kept the party going while Yella Boy, and Nala took a walk along the shore. Rico looked around at the couples then looked at Erica. He hadn't spoken to her since that night, and felt that maybe now would be a good time, so he approached Erica saying,
"Erica let me holla at'chu for a minute." Erica was extremely hesitant at first, but decided to hear him out. When she stood up everybody started acting like third graders with all the ooh's and kissey sounds. Erica found their silliness amusing, but she smacked her lips, and said,
"Whateva! Y'all need to grow up." Then she gave Ug a playful push, and walked off with Rico. Once they were out of listening range, Rico said,

"First off Erica, I want to apologize fo what happened at my crib dat night." Erica instantly tossed her hand in Rico's face to stop him from talking, and said.

"So, is that wut'chu was gone tell my family after Racks put a mufukin bullet in my head?" Rico looked away, and became absolutely speechless. Erica then said, "Yeah dats right, gone and turn yo head. Dats tha same shit you did dat night when they was talkin about killing my ass, but for real Rico, I ain't even mad at'chu, we can be friends, we still cool, but if you tryin to make this anymore than wut it is, you can let *that* go!"

"Com'on Erica, why you trippin'? I'm trying to make dis right. I'm still feelin you."

"Well I *ain't* feelin you! And to be honest, I got more respect for Racks, at least he know how to stand on something. All you had to do was a least try to stand up for a bitch Rico. Now it is what it is." Rico respectfully listen to Erica's words in spite of the fact that he *did* try to convince Ug not to kill her. Buy after hearing her vent, he just decided to let it be. Rico knew Erica was completely scarred, and there was absolutely nothing he could do with damaged goods, so he put his hand on Erica's shoulder, and softly said,

"Relax shawty, I feel you. I didn't mean to get'chu all upset and errythang. It's just, you know we on the islands and shit, smokin exotic weed, getting drunk and all. Lookin at'chu made me feel some type of way."

"Look Rico, we had our fun, and it was nice while it lasted, but I just wanna put dat chapter of my life behind me, you know?"

"It's all good lil mama." Then he took a step back with his arms opened, and said, "Can a nigga at least get a hug out'cho mean ass?" Erica giggled, then walked into his embrace. Once they let each other go, Rico looked into her eyes, and held her chin as he said, "Erica you a bad bitch, don't you ever forget dat. You one of us now, so anytime one of dem sucka ass niggas out there try to take advantage of you or do you dirty, come holla at'cha boy, you hear me?" Erica shook her head up and down then Rico said. "Dats what I'm talkin bout. Welcome to the family." Then he put is arm around her shoulder, and they walked back to the bond fire to join the rest of the crew.

Chapter 77

The next afternoon everyone was out playing in the warm Jamaican sun. While some swam in the crystal clear water, and others floated through the water on jet ski's, Ug sat on the beach building a sand castle. He was creating his masterpiece until Nassir, Maria, Toni, and Candice walked over and watched as Ug molded the sand. Nassir snickered, and Maria gave him a playful elbow in the ribs. Then Ug said,

"Wut tha fuck so funny Nas."
"Nuttin I just didn't know you had such architectural skills." Then they *all* began to snicker, except for Ug. He look down at his pitiful work of art, then kicked his castle busting sand everywhere. Toni instantly jumped to Ug's defense saying,

"See wut you did Nas? Com'on Ug, me and Candice gone help you build a new castle." Then Candice stuck her tongue out at Nassir, and said,

"Scram bum." Nassir just laughed then held his elbow out as Maria latched on, then he looked at Ug, Toni and Candice and said,

"Dats ok, I ain't wanna play wit'chall lames no way! Maria tilt yo head back."
"Like this?"
"A little more. Yup like dat. Now lets roll." Nassir then tilted *his* head back, and the both of them walked away looking like Beverly Hill's snobs. Candice laughed when she said,

"Silly and *sillier*! I don't know which is which between them two. They are definitely made for each other." As they sat in the sand remolding the castle. Toni kept sneaking peeks at Ug's chiseled body, and every now and then she would grab Candice's titty to get her feels off. Halfway into remolding the castle Toni said,

"Candice, wont'chu run in tha beach house, and grab us sumtin cold to drink," Since Candice was thirsty, she thought that was a great idea, so she took off, and as soon as she was gone, Toni said,

"Ug I understand about Nitty, but wussup wit tha otha two?"

"Com'on Toni you ain't gotta beat around the bush wit me. Say wut'chu feel."

"You know Im'ma 'ride to tha otha side of the moon wit'chu, but I think some of tha guys feel a little threatened."

"Fo what?!" Toni leaned back on her knees and said,

"Ok, this all started out wit *you*, me, Yella boy, and Nassir, right? Then came Bino, Gacy, Lil stone, and Rico. That I understand too, but then out of nowhere you bring in Racks, Nitty, Erica, and Chico."

"Niko!"

"Chico Niko, wut's tha difference? Point is you need to holla at the guys and let dem know they spot still all good, you know wut I'm sayin'?"

"I feel ya T, good lookin out."

"It's all good Ug. I told you, I got'cha back."

Chapter 78

On the fifth day of our vacation, I woke up to the smell of maple bacon. I made my way to the kitchen to find the ladies preparing breakfast. Since the food wasn't ready I grabbed the remote, and turned to the news channel. Candice got upset cause they were watching some bullshit talk show about butt lifts and shit. Oh well, I know they didn't think I was going to sit there and watch that crap, so I paid them no mind and turned to CNN. As the news reports kept flashing, I couldn't help but notice that we were living in a fucked up world. Every report that came up was negative. That is until the report about the war in Mexico came up. This had to be something good for *somebody*, cause the citizens of Juarez were celebrating in the streets instead of laying in the streets dead. I just wondered how the ending of the war would affect business back home, or if it would affect our business at all.

By the time the news looped back around breakfast was done. I changed the channel back and tossed the remote on the table and said,

"Here, yall can have y'all butt lift channel back, I'm goin out on tha deck to eat like a real boss. Erica, wake Bino, Gacy and Lil Stone up. Tell them to meet me on the patio for breakfast."

While I sat at the table eating my food and watching the waves in the ocean, Bino, Gacy, and Lil Stone came out with their plates, and sat down. Toni was right behind them with a bowl of exotic fruit, and Maria was in tow with a couple carafe's of orange juice. After Maria placed the orange juice down on the table she said.
"Now you look like a *real* boss Señor Adonis. Would you like anything else?"
"Uhhh, Naw we good fa na baby girl, good lookin'." Then Toni said,

"Well then gentlemen, enjoy your breakfast." Then Maria, and Toni walked backed into the kitchen while me, Bino, and Lil Stone ate our breakfast. Gacy didn't touch his food yet, instead he fired up a blunt, and said,

"Shit, I gotta get high before *I* eat." Bino then replied,

"Fuck dat, pass dat shit! Im'ma get high *while* I eat." Right then, Lil stone took a blunt from behind his ear, and lit it. He hit it a couple of times, then he passed it to me. I thought about the last time I got high, and I really didn't want to take it, but before I knew it, I had the blunt in my hand taking deep long pulls.

As we sat there getting blowed, and eating breakfast, I decided to go ahead and get down to business, so I hit the blunt once again then said,

"Shit changing y'all." And Gacy said,

"No shit. Wussup wit da add on's. I thought it was gone be just tha eight of us at the table?" And I replied,

"And it will be just the eight of us at the table, only Nassir won't be there wit us." Lil stone immediately said, "Why, wussup with Nassir?" All of a sudden, I got lost in my thoughts until Bino G called out my name.

"Ug!" I looked around trying to remember what the fuck I was talking about, then I said,

"Uhhhh damn wut was I saying'?" Then Gacy said,

"You was about to tell us why Nassir ain't gone be at tha table wit us."

"Oh yeah!" Then out of nowhere, I just started cracking up. Bino wipe his face in a frustrated manner, and said,

"Dis mufucka high as hell!" I took one look at Bino, and said,

"Bino, did I ever tell you dat'chu look like… sugar bear?" Lil Stone, and Gacy started cracking up laughing until Bino said,

"Com'on man for real, lets get serious." I pulled myself together, straighten my face, then said,

"My bad, my bad, you right. Look, dis my serious face right here." I looked at the guys with an expression that said playtime was over... then I exploded with laughter again, saying,

"Where the fuck y'all get that shit from! I can't stop laughing'!" I leaned back in my seat, and held my stomach as if my guts were going to spill out. I didn't even know what the hell was so funny, and before I knew it I was the deck rocking back and forth, tickled with laughter. In the middle of all the giggles, I managed to get up off the deck right around the time Nassir stepped out on the patio. He took one look at me, and said,

"Fuck y'all do to my man Ug?" Lil Stone blurted out,

"He only hit tha weed a few times, and tha nigga ain't stopped laughing since." I got up from off the deck and walked up to Nassir still laughing. I leaned on his shoulder, and held my stomach, then said,

"Nas, don't Bino look like Sugar Bear?" Nassir snapped his head back with a look of confusion on his face, and said,

"Sugar bear?!" He looked at the guys then he looked at me. He looked at the guys again, then back to me. Finally, he looked at the guys one last time, then reached his arm out and said, "Yo, pass that shit! Bullshit ain't about nuttin'! I'm tryna get like dis nigga *right* here!" Then Nassir grabbed one of the blunts, and sat down at the table to eat. When I finally got my shit together, I explained to them the situation with Nassir, I also let them know that Nitty would be taking Nassir's place. When I saw the looks on their faces, I said,

"If y'all got sumtin on your chest, speak on it." Lil Stone spoke first saying. "So, who takin my spot?"

"Nobody" Then he said,

"Oh, well shit I'm good. I ain't got no problems wit it as long a I'm still eatin, ya feel me?" When I looked at Bino G he simply tossed his hands up saying,

"Hey, you ain't steered me wrong yet so, I ain't got no beef wit it." But when I looked at Gacy, I could tell that he was really the one with the issue, so I said,

"Gacy wus tha word, you gotta problem wit dis?" Gacy didn't hold his toungue, he came straight out and said,

"Man, fuck dat shit! We out here grindin' and putting in work! How anotha mufucka dat ain't even from Robbins gone come along and go straight to tha top?! Dats some bullshit! I ain't feelin it! I feel cheated!" At that moment, there was only one question that was on my mind. All I thought was, who the fuck did he think he was talking to?! But after I took a quick second to calm down, I took a deep breath, and said,

"So, you think you deserve dat spot Gacy?"

"I ain't sayin it should be me, but it could've been anybody dat been at the table already!"

"Ok, well since you speakin for *anybody*, is you or *anybody* willin to take a hit for 20 or more years in a fed joint? Huh? Cause Nitty is! Look, I made dat decision to protect dis dynasty, and I want' chall to start making tha same kind of decisions in yo area. When shit start hittin tha fan, I want tha table to be protected. But when shit start getting fucked up at the table, I gotta be able to cover my ass to keep shit from getting to my connect. Is dat makin sense to you?" Then Gacy said,

"I guess I can see yo point. I just needed to know wut tha bidnis was. You my nigga tho, I trust you."

"Gacy you ain't *never* gotta question my loyalty, my shit official through and through, and as long as yours stay tha same, you ain't never gotta worry about nobody replacing you, and dat goes for all y'all… Now, roll up some mo of dat mufukin weed."

Chapter 79

It was a beautiful evening across the island as a huge full moon brightened the night. The crickets chirped, the waves splashed, and Erica sat on the deck of the beach house in an ever so serene mood. Being away from the city bustle had her seriously thinking about where she was in life. It also had her thinking of Moony. She was beginning to question what is was she truly felt about him. Did she love him unconditionally, or did she love the lifestyle he provided for her, cause Moony hadn't been gone six months, and yet the thought of having 1,000 kilos of heroine, had her slowly putting Moony out of the back of her mind. She was focusing on the future.

While she sat there smoking a cigarette, and reveled in her thoughts, Racks came out on the deck, and as soon as he noticed her sitting there, he smacked his lips, and said,

"Damn, I thought I was here by myself." Then Erica spoke to him sarcastically saying,
"Trust me, in the world you live in, you *are* by yourself." For the first time, Racks wasn't looking to argue, he was just trying to smoke some weed and chill in the warm summer breeze, but it was killing his ego to not have said anything back to her, countering her comment. He just looked at her, then shook his head. When Erica noticed the gesture he made, she blurted out, "Wut tha fuck you shakin *your* head for?!" Racks then exploded,
"I mean damn! Do you always gotta be a bitch! I wasn't even on dat wit'chu tonight, but everytime you open yo mouth, you make me wanna…"
"Wanna wut Rack's?" Erica said as she junped in his face cutting him off. Racks was pissed! They stood thier face to face mean mugging each other like two heavyweight boxers. Erica egged it on saying, "Wanna wut mufuka?! Don't bitch up now nigga!" Racks stood there breathing hard as hell. His face

grimaced up as he stared into Erica's eyes, but it didn't faze her one bit. She felt like she had *already* met death face to face, so there was no more backing down. She just stood there as she folded her arms, rolled her neck, pursed her lips, and looked Racks up and down. He took a step towards Erica ready to slap the shit out of her. Surprisingly, she still didn't budge. That only fueld Racks even more. He clenched his fist, and looked Erica square in the eyes and said,

"Damn you sexy as hell!" Erica held a look of shock, *and* disbelief on her face. Racks was one hundred percent embarrassed. He closed his eyes momentarily and said, "Oh shit did I just say that out loud?"

"Umm yeah, and I can't believe it came out'cho mouth!" Not only was Erica shocked by the comment, but she was actually flattered. The compliment alone instantly gave Erica a change of heart about him. Racks stood there with his head hung low until Erica leaned in to look him in his face. She pulled his head up by the tip of her finger, and softly spoke, "Racks it's ok, you ain't gotta be embarrassed." She took a deep breath then continued, "Look, why don't we just let that past be the past, and start all over, aight? I'm willin to if you are." Racks still stood there speechless, and drowning in embarrassment. Erica could see the shame scribbled all over his face, so she smiled then held her hand out and said,

"Hi I'm Erica."

An hour later, Ug stood in the doorway of the deck. He couldn't believe his eyes when he saw Racks and Erica all up in each other's space, deep in conversation. He was used to seeing them at each other's throat so much, that seeing them actually conversing didn't look right. He didn't want to disturb them, so he faded back into the kitchen, and just watched like a private investigator. After watching them for fifteen minutes, Ug saw Erica and Racks stand up and give each other a rather long and somewhat passionate hug. To Ug, shit was getting juicy, but he figured he'd let them have their moment, so as Racks began to walk away, Ug ducked behind the island counter smiling like a mischievious little kid until Racks disappeared into the house, and once Racks was gone, Ug strutted on out on the deck and sat next to Erica smiling hard as hell. Erica took one look at Ug and giggled, saying,

"Wussup wit tha big ole smile?"

"I gotta secret." Ug replied, sounding like that mischievious little kid.

"Oh yeah? Wus yo secret? I won't tell."

"You tell me yo secret first, then I'll tell you mine." Erica was still smiling when she dropped her head saying,

"You saw me an Racks out here didn't chu?"

"Bingo! Oooh wee! Y'all two some frontin mufukas! So how long y'all been fuckin'?"

"It ain't like that Ug! I mean... we was just talkin'."

"Hey, call it wut'chu want, but I seen y'all two mufukas out here stuck together like twizzlers!"

"Look Ug, just don't say nuttin' aigh't, I don't want nobody getting' the wrong idea."

"Yeah, especially if they catch y'all all hugged up like I saw y'all. But who knows they might just think Racks was trying to burp you." Erica laughed while playfully pushing Ug saying.

"Wuteva nigga, just keep dat on the low fo ya girl." He smiled saying.

"I gotcha." As they sat there in silence for a few seconds, Erica decided to try and get a little personal. While looking out at the caribean sea, Erica spoke,

"Wut he do to you? If you don't mind me asking?" Ug smiled cause he knew exactly what Erica was asking. He leaned back in his seat, clasped his hand together, and said,

"He was a fuckin rat, and he was gone bring all of us down... And to think, me and dat bum mufuka had tha same blood." Erica's attention was instantly raised, and she yelled out,

"Wut?! Wait a minute! So, you and Skeezo was related?!" Ug spoke somberly when he said,

"Yeah that was my chump ass cousin." Erica couldn't believe what she had just heard. She grew up with the belief that family sticks together no matter what. That's when it dawned on her that Ug was *not* to be fucked with, and if *he* would have his own cousin killed, then what would he do to her if she ever fucked up? But she finally understood why he asked *her* to kill Skeezo. After a long period of silence, Ug finally spoke,

"You probably think I'm fucked up don't chu?"

"I ain't sayin dat, I just don't think I could ever do that to my own family." Ug turned towards Erica and broke it down.

"Did I have love for my cousin? Yeah... Do I feel bad about the outcome? Fuck yeah! But in dis game, you gotta be willin to sacrifice for *the* bigger picture. Skeezo was only willin' to sacrifice for *his own* big picture. Dats tha shit I ain't got no love fo! Loyalty is everything to me Erica. Dats wut I was brought into dis game on, and dats wut I brought'chu into dis game on. You got blood on yo hands now baby, and as long as you keep it one hunnid wit me, sky's the limit. But if you fuck me, then the grave is yo *only* option." Then Ug got up from his seat and walked away leaving Erica to think about what he'd just said. He was hoping that she got the message loud and clear, cause her third strike was going to land her right at the last and only option.

Chapter 80

The next morning, I rented a yacht, and got the crew together for a cruise up the Carribean coast. Everybody was having a ball, and enjoying themselves, you know, just living life to the fullest.

As we were taking pictures and acting silly, something pulled my attention towards Nassir. While he leaned on the guard rail watching all of us. I quickly saw him wipe a tear from his face as he forced himself to smile. All of a sudden, the fun didn't seem so fun anymore, so I called him out and waved him over.

"Yo Nas! Com'on, come kick it wit me fo a minute" I led Nassir into the living room cabin of the yacht, and closed the door. As soon as he sat down, he sparked a blunt while I made both of us a drink. In the process of pouring the liquor I spoke,
"Nas wussup fam, you aight?" Nassir hit the weed and said,
"Yeah bro I'm all good, you know me."
"Yea I do know you, all to well as a matter of fact. Bro I saw you wipe dat tear off yo face, holla at'ch boy." Nassir fell silent for a moment then spoke with an emotionally shakey voice, and said,
"Ug I ain't got no problem wit doin tha time and holdin my weight. It's just… Im'ma miss you bro. Im'ma miss all of y'all. Im'ma miss dis!" Then he held his arms out looking around the cabin. "Man Ug, I'm livin' a dream right now bro, and soon Im'ma be walkin straight into a mufukin nightmare!"
"I feel you fam, but'chu gotta believe everything gone be all good. The only thing that's gone stand still is those prison walls. You still gone get paid like everybody else, I'm just gone split'cho cut wit Nitty, but dats only til you touch back down, but'chu still gettin' paid, ya feel me? Don't trip, Im'ma hold you down in every way possible bro. Whateva you need, wheneva you need it, I

got'chu. Just stay focused, keep yo eyes and ears open. Don't look at dis like you goin to the grave. Look at it like an opportunity! You gon be bumpin into dudes from all over the United States. Use dat to yo advantage! To *our* advantage! Mufuka's out there getting' stupid money bro, its time to start thinkin outside tha box and rock dis shit from coast to coast, ya feel me? Nas, if anybody can make dat happen, it's you." I know Nassir was fucked up about having to do time, but he had to realize that this is what comes with the territory. Nothing in this world is free, and like any hardworking citizen, the dope man had to pay his taxes too. The sad part is that the dope man doesn't get the chance to choose how he pays. The hardworking citizen get to choose between check or cash, but the dopeman has to face the consequence of death or imprisonment. It's a hell of a game to play, but if you cut like that, then you're always up for the challenge.

****

Another day was gone as Ug, and the crew spent they're last night on the island. Everbody was exhausted after the yacht cruise and just wanted to chill on the beach. By tomorrow night, they'd be back at home battling with the cold November weather in Chicago, so they wanted to soak up as much paradise as they could.

As eleven o'clock at night approached, Candice let out a long exasperating yawn and it became infectious among the crew. She then stretched saying,

"Toni baby. I'm about to go to bed. I can't fight it no more." She stood up, gave Toni a kiss, then said. "Alright y'all. Peace out." She then threw up the deuces, and began heading back to the beach house. It wasn't any surprise that the majority of the group followed right behind her. Everyone except Ug, Nassir, Yella Boy, Nala, and Toni. That's when Yella Boy grabbed Nala by the hand, and took off to their favorite little rendezvous spot on the other side of the beach.

Yella Boy walked along the shore with a blanket in one hand, and Nala's palm in the other. He was trying to find a way to let her know that they would be leaving tomorrow, but he couldn't find the words to say it. Mainly because he wasn't ready for their time to end.

Once they met their destination, Yella Boy laid the blanket across the sand, then pulled Nala into a tight embrace as he kissed her slow and passionately under the cheerful moonlight.

After their kiss, they held each other's embrace as if they'd just reunited after ten long years. He was even seriously thinking about *staying* in Jamaica to be with her. He figured he had *more* than enough money to start a new life, but he didn't have the will power to walk away from the game, especially when he knew Ug depended on him to play his part.

Yella Boy sat down on the blanket, then pulled Nala between his legs, and put put his arms around her waist. When he kissed her on her neck, she spoke,

"It's time for ya ta go isn't tit?" Yella Boy didn't have it in him to answer the question, he just held her tighter and she said, "It's ok, I knew this day woood caam." Nala broke their embrace, then spent around to look Yella Boy in his face, and said, "Yella Boi, I don't want'cha ta forget about me."

"Com'on na lil mama, I ain't gone neva forget about' chu."

"I know, cause I'm gonna make sure ya don't!" Then Nala pulled her shirt over her head exposing those dark round tits that Yella Boy loved so much, she then leaned into him and started licking around his ear, and it drove Yella Boy Crazy! He was loving every minute. That's when he flipped her over on her back, and took *his* shirt off. Nala was extremely turned on by the tattoo that lined his collar bone saying. 'Death before Disloyalty', and it made her wild. She jumped up and stripped down to nothing, then said, "Catch me if you can." And she took off running towards the water leaving Yella Boy to play catch up.

Back on the other side of the beach Toni, Nassir, and Ug were still chillin, and talking. They were mainly speaking on how much they really needed this vacation, until Nassir felt it was time to excuse himself saying,

"Well y'all, it's been a hell of a day. Now I'm about to go in here and eat dis spanish omlette ya feel me?" Ug didn't quite catch on, so he said,
"Oooh hell yea, make me one too!"
"Naw Ug, you might wanna move around tha island and find you some jerk chicken head or sumtn, know wut I'm sayin'?"
"Oh! I get it. Well ride out den wit'cho freaky ass." Then Nassir walked away dancing the cha-cha.

Once Nassir was out of sight, Toni pulled out here last blunt and asked Ug if he wanted to smoke it, and he more than willingly said yes. As Toni hit the weed, Ug stared at her out of the corner of his eye thinking to himself what he would do to her if she *wasn't* Candice's girl, and Toni sat there clad in a two peice bikini thinking those exact same thoughts. The energy there on the beach was *dynamic,* and the ambience of romance began to cloud their better judgement, but neither took the liberty to act on what they felt. Instead Ug just asked,

"Why you so quiet? Wut'chu over there thinkin' bout?"
Toni's inner goddess popped out of nowhere screaming,
"Bitch wut'chu waitin on? You know you want some of that dick, tell him wuts on your mind girl." Then her subconscience kicked in saying,

"Girl don't listen to her, she gone get us in some shit just like always, do the right thing girl." Toni finally got her head together and said,

"Ummm nothing." Ug looked confused when he said,

"It took you two whole minutes just to tell me nothin'." Toni's subconscience jumped in saying,

"Oh shit! I think he's on to us girl!" While her inner goddess was bent over shaking her ass screaming,

"Get it girl! We gettin that *tonight!*" Toni shook the both of them out of her head and quickly stood up. She looked down at Ug and said,

"Here Ug you can smoke the rest of that. I'm about to ride out." Then she turned and began to walk away. Ug jumped up out of his beach chair and grabbed Toni by her arm and turned her around. When they looked each other in the eyes, Ug said,

"Toni, you aight?" Toni had looked Ug in his eyes many of times, but somehow this time he had her completely mesmerized. She didn't blink, nor did she speak, she just leaned in and kissed Ug tenderly on the lips and her inner goddess went *bananas*! That's until Ug pulled away saying,

"Toni dis ain't right. I can't do dis." Toni stood there feeling embarassed and looking ashamed. She couldn't believe that she had actually kissed Ug! She was now fluttered with a gang of mixed emotions. Part of her was excited because it felt oh so good, but the other part was now trembling in fear and praying that Candice would never find out. That's when her subconscience kicked in again saying,

"See, I told you she was gone get us in some shit. Just... like... always!"

After a playful game of marco polo, Yella Boy chased Nala back to the blanket. She giggled as he grabbed her from the back by the waist, and when Nala turned around, she bit her bottom lip as she watched the water glisten off of Yella Boy's chest and arms. She reached out and touched him as if he were just a figment of her imagination, but feeling on his rock hard abs, let her know that he was *all* too real.

    Nala grabbed a hold of Yella Boy's belt and yanked him closer as they began to lustfully kiss. Their breathing became shallow, and their kiss had gotten wilder, all while she fidgeted with his belt until she got the buckle loose and unzipped his shorts. She slid her hands around the sides of his waist until her hands cuffed his butt cheeks, and his shorts hit the blanket. Yella Boy stepped out of the shorts and picked her up like a newborn baby as she wrapped her arms around his neck and legs around his waist, then he slowly took her down.

    Yella Boy looked at her entire body from head to toe, then started kissing all over her neck. He took his time cause he wanted to taste every inch of her body.

    After nibbling on her neck, he turned her over onto her stomach. He took the tips of his fingers and softly began to make squiggly lines from the top of her neck, straight down to the center of her spine, sending chill shocks throughout her body. Once he got to the small of her back, he gently began to kiss her right above the neck as he massaged her back. When he slid his hand between her legs, he saw that she was as wet as Lake Michigan, and that let him know that she was way past ready.

    When Yella Boy turned her back over and entered her honey pot, he started off with short slow strokes. She was crazy wet and it made Yella Boy softly call out her name. Once he felt her body respond, he grabbed hold of her hands as their fingers intertwined, and stretched her arms over her head. He then began to go deeper. In the midst of their flow, Nala yelled out.

    "Stop, stop, stop!" Yella Boy did as she asked and gave her a *very* confused and pleading look. Nala placed both of her hands on the sides of his face, then looked him in the eyes and said.

"Yella Boi, I don't want'cha to make luv to me, I want'cha to *fuck* me, ok?" Yella Boy smiled, then flipped her back over to her stomach as she raised up on her hands and knees, ass up!

Yella Boy looked down at Nala's big round ass and gave a playful and seductive giggle, he eased into her as she backed that *thang* up, then she pantingly said,

"Fuck me, fuck me!" That's when Yella Boy grabbed a hand full of her hair and wound it up around his fist until he had it gripped in a knot. When he saw that it had her going crazy, he gave her what she asked for.

Once the morning came, everyone was packed and ready to go. Nala made sure that she stayed by Yella Boy's side up until the moment he left the island. On another note Ug and Toni were back in another awkward situation, and Toni wanted to ensure their secrecy, so she pulled Ug to the side and said,

"Ug, about last night, I wasn't in my right mind, I'm sorry. I ain't mean to take it there. I just really don't want Candice to find out, ya know? So *please* don't say nothin' alright?" Ug looked away in a nonchalant manner and said,
"I got tha slightest idea of wut'chu talkin about Toni."
"You know wut I'm talkin about Ug!" This time Ug looked at her and said,
"Like I said, I don't know wut'chu talkin about." Then he got up and walked away. Ug knew in his heart he loved Brittany, but couldn't help but feel something for Toni. So. could he keep his mouth shut about the kiss? Yes. But he would never forget that brief passionate moment that they shared under the moonlight on this exotic island off the Carribean Sea. Never!

Chapter 81

We were back in the hood and we were all pumped up and ready to get back to the money. Things were still a little funny between Toni and I, but I'm sure that in do time it'll work itself out.

When Nassir and I stepped in the crib, I tossed my luggage near the front door and went to grab my cell phones. Although we had spoken everyday while I was gone, I had to hear Brittany's voice. I could never get enough of the soft and sexy words she spoke to me.

As we talked on the phone, she became extra excited to know that I was home. I took it that she'd missed me as much as I missed her. We made plans to see each other later on in the evening, after I handled some business.

My next call was to Carlos. I wanted him to know that I was back in town, so I switched phones and dialed his number. When he answered, I said,

"Yo, wusup! I'm back in tha hood!"
"Ah wonderful, how was your trip?"
"Aw man, Jamaica was live! I definitely enjoyed myself."
"I'm glad to hear that, you sound refreshed. Well, I I don't want to rush you off, but I gotta get back to a few things, so call me in the morning and I'll get you squared away, ok?" Just as I hung the phone up, Bino G hit my line.

"Ug, sumtn ain't right out here G!" I saw about twenty or thirty police cars lined up over here on the otha side of the Kedzie bridge! I don't know who they bout to hit, but they bout to hit hard!" I threw my phone onto the bed and ran to the front room where Nassir was sitting and said,

"Dem people bout to hit tha town!" Nassir calmly lit a blunt and said,

"Oh well, fuck'em! If it's my time to roll, I wanna be high when I go." I grabbed the pistols that were in the house, and ran them across the street to the apartment building. On my way over, I yelled out.

"Blue! Blue! Blue! ... Blue! Blue! Blue!" To let the guys on security know that a raid squad was in the area.

On my way, out of the building I saw Nassir leaning aganst the mailbox smoking his blunt looking like he didn't have a care in the world. I walked to the edge of the curb and looked around, and that's when my phone rang, it was Bino G again.

"Ug, they over there in tha Old Projects famo. I'll let'chu know wus goin' on as soon as I get word."

"Aight bet." Aw man, I was relieived. I thought they were coming to get Nassir. Well one thing is for sure, and two things were for certain, Nassir was living on borrowed time and we all knew it, and that's what scared me the most.

Later that night I ended up at Brittany's place, and after eating, Brittany and I cuddled up under a blanket and watched old re-runs of Sandford and Son until eventually she dozed off. The heat between our bodies was so warm and comfy, I began to doze off myself. That's until my phone started to vibrate, and when I checked the screen, I saw it was Alexis. I then looked at the time and saw that it was 1:30 am. There was no way in hell I was going to answer this call, so I let it go to voicemail. At one-thirty in the morning what could she possibly want? Regardless, she had to wait, time with my girl was far more important to me right now.

When I opened my eyes, I looked at my watch to see that it was 7:08 am. As I went to take a leak, I realized Brittany was not there. After I took a piss, I sat down on the living room couch and noticed a note.

Good mornig baby! I had to take care of some early morning business. I didn't want to wake you because you were looking so peaceful. Anyway, if I don't see you tonight I want you to know that I love you so much.

Brittany

After I read the letter, I put on my clothes and hit the door. I was kind of glad she left out early because if not, she might've tried to slow me down with a little morning sex, and I *had* to get on top of this money.

While I let my car warm up, I checked my voicemail. One message was from Carlos wanting to know what time was I goning to be ready, and the other messages were from Alexis saying she needed to see me A.S.A.P, but before I could get a chance to call her back, Yella Boy called, and when I answered my phone I said,

"Wut up boi? I see you up early ready to get dis paper."
"Ug, the FEDS just snatched Nassir up jo, and they all up in y'all shit right now!"
"Fuck, I'm on my way right now!"
"Naw, naw, naw! Just stay where you at, Im'ma hit'chu when they leave."

While I laid low, Leonard and Candice met downtown at the Dirkson building for Nassir's arraignment. Come to find out, the three dudes from yesterday's raid were brought in as being co-conspirators in a crack distribution ring *led* by Nassir. The weakest part of the entire situation was that the total amount of crack distributed in this conspiracy didn't even exceed 250 grams!

Later on in the day, Leonard called my phone to give me an update on Nassir's case. He was talking a whole bunch of federal mumbo jumbo, but I relaxed when he said,

"Things don't look *that* bad. The case actually looks weak, nonetheless it *will* stick, all I can do is soften the blow. This conspiracy charge won't hold, it's just a formality, but I won't know anything else until the indictment is formally filed by the government.

So far this was good news. It didn't sound like Nassir would be doing *that* much time, but I know how the FEDS operate. The feds don't hand out no lessons in right or wrong, and they could give a fuck less about rehabilitating you, so just know that if you're the pettiest hustler this could happen to you also. The FEDS have time and space for a gram or better of any drug. Just remember that while you're getting money.

Chapter 82

By the time 6pm rolled around, the hood was dark, quiet and cold. All the dope spots in the hood were shut down. Everybody was shook. They didn't know if the FEDS were going to come back for more people. It was better to be prepared and safe than pre-seasoned and cooked. That's what I say anyway.

When Yella Boy and I walked inside my house I looked around to see shit everywhere. I scratched my head and told Yella Boy we were going to need some help, so he called Toni over to help.

As I walked around trying to figure out where to start, I looked in Nassir's room and noticed a big dumb ass hole in the wall. The shit looked like the kool-aid man had been to visit. I just shook my head and kept moving up the hallway until I walked through a patch of soak and wet carpet. I looked to my right towards the bathroom and noticed that they smashed the toilette, water was everywhere!

Ten minutes later, Toni and Candice showed up. As soon as they walked in Candice said,

"Dang, they fucked y'all shit up!" Toni shook her head saying,
"Dis don't make no damn sense! Why they ain't just bring some police dogs to sniff around dis bitch?" I didn't even try to answer her question, I just said,
"Aight look, me and Yella Boy gone start in the rooms, y'all two go ahead and knock out the living room and kitchen."

A little past eight thirty we all plopped down on the sofas in the living room tired as hell. Since the living room and kitchen weren't that bad Toni and Candice finished up early then helped us out in the rooms. As I glanced around the living room thankful that we were done I said.

   "Man, now I need a drink." Toni then blurted out.
   "I second that motion!" That's when Candice got up and said,
   "I'll go to the store. Toni, let me see your keys." Toni handed over her keys and Candice left to go get us all a drink.

Chapter 83

While Ug, Yella Boy, and Toni sat back recanting their trip to Jamaica and and feeling down about Nassir, Ug yawned and said,

"I know dat shit seemed fucked up right now, but trust me, shit bout to get betta. I gotta surprise for y'all, just call it an early Christmas gift." Yella Boy responded saying.
"Oh yea? Wut'chu got fo us big bro?"
"I'm dropping the price on dem thangs for y'all." Yella Boy perked up with excitement saying,
"So wut price we gone move'em at?"
"Shit dat's on y'all. Y'all can stay consistent with y'all four thousand a brick profit and sell for 20, or y'all can keep the ticket at 23 wit a seven thousand a brick profit, but only for the next five tons. After that y'all gotta take a five hundred dollar cut and move'em at 19,500. Y'all two make the call." And before either one of them could speak another word Ug heard a barrage of gunfire erupt sounding like a war in Iraq. Ug held a confused and angry look while saying, "Wut tha fuck was dat?!" They all ran to window trying to see what was going on, but all they saw were the guys on security coming off their post looking around just as confused. Ug turned to Yella Boy and said, "Get Rico on tha line and tell'em to go check dat shit out!" A few minutes later, Ug's phone rang, It was Rico, and Ug said,
"Rico tell me sumtn good. Who tha fuck out there poppin' off like dat?" And Rico sadly said.
"Ug, niggas just killed Toni fam." Ug, looked over at Toni and said,
"Wut tha fuck you talkin' about? Mufuka Toni right here fool!"
"Bro, I'm looking at her body leaning over ther steering wheel of her whip right now." Just then it all clicked in Ug's head.

It wasn't Toni's body Rico was looking at, it was Candice! Once he realized it, he yelled into the phone.

"Where you at?!"

"I'm on the 5th at the corner of Ridgeway." Ug dropped his head for a quick second, then jumped up and slung his phone into the wall then stormed out of the house leaving Yella Boy and Toni in suspense. Toni felt something wasn't right and yelled out,

"Ug, wut tha fuck is goin' on?" Ug never answered, he just headed straight for his car. Toni ran up to Ug and grabbed his arm to get his attention saying, "Ug, tell me wuts goin' on!" Ug just looked at her and said,

"Is you comin' or wut?" Then got in his car.

As soon as they all jumped in Ug's car, he took off like a bat out of hell. When they reached the corner of the block, they looked up the street to their left where they could see Toni's car sitting slanted up against the curb. Ug then made a hard left and punched the gas. Toni started slamming her fist against the dash board screaming.

"No, no, no!" Ug just gave Toni a quck glance, then kept driving.

When they reached Toni's car they all hopped out and Toni took off running towards Candice's lifeless body. Ug just stood there leaning against his car as his knees began to buckle. Yella Boy ran up to Toni trying to hold her back from looking at Candice, while Rico walked over and hugged Ug in an attempt to console him saying,

"Don't trip my nigga, we gone handle dis shit, I promise."

By this time police and fire trucks started flooding the scene. Ug stood there with his head spinning. He was so deep in shock that he couldn't even shed a tear. He just stared at Toni as she cried her eyes out, not able to do anything but feel her pain. He then looked up and began to scout the crowd that had gathered up, hoping he would get a feel for the motherfuckers that had just stolen his best friends life. All he saw were faces full of tears and sorrow. When he looked back at Toni's car, he began to pay attention to all the bullet holes that riddled the car, then he stared hard at Candice's body. Right then was the moment he felt the first tear fall from his eye, and that was the moment he fell to his knees and let it all go.

While Ug was still going through his moment of greif, Rack pulled up and began to talk to Rico. He looked over at Ug and knew exatly what he was feeling, so he decided to just give him a little time. Then out of the crowd a short skinny guy walked up to Rico and said,

"Ay fam." Racks instantly grabbed the handle of his gun and said.
"Wut?! Wut tha fuck you want?" He walked up to the guy and grabbed his shirt yelling. "You had sumtn to do wit dis shit nigga?!" The guy hysterically blurted out.
"Naw fam, fuck naw! I just saw it all go down!" Rico stepped in between Racks and the guy then shoved Racks away. He then walked back to the guy, put his arm around his shoulder, and walked towards his car and said,
"Get in." As they drove away Rico fired up a blunt and asked,
"You smoke?" And the guy replied yes, then Rico past him the blunt saying. "So wut'chu see my dude? I mean I wanna know errythang in full detail." Dude hit the blunt a few more times then passed it to Rico and said.
" Aight, I was parked in the alley right there gettin' my dick sucked. You know it aint no house on the corner, so you could see everything. Anyway, dis van pulled up on the otha side of the 5th, I thought it was dem people, but I was gettin' sucked up, so it ain't matter to me. Then all of a sudden the headlights popped on and it just shot out in the middle of the street right in front of dat Impala!

The Impala tried to back up but dis suburban rode up out of nowhere and slammed in back of it! The Impala tried to cut the wheel and go forward again, but I swear about seven or eight niggas jumped out wit big ass choppa's and just lit tha Impala up!"

"So, you ain't see no faces or nuttin?"

"Naw, I couldn't see no faces, but I could tell niggas ain't have no masks on."

After Rico got the description of the truck and van, he dropped dude off at his home so he would know where to find him in case he needed him again, but before dude got out, Rico reached in his pocket and broke him off a stack of hundred dollar bills and said,

"Ay, don't say shit to nobody! You ain't seen shit and you don't know shit, got it?"

"Yeah, I got'chu big homie." Rico watched him until he went into the house and closed the door. He wanted to make sure he wasn't faking about where he laid his head, and after he went in, Rico fired up another blunt then leaned his head back as he blew out the smoke. He then took a deep breath and threw his car in drive, cause now it was time to return to that horrific scene to join his crew in agaony, but before he drove away, he ashed his blunt and simply said,

"Damn, when it rains it mufukin pours!" Then he took off to make it back with the rest of the crew.

Chapter 84

It was 12:30 in the morning, and I was on the elevator on my way up to Alexis' condo. I tried calling Brittany's phone several times, but I kept getting her voicemail. I couldn't wait any longer, I had to get away. I needed to be in someone's arms while they told me everything was going to be alright, cause right now, I beleive I needed to be lied to.

I got off the elevator and knocked on Alexis's door, when she answered I walked in. She took one look at me and said,

"Oh my God Adonis, you look a mess! Have you been crying? Sit down I'll fix you a drink."

Alexis sat on the sofa quietly as she watched my hands shake uncontrollably while I sipped on the glaas of vodka she gave me. I could tell that she didn't really want to press the issue. However, even if she did, I don't think she knew what to say.

As we sat there I could feel Alexis's eyes beaming in on me, but I couldn't take my eyes off of the glass that I held. Subsequently, Alexis put her hand on my shoulder then rubbed small soft circles into my back, and it felt soothing. I felt understood. I appreciate the fact that she didn't try to push me to talk. So, I went ahead and opened up to her saying,

"Mufukas killed my best freind today."
"Oh my God, Nassir?"
"Naw the FEDS snatched Nassir up dis morning, I'm talking about my girl Candice. Me, her, and Nassir grew up together. After tha FEDS raided the house we spent the rest of the day cleaning up. When we finished, Candice made a run to tha store to get a drink and got gunned up in her girlfreinds car."

"Oh Adonis, I'm so sorry to hear that. I can't begin to imagine what you are going through right now." Then she cuddled my head into her breast and I began to cry again."

After a few drinks, I became a little more tipsy, and a lot less emotional as I told her stories of our childhood. The stories brung back some funny memories and we began to laugh. That is until the emotions began to resurface and brought about an ungainly silence, leaving Alexis to intervene.

"Oh shit, I almost forgot. I have something for you." And she got up and walked out of the room.

Moments had passed and Alexis walked back in the room with a tan sashay case saying,

"I've been trying to get a hold of you for a few days now to show you what I was able to come up with." Then she began pulling papers out and spreading them across her coffee table saying, "Ok, are you familiar with a Nicole Stansbury?"

"Naw, dat name don't ring a bell."

"Well she's the confidential informant who set up four purchases with this guy here." Then she showed me a picture of Nassir and some other dude in a drug transaction.

"So wus his name?"

"His name is... Darnell Turner. Nicole set up four controlled buys with this guy, and all buys were of the same quanity."

"You ain't got no picture of tha girl?"

"Nope. She was never arrested. She was just doing some C.I. work to help her brother get a lighter sentence."

"Damn, dat's fucked up."

"There were a few other federal complaints filed, but the FEDS weren't able make anything of it, so they just decided to go with what they had."

"So, wut'chu think gone happen to Nassir?"

"Well, those controlled buys were the least of his problems. After those buys were setup by the C.I., the FEDS tapped Nassir's phone and linked in three other guys who made plans to purchse crack cocaine from Nassir as well, and those conversations were recorded. Those three purchases were equally in the amount of 62.5 grams, and the government is seeking conspiracy charges, but in my professional opinion the conspriacy will be dropped. So, to sum it all up, Nassir may be looking at ten counts of indictment, now how it all plays out is totally up to him"

"I thought you said it was four controlled buys and three dudes was trying to buy 62.5 grams? Dats only seven counts."

"Right but there's also the three counts of phone facilitation from the phone taps."

Damn, all this shit was too much to handle. First, I loose my best friend to the chain game and the other for life. What's so special about me? I'm the one who started all of this shit. So why is it that I'm the only one free and alive.

Minutes into my thoughts my phone rang. It was RIco.

"Yo, rico wusup?"
"Ug, where you at?"
"I'm just in tha cut chillin', why wusup?"
"Ay, remember dat nigga off tha corner dat Toni popped in tha feet?"
"Yeah, wussup?"
"Man jo, we just ran in dat nigga spot and found a gang of loaded guns. I *know* he had sumtn to do wit Candice gettin' killed."
"Aight, hold his ass down til I get there."
"It's too late, we al-"
"Who, whoa, whoa! We gone holla bout dat whcn I get there." After I hung up, Alexis asked if everything was alright. I sat my phone down, took another sip from my glass then gave her a devilish grin, and said, "Yeah, I'm all good. I think the healing process just started."

"Good cause I wanted to talk to you about something else."

"Go ahead, knock yoself out."

"Well in the process of looking into Nassir, I also did a little homework on you as well. Adonis, when you were locked up, did your mother come to see you at all?"

"Yeah, a few times."

"Did she ever speak to you about anything out of the ordinary?"

"Naw, nothin' that I can think of."

"I remember you told me your mom passed away."

"Yeah, about a year and a half after I got locked up."

"Did the prison let you attend her funeral?"

"Wait a minute, hol'up! Wus all deez mufukin questions about my mama fo?" Alexis held her hands up in a surrendering manner and said,

"I'm sorry, I'm sorry." Then she slid an unfamiliar picture saying. "Have you ever seen this man before?" I told her no, because truthfully I hadn't, but then she slid another picture photo in front of me. This time I did recognize it. "This is the man you were with when I first met you. How much do you know about him?"

"Nuttin' much, we was locked up together."

"Locked up?"

"Yea, he was my celly."

"Ok now *I'm* confused."

"   About wut? We lived in tha same cell togehter, wut is there to be confused about?"

"Adonis this is Carlos Alcantara, he has diplomatic impunity! A man like this doesn't go to prison. A man like this doesn't even get a traffic ticket. How the hell does he end up being your cellmate?"

"Fuck if I know, I ain't no detective." She sat there in deep thought for a second before she said,

"Adonis, years ago the Cheif of police in Robbins was suspected in being invloved in a cocaine distribution ring. We were never able to prove it, but we knew he was living way above his means. However, through surveilance, agents were able to link your father and an unidentified man together by association which confirmed our confidential informants statement. Now our files speculate that this man here acted on behalf of the cheif of police and murdered your father when word of the investigation leaked." That's when she showed me a picture of that punk bitch detective Ross. No wonder he was always trying to lock me up. His bitch ass didn't want me to ever find out he was involved with my father's murder. I knew I should've smoked his ass myself when I had the chance. Oh well, it's all good, what goes around comes around.

Alexis remained quiet for a moment giving me a chance to think about everything she had just told me, but then she went on to finish.

"Adonis. we believe this man supplied your father with drugs." That's when she went *back* to the picture of the man that I didn't recognize and lined it up with a picture of my father, *and* the mayor of Robbins, so I had to ask.
"So wut do tha mayor of Robbins have to do wit all dis. I thought'chu said this had sumtn' to do wit tha cheif of police?"
"It does Adonis, and *that* cheif of police is *now* the mayor of Robbins. Now I know this is a lot to take in at a time like this, but I have to say this. A little over a year after your dad died your mom contacted the F.B.I and gave them info regarding the city's corruption and you father's murder. Not only did she confirm it but she was willing to testify in court. That is until the government recieved word that she had died. Now database shows that there *is* a death certificate on record. However, there is no physical proof that supports her death."
"So wut'chu sayin'."
"I'm saying that I beleive that somewhere out there your mother is still alive Adonis. If we can find this man *here*, we may have a chance to find *her*." Again, she went back to the picture of the man that I did not recognize.

I was now beginning to feel like I was in the twilight zone. Emotionally none of this made sense, but mentally it was all reeling me in. There were still a lot of missing parts to this puzzle, but my brain was too fried to even think of where to begin.

I got up off the sofa to go take a leak, and as soon as I got in the bathroom I heard Alexis yelling out,
"Adonis your phone is ringing!"
"Just let it go to voicemail!" When I returned from the bathroom Alexis was sitting there with this weird look on her face. When I asked what was wrong, she held my phone up revealing my screensaver saying,
"The woman in this picture..."
"Oh yeah, dat's my girlfreind Brittany."
"Brittany! Adonis this is Agent Valencia Williams! She was the undercover agent assigned to Nassir's case!" What... Wait... What *the* fuck! All of a sudden, my mind began to process, then it clicked. Nicole Stansbury had to be Nikki, the girl Nassir hooked up with the night after Rack' brother was killed. That was the night I met Brittany, or Valencia, or whatever that bitch's name is. How could I have been so blind and stupid? The whole time I'm trying to find out who was doing us dirty and I was sleeping with the enemy all along. I guess it *is* true when they say that love is blind, cause for the life of me, I did *not* see this coming. All the signs were right in my face, but my heart wouldn't let me recognize them.

Listening to everything Alexis said only frustrated me and made me get sloppy drunk, so I called Carlos and had him send the limo over to take me home.

The ride home seemed to take forever, because all I wanted to do was lay my head down, but when we pulled up in front of my house, I sat there as the tears rolled down my face. I couldn't understand why this had to be happening to me. I guess when you make a deal with the devil, you have to dance with demons. When

I made that comment about Ross I said, what goes around comes around. I guess karma *is* a bitch, cause shit came back around on me hard as fuck!

Just when I was about to reach for the door handle I heard the privacy window between the driver and I rolled down, then I heard the driver say,

"Long day huh youngsta?" I wiped my face and said,
"Man, you wouldn't fuckin' believe me if I told you." He chuckled a little then spoke.
"Yea, I remember them kinda days." I was drunk as hell, but the voice of the driver sounded so familiar. It was sort of raspy, kind of like Dizzy Gillespi. The driver must have recognized the expression on my face when I remembered the voice. He laughed and said,
"I see ya mind startin' to work again." It was the same old man that drove me home from prison when I first got out. Was this a coincidence or was I still not seeing something bigger at work. I pulled myself together enough to say,
"Hey old man, ain't 'chu tha same dude dat drove me home from tha prison?"
"You got it youngsta! You remember wut I said to you before I drove away?" I tried to think, but I couldn't remember, so he kept talking. "I said dat it was all about'chu, and it still is. Wut don't kill you only makes you stronger. Well guess wut youngsta, you still standin'. Things gone happen dat we can't control, dat's life's design. Every experience is meant fo ya to learn from, so dust yaself off youngsta, dis game ain't over."

We loked in each other's eys through the rear-view mirror, then he rolled the security window back up. That's when I got out and went into the house.

When I opened the door, I saw Toni and Yella Boy asleep on the couches. I didn't wake them, I just headed straight for my bed and fell face first into my pillow. I laid there in a daze until I eventually cried myself to sleep. Tommorrow was a new day and I needed all my strength to deal with it.

When I woke up the next mornig Toni and Yella Boy were gone. I stepped outside just to look around and get some air until one of the seciruty guys said,
"Ay Ug, yo girl came by and left something in yo mailbox." I walked over to the mailbox and got the mail she left. I looked at it not sure if I even wanted to open it, but my heart was fighting hard for me to do so. So, I grabbed the rest of the mail and went into the house.

Once I got in the house, I tossed the bills on the table and looked at Brittany's. I mean Valencia's letter again and decided to open it. When I did it read:

Dear Adonis

There are going to be some things that you're going to find out, and I wanted you to know that for whatever it's worth, I will always love you. I know the person you learned to love isn't real, but what I feel for you is. The only regret I hold is not being honest with you, but you have to know. I wanted to tell you. All I can say is I'm sorry. I'm relocating to a different state so you won't be seeing or hearing from me again. I wish things were different. I don't know, maybe I'll see you next lifetime, until then, you will always have a place in my heart.

Love

Brittany/Valencia

P.S. Get out while you still have the chance.

While I sat holding the letter, my phone started vibrating in my pocket. I was hoping so bad that it was Brittany. Fuck, I mean Valencia, so I could give her a piece of my mind. But when I pulled my phone out I saw it was an unknown caller. Still hoping that it was Valencia, I answered and said,

"Hello?" Then the voice on the other end said,
"You wanna know the difference between me and you?"
"Who tha fuck is dis?"
"Aw com'on Ug. You try to have a nigga killed and *now* you don't know me? See, the difference between me and you is dat I got *real* killas. How you like they work? I hear dat 50 caliber is a bad mufuka. I know my voice sound a little slow and fucked up, but dat's wut happens after tha doctors put a metal fuckin' plate in yo head! Dis shit ain't over nigga! Yesterday was just to let'chu know that you *can* be touched." I closed my eyes and breathed in deep, then calmly said,
"Black Pooh huh? Boy, I swear to fuckin' God, you betta just run as far away as you can, cause Im'ma kill you. And when I'm done killin' you in the worst way possible. I'm gone throw a fuckin' grenade in whateva church that's holdin' yo weak ass funeral and kill every fuckin' person dat got love fo you. I promise, I'm gone be tha last person you ever lay eyes on. It ain't gone be no send off and it ain't gone be no hitman. Just me, nobody else. Dat's tha difference between you and me bitch!" The only comeback Black Pooh had was,
"Fuck you nigga! See me in these streets!" I just chuckled and said,
"Oh, don't worry, I was plannin' on it!"

To Be Continued...

Author Bio

Author J.Hitz was born a Chicago native, March 29, 1977 He was conceived by the union of Syverina Moses & Jeffrey Clair. As a young child, HITZ was intrigued by the sound of music. So much that he joined the school orchestra at the early age of 8. HITZ began with the cello, but later took on the challenge to stretch his repertoire by playing the: violin, viola, string bass, timpani, chimes, marimba, and xylophone.

1991, HITZ reached high school and elevated his arsenal by joining the schools marching band. During this quest, he learned to play the: snare drum, bass drum, crash symbols and synthesizer. But high school wasn't all about playing instruments. HITZ went on to join the mixed choir and men's ensemble where sing becoming a flash of his life as he held on to the newly found love of the synthesizer. He also engaged in high school sports such as: football, wrestling, and track and field.

1993 HITZ's synthesizer playing began to pay off as he began to make house music tracks. This led him to join De Juan Frazier in a venture to start a dance group by the name of House Arrest II. HITZ served as the Vice President and later became one hell of a dancer. This group went on to multiplying chapters in different states.

When year 2000 came the dancing slowed down. HITZ began to center all of his energy on producing house music. Until one day he mistakenly hit the tempo button on the keyboard and it slowed his beat down. As he went to speed it up he stopped. He leaned back and listened to it, and house music became an era of the past, as hip-hop music became his new future.

HITZ went on to produce many hip-hop tracks and even released his first album as an artist in 2008 entitled "Ignant Az Hell" with the leading single "That's Wut I Like. " As his career as an artist began to heighten, he was introduced to the world of concert promoting as a marketing tool.

All of HITZ's dreams as an artist and concert promoter were short lived when he was taken into custody in 2008 for firearm and possession charges. HITZ was threatened with 12 yrs but as a first time offender he was sentenced to 30 mo probation plus community 30 days service.

During the period of his probation HITZ continued to strive as an attitude and promoter, but as the saying goes "when it rains it pours". He was 8 months short of finishing his probation with the state when he was taken into custody by the FBI in 2010. HITZ somberly took a blind plea for 11 yrs, but was later re-sentenced under the "new crack law" and was sentenced to 6 years in a federal prison.

Narrowing in on his release HITZ began to worry about his career as an artist. He was nearing 40 years of age and didn't think he'd be able to match current sales because of his age, so in keeping his creativity going he decide to write.

     May 2015 HITZ finished writing his first novel "Tha Hood Tha Bad and Ugly." He was later released in November of 2015. Around this time HITZ spent much of his time tightening up his graphic skills and shopping his novel. He was later picked up by Shaunta Kenerly of Kenerly Publishing. And the rest shall be history.

Now Available

Escaping the Allure of The Game (series) by Shaunta Kenerly

Sex Therapy by Shaunta Kenerly

Damaged Goods by Terrie L. Branch

Gotta Be Shiesty (series) Terrie L. Branch

The Ultimate Break by Rio Jonz

Split Decisions by Anitra Hill

Hanking: In Love With The Game by James Turner III

And Many More…

Made in the USA
Coppell, TX
03 October 2025

60789155R00229